Praise for th

"Deese's latest is a beautiful story of faith, family, and the power of forgiveness.... [It] will appeal to women's fiction readers as a Dolly Parton–esque tale of hard-won fame."

—*Library Journal* starred review

"This is a vivid and emotional journey that readers will remember for a long time after it's over."

—*Booklist* starred review

"Deese is a master wordsmith, deftly weaving a story that readers won't be able to put down. This latest book has crossover appeal for fans of contemporary romance seeking realistic and endearing characters."

—*Library Journal*

"Sometimes a love story ends in tragedy, and a tragedy leads to a love story. And sometimes a hero turns a bit villainous, and a villain turns a bit heroic. In this unique story within a story, Deese delivers all of the above with the finesse of a clever storyteller. *The Words We Lost* is thought-provoking and tender, capturing the transformative beauty of surviving."

—T. I. Lowe, bestselling author of *Under the Magnolias*

"A poignant, masterful exploration of the enduring power of friendship and love, and the links that sustain and nurture us through all of life's complications and losses. Deese once again takes readers on an emotional journey filled with heart and hope."

—Irene Hannon, author of the bestselling HOPE HARBOR series

"Few things in life can be depended upon as reliably as the magic of a Nicole Deese book. No one breaks my heart and pieces it back together, better than before, quite like Nicole. *The Words We Lost* more than lives up to the standard of beauty and brilliance we've come to expect."

—Bethany Turner, author of *Plot Twist* and *The Do-Over*

The Voice We Find

Books by Nicole Deese

Before I Called You Mine
All That Really Matters
All That It Takes
The Words We Lost
The Roads We Follow
The Voice We Find

Novellas
Heartwood from *The Kissing Tree:*
Four Novellas Rooted in Timeless Love

A FOG HARBOR
······ ROMANCE ······

The Voice We Find

NICOLE DEESE

BETHANYHOUSE
a division of Baker Publishing Group
Minneapolis, Minnesota

Published by Bethany House Publishers
Minneapolis, Minnesota
BethanyHouse.com

Bethany House Publishers is a division of
Baker Publishing Group, Grand Rapids, Michigan

Printed in the United States of America

Library of Congress Cataloging-in-Publication Data
Names: Deese, Nicole, author.
Title: The voice we find / Nicole Deese.
Description: Minneapolis, Minnesota : Bethany House, a division of Baker Publishing Group, 2025. | Series: A Fog Harbor Romance
Identifiers: LCCN 2024045349 | ISBN 9780764241208 (paper) | ISBN 9780764244520 (casebound) | ISBN 9781493448906 (ebook)
Subjects: LCGFT: Christian fiction. | Romance fiction. | Novels.
Classification: LCC PS3604.E299 V65 2025 | DDC 813/.6—dc23/eng/20240930
LC record available at https://lccn.loc.gov/2024045349

Cover design by Susan Zucker

Baker Publishing Group publications use paper produced from sustainable forestry practices and postconsumer waste whenever possible.

25 26 27 28 29 30 31   7 6 5 4 3 2 1

This book is dedicated to every
father, mother, sister, brother, spouse, relative, or friend
who has ever prayed for a prodigal's return home.
May your hearts be encouraged and your prayers be answered.

*"For I am convinced that neither death nor life,
neither angels nor demons, neither the present nor the future,
nor any powers, neither height nor depth
nor anything else in all creation,
will be able to separate us from the love of God
that is in Christ Jesus our Lord."*
—Romans 8:38–39

1

August

I duck dive the nose of my surfboard under the next breaking wave using the same technique my dad endeavored to teach me back when I was a know-it-all punk who believed time was something to exhaust, not cherish. And back before I realized that practicing pop-ups with him at dawn wasn't a punishment, but a privilege. But I suppose that's the ugly truth about regrets: They never arrive until after it's too late.

I paddle hard for the next surf-worthy lineup, timing the enormous swell ahead with the same precision I once applied to mastering albums for artists in Los Angeles. As soon as I close in on the shoulder of the wave, my adrenaline surges. *Three, two, one.* I pop up on my board. Despite my muscle fatigue, my core holds taut, ready for one last battle for balance. Fiery heat licks the length of my spine as I pick up speed to ride the wave's power source.

The instant I slip into the pocket of the massive curl, the static in my brain is replaced by instinct. And it's this moment that is both everything I crave and everything I need all at once. Here, in this temporary cocoon of peace, there are no overdue medical bills screaming for attention, no home-based business investments lacking clientele, and no teenage dependent relying on me to keep us afloat.

The familiar tremor in my quads urges me to ride this wave back to shore and recover on the beach with a bottle of electrolytes and a protein bar. Only I'm not ready to go back to the noise yet. *I never am.*

I maneuver the board and cut back into the pocket, riding high on the momentum and gaining confidence with every second I'm on top. But when the next swell crests and breaks, the calm inside my head begins to slip, uncovering each stressor I'd hoped to drown. A single misstep later and I'm on the wrong side of the churning foam.

I have less than a second to tuck my head before I'm plunged into the dark waters with a force that depletes my oxygen reserve. On impact, I tumble head over feet, plummeting deeper and deeper into the abyss of the Pacific until I'm nothing more than a disoriented tangle of heavy neoprene limbs and spasming lungs.

But it's silent down here.

An enticing, addictive, weightless kind of quiet.

And for a moment, I will the panic clawing for my next breath to stop.

I will it all to stop.

The regret. The pain. The guilt. The grief. The shame.

My bearings and vision grow dim as a single thought closes in: *What if I just let go?*

The question barely has enough time to register before a spear of light illuminates the crashing waves above me, and with it, a primal, almost savage instinct takes over. *I can't leave my sister alone.*

I grasp for the leash around my ankle.

Desperation drives me as I climb the safety tether with a strength that consumes me. It's unnatural, and yet I'm positive it's the very thing keeping me alive. With every pull toward the light, the burn in my lungs intensifies. The urge to inhale is relentless as my vision spots and tunnels.

And then I see it: the shadowy outline of my board directly above me.

I break the surface.

I gasp for air, but I'm too weak to do anything more than cling to my board like the lifeline it is until I've recovered enough to float on my back and breathe.

It's okay.

It's okay.

It's okay.

I chant the words over and over again in my mind until I almost believe them.

Once the trembling in my chest subsides, I heave my upper body onto my surfboard and drag my dead-weight legs to follow suit. Though my body is thoroughly trashed, my mind fights to make sense of that suspended moment underwater. *How close was I to . . . ?* I don't allow myself to finish the question, but much like the waves rolling beneath me, my thoughts collide, one after another, and soon I'm picturing my sister outside the Welcome Lodge of Camp Wilson yesterday, waving good-bye.

The irony of our last conversation plays over in my mind.

I hadn't even put the gearshift fully into Park before I'd started in on her again. *"No surfing, no diving, no trampolines—on land or on water—"* I amended after I saw the glint of mischief in Gabby's dark brown eyes. *"No go-karts, no rock climbing, no mountain trails without adult supervision, and no horseback riding without a secure helmet."*

"Do you really think I'm going to forget your long list of no-no's the second you pull away?" My sister fiddled with her right hearing aid in the visor mirror before moving on to her left side. *"I had a head injury, August. Not Alzheimer's. Besides, I know you wrote an entire essay to the camp nurse about me already."* She flipped the visor closed and gave me a look that dared me to deny it. I couldn't.

"I'm just saying, I know how difficult peer pressure can be at your age. It wasn't so long ago that I was sixteen, and—"

"Oh wow, okay. I'm gonna go now." She popped the passenger door open, and I felt a distinct pinch in the center of my chest.

"Wait, *Gabs.*" I placed a firm hand on her knee. *"If you need any-thing, and I mean anything at all, promise you'll call me. I don't care if it's three in the morning or if you have to walk half a mile to find cell coverage—you call me, alright?"*

She stared at me for the longest time without saying a word and then finally laid her hand on top of mine, patting it twice. *"I'll promise, but only if you promise me something, too."* She raised both her eyebrows until I gave a slow nod in reply. *"You have four whole weeks without me at the house, so please go do something fun. Live a little. I better not come back and find you . . . well, like this."* She pulled a sour expression I assumed was meant to represent me and then proceeded to drill her pointer finger into my cheek. *"Promise me you'll free these dimples from the prison of your chronic grump face and find something real to smile about."*

I batted her hand away, but she held my gaze until I said the words out loud. *"Fine,"* I sighed. *"I promise."*

And then she was gone, hauling her overnight bags to the Welcome Lodge as if being away from home for longer than the one weekend a month she spends with Aunt Judy was a normal part of our routine.

As the memory fades, I blink the shore into focus. I'm much closer than I realized. And so is the familiar figure standing on the beach: Chip Stanton. My oldest friend, and the one person who never fails to show up when I'm at my worst. I have no idea why he's here or how long he's been waiting for me on that shore, but I stopped questioning Chip's uncanny timing years ago.

The surf approaches quickly, and though I'm as prepared as I can be, gravity hurts. There's no way around it, the hike back to my dad's rebuilt 1972 Bronco—affectionately named Maverick—is really gonna suck.

On rubbery, boneless legs, I limp my board onto the dry sand where Chip, in his pressed chinos and loafers, shields his eyes from the sun's glare. He's never been a fan of the beach, which makes his appearance here all the more curious.

When I speak, my voice sounds as torched as my lungs feel.

"Hey." I clear my throat. "If I'd known you were coming, I would have brought you my extra board."

Given that roughly ninety percent of Chip's worst fears reside in or around the ocean, I've spoken some version of this recycled joke more than a dozen times in the last decade. Only today, it falls flat.

"Dude, what happened out there?" He stalks toward me. "When your board surfaced without you . . . well, I thought . . ." He stops and blows out a hard breath. "Are you okay?" For all Chip's idiosyncrasies and quirks, he's not typically a worst-case-scenario guy. That's my role.

For a split second, I consider telling him about the light, and the superhuman strength that propelled me to the surface long after I should have been unconscious. But I can barely understand it myself. I need more time to sort it out. So instead, I shake my head and bend to disconnect the leash from my ankle. "I'm good."

Chip steps in to stabilize my board.

"I misjudged the size of the wave," I explain. "Lost my footing." Droplets of saltwater drip from the ends of my hair and disappear into the sand at my feet. I work to mask the shake in my legs, my arms, my hands, my voice. "Wipeouts always look worse from shore." The lie is so easily spoken, and yet it rebels inside my chest with the force of a hammer strike. Seeing as my smile's been out of commission for the better part of two years, I reach for the next best thing. "I'll try to work on my performance for next time."

Chip ignores my sarcasm and scans the scarcely populated bay around us. Other than a few cars on the street and a couple kiteboarders on the opposite side of the tide pools, there's no one else.

"Isn't there some kind of warning in the Surfer's Handbook about surfing alone?"

"Probably," I quip. "I'm betting it's right under the warning about wearing loafers in the sand." I point to his shoe of choice. "Those are meant for a library, not a beach."

He flexes the sandy toe of his shoe. "According to the website, these are considered a multipurpose loafer."

"What website? BookNerdFashion.com?"

This earns me a laugh.

Chip has worked as an editor for a big publishing house in San Francisco since college, but the truth is, he's one of those lucky guys who found a way to monetize the thing he loves most: reading. I suppose, in my own way, I was one of those guys once, too. Only, instead of books, it was music. Playing it, recording it, mixing it, producing it.

It's strange to think that once upon a time music made up the bulk of my world. *Before Gabby.*

A cool breeze whips dry sand against our calves, and I motion to the backpack I left near a chunk of driftwood by the trail up to the Bronco. My body is in dire need of electrolytes. "How'd you know I'd be out here this morning?"

Years ago, I kept a consistent Saturday morning surfing routine, but my time for hobbies, as the sole guardian of a sixteen-year-old, is a rare luxury. There's always something more pressing to focus on.

"Gabby's away at camp," Chip answers with a shrug before he takes my surfboard once again so I can swipe my backpack off the trail. I pull out my premixed drink and take a long pull as he continues. "When you didn't respond to my text about grabbing breakfast this morning, I checked the surf conditions and tried my luck. As soon as I spotted Maverick, my rideshare driver pulled over and let me out."

We've only just begun our trek, and already my legs have waved the white flag of surrender. Twenty-eight has never felt so old. "So you came all the way out for breakfast?" It's certainly not the strangest thing he's ever done, but the further we climb, the more I begin to crave a sausage omelet with a juicy side of bacon and hash browns smothered in—

"Not exactly," Chip hedges from behind me. "Breakfast is just the vehicle to discuss a business opportunity with you."

"How many timeshare presentations are involved in this business opportunity?" I toss back.

"None. Although, I hear Turks and Caicos is stunning." He attempts to jog in the sand beside me, which only makes him look like he's mimicking a slow-motion cartoon chase. "Actually, I was hoping we could discuss your recording studio."

I crane my neck and narrow a questioning gaze at him. I've been careful not to reveal too much when it comes to my work these days. Not because I don't trust him or because I'm attempting to save face—an impossible task considering the number of spit-wad wars we've engaged in over the years—but because Chip's the sort of guy who would auction off a kidney to help a friend in need. And I've been that friend more times than I care to admit since the accident.

"The recording market is different up here than it was in LA," I say with more ego than I intend as soon as my foot touches the pavement. "Finding the right clientele has been . . . challenging." It's why the bulk of my current workload is spent producing single EPs with run-of-the-mill studio musicians instead of engineering projects that could keep us afloat for an entire year.

"I'm sure that's true," he readily agrees. "California wine country is certainly not Hollywood." We're only steps away from Maverick when I sense him hesitating. "I'm also sure you've had more outgoing expenses than what you've let on for a while now." I don't confirm his suspicions, but Chip continues, undeterred. "I know you don't like talking about Gabby's prognosis, but I'm not ignorant enough to believe insurance has covered the bulk of her medical bills." He lowers his voice. "I know what you did to pay for her special hearing aids. And while that's commendable, there's only so many vintage guitars you can sell when it comes to—"

"Where is this going, Chip?" I can feel my defenses rising, and I'm certain Chip can, too. I grip my board and prepare to secure it to the roof of the Bronco.

"Audiobooks," he replies triumphantly.

I pause mid-lift and stare at him blankly. "Audiobooks."

"Yes." He holds out his hands. "Hear me out."

I say nothing as I swipe the damp hair from my eyes and hop onto the back bumper to tie down my board.

"Fog Harbor Books just gave me the green light to spearhead our first audiobook imprint, and you're my top pick for a producer.

I can do all the preproduction legwork—vetting the narrators and sending you demos so you can check the quality of their home studio equipment, and then once you approve them, I'd send you the raw cut recordings so you can do what you do best: produce a killer product."

After tightening the last strap, I drop down to the pavement and open the back of the Bronco. All I want is to peel this wet suit off, pull on my dry clothes, and drive to food. But first, I need to address Chip's random request. "While I appreciate the thought, Chip, I'm a sound engineer. I work with bands. Singers. Musicians. Wannabe rappers with too much disposable income. I don't do read-a-thons."

"Listen, I get that you're overqualified," he challenges. "But that's what makes it so perfect. You're already set up with everything you could possibly need. Depending on the length of the book and the edits you might require, you could crank out several projects a month. It would be flexible hours you could work around your current studio clients and Gabby's schedule."

"I don't know the first thing about books."

"You don't have to know anything about books. Some of these narrators are award-winning actors—their talent is incredible. I'm telling you, this gig is custom-built for you. And the pay is pretty great, too."

"How much is 'pretty great'?"

I swear his left eye twitches as he tells me the cut I'd make per finished book. It's decent. Maybe even a tad better than decent. And by his grin, he knows I know it, too.

"What kind of commitment are we talking about here?"

Chip laughs. "How did I know that would be your next question?"

I toss my stack of dry clothes onto the bumper and yank the extended zipper pull on the back of my wet suit until it reaches the top of my swim trunks, then work to break the fabric's suction on my arms and chest.

Chip leans his back against the Bronco, facing the water as he speaks. "I could start you off with a ten-book contract. That's the

NICOLE DEESE

minimum I can offer as there's a good size list of bay-area producers who wouldn't turn this opportunity down. Once you complete the first contract, we can renegotiate terms."

Ten books. I multiply the number Chip gave me earlier by ten. That would go a long way in recovering some of our savings.

Just the thought eases something tight in my chest. When I became my sister's legal guardian overnight, I didn't have a clue how fast we'd burn through my life savings and the majority of the insurance policies our parents left to us. But between my relocation costs, funeral expenses, medical bills, and the home studio I was certain would take off just as soon as the dust settled on my renovations to our parents' detached garage . . . we're running dangerously low.

It's tempting to recall the cushy paychecks I left behind in Los Angeles and the recording studio that was more like a glorified amusement park for music and tech geeks everywhere, but I can't afford to linger there for long.

The few highlights of that life had cost me so much more than they ever gave.

And that life never could have included Gabby.

A sixteen-year-old girl mourning the loss of her parents needs security: a real home in a good neighborhood with familiar friends at a familiar school. Not to mention the world-renowned medical care she's received at Stanford Children's in the wake of everything else the accident stole from her.

I pause my undressing and peer at the back of Chip's head. "Is there really a market for people too lazy to read for themselves? I mean, I'm no expert here, but reading a book versus listening to one seem like two completely different experiences. Does it even count as reading?"

Chip whistles low. "I'd highly recommend never repeating that question, especially in the presence of a reader. Brawls have broken out over lesser aspersions in the publishing world. But to put it mildly, yes, audiobooks do count as reading. It's been proven multiple times over in multiple studies. The brain responds similarly to the power of a good book whether it's listened to with the ears or read with the eyes. Plus, think about what an audiobook provides for a reader with a vision impairment."

The word *impairment* thumps at my shame.

Inch by slow inch, I peel down the thick layer of neoprene suctioned to my quads and calves until I can finally step out of my suit. I'm standing in nothing but my swim trunks when a convertible of college-age girls drives by. I reach for my T-shirt, but not quickly enough. The car reverses until it stops on the street near my Bronco. The driver honks her horn, followed by the waves and catcalls of her passengers. A scrap of paper is tossed in our direction. It flutters to the ground.

In two quick moves, I yank on my shirt and reach for a towel to dry my sun-bleached hair. The *beep beep* of an oncoming car causes the convertible to squeal forward.

"Well, that was exciting." Chip jogs around the front of the Bronco and picks up the paper from the road. He opens it.

"Samantha says to call her." He shows me the scribbled phone number next to a blotted lipstick mark. He tries to hand it off to me, but I give him a stare that has him wadding it up in his fist. "You're not interested. Got it."

"My life is complicated enough as it is." I slam the back hatch closed. "And that's without the added stress and misery of dating."

"Ya know, my offer might actually help you *uncomplicate* some things if you were willing to give it a chance." He quirks an eyebrow. "But since we're on the subject of dating, might I also suggest you stop thinking that every woman could be Vanessa in disguise."

He shudders, and I flash him a look that conveys exactly what I think of discussing my ex so early in the morning. I'm starving, but even the sound of her name brings back memories so nauseating they nearly kill my appetite altogether.

"Fine," he chuckles. "If I swear not to bring her up again, will you at least *consider* producing for Fog Harbor Audio? I'll need an answer soon."

When I nod in acknowledgment, Chip strides to the passenger side and climbs in. But instead of moving closer to the SUV, I take a final glance at the water, as if in a private consultation with the ocean. But there is no mystery to the decision I will make. Spoiler: It's not one where I keep trying to resuscitate a dying dream. The hours I've logged in a production studio don't matter, nor do the artists who've publicly recognized my creative ingenuity. *That* August Tate doesn't exist anymore. Truth is, he hasn't existed since the day he got the worst phone call of his life and took custody of his adopted sister.

I might have declined opportunities in the name of ego and pride in the past, but I'm not foolish enough to do it again. I have enough regrets. So I cut my gaze from the ocean, yank open the driver's side door, and accept the lifeline my friend anticipated I'd need even before he watched my head go under water.

2

Sophie

The instant my rideshare driver unloads my suitcases from the trunk of his Kia Sportage, I'm tempted to ask if he'll please put them back and take me somewhere else. But thanks to the many hours I've spent processing my massive life setback with my best friend, I'm too self-aware to mistake a different destination for what I really want: a different future than the one in front of me.

Right on cue, the phone I'd slipped into the pocket of my long skirt buzzes. And I know it's her before I even check the screen.

Dana:

You in Cali now? Did Phantom do okay on the long flights? How did the reunion go with your family? Also, I don't know how it's possible to miss you this much already when it's only been twelve hours. I just got home from tech rehearsal, but I'll be up for a bit if you want to chat. Xoxo.

It's not every day a text brings tears to my eyes, but I suppose it's also not every day I say good-bye to the best friend I've ever had and move across the country, either. I shoot back a quick reply, assuring her all is well and that I'll text her in the morning. There's no possible way she's not bone-tired after a full day of tech rehearsals. It wouldn't be fair or kind of me to ask her to wait up. I wonder how long it will take us to adjust to living in two different time zones . . . not to mention two totally different worlds.

I work to silence the pang of loss reverberating in the pit of my belly. This may not be the outcome either of us wanted after my acting career took a sharp nose dive, but I'll never forget how hard Dana fought for me to stay with her in New York. Even going so far as to take on my share of the rent to try and buy me as much time as possible on my job hunt. Ultimately, in the current economy and with living expenses what they are, not even our combined efforts were enough. Which is why I'm standing in the middle of the same brick driveway I pulled out of eight years ago on my eighteenth birthday.

The pathetic *meow* coming from my back—or rather, from inside the clear cat carrier strapped to my back—reminds me I'm not the only one who's traveled across the country today.

"Okay, Phantom, I hear ya, buddy." I banish my mental pity party and try instead to focus on the positives I'd rehearsed during our long flights here. I grip the handles of my roller bags and start for the moss-covered chateau at the front of the winery, my childhood home. Hanging lanterns illuminate the path in the dusky light, and I veer my suitcases around the large ceramic fountain where I used to sing with my Gigi while she planted poppies and marigolds under the welcome sign for Bentley Vineyards. She'd tell me to take the melody so she could harmonize with me. And at the end of every song, she'd say the same thing: *"The joy in your voice is a precious gift from God, Sophie. I pray you'll share it with the world someday."* The reminder causes my chest to ache. Memories of my grandma Greta—Gigi, as I called her—have always brought me comfort, and considering her fingerprints can be found everywhere at—

I halt to a stop and feel poor Phantom press into my spine. My eyes widen and then promptly narrow as I read and then reread the new words on the welcome sign: *Wilder Wines: Same vintage taste; new modern twist.*

I rotate in a complete circle, and my long eyelet skirt flares out as I look for clues to indicate my tired travel eyes aren't playing tricks on me. Of all the glowing reports my mother has shared regarding the changes my brother has made to the winery since my father's semi-retirement two years ago—she'd failed to mention a full re-branding of Gigi's legacy.

Befuddled, I approach the arched wooden doors of an estate I used to call Gigi's castle before we moved in with her when I was just six years old. My parents took on the bulk of the vineyard's responsibilities and eventually the small winery she'd started out of necessity in the late '60s. Before I push open the door, I begin the deconstruction process of transforming Fanciful Stage Sophie back into Family Winery Sophie. I take off my favorite dangly ear-rings and the secondhand vintage scarf I've wrapped through my hair like a headband, then step into a dimly lit grand foyer, one that looks as if it's already been tucked into bed with no plans to awaken till morning.

"Hello?" My voice echoes through the vast foyer with the same level of uncertainty as Belle when she first entered Beast's castle. Although Belle, at least, had magical furniture to keep her company.

"Mom? Dad?" Though my parents moved into a luxury condo only a short distance away after my brother and his wife took over the private living quarters upstairs in the east wing, I'm still hopeful they might be here to greet me. After all, I haven't seen either of them since my brother's wedding in Maui just over two years ago.

My footsteps reverberate in the wide empty corridor as the setting sun sweeps in from the large, west-facing windows overlooking the vineyard and tasting room. Golden light glistens on the high-gloss hardwoods of the main floor as I take an inventory of the modern tobacco-colored furniture that's replaced Gigi's carefully curated antiques. Everything is stone and leather, dark colors and straight lines. *Cold*, I think. Everything looks so cold.

A knot forms in my lower abdomen as I think of my mother having to part with Gigi's possessions after so many years. There are few battles I ever saw her engage in as a child, especially if the opponent was my headstrong father. And maybe that's why the loss of my grandmother hits me so hard in this moment. It was much easier to ignore the circumstances I left behind when I lived three thousand miles away.

I watch the way the shadows bend and move across the floors, remembering how Gigi used to shine them so I could practice my twirling. She always had a meticulous eye for detail, as well as a particular aspiration to keep her winery small and sustainable despite the pull of the booming industry around us. Unfortunately, after she died, my father and brother had other plans.

I spare a final glance into the parlor and then into the formal dining and living areas that, for a steep price, can be rented out to private wedding parties and special gatherings. When I see there are no lights aglow in the staff kitchen and can't make out a single muffled voice within the residence, I realize what I probably should have known all along: There is no one waiting for me.

It's not as if I'd been expecting some big sentimental homecoming, but I suppose there's nothing like the silence of a six-thousand-square-foot mansion to remind you of the reasons you moved away in the first place.

I roll my luggage to a stop at the base of the stairs, figuring I'll have to finagle them up the steps one at a time, when I see the door to my father's old study framed in light. Of all the family members I'll be reconnecting with during my stay here, it's my father's protégé who I've lost the largest amount of sleep over: my brother.

And it looks as if he's the only one here.

Gingerly, I slip off each strap of my backpack and ease Phantom's bag to the floor. I reach into one of the arm holes and scratch his fluffy black head and white ear. "Just a few more minutes. I promise." I smooth my hand over his back and help him get comfortable

23

again. The vet I brought him to after I'd found him on the street outside the theater estimated his age at ten. But right now the poor geezer looks as if he's lived all nine of his lives, plus a few extra. "Believe me when I say it's for the best to wait on making any formal introductions tonight."

I lift my timid gaze to the staircase and straighten my rumpled blouse and flowy skirt. A dozen or so hours ago when this day began, Dana had described my travel outfit as *enchanting*. Now it looks as if . . . well, as if I've been traveling for twelve hours.

As I take the stairs to the office Jasper now inhabits, the anxiety I've pushed down for weeks rushes in at once. Though I've tried to explain my apprehension to Dana numerous times, my words never come out right. On paper, my brother is the celebrated golden boy I've never been able to measure up to in the eyes of our parents and their affluent friends. I was often made to feel like the quirky, over-dramatic secondborn who struggled in all the areas that seemed to come naturally to my distinguished older sibling. But the thing is, even after that golden boy grew up to become a golden son, husband, and respected business mogul, he's never shown any interest in becoming a golden brother. Jasper's never really shown an interest in being a brother at all.

I pause at the top of the stairs, remembering one of the last conversations I'd had with my father, standing right here. He'd thundered out of his office, fisting my hard-won acceptance letter from NYU Tisch School of the Arts and demanding that I "stop this silly non-sense at once" even though it had taken me months to record and edit my audition videos and meet the requirements to apply online.

My father was not a yeller by nature, but I suppose that's because nobody ever dared to disobey him. I certainly never had. But I was even more certain that if I forced myself into the mold he'd cre-ated for me, it wouldn't stop there. *"You will go to Stanford like your brother, and you will let this foolishness go, do you hear me? I told your mother she would regret indulging you in this drama hogwash, and I was right. But I won't stand for it another minute. I did not raise you to become a glorified showgirl, and I certainly will not pay for it."* He tore my letter in half and flung it over the railing. For a man so opposed to dramatics, he put on quite the show when he wanted to. *"Your future is here. End of story. Now go get dressed for dinner."*

It takes more courage than it should to blink the memory away and knock on a door I was rarely welcomed through growing up. But now that my father has passed the baton off to Jasper, I've been given little choice as he's now the official gatekeeper to the next six months of my life.

"Come in."

I push the door open, and immediately I feel myself shrink back into the insecure teenager I'd hoped I left behind. There are only five years between Jasper and me, but in many ways, he's always felt like an equal to our father.

"Hello, Sophie." There's a smirkish smile on my brother's face as he takes me in from behind his desk. The setting should feel familiar, given how my father occupied this same space eighty-plus hours a week when I was growing up. But unlike the renovations made to the downstairs, I can't discern what's been upgraded verses what's twenty years old. My gaze makes a quick zigzag from the imported liquor that sits high on the shelf behind his desk, to the leather recliner in the corner, and then finally to the small wooden table displaying a magazine on an easel.

My brother's sharp jawline and intimidating brown eyes steal my focus. He's there, on the front cover of *Wine Spectator Magazine.* Another professional victory, another milestone of success met. Another reminder that Jasper has always belonged here.

"H-hi," I say around the thickness in my throat. "I just got in." The statement is so obvious I wish I could rewind the last fifteen seconds of this interaction and start over with the same level of confidence I possess on stage. Or rather, the same confidence I *used* to possess on stage. "I didn't want to bother you, but I figured I should check in tonight so I don't startle someone when I come out of my bedroom in the morning."

I once took a class on the power of microexpression during my studies, but my brother's blur the lines of several categories. When at

25

last he gestures to the chair across from him, I note that the creases around his eyes appear agreeable enough. "Please, take a seat. I'd offer you something from the kitchen, but our staff has already gone home for the evening."

"That's alright." I take a seat, trying to ease the tension in my shoulders. "I grabbed a bite before I left the airport. I'm more tired than anything else. It's been a long day."

"By the sound of your email, it's been a long few months." His piercing eyes appraise me with the same unsympathetic gaze of our father's. "It's a shame things didn't work out for you in New York."

But New York is quite possibly the last thing I want to discuss with my brother. I grip and twist my hands in my lap. "Do you know if Mom and Dad are planning to stop by tomorrow?"

"I'm afraid they left yesterday and will be gone for close to four weeks." He studies me. "I assured Mom you'd understand, considering my request for them to take my place on a networking cruise to the Mediterranean was rather . . . recent."

I blink, working hard to process this new information. He'd asked them to leave the same week I was coming home? "They're networking for Bentley Vineyards?"

"No," Jasper says with what sounds like a hint of pity in his voice. "They're networking for Wilder Wines. Bentley Vineyards was phased out at the end of last year."

"When was that decided?" When he quirks an eyebrow at my boldness, I rephrase. "I just mean, I thought Gigi's trust required a vote on any matter that affects the winery's future."

Due to a long-standing grudge held between Gigi and my father, she'd changed the structure of her estate to prohibit him from being one of four appointed trustees near the end of her life, limiting his power and control. Those trustees are named as Mr. Adams—Gigi's original attorney—my mother, my brother, and me. Though I forfeited my position and vote, as well as all my financial gains, the second I drove away from the winery. A fact my father recited at length when I told him that the acting hobby I loved had become the future I wanted to pursue.

My brother leans back in his expensive chair. "It does, and we did. It was a majority vote in favor of the rebranding."

Meaning that my mother, once again, cowed to the men in her life in order to keep them happy. Nothing new there.

Before I can comment further, my eye catches on the eerie artwork to the left of the table with the displayed magazine. Framed in a raw, dark wood, the abstract painting holds randomized textures and patterns of a neutral palette. With the exception of a blood-red smattering that divides the canvas in half.

"It's one of a kind," Jasper acknowledges as he stands. "All of Donnella's paintings are. It's what makes them so valuable." Hands clasped behind his back, he strolls over to it. "It's subtle yet profound, each stroke a testament of the artist's skillful eye and to the technique he's mastered with the manipulation of light and dark from every angle." His gaze cuts back to mine. "The English translation of the title from Italian is 'Blood and Shadows.'"

"I didn't know you'd taken an interest in art."

His smile is loaded when he says, "Eight years is a long time to be away from home." He moves toward the desk, leaning against it's surface directly across from me. Even at the late hour, his slacks and dress shirt remain free of wrinkles. "Upon closer inspection, you'll find we've evolved on nearly every front since you left, and it's my top priority to make sure things continue on in that direction. Without any unnecessary distraction." Jasper lets the word linger between us. "Your current financial situation is unfortunate, Sophie, but you were the one who made the choice to disengage from this family and from the industry we've invested in." His stare is unblinking, and I'm one-hundred-percent sure that if he wasn't bound to the rules of the Bentley trust, I wouldn't even be sitting here. "So let's both do each other a favor and not pretend like you've come back for any other reason than to collect your share of the biannual payout from the trust before you're on your way again."

Shame pricks my cheeks because I wish I could deny it. But the hard truth is I'm broke and homeless and in desperate need of a career path that won't cause me to freeze every time the lights go out. "I'll do my best to be a valued employee in the time I'm here. I've gained quite a bit of experience working in the food service industry between shows, so I'm confident I can assume almost any position here with minimal training." Per the conditions of the trust, I must work for the family a minimum of twenty hours per week for a duration of at least six months in order to receive a single cent of the next biannual payout. It's a substantial amount of money. Enough to pay my debts and start over somewhere new as long as I invest it well.

"Also," I add with my best attempt at a smile despite his scowl, "I really appreciate being able to stay at the house while I'm here." There's no way I'd be able to pay current rent prices in the area on the minimal wages I'll be earning until the payout hits my account next January. "My old bedroom will be plenty of space for me and—"

"Actually," he cuts me off, "your old room was recently remodeled into a home gym. I'll be sure to have Natalie provide you with a schedule of the various remodeling projects we have going on this summer. For now, she's made accommodations for you in the pool house."

My lips part and then close. "The winery has a pool?"

"It's currently in progress." He pushes off the edge of the desk. "I suggest you invest in a good white noise machine if you intend to sleep past six." He takes a seat at his computer again and taps his mouse. "Starting Monday afternoon, you'll work in the tasting room and report directly to Natalie. She'll handle your hours and set up your direct deposit for every other Friday, as well as provide you detailed instructions on how to check out a vehicle from our fleet, given you don't have your own means of transportation. That is, after you renew your California driver's license."

Despite the low dip in my stomach at the mention of a sister-in-law who's felt as much like a stranger to me as my own brother, I'm in no position to negotiate anything. And Jasper knows it. Without his signature, confirming I've met all the outlined conditions, my share of the trust payout will be denied, and I'll have absolutely nothing to show for what will likely be the toughest six months of my life.

"Thank you" is all I can say as I stand to leave.

With a final glance in my direction, he nods. "Please close the door behind you."

On the way out, I collect my cat and bags and trail down a new path to a pool house I hadn't known existed until a few minutes ago. The tiny cottage-like structure sits twenty feet from a giant crater in the earth wrapped in neon orange fencing. If only I could protect the hollow center in my chest in a similar fashion.

As soon as I open the door and flick on the light inside my new living quarters, I take in the functional yet soulless outbuilding. I swallow back the raw emotion lodged in my throat and try to imagine what Dana would say if she were here with me. It's not hard. I know she'd tell me to start by adding the colors and patterns I love to these blank walls while encouraging me to *make this space my own.*

But Dana is three thousand miles away, and this space isn't mine. Nothing here will ever be mine.

On a sigh, I unzip the cat backpack and reach for Phantom. Snuggling him close to my chest, I sit on the bed and fight back tears. "Welcome home."

3

Sophie

It only took six quiet nights in the pool house and four deep cleaning shifts in the tasting room—under the supervision of Natalie, my aloof sister-in-law who has yet to speak more than fifteen total words in my presence—to motivate me to spend yesterday reinstating my California driver's license. Considering there are one hundred and sixty-eight hours in any given week and only twenty of mine are accounted for at the winery, I'm left with a whole lot of soul-shriveling silence to fill. And this Saturday morning seemed like the perfect time to escape.

When I first signed out one of the twin black Escalades from the winery's small fleet of vehicles, I was surprised by the vibrant 3-D wrap advertisement featuring a giant bottle of Chardonnay with our new wine logo. My brother certainly wasn't going for the understated look when he ordered these. But once I started driving, it wasn't long before I forgot all about the obnoxious exterior.

It also wasn't long before I felt a familiar pull to a long-ago place of comfort for teenage Sophie. And while I can't say my destination wasn't planned, I can say I've had a theory I've wanted to test ever since the night I fell catatonic in front of an audience of twelve hundred people: *Did what happened to me in New York stay in New York?*

I sincerely hope so.

I stare at the *Summer Showcase Auditions Happening Today!* sign hanging on the front doors of the same community theater where I fell in love for the first time. Not with a person, but with a passion that had given me a purpose beyond the life constructed for me. It had also given me a family.

My fingers twitch for the phone in my purse. I want to call Dana, but then I remember the pictures she sent of the cast and crew party last night—all those happy faces I used to joke with, laugh with, run lines with, share a stage with. *No,* I think. *It's better if I do this on my own.* Dana has met her lifetime quota of Sophie pep talks this year, and honestly, I can't bear to let her down if I fail again.

On a shaky exhale, I approach the ornate door of the old community theater in Santa Rosa as if I'm expecting it to come to life, shrink me down to size, suck me through its keyhole, and label me an imposter. Before I decide to reach for the handle, the door creaks open.

I leap back just in time for a petite Latina woman—who looks to be around forty, with sleek dark hair and deep fuchsia lipstick—to peek her head outside.

She stares at me through round, apologetic eyes. "Well, this is embarrassing." She pushes the door the rest of the way open. "I keep telling our handyman—who also happens to be my husband—that this door is cursed. It always decides to jam at the most inopportune times. Glad I checked to see if there was anyone else out here before we got started." She beckons me closer. "Please, please, come in, and don't hold our faulty hardware against us. We're still getting things in order since the reopen." She props the heavy door open with her hip and then looks from me to her watch. "Auditions for our One-Act Summer Showcase start in nine minutes. Am I right to assume that's why you're here?"

I start to shake my head no, but my mouth betrays me. "Yes, ma'am."

"Great!" She beams and then drops her voice to a conspiratorial level. "Here's a hot tip: The regulars usually come through the side door by the alley." She points stage left and winks. "And they usually bring donuts and plenty of drama to keep us well entertained."

"What's not to love about donuts and drama?"

"Exactly." Her smile broadens as she ushers me inside. "I'm Portia Pimentel."

For a split second, I see a vision of myself tucking tail and running back to where I parked without taking a single step farther inside this theater. But instead, I remind myself why being here is absolutely critical to my mental health. I need to test my theory. If I succeed today, then I might just have a chance at keeping some form of the dream I've held for a decade and taking it with me to whatever and wherever comes next.

"I'm Sophie." I extend my hand and work to find my professional side. "Sophie Wilder."

"It's so nice to meet you. Also, may I just say, *you are stunning*," Portia adds appraisingly. "I'd kill for your height."

Unexpected heat floods my face. Five foot nine may be on the taller side for the average American woman, but given that the top of Portia's head barely reaches my shoulder, I can see how she might consider my height an impressive feat.

"I'd ask if this is your first time here, but seeing as we just purchased the Twilight Theater back in April, *and* seeing as I'm pretty much familiar with every thespian in the area currently gossiping inside that auditorium, I know that it is." Her quirky laugh is followed by a wink, and I decide against telling her about the theater camp I attended here my junior year of high school or how it became a second home to me that summer.

"Just stick by me," she says. "I'll be happy to introduce you to your friendly competition today."

I glance over her head into a dim lobby, and my heart double-taps against my ribs. "Wait, are these *open* auditions?" As in, everybody here will be watching me get up on stage for the first time since February?

She nods. "We've done it the same way since we were a tiny crew of drama nerds who used to meet in a church nursery over fifteen years ago now. But I promise, you'll find this group to be super supportive. Our Summer Showcase is three different one-act plays that will run the last weekend in August—they're a community favorite, and we're thrilled to finally have a theater to perform at." Her gaze drops to my hand. "Ooh, is that . . . did you bring a portfolio with you? I'd love to take a look if you don't mind?"

It's not until she points to the yellow folder pinched between my fingers that I even remember I brought it with me, and I can't be sure if I actually hand it over to Portia or if she coaxes it from my gummy fingers. But within two blinks, she's scanning my headshots.

She whistles. "These are next level. Did you get them done around here?"

I try to swallow, but the roof of my mouth is drier than the outside of a cotton ball. "I, um, no. I had them taken in—"

"New York?" She's perusing my resume now, and I go from hot to cold to hot again. In New York, its second nature to bring a portfolio everywhere . . . but I'm realizing only now just how overkill it was for me to bring it to a small community theater.

"Wait." Her eyes narrow and then promptly widen as she looks from the thin piece of paper where I've conveniently left off my most recent show. "You've been on Broadway?"

"Minor roles only." For four years straight, until I landed my big break.

Which I'd promptly destroyed in the first act.

"Still, that's . . ." She shakes her head and gives one of those breathy laughs as if she doesn't quite know which emotion she should be displaying at the moment. "It's an honor to have someone of your caliber auditioning with us. I'm positive there's so much we can lean from you and your experiences. Don't let our size fool you—there's a lot of talent here. And wouldn't you know it, but we're short on female leads who can sing and dance."

Mutely, I open my mouth, uncertain of what I should say to assure her that I'm actually a total failure of an actress, and that my name is likely blacklisted with every major director back east, and that I'd be thrilled to walk away from her cast as a bleating goat if it means I'm not completely broken. "I'm actually not looking to land any kind of lead role, I really only came to—"

But she's looped my arm through hers and is practically skipping us toward the auditorium doors. "I absolutely cannot wait to introduce you to everyone, Sophie! You are an answer to prayer."

With a strength that doesn't match her stature, Portia flings open the auditorium doors, and every happily mingling thespian down below cranes their neck to stare back at us. I feel my body temperature rise as they assess my threat level. I'm about to attempt my meekest win-them-over smile when I catch sight of the stagehand flicking the giant spotlight on and off on center stage.

I can't look away.

And just like that, the memory is here in present tense, clawing at my peripheral vision and scratching away the surrounding detail of this room until I'm forced to revisit a scene I've tried to forget since February. A wide-eyed audience. A wildly gesturing director. And a pair of lungs too frozen from fear to utter even a single word after the curtain opens.

My frozen lungs.

Even now I can't make them inflate.

I can barely make myself do anything except for the one thing I want to do most. *Escape.*

Before Portia even has a chance to ask me if I'm okay, I've unhooked my arm from hers, muttered an intelligible apology, and stumbled my way back through the dark lobby and out the theater doors.

My theory was wrong: What happened in New York didn't stay in New York.

Likely because New York isn't where my nightmare originated.

California is.

When I get home later that afternoon, after driving aimlessly for hours, I head directly to my living quarters on the far side of the construction pit surrounded by heavy equipment. Jasper wasn't exaggerating when he said the workers started at six in the morning to allow for peace during the hours when the tasting room is open. From what I could eke out of Natalie, the luxury pool and spa project should be finished in four weeks' time. But by the looks of it, construction time seems to be on par with God's time.

As soon as I'm inside the pool house, I call for Phantom and hear his quiet purr in response. Naturally, he's been hiding under the bed. He's about as big a fan of the construction zone as I am. My black, long-haired rescue cat with the white patch of fur around his blind eye circles my ankles. I bend to scoop him up and snuggle him close.

"It was awful," I whisper in answer to his unasked question about my day, something I've been doing more and more of since I moved back. I take a seat in the small desk chair and proceed to nuzzle my face into his fur. Yet another thing I've been doing as of late. Somehow, it keeps the tears from falling. "I should probably add the words *coward* and *fraud* to my résumé after today." A thick ache builds in my throat. "And maybe *aimless*, too, while I'm at it."

Apart from working as a waitress on and off over the last few years, I've had the same dream since the summer I found a way to be a million other people besides the one person I didn't want to be. I suppose that's the hardest thing about dreams coming true at a young age: Once you've lost them, it's impossible not to wonder if you've also lost yourself.

My phone rings, and I let it go to voicemail.

When it rings a second time, I know that if I ignore it again, my night could end with a wellness check from the local police, courtesy of Dana.

I answer and try my best to sound like I haven't been facedown in cat fur. "Hey," I say with forced cheeriness. "How are you?"

She doesn't respond.

"Dana?" I pull the phone away. Check to see the call is still connected. It is. "Hello?"

"What's wrong with your voice?" Her tone is calm, but I hear the suspicion behind it.

I quickly set Phantom on the floor as if he's the thing responsible for giving me away. "Nothing, just a long day." Thank goodness we're not on video call.

And then she's calling me on video. Dang it.

I swipe at the dampness under my eyes with the hem of my shirt and then answer with a smile. "Hello again."

"Oh sweetie, you look awful. What's wrong?"

I almost laugh when I see the mascara smudges under my eyes. Her assessment isn't wrong. I look about as good as I feel. "I promise, I'm just having a bad moment. Mostly hormones."

"Nice try, but you still have eleven days to go before you can claim PMS. We're still cycle buddies, remember?" She narrows her fan of false eyelashes at the camera. "Did something happen with Natalie?"

This time I actually do laugh. "Other than her playing the ignoring Sophie game? No. She's winning by the way."

"So what is it?"

I bite the quiver from my bottom lip before I speak, knowing that once I say these words out loud there will be no taking them back. "I went to an audition at my local community theater today, and I couldn't go through with it."

"You did *what*?" She looks directly at me through the camera. "Why didn't you call me?"

"Because I needed to see if I could do it on my own." I flop back on my bed and hold the phone above my head. "And I couldn't. It's . . . it's really over."

I've avoided this truth, tiptoed around it for months now, even though everything in my life pointed to the same blinking neon sign of my failure. But hope is strange thing. It keeps right on living even when you feel like dying.

"No it's not, it's just . . ." Dana's eyes shift as if she's searching for the right vocabulary words. "You're dealing with the stress of a difficult transition period right now. Give yourself some time. And remember, this isn't your forever, it's just temporary."

"But what happens after I leave here? I have nothing. No plans. No dreams. No connections outside of—"

"You still have me."

I sigh, thankful to be reminded of that. "I do, I know. But you're in New York."

"For now, yes." She shrugs. "But it's not as if my contract is indefinite. Besides, you know I'm a nomad at heart. Maybe we'll find that traveling theater gig we've always dreamed of doing together."

"Maybe," I say, hoping I sound more optimistic than I feel about such an unrealistic opportunity. "But you're living your dream right now, and I'd never forgive myself if you left it for me."

She purses her lips and tilts her head. "You need something that excites you, Sophie. Something you can look forward to while you're stuck in limbo."

I tug a pillow close. "Like what?"

"Like an in-between dream—something you'll do while we figure out how to fix you on stage and get you out of California." Dana is even more of a diehard when it comes to hope than I am. "I'm thinking through possible hobbies. Hang on. I'll come up with something."

I flip over on my tummy. "Please don't suggest I give crocheting a try again. You remember how horrible that lopsided hat I made for Jason's birthday was." I laugh now, remembering Dana's ex-boyfriend walking around with a mismatched striped hat that looked like something from a Dr. Seuss book. I think I was more upset than Dana when they broke up. He was such a good sport, which is probably why they remain close friends.

I expect Dana to throw in a quip about my poor crafting skills, but instead she seems to be contemplating something else. "How weird you mentioned him—I just saw him last night."

"Why is that weird? You see him at auditions all the time."

She shakes her head as if she's trying to recall something. "I know, but he was telling me about a gig he just got. Honestly, I was only half listening because it was karaoke night and you know how focused I get. But anyway, I guess he's reading books for like a publishing house or something. Said he loves it. Maybe that's something you could look into? You love books, and you're a pro at character voices."

I try to piece together her words. "You mean he's narrating audiobooks?"

"Yeah, that's it." She nods enthusiastically. "Although I'm pretty sure he called it 'voice acting.'" She sounds more excited by the second. "Never know, maybe it could be the thing that gets you out of that pit of despair you're living in and keeps your talents from getting rusty. Plus, he seemed pretty happy with the paycheck, too."

"Interesting." I nod in solidarity, even if the idea feels wildly over-dramatized. "Did he tell you how it works—how he got started?"

"I didn't ask a whole lot of questions, but from what I understood, it sounds like actors submit a demo to various websites, and once they're selected, they record the books in their home studios. Jason soundproofed his closet."

And just like that, my brand-new in-between dream dies. I flip the camera to show her my living space. "The closest thing I have to a closet is my shower, and even if I did have one, there's construction going on most of the day and I work most evenings."

I can tell I've stumped her. "Listen, I don't have all the answers, but I'll ask Jason to send you a link. Maybe there are solutions for someone in your exact scenario. You can't be the only down-on-her-luck heiress looking for a way out of her castle." Her mischievous grin is marked by amusement. "You do realize you're living out the real-life equivalent to several Disney movie plots, right?"

I laugh at this. "So you're saying I either need to find Aladdin's lamp or a dashing prince to ensure a happy ending?"

"Either of those options would be acceptable."

"Okay," I say decidedly. "I'll look into it."

Dana grins her most winning smile. "I have a good feeling about this, Sophie."

"You said that about pickle ice cream once, too."

She pulls a face and gives a full body shiver. "*Please* never bring that up again. I still don't know how you can eat that stuff."

"Get him to send me the link." I return to the desk and reach for my laptop.

"On it. Bye!"

Before I've even finished typing in my password, I receive her forwarded text from Jason, and soon I'm lost in a perusal of an entire industry I'd never given a single thought to in the past. Halfway down the page, I notice a sentence that hooks me like the desperate, gullible fish I've become since I moved back to California.

Are you an out-of-work actor looking for a reliable, flexible income? Click here to learn more information about one of the fastest-growing industries in entertainment today.

I hover my finger over the attached mini trailer of a woman wearing headphones and smiling like she's living her best life as she talks into a radio mic while peppy music plays in the background. I refresh the page to watch the video a second time and then scan the Q&As below it. Apparently, some narrators prefer working in a studio outside their home. I click on the *more details* section and read that a narrator's pay scale is based on experience. Does stage acting count?

Phantom watches me through his one good eye as I learn how to upload a sample using my iPhone. The quality won't be stellar, but it's a start. At least I'll be able to register a profile and search the current job openings in my area.

I click the flashing headphones dancing on my screen next to the *enter your zip code* prompt. Immediately, I'm redirected to a page of local and national job openings for voice actors. I scroll through the list, reading each description and requirement carefully. I sort the postings that require fancy equipment I don't own—which, as it turns out, are most of them. By process of elimination, there are only a couple that meet my limited criteria. And only one that catches my eye enough for me to upload my résumé and figure out how to send in a sample to Chip Stanton, the contact at Fog Harbor Audio in San Francisco.

And then I send it off and say a prayer to the same God my Gigi loved with her whole heart and hope He'll guide me.

4

August

My phone lights up next to my soundboard, and I quickly press Pause on the male narrator I'm listening to as he describes the color patterns of Canada geese along a riverbank. While I've never made a habit of checking my phone on the job, I've also never had to listen to someone read for eight-plus hours until recently, either. Checking my phone notifications has become somewhat of a needed palate cleanse for my ears as this is the third audiobook I've produced for Fog Harbor Audio. So far, staying alert when my mind wants to drift has proven to be the most challenging part of this gig.

But it's a solid paycheck. And that's what matters most.

I glance at the screen and smile when I see her name.

Gabby:

> How many energy drinks have you consumed today? Don't lie.

I chuckle at my sister's familiar text greeting. She's either found a signal due to a camp excursion, or our aunt has popped in with lunch for her and her friends again. I side-eye the sixteen-ounce beverage on my desk.

> Not that it's any of your business, but I'm still on my first can.

Gabby:

> The jumbo size or the regular?

I groan.

> Are you doing anything useful today besides monitoring my caffeine intake?

Gabby:

> Aunt Judy brought five batches of mom's famous peanut butter fudge to camp, so we took our lunch down to the water. I forgot how delicious this stuff is!

The twinge of grief is fleeting, but it still takes me a moment to reply.

> I'd ask you to save me some, but given you're not even halfway through camp yet, I won't be so cruel. You'll need something to snack on the next time you pass on pizza night.

Gabby:

> Urgh. That pizza was foul. 🫠Also, don't tell Aunt Judy I told you, but she made a batch for you, too. She's headed your way on Saturday so I asked if she'd mind picking up a few things for me from my closet. I could use an extra pair of shoes.

Gabby:

> I'm LOVING it here though (other than the pizza) and I'm learning SO MUCH! I feel like my brain is

absorbing ASL three times faster since the camp is total immersion. Tyler says I've picked it up quicker than anyone he's ever known. Thank you again for letting me come 🙂

Gabby:

What about you? Are you keeping your promise to me? Are you having some real fun?

I blink at her rapid-fire texts, remembering when her team of doctors pulled me aside to tell me they couldn't be sure how well her brain would recover after the trauma she suffered in the accident. And yet here she is, typing three times faster than I can think and exceeding all the best-case scenarios. Except for one.

When I don't respond to her last text with super human speed, she sends another.

Gabby:

Auuuguuuusssssttttttt????

Fun is relative at my age. Chip is on his way over in a few. We'll probably grab takeout after we finish up a work project at the studio.

Gabby:

You always get takeout with Chip. So no, that does NOT count.

Gabby:

And what work project?

When did I become so predictable? I take a second to consider how to tell her I've taken on a new job since I dropped her at Camp Wilson. What's the least nerdy way of saying I listen to people read books for a living now?

There's this new trend in literary entertainment, integrating voice actors into the book world.

> Chip's super pumped about it, so I'm helping him out for a while.

Gabby:

> You mean like audiobooks?

So, basically, I am exactly the nerd she thinks I am.
I provide her with a thumbs-up emoji, hoping she'll leave it alone.

Gabby:

> Okay, well . . . if you don't send me a pic of you doing something fun soon, I'm gonna send you some pictures of me riding a stallion bareback down a beach without wearing a helmet. Gotta go!

She's joking, I assure myself. But even still, my pulse kicks up a notch as an unwanted image of my sister endangering herself plays across my mind in slow motion. I tug my studio headphones off, feeling the need to take something apart just so I can put it back together again. I do a quick scan of my work area, looking for such a project, when I notice the takeout box from last night's dinner sticking out of the too-small trash can. Another bad habit I've developed as of late: eating in my studio instead of going into the house, which is only on the other side of the driveway from my remodeled studio. But on the upside, working through dinner has helped me log more hours in my new side hustle as I flag mouth pops, slurred words, harsh consonants, and weird exhales, and take note of any area that needs to be rerecorded.

I've found that pumping myself full of caffeine helps me stay focused on the reader, rather than on the sound effects I can imagine adding to each scene—wind instruments, percussion, and some creeping bass notes for dramatic intrigue. Maybe in the same way I can hear music where it doesn't exist, a reader can create connections to characters who also don't exist. What a bizarre thought.

I drain the last of my drink and toss the can into the overflowing recycle bin near my thinking couch. I should probably take that out. Otherwise it might actually look like I have a problem.

I glance at the clock above the recording booth and note that I have approximately fifteen minutes before Chip arrives with a local narrator he's looking to contract. He asked me to record a fifteen-minute demo he can send to his author for approval. My hesitant agreement came with the caveat of *just this once*, as I don't wish to make a habit out of hosting story hour in my one and only equipped recording booth reserved for musicians. It's one thing for him to send me the raw cuts of his narrators. It's another to have them invade my personal space. In the future, I'd love to outfit a second booth as the space is already framed in, but at the moment, it's nothing more than a storage closet.

With the overloaded recycle bin gripped in my right hand, I head to the door, throw it open, and bump the bin directly into a pair of legs. Decidedly female legs. There's only a fraction of a second to ponder this as our bodies collide and then promptly bounce apart, sending a spray of cans through the air like confetti in the process.

"Oh no! I'm so sorry!" the woman blurts as we both attempt to collect the flying objects before they begin their final descent onto the driveway and roll into the street.

She catches the two at her feet while I jog after the ones that got away. In an instant, we've become teammates, successfully retrieving my recycling and making goal shots into the bin I've set against the outside wall to deal with later.

When I finally stand upright and face my surprise visitor, I can't even pretend not to notice how arrestingly beautiful she is—like some sort of fairy-tale maiden straight out of the princess books my mom used to teach my sister English. Her caramel-brown hair is long and wavy with streaks of light and dark, half bound with a thick blue ribbon tied near the crown of her head. The tails swish every time she moves. With that and her intriguing wardrobe of layered fabrics and colors, there's literally too much for me to capture in a single glance. I'm not even sure a full five-minute study of her would do the job.

"Hello," she says with a voice that seems to pry open a chasm in my chest. "Are you August Tate, the audio engineer?"

"Yes, I'm . . . August." I have never sounded so unsure of my first name. Was she here to inquire about my marketing ads online? A singer, maybe?

"Oh, good." She sighs and smiles at me in a way that makes my lips follow suit of their own accord. "I'm glad I found you. I'm Sophie Wilder." She adjusts her stance, then holds out her hand to me in greeting. I hesitate before taking it, but when I do, our hands remain connected a beat longer than two strangers meeting for the first time should. The instant we break apart, I'm already hoping it won't be the last time I get to touch her. "I believe Chip Stanton scheduled me to record a demo here today at two?" She glances at her watch. "I was worried I'd be late, but since there was little traffic out this way, I'm actually here a few minutes ahead of schedule."

Wait. *Sophie* is the narrator Chip scheduled? Had he mentioned that she was a . . . *she*? If so, he'd conveniently left out a few key adjectives.

She hooks her thumbs under the padded straps of her backpack and gives me a questioning look. "I'd be fine to wait outside until Chip arrives."

It's only then I realize I haven't uttered a single word since I caveman-spoke my first name. *Pull it together, Tate.* "No, no. That's okay. Please. Come in." And just like that, I'm suddenly regretting not doing a more thorough cleanup of the studio. It's been a long time since I've invited an outsider into the messy state of my life, longer still since that outsider has been a woman unrelated to me. "I'm afraid I don't get many guests, but you're welcome to make yourself comfortable on the sofa there. I doubt Chip will experience the same traffic luck, coming from the city."

As soon as she steps past me, I'm hyper-aware of the sweet, intoxicating fragrance that trails after her. Something floral maybe?

"Traffic is so fickle, isn't it?" She gives a half laugh, half groan. "In New York, it seemed like the more pressed for time you were, the more delays you were sure to have."

"New York?" I ask, surprised. "Is that where you're from?"

"Originally? No." She takes in the various instruments on my wall with curious eyes, and I suddenly wish I was a mind reader. "I actually grew up just outside of Santa Rosa, but I went to college at NYU and lived there for the past eight years. I only moved back recently."

There's a story there, I'm sure of it. But seeing as I'm probably the last person on earth to ask a stranger something so personal, I just say, "That's a big change."

She lowers her eyes to her metallic gold sandals that tie in bows at her ankles. One peeks out through the slit in her long denim skirt every now and again as she gently sways left to right. "It's been an adjustment, to be sure."

I pick up on the somber note in her tone even as her lips tip north. I rarely allow myself to think about what I might miss about living in LA. Instead, it's easier to focus on the traffic, the smog, the constant crime and ridiculous crowds, the ex-girlfriend who exploited my regrets like trophies. But there were other parts, more significant parts, that feel as if they were amputated from my life without permission. I suppose, in a way, they were.

"May I offer you a drink?" I open my fridge and then immediately wince, wishing I'd taken the time to restock the sparkling waters Gabby always adds to the grocery list. Or, you know, shopped at a grocery store. "Unfortunately"—I run a hand through my hair—"my selection is fairly limited at the moment."

"Unless I'm in the mood for an energy drink, you mean?" she says with a smirk. "You know, the first step to help is admitting you have a problem."

"Then I'm definitely not on that step yet." I hold up my favorite flavor. "But I am willing to share."

She flashes me another grin, and I honestly can't remember the last time I've been so affected by, well, anyone. Maybe this is a side effect of the caffeine. If so, I might never stop. "Thanks for the offer, but I try to stick to water as much as I can—vocal chords are pretty boring that way."

I watch her twirl a long strand of hair around her finger as she studies the framed pictures on my wall: Most of them are bands I worked with in LA, some of them are album covers; all of them are signed to me. Gabby had found them shoved into a moving box around the same time I was finishing up the renovations on the detached garage. She'd come to me one night with an armful of frames and an idea of how to hang them. I couldn't say no to her. She was too happy to find something she could do to help that didn't require her being in the center of a construction zone. *"It's good marketing to show your work history, August,"* Gabby said as if she was keen on good business practices at her age. *"You never know who might wander in here someday and need a sound engineer with your exact qualifications."*

I can only imagine what Gabby would be thinking if she could see Sophie in here right now. Undoubtedly, she'd like her. The woman's artsy style alone would draw my sister in like a—

"Wow," Sophie says. "You've worked with a lot of artists. Where was this big studio located?"

"LA," I say, working to scratch the thoughts about Gabby meeting Sophie from my head. This woman will be here and gone in thirty minutes with nothing but a demo to show for it.

I've just fished out the single bottle of water from the back shelf of my fridge to give to Sophie when a peculiar sound pricks my ear. A low, soft rumble.

The volume increases incrementally as I approach Sophie standing near the picture wall. I hold out her water.

"Here's your—" But I can't finish the sentence because I'm too busy seeing something that simply can't be. I blink to clear my vision, but the transparent orb strapped to Sophie's back is still there. And so is the purring black-and-white cat inside it.

I leap back. "That's a cat."

The words come out stilted, only there is nothing stilted about the memory of my aunt's demon tabby attacking me in my sleep more than a decade ago.

Sophie twists to face me. "What?"

She can't be serious. I wait a beat, then two, thinking maybe Chip has put her up to this? Is this woman nothing more than an innocent bystander to a prank involving one of my most traumatic childhood memories?

"You have a cat strapped to your back," I repeat.

"Oh! Right," she exclaims with a laugh. "Yes, I'm sorry." She slips one shoulder strap down and then twists the whole weird contraption around to her front. "This is Phantom." She then plunges her entire hand through a hole in the side of the bag with seemingly no fear of losing her extremities and then . . . strokes its head. "Phantom, this is August." She lowers her voice as if to keep her confession between us. "He's adjusted to the backpack pretty well, but the last time he was in it was for a super long day of travel I'm sure neither of us wants to repeat anytime soon."

I'm frozen. My limbs are stuck in this awkward mid-movement state, hands poised to cover my vital organs, water bottle wielded like a sword. I stare at the feline for what feels like all nine of its lives before I look up to its owner and simply ask, "But why?"

She tilts her head, her concerned expression directed at me. "Why what?"

"Why is he *here*? In my recording studio. Is he some sort of . . ." I search my mental files for the proper terminology. "Emotional support cat or something?"

Sophie laughs. "More like I'm his emotional support human—although lately I suppose it's about fifty-fifty." She must pick up on my confusion by this point, because her smile dims. "I'm sorry. I was under the impression from Chip that it wouldn't be a problem for me to bring Phantom today. I emailed him this morning to ask and—wait." Her eyes widen as if only now being struck by the horror of this situation. "You aren't allergic or anything, are you?"

Does phobia count as an allergy? I shake my head and watch as her neck splotches pink.

"Just not a cat person then . . ." She swallows at whatever nonverbal answer she discerns in my expression. "Right . . . and I suppose you probably think I'm some sort of crazy lady who always takes her cat out in public—but I promise you, I'm not. Crazy, I mean. At least, not about cats. Phantom is a special case; he's a rescue cat, and he's super old and practically blind in one eye, and my brother has this giant construction project going on right next to where we're staying, and this morning the walls were actually *vibrating* from whatever jackhammer thingy they were using, and I truly thought Phantom might not survive the day if I left him alone." She sucks in a huge breath. "Normally, I would be fine leaving him in the car for a bit, but there was no shade on the street where I parked, and it's too hot in the sun, and so yeah . . . that's why he's here."

The second Sophie's finished speaking, a cloud of awkwardness descends, leaving us at an impasse. While her persuasive speech might have moved the proverbial needle a notch or two closer to Team Phantom, it doesn't erase the fact that cats are shifty and unpredictable.

This whole thing is such a signature Chip move. Naturally, he would think nothing of inviting a woman *and her cat* to what is essentially a job interview—why? Because he's a genuinely nice person who is rarely, if ever, put out by anyone. His bachelor-led lifestyle is full of fast-paced, spur-of-the-moment decisions that offer little in the way of consequence and a lot in the way of freedom. And sometimes it's difficult not to feel the least bit envious of the autonomy he holds over his own life.

I've only just begun to calculate the ways he will need to make this up to me when the devil himself bursts inside.

"Hey, August." He holds up a palm in greeting and then spots my surprise guest on the sofa. "And you must be Sophie. It's so good to meet you." He takes her free hand as if she's a celebrity, grasping it with both of his and shaking vigorously. "I sincerely apologize for my tardiness. I always refer to rush hour as sloth hour." Chip says all this as if it's completely normal to greet a woman who is petting a geriatric cat inside a giant plastic bubble with air holes.

"No problem at all," Sophie says with notably less brightness in her voice than she had three minutes ago. "It's nice to finally put a face to all the emails we exchanged last week."

Chip squats down then, eye level with the cat he approved for a playdate in my studio. "And this handsome fella must be Phantom." Chip grins and rocks back on his heels to smile up at Sophie. "Genius name. He looks exactly like him."

I scrunch my eyebrows together. *Like who?* How many black-and-white cats has Chip been introduced to?

"Ya know, that was my first experience with live theater," he continues, hand to his heart. "It made a big impact on me as a teenager."

"I never got to see it live," Sophie chimes in. "I so wish they'd bring it back."

I look between them both, waiting for someone to clue me in on the last twenty seconds of this conversation, but they've already moved on. Chip invites Sophie back to the recording booth—*my recording booth*—at the far end of my studio while he chats up a storm regarding how pleased he was with her submission and how he has high hopes for this demo.

Meanwhile, the cat has been left in his see-through prison on the sofa, pawing to get out.

Not going to happen, buddy.

"August?" Chip rotates to face me as if I've just returned from an extended vacation. "I'd like for Sophie to read the sample chapter I sent her last night. You mind helping her get situated in the booth?"

There is no interpretation needed for the look I laser into Chip on my way back to get Sophie *situated.* But I suppose the sooner she reads, the sooner she and her cat backpack will be on their way, and the sooner I will make it abundantly clear to Chip that this scenario will never happen again. I signed a contract to produce unfinished cuts from the narrators he sends me, not to escort them into my booth after what might be one of the most uncomfortable interactions I've ever had with another human.

"I'm happy to read this for you, Chip," Sophie says hesitantly, "but I'm sorry in advance if Phantom throws a fit. He can get a bit temperamental when he feels trapped."

That makes two of us.

"How 'bout I hold him while you're in the booth?" Chip offers.

"It shouldn't take more than ten or fifteen minutes. I'm interested to hear how you interpret each character description I emailed you last night. There are six characters in the reading I've chosen. Feel free to take a moment."

"Thank you." Sophie appears to be studying the script on her phone carefully.

I hand her a pair of studio headphones. "I'm guessing you're familiar with this process?"

She looks up at me then, and I feel a distinct, radiating pinch in the center of my chest. "Actually, no," she says as if this is a confession booth instead of a recording booth. "This is all new to me. I used my iPhone to record the audition for Fog Harbor's submission opening. I don't have a home studio like a lot of the narrators I've researched online. My living situation is too temporary for something like that."

I nod, and to my surprise, compassion rises to the surface more quickly than I anticipate. I may not understand her choice in animal companions, but I can offer her some pointers on recording booths. "This mic here is incredibly sensitive, so you won't need to speak loudly, just clearly." I demonstrate how close she should be for the best quality and how to minimize unnecessary mouth noises, which I will be working to eliminate on my end as well. She nods like I've told her the secret to immortality, and it takes a Herculean effort to cut my gaze away from her piercing green eyes. *Jade*, I think to myself. That shade is called jade green.

At least these tips will be useful to her if she decides to make a career out of this.

"Thanks," she says after she swipes to another page on her phone. "I think I'm ready."

I exit the padded booth and round the corner to find Chip fishing the cat out of the pack. I don't even bother with a sarcastic comment. I'd rather pretend neither of them exists at the moment.

"Do we wear headphones out here, too?" Chip asks as Phantom attempts to crawl up his arm.

I hand him a pair and say, "Don't even think about taking these off and leaving them where they'll get chewed on or clawed. They're not replaceable." With my current savings, none of my equipment is.

"He's a cat, August, not a wolverine."

"Tell that to the three-inch scar on the back of my neck."

I can almost hear his eyeroll.

I instruct Sophie to say the ABCs so I can get a baseline for her levels and adjust the controls accordingly. For a woman her age, the mature texture of her voice is unusual. It has the same velvety quality that a professionally trained singer might possess.

Chip taps me on the shoulder, and I slip my left ear out of the headphones. "Did she tell you about her impressive résumé?"

I shake my head once.

"She's an actress."

"As is most of the population of southern California." I adjust the EQ.

Chip is undeterred. "No, like a *real* one. She majored in theater and has worked on many live productions in New York, including on Broadway."

Ah, so that's how New York fits in. So why on earth would she choose to record books over acting on a stage? She certainly has the look of an actress. I bring up the master mix when Sophie reaches *W* in the alphabet and cut Chip off when I press the intercom and tell her I'm all set to record whenever she's ready. This time when she smiles, all I have to do to fight off the pinching sensation is look at her cat.

I tap the red Record button and then point at Sophie through the glass window that separates us.

She starts to read, but my concentration is divided due to Chip tapping me on the shoulder. Again.

"Yes?" I pull back an earphone.

"If I get the green light on Sophie from my author, she would get a ton of positive exposure as well as an immediate second contract for the sequel. It's a rapid release that will be ready for preproduction in early winter. But we expect Allie's launch will be epic."

"Allie? As in *Allie Spencer*?" I give him a baiting look. I've heard her name come up dozens of times since I moved back home. Supposedly, she's a young author who lives in Washington State but interned at Fog Harbor Books while finishing up her creative writing degree last year. Chip swears there's never been anything unprofessional between the two of them—seeing as he's been her editor—but I haven't heard him talk about any of the women he's casually dated even half as much as I've heard him mention Allie.

"I'm choosing to ignore the implication in your tone," he says dryly. "But yes. Allie Spencer, one of my authors."

"And what happens if you get promoted after all this? Will she still be off limits?"

He opens his mouth, closes it, and then shakes his head as if it's the first time he's even entertained the idea. "Let's just focus on the demo."

"Fine." I slip both ears back on and work to concentrate on Sophie's voice, careful not to meet her gaze through the glass, which is far more difficult than it should be. I stare at my controls while I take in the quality of her enrapturing cadence for nearly a minute. I have no idea what this story is about, but somehow, I feel like I'm in it right beside her. Seeing what she sees, feeling what she feels—

Tap, tap, tap.

I push aside my headphones and sigh.

"She's really good, isn't she?"

"I wouldn't know, you keep interrupting."

"Listen, August, I know you don't prefer to make decisions quickly, but if Allie likes Sophie's voice as much as I think she will, the turnaround on this project is gonna be tight."

This garners my full and undivided attention.

"Meaning?"

"Sophie needs a studio to record in." He holds up both hands. "Don't say no yet. I know you need time to overthink it, but it would just be temporary. A few weeks tops until we can secure a better option for her somewhere else. It sounds like Sophie's only in the area short-term anyway."

While I'm imagining what life will look like when Gabby returns from camp and I've once again assumed the role of a single parent—rides, appointments, meal-planning, etc.—he continues. "We'd compensate you for your booth time and the production time if you agree." He lowers his voice, even though Sophie's in a soundproof room with headphones on. "And from the little information I've gathered from Sophie, it sounds like she could use a good break."

I don't want to feel anything at his words, especially since her cat is staring at me through predatory eyes. "This isn't a rent-by-the-hour studio, Chip. It's one thing for me to produce audiobooks in the evenings at my soundboard, but my priority is Gabby. I need to be available for her."

"Of course." Chip's quiet for all of five seconds before he flicks his eyes from the booth to me. "You can't tell me Sophie isn't talented."

"I never said she wasn't."

Chip smiles as if he's won. "Think on it."

When we slip on our headphones again, I picture the other studios I've researched in a sixty-mile radius, knowing full well that none are closer to Santa Rosa than mine. And even if she were lucky enough to find an opening in San Francisco, her commute would be arduous.

In my right headphone, I hear a distinct shift in Sophie's cadence that draws me back in. She slips into an accent I can't place, likely because she's just invented it on the spot. Her voice registers in the tenor range on my levels and holds a gravelly quality I never would have guessed could come out of someone who looks like her.

It's captivating. Correction: *She's* captivating.

In just over eight years of producing music, I've only experienced this ravenous sensation in my gut a handful of times. And with each one, the unknown artist went on to break record after record with the EPs I produced for them.

It's the same sensation I feel now.

Sophie masters the tight dialogue flawlessly, slipping in and out of multiple dialects with ease. Every character she creates for these magical woodland creatures is distinct and memorable, stirring my imagination in ways I didn't know possible. Soon, every cell in my body is attuned to her voice, so much so that I feel the exact millisecond when something inside me yawns awake after years of hibernation.

It terrifies me.

Chip taps me on the shoulder again, but this time I can't bring myself to remove my headphones, not even after she's finished reading. I may not understand much about this medium of entertainment, but I *do* understand that the caliber of talent Sophie Wilder possesses is rare. The kind of rare my home studio has been lacking for the past two years.

The same kind of rare I'd almost convinced myself I'd never find again . . . before she spoke word one in my sound booth.

5

Sophie

As soon as I finish reading the final words of the sample chapter in the recording booth, elation fills my chest like an overinflated balloon. It's been so long since I've felt anything close to a *win* when it comes to acting that I'm almost afraid to remove my headphones for fear the feeling will float away. After months of trying to reclaim the confidence of the woman I left behind in New York, I found it in the most unlikely of places. A place where there are no stage lights, costumes, cast, or crew members to contend with. Instead, the only things in view are a microphone, a deliciously intriguing fantasy novel on my iPhone, and the painfully attractive producer who isn't a fan of my cat. And by the flat expression he wears now, he doesn't seem to be much of a fan of me, either.

Despite Chip's arrangement of today's demo, it's clear from the accolades on August's wall and the variety of instruments stationed at the far end of his studio—not to mention the way I saw Chip defer to him through the viewing window—that his opinion is highly esteemed. Chip's reaction to my reading may have been an enthusiastic thumbs-up whenever I raised my gaze to the glass, but August's brows have remained permanently pinched.

Obviously, whatever favor I lost by surprising him with Phantom hasn't been recovered in the last twelve minutes. I tell myself that this is fine, that his opinion of me doesn't lessen the breakthrough I experienced while performing today. I tell myself that even if he rejects the idea of me recording in his studio in the future, I can still pursue this in-between dream with the time I have left in California. I tell myself that I am not as lost as I thought I was when I first arrived back in my home state.

And it's for this reason, more than any other, that I vow to leave this studio with my head held high.

I slip off my headphones, square my shoulders, and then crack the booth's door open.

One step out into the short hallway, I hear a phone ring.

"Dang. I have to get this. It's the office." The voice belongs to Chip. "A deal is going south. Here, take Phantom."

"What? *No*," August hisses. "I'm not about to—"

"Talk to Sophie until I'm off," Chip says, his voice growing closer. "This shouldn't take too long."

"Chip," August growls. "Don't you dare leave me with—"

But then Chip scoots past me, ducking into what looks like an unfinished recording booth directly across the narrow hall from the one I just exited. With his phone pressed to his ear, he gives me another thumbs-up as he begins to converse with whoever's on the other end of his call.

Nerves gather in my belly at the thought of facing August's disapproval alone, but then I remind myself that I'm too grateful to be a coward today.

I school my expression into something light and pleasant as I walk the short hallway and prepare to see August again. The studio isn't large by any stretch of the imagination, but the rectangular building is well laid out. From what I've seen, August has two recording booths, a private restroom, an open lounge area loaded with instruments, and a desk that holds a soundboard filled with more gadgets, knobs, and buttons than I can name.

Even after I see the grimace August wears as he holds Phantom far away from his body, I keep my smile locked on tight.

"I can take him from you, sorry," I say, relieving him of my cat while doing my best to ignore the current of electricity that skips up my spine when our fingers brush.

I twist away quickly and head to the sofa, where I give Phantom a single reassuring squeeze before tucking him safely inside his backpack. What I wouldn't give for my own little bubble of safety to crawl inside when I need it most.

From behind me, I hear a throat clear and hope it's Chip returning from his emergency phone call. I glance over my shoulder. No such luck.

"So, um," August begins while scratching the back of his head. Golden strands of sun-bleached hair slip through his fingers and sweep the tips of his ears. "About your demo, it was good. . . ." His long, awkward pause has me rotating in full to study him. "I mean, the voices you invented when you were reading were, uh, creative and . . ."

It would appear that while this guy might have the best beach hair I've ever seen on a human being, small talk is not his forte. Nor is acting. The least I can do is put him out of his misery.

"I really appreciate you opening up your studio so I could try something new—and for putting up with my cat." I give him an apologetic shrug. "Sorry again about the miscommunication on Phantom. You can't know how much I needed this experience today. So thank you for the opportunity." I lift the backpack off the sofa and slide my arms through each strap before craning my neck to glance down the hall. Chip is still on the phone, and by the sound of it, he won't be off any time soon. "I'd be grateful if you would tell Chip the same for me. He has my number if he wants to follow up."

August's storm-blue eyes scan my face in earnest. "I don't think you should leave without talking to him." August grips the back of his neck and blows out a hearty breath. "He's better at this kind of thing."

Better at what *kind of thing?* I wonder. Unless . . . unless August knows something I don't. Understanding dawns then. Perhaps August is so uncomfortable because he's afraid to tell me the real reason Chip wants me to stick around. Perhaps August knows Chip doesn't need to follow up with me because I'm not what he's looking for after all.

My cheeks prickle with an all-too-familiar heat. If this guy only knew how many times I've been booed off stage, cussed out in parking lots, and ripped apart in online reviews, I'm certain he'd speak more freely. I'm well practiced in the art of rejection.

At the thought, a seedling of doubt begins to take root. What if the breakthrough I experienced today while reading is little more than a fluke? A first-timer's high? Worse, what if I won't be able to recreate it in another studio for a different publisher?

"Is something . . . wrong?" August tilts his head to catch my eye. It's only then I realize how long I've been silently staring at the closed door behind him.

When I shake my head a little too enthusiastically for a trained actress, his eyes narrow.

"No, I'm good, I was just pondering how trying new things can be compared to a . . . a sports analogy."

What am I even saying?

He glances behind him at the door, as if trying to connect the dots. But it's actually the tiny print of a sports brand on the cuff of his light blue sleeve that did it. "Which analogy is that?"

I rack my brain for literally anything having to do with a sport. "The one about how it's better to play the game and strike out than to never have played the game at all." I have no clue where this comes from or if it's even a real saying, but I do my best to play it off before I edge closer to the exit.

"That's love."

My hand freezes partway to the doorknob. "What's love?"

"The saying goes, 'It's better to have loved and lost than never to have loved at all.'"

My smile slips as his words circle my head with an entirely new meaning. Is that how I feel about theater after losing it the way I did? Would I choose to do it all over again now that I know the outcome of my stage dreams? Before I can form an answer in my head, a rush of honesty escapes me. "I'm not sure if I believe that."

"I'm not sure if I do, either."

Neither of us break eye contact for what feels like a thousand heartbeats. Surprisingly, August is the one to speak next. "I don't really feel qualified to give you feedback, as this isn't my area of expertise."

I begin to shake my head, to tell him I don't require feedback, when he cuts me off.

"I've never cared much for fiction, but that—what you did back there—made me want to keep listening." I watch the way his neck thickens when he swallows. "I'm not sure how you managed to bring those characters to life in just over twelve minutes, but that's what you did. You made them real, which made the story real. And while I can't speak for Chip, I think your talent is . . . something special."

My jaw actually unhinges, and it's all I can do to keep from gawking.

He shifts uncomfortably. "Why are you looking at me like that?"

Dumbfounded, I shake my head. "It's just, is that really what you were thinking while I was in the booth?"

His nod is hesitant, as if I'm trying to stump him with a riddle, but I'm the one who's stumped at the moment.

"It's just"—I try to clarify—"your face said something very different."

"How so?" He scowls.

It takes me half a second to re-create the expression he wore, and to my shock, he has the decency to look . . . self-conscious? He runs a hand from his eyebrows to his chin and releases a slow exhale. "Not to play the victim card here, but I have recently been diagnosed with RGF."

"RGF?"

"Resting Grump Face."

I press my lips together, refusing the laugh that tries to bubble up my throat at his unexpected confession. "Oh, well, I'm sorry to hear that. Is your condition reversible?"

"Only time will tell."

He drops his gaze to the small space of floor between us, and I note his perfect fan of dark lashes. "My condition tends to worsen the more I concentrate. And today I was concentrating rather hard on the specific tones and layers that make up such a captivating voice."

When he meets my gaze again, my knees go soft.

"Captivating?" I all but whisper.

He nods.

It's such a simple response, and yet the significance of it is anything but.

He clears his throat and braces his forearm against the doorjamb. "Like I said, audiobook production isn't my forte. It's new for me, too. But artistry isn't new for me; neither is talent. And you have both."

Just as my smile melds into something real, Chip rounds the corner, then halts abruptly. We turn our heads, and I watch as he takes the two of us in: August leaning against the doorframe, gazing into my eyes as I peer up at him with a look that likely doesn't qualify as professional.

August drops his arm and takes an immediate step back. I do the same.

Chip drags an assessing gaze from me to August. "I take it you told her we were impressed with her work?"

August avoids eye contact as he says, "I'll have the demo ready for you to send off within the hour."

"Great." The awkward moment ticks on until Chip crosses the room to shake my hand. "I'll be in touch soon, Sophie. I think Allie is really going to love what you've done with her characters. In the meantime, I'll work on securing you a studio space to—"

"She can record here," August says, sparing a glance in my direction. "That is, if she wants to."

Surprise pebbles my skin, and it takes me a moment to find my voice. "I'd like that, thank you."

Chip's expression is one of excitement with an overlay of befuddlement. "Well, great! Then I'll leave you and August to work out the schedule as soon as I get the green light from Allie. But one thing's for sure, whether it's this project or another, I want to get you contracted as a narrator for Fog Harbor Audio, Sophie. No doubt about it."

The floaty feeling I experienced in August's studio carried me through the night and into my eight-hour shift at the tasting room the following day. Saturday afternoons are typically the busiest shift of the week, considering we're closed on Sundays—yet another stipulation of the Bentley trust. Even so, there's rarely enough work for more than three employees at a time. One to plate the charcuterie boards in the kitchen, one to serve and bus tables, and another to work the tasting bar—a job I've yet to be scheduled for even though I grew up memorizing the tasting notes in each of our family wines the way most children memorize their capitals and states.

Along with serving the wine to our guests who pop in for an hour to sit on the patio or wander the property with a glass in hand before they're off to their next stop, there are also walk-ins who range in number and purpose. Girls day out? Often. First dates? Absolutely. Celebrations for anniversaries, birthdays, graduations, job promotions? Regularly.

Today's been a mixed bag of all of the above, and I find myself smiling and laughing and engaging in small talk with the patrons more than I have since I arrived. Some might guess my ease with customers comes from my years working in the food industry, but I know today's mood has less to do with my experience and more to do with . . . *hope.* It's incredible how a small dose can have such a drastic affect on a person's outlook, even if their immediate circumstances haven't changed at all.

I slip my phone from my pocket and review the text thread August initiated this morning. I bite the inside of my check as I anticipate his next message.

August:

> Hi, Sophie, this is August Tate. Sounds like Chip got the green light from Allie last night. Are you available to start recording next week? How much prep time do you need?

> Hi, August! Yes, Chip sent me the full manuscript this morning. I can't wait to read it! I plan to do nothing but read tonight and tomorrow. I can be ready as early as Monday, if you are? I'm free most mornings and afternoons. Thanks again for being so accommodating with your studio. I promise to leave Phantom at home during recordings. (Barring a natural disaster.)

August:

> Seeing as we're both Californians, we should probably define "natural disaster"?

> You forget I lived in NYC where I survived brutal winter storms and blackout-inducing heat waves. I assure you, Phantom will be happy at home. For your peace of mind, I've recently purchased him a white-noise machine to help drown out the construction chaos near our living quarters.

August:

> What a relief indeed. I'll sleep better knowing that. How does Monday at 9 a.m. sound? (Barring any real natural disasters, of course.)

August:

> I just opened Chip's attachment. Did you realize this manuscript is 539 pages? 😨Maybe we should push back the start date a few days?

I discretely type out a cheeky reply.

Two things you should know about me: 1. I love reading challenges! 2. The only award I ever won in school was for my speed-reading abilities in the third grade, Mrs. Deitz's class. It came with a gold star-shaped button I pinned to my backpack that read, "I'm a superstar reader!" Unlike my math skills, my reading skills have only improved with time. Monday will be great.

I'm about to slide my phone back into my pocket when it buzzes in my hand.

August:

If you manage to read all 539 pages by Monday morning, you definitely deserve a superstar button. You can add it to Phantom's backpack. A bright yellow button can only improve his habitat.

I'm still grinning as I wave good-bye to our last customers of the day, a delightful mother-daughter duo on an epic West Coast road trip. I then clear their table in preparation for the catering crew covering tonight's private event—yet another change since my brother took the reins. From what I've gathered, there are only a small handful of staff on the winery's payroll; the rest are contracted from a local catering agency as needed. I've yet to work with the same employee twice.

I'm humming along with the happy tune on the playlist when Natalie walks into the dining area. Like usual, she's dressed in top-tier designer fashion: a flowy, high-collared jumpsuit and strappy, red-soled heels. Even if I could somehow tally the retail prices of my favorite curated consignment pieces, my eclectic boho selections wouldn't hold a candle to her sophisticated, tailored wardrobe. I remember nearly choking to death on a coconut-battered shrimp when my mother slipped about the cost of Natalie's wedding dress during their three-day wedding extravaganza in Maui two summers ago. My brother had spared no expense when it came to the big event—except, of course, when it came to my plane ticket from NYC. If not for my mother's unexpected deposit in my money app, my brother's fancy nuptials would have cost me more than six months in tip savings.

I assume Natalie's purpose for stopping by ranks higher than my need-to-know status, so I'm more than a little surprised when she beckons me to follow her into the butler's pantry behind the wine counter. Perhaps if I wasn't riding so high on endorphins, I would be more alarmed by her assertiveness, but I'm too curious to be cautious. This is the most interaction the two of us have had since she went over the rules of my temporary employment.

Once we're tucked into the pantry next to shelves of catering supplies and stemware, Natalie sheds the outer layer of her aloof shell and speaks to me directly. "Is there any chance you can work another shift this evening? One of my regulars called in sick. I can double your hourly wage and offer you a fair split of the tips at the end of the night."

Given my debt-to-income ratio at the moment, I'm hardly in a position to turn her down, but oddly enough, I'm not thinking about my overdue bills when I agree. "Sure, I can help." My plans to start Allie Spencer's romantasy novel will have to wait until tomorrow. I'm definitely gonna put my elementary school button to the test. "Where would you like me?"

Before she answers, I note the flicker of relief that crosses her features. "Mason and Brianne will tag-team food prep and plating in the kitchen, and Christina prefers to work the floor, so I'd like you stationed at the wine bar. Is that alright with you?"

I employ my best acting skills and nod as if she isn't going against my brother's wishes to have me front and center. "That's no problem at all." I study the way she's styled her dark hair into a slicked-back twist that makes every feature of her face all the more striking. I was thirteen when my brother brought Natalie home for the first time his senior year of high school, and I remember thinking that she was the most beautiful woman I'd ever seen. My opinion hasn't changed. Unfortunately, her outside appearance and her choice in men are the majority of what I know about my sister-in-law, even after all these years.

"What's the event?" I ask.

"It's a VIP networking social for some of Jasper's business associates."

My stomach dips as I realize what this means: My brother will be in attendance. We might be able to avoid each other due to the size of the winery, but the tasting room was designed to be intimate—with richly textured walls and an open floor plan, barring the large wine cellar below the stairs. I push the unwelcome fact from my mind and recall, instead, the only exception I'd requested from Natalie the day she became my official supervisor. *I'm happy to do any task you assign in order to fill my hours, but I'd like to request that any job involving the wine cellar go to someone else.* She didn't bother to ask any follow-up questions; everybody in my family would know the reason, even if some refused to acknowledge it. Still, she'd simply bobbed her chin and said, *"We can work around it."*

"Tonight's patrons are," Natalie begins with obvious hesitation, "important to your brother and to the winery. We do our best to accommodate any requests from our guests."

The statement is odd, but I suppose there's little about this pantry conversation that isn't. I can only hope Jasper will be too busy schmoozing with his carbon-copy friends to notice me behind the bar.

Before I can ask anything else, we hear voices, and soon Natalie is instructing the per diem employees—Mason, Brianne, and Christina—about the evening. It's obvious by their familiarity with one another and with Natalie that this is not their first time working a private event. I have just enough time to grab a quick snack in the kitchen, refill my water bottle, and check my phone—no new texts—before returning to the tasting room and setting up for a night behind the counter.

Over the next three hours, a couple dozen men wearing different versions of the same designer suit fill the tasting room. Thankfully, the steady stream of wine orders is enough to keep me on my toes but not enough to completely overwhelm me. Staying busy is a good buffer between me and my brother. Jasper is in full public mode tonight: mingling, joking, smiling, and of course, charming and wowing his captive audience with his brilliance.

I'm uncorking a vintage bottle of our reserve Sauvignon Blanc when a clean-shaven man I served early on in the evening approaches the counter. He unbuttons his suit coat at the waist and casually leans an elbow on the bar top. Between his carefully groomed hair, smooth, easygoing grin, and over-confident demeanor, I know his type well. And it's far from the type of man I want to engage with. Almost immediately, I see someone else in my mind's eye. A man with striking blue eyes and a rough-around-the-edges personality. Or maybe that's not quite a fair assessment of August. He invited me back to his studio, after all, and his texts have been surprisingly personable. And fun.

"Good evening, again," coos the gentleman, resembling the majority of my brother's acquaintances from Stanford. "You wouldn't happen to have a bottle of Pellegrino back there, would you?"

"You're in luck," I say amenably as I turn away to retrieve the chilled glass bottle. "Would you like that over ice?"

"You read my mind."

I twist and pour and place the short glass on a cocktail napkin for him, but instead of reaching for the drink he's requested, he holds out a hand to me. I don't miss the way his sleeve inches back to reveal his designer watch. It's the same brand my father wears. My brother, as well. "I'm Clinton Owens." He flashes a grin I'm sure any orthodontist would proudly hang on their wall and shakes my hand. "And you are Miss Sophie Wilder, the younger and, dare I say, most intriguing Wilder of the bunch to date." Though his voice registers low on my creep radar, his boldness is unnerving. I'm not wearing a name badge, so I'm not exactly sure how—

He unclasps my hand but keeps his eyes trained on me. "Forgive me. I couldn't help myself." He winks. "Your brother gave up your identity when I complimented the spot-on wine pairings you recommended to me at the beginning of the night. Good taste must run in your bloodline, although I'm curious as to why you're back here and not out there." He tips his head to the patio, where the majority of the VIPs have migrated. It's only then I realize how few people remain in the dining area. Three, no four, men occupy a corner table. All on their third or fourth round of something or other.

It's then I pull out my bag of tricks and aim to play the part of a woman with far more confidence than I possess naturally. It's always been easier to assume the identity of a character I create than play myself, especially while in proximity to my family. "I'm afraid my good taste doesn't count for much outside the realm of wine pairings. You should know I've been known to indulge in pickle-flavored ice cream when the mood strikes." I shrug to say, *See, this is why you shouldn't be impressed* and wait for him to pull a sour face. But the expression he pulls is not sour at all.

"A bit of a daredevil, then? I like to walk on the wild side myself. I didn't become a stockbroker for nothing." He scans my face in a way that feels too familiar. "Without risk, there's no reward." He lifts his glass as if to make a toast, then sets it down when I don't follow suit, as I have no beverage. Or interest, for that matter. "I'd offer to buy you a drink, but considering you're the one pouring them tonight, it's hardly an enticing offer."

He's good, I'll give him that. "I don't drink while on shift, but thank you anyway." I smile politely and reach for the damp rag I keep under the counter. Nothing needs cleaning at the moment, but I could use something to do with my hands. "May I get you anything else? Another Chardonnay or a—"

He rotates toward me fully. "I'm still waiting to hear the reason you're stuck working behind that counter tonight."

If my pulse were a color, it would be a flashing yellow light.

"I don't care much for crowds." It's a blatant lie, but one the character I've created believes wholeheartedly. And by his studious nod, Clinton buys it.

He plants an elbow on the custom bar top and stares into my eyes. "How about a private tour, then?" A subtle eyebrow raise followed by a once-over assessment. "I've been waiting—not so patiently, I might add—to see your brother's art collection in the cellar." He rocks in closer until the arms of his suit coat pull taut.

At the mention of the cellar, something inside me begins to quake, and it takes every ounce of my acting skills to keep my voice steady. "I'm sorry to disappoint you, Mr. Owens, but I'm afraid I know nothing about my brother's collection and even less about art. You'd be much better off asking him for a tour."

"No offense to your brother, but he's not my type." Clinton gives me yet another wink. "However, I'd be up for negotiating a trade. If you escort me to the cellar, then I'd be happy to give you a lesson in fine art. I keep a few of my favorite pieces aboard my yacht in the bay." His voice drops to a suggestive whisper. "You'd be welcome anytime."

Just as I open my mouth to refuse him, my gaze collides with something else. Or rather, on someone else. My brother. The over-seer of my future. He's eyeing me expectantly as if he's somehow heard every word of this conversation. Natalie's instructions at the beginning of the VIP event boomerang back to my ears in full sur-round sound: "*We do our best to accommodate any requests from our guests.*"

I ball my trembling hands into fists under the counter and fight against the way my vision collapses in on itself. I can't act my way out of this one. And I also know I cannot go down to that cellar. No matter what.

"Come on, Sophie." Clinton eyes me with a level of presumption that twists my stomach. "I'm sure your brother won't mind if you step away for a few minutes."

"I'm—"

"Actually, Mr. Owens, I'm afraid Sophie has a previous engage-ment to get to tonight, but I'd be happy to give you a tour of the cellar and answer any questions you may have regarding Jasper's collection." Natalie turns to me and makes a show of checking her tiny gold wristwatch encrusted with diamonds. "You'd better be on your way. Thanks for stepping in tonight."

Though I have no clue what prompted her fabricated tale or her willingness to stick her neck out for me, when she gestures to Mr. Owens to follow her, he does. Albeit with more than a little reluctance. "It was nice to meet you, Sophie. I hope our paths cross again someday."

I want to tell him I hope the opposite, but instead, I check the corner of the room where my brother was only moments ago. He's gone, and I have a strong feeling Natalie timed her intervention accordingly. But why? I don't know.

I also don't wait around to find out.

6

August

It's not until I'm balancing on the top rung of a ladder leaning against the warped roofline of my mom's old greenhouse that I consider the repercussions of taking on such a project alone. Perhaps my confidence is riding higher than usual this morning after an evening spent researching the ins and outs of a side gig I hadn't put much stock into—that is, until a remarkable brunette entered my studio and pulled the rip cord on my expectations.

The cumbersome roof vent I'm holding above my head tries its best to rock me off-center, but I'm no lightweight. I didn't recover this thing from the back acre of my neighbor's overgrown property just to lose it to the wind again. And I didn't agree to let Sophie record in my studio only to muck it up on account of my ignorance on all things fiction. No matter how long she intends to stay in the area, I know she's something special. That moment we shared before she left my studio was the closest thing to hope I've felt in approximately two years.

With my father's drill in hand, I strain to slide the problematic vent across the exposed opening. Before I can secure it fully, my vision snags on the herb garden my mother once meticulously maintained inside these weathered walls. Though my father built this greenhouse as an anniversary gift for her, my mom's presence looms in the handwritten signs that hang from the rafters, indicating the location of each variety.

Perhaps, in her own way, that's what Sophie is, too. A sign to point me in the right direction after so many wrong turns and dead ends. *A sign?* I shake my head at the random intrusive thought. But before I can blink them away, a pair of gorgeous green eyes looms steady at the forefront of my mind, shimmering with the kind of enchantment that both enthralls and terrifies me. And it's then my braced knee slips from its post, kicking my only ladder to the ground.

I scramble to find a foothold as my hands claw for anything that might keep me on this roof when something sharp rips through the flesh of my left palm. Yet I can't lose my hold. To do so would require me to let go of my dad's favorite possession.

I stare at it now, dangling above the earth like a trick question.

Hot, sticky blood trickles down my fingers as I assess my predicament. Particularly how to perform a slide, tuck, and roll maneuver without having to release the goods in my right hand.

Much like surfing, I tell my mind to take a back seat to my body. And then I just . . . let go.

The ground meets me sooner than I predict, and my landing is far from graceful, but at least everything is intact after impact. Including my dad's drill.

Chest heaving, I lie flat on my back in the dead grass and slowly take inventory of each appendage. *No breaks. Good.* Seeing as I still have a dishwasher to unload and three piles of laundry waiting for me to fold before Aunt Judy shows up to refresh Gabby's camp attire, I don't have time for a medical emergency. The last thing I need is for my aunt to question my ability to run a household.

As soon as I regain use of my faculties, I'm up on my feet. And other than the flesh wound on my palm, I'm fine. That is, until I pull back the patio slider into the kitchen and see a container of my mother's peanut butter fudge on my parents' dining table. The sight sends a splinter through my chest.

"That you, August? I saw your car in the drive but didn't want to disturb you if you were in the middle of recording something in the studio." Before I can respond, Aunt Judy strides into the kitchen from the living room, holding up a pair of my boxer briefs.

My eyes narrow on the object clutched in her manicured hands. "Is there a reason you're holding my underwear, Aunt Judy?"

"What? Oh! Oh my. Sorry about that." She laughs and sails them into the other room as if that's all it will take to erase the image permanently tattooed to my brain. "After I collected your sister's things from her room, I saw the baskets of clean laundry on the sofa and thought I would make myself useful while I waited."

"Thanks," I begin, "but you really didn't need to—"

I'm interrupted by a yelp that's delivered in an octave not suitable for human ears at the sight of the blood pooling at my feet. And now it's my turn to look sheepish.

I book it to the sink. "It's nothing. Just a little cut."

"That is *not* little!" Aunt Judy sputters as she runs ahead of me to flip on the tap. "What on earth did you do? Did this happen in your studio?"

"No. Outside." The shorter and more vague my answer, the better.

"Where specifically?" she presses, grabbing my wrist to place my injured palm under the stream and examine the injury as if she were a nurse and not an accountant. But on second glance, the cut does appear more gnarly than I first surmised.

"The greenhouse."

Though I'm purposefully avoiding her gaze as I angle my hand out of hers, she isn't deterred. "*How?*"

"The roof vent blew off in the storm last night. I was reattaching it."

I cut my gaze away, but not before I see her horror-rimmed eyes. "Please don't tell me you were up on that old roof alone."

I say nothing.

"*August.*"

"I'm fine," I say again, knowing full well she won't accept this as fact. Neither would my mother. The stray thought rubs at me like sandpaper.

"Clearly." She heaves a sigh as she opens and closes five drawers looking for what I can only assume is a kitchen towel, which she won't find seeing as every towel in this house is currently piled on my sofa, waiting to be folded. "You've had a tetanus shot within the last ten years, right?" Another drawer opens and slams to the side of me. "I don't even want to think about what kind of bacteria you could have picked up from that ancient, moss-ridden thing." Empty-handed, she rotates to face me. "I think I should take you to a doctor. There's a good chance you'll need stitches."

With my good hand, I reach across my body to collect a wad of paper towels and wrap them around my palm. The sting of pain pales in comparison to the sting of my pride in this moment.

Aunt Judy has always been a little over-the-top when it comes to nurturing. As my father's older sister, fussing over her family comes naturally, I suppose. But after the accident, that particular trait is what held us together even after our world broke apart. She'd organized meals through the neighborhood church my parents had attended for decades, sorted the gifts and endless barrage of cards, navigated Gabby's female needs, and offered an endless supply of maternal affection I was in no way qualified to give.

Somehow, this nightmare we shared had blurred days into weeks, weeks into months, and finally months into nearly two years. And while I appreciate everything she's done for us—for my sister in particular—I also recognize how different the two of us are as people.

Case in point.

I tick my head toward the dining table, hoping distraction will tame Aunt Judy's hyper-fixation on my wound. "I appreciate the fudge. That was thoughtful of you."

"You're welcome." She moves her hands to her hips. "But if that's your sneaky way of trying to change the subject, it won't work."

I feign innocence. "Never."

Another hearty sigh from my only blood relative in California. "Just promise me you'll watch for infection, okay? If your mother were here right now, she'd—"

At her abrupt stop, the ever-present chokehold around my throat tightens. If my mother were here right now, everything would be different.

"I'm sorry, that wasn't . . ." Aunt Judy takes a moment to re-calibrate. "All I'm trying to say is that you are important to this family—to me and to your sister, especially. She counts on you."

"There is nothing I think about more than Gabby." The statement comes out stronger than I intend, but between the throb in my palm and the insinuation that I might be unaware of Gabby's dependence on me, I leave it as it stands. Without apology.

"I know," she says, backpedaling as she reaches to touch my arm. "You are a wonderful big brother, August." She smiles then, as if she's called a silent truce. "You made the right decision allowing her to attend this camp, you know? When I popped in on her a few days ago, she looked so happy. I think spending such a concentrated amount of time with the deaf community has been good for her."

We both know it was Judy's persuasive phone call and camp fee donation that got me to agree, but I can't help but feel relieved at her report, even if I don't fully agree with her reasoning. "She's always made friends easily. And I'm sure it helped to know a couple familiar faces when she arrived."

"I'd say that's true." Her expression shifts into something almost mischievous. "Although, you should probably know she seems to be drawn to one face in particular."

"What do you mean?"

"I mean Tyler seems to have become more than a friend."

My mind refuses to compute. "Tyler? As in her ASL and speech tutor's son?"

"Yes." She nods. "Of course, I'm sure that's not too surprising, considering you've allowed him to give her rides to church events over the last few months."

My tongue has suddenly been sucked free of moisture. "That's only because they live five minutes from us. We're literally on the way."

She hikes an eyebrow, and I begin a mental moonwalk back through the last year, to when Gabby first saw the flyer for the big church in town with the "deaf-friendly culture" and ASL interpretation of the sermons at her tutor's office. Gabby begged me to let her attend, and I simply didn't have the heart to say no to her even if church was the last place I wanted to be.

"Tyler's eighteen," I protest. "He just graduated. He's too old for her."

"She's half a year away from turning seventeen. Technically speaking, they're only a grade apart."

Of all the topics we've discussed in relation to Gabby—my household budget, my job security, my sister's medical needs, her grief therapy sessions online with a captioning system that Aunt Judy financed before summer break—the subject of *boys* has never come up.

A nervous prickle sweeps my spine. "Gabby has goals. She isn't interested in . . . in a relationship like that." But even as I say it, I hear how idiotic I sound.

Aunt Judy glances at the blood-soaked paper towel around my left hand, then grabs the fresh roll off the counter. She offers me a few more squares, and I do a wordless exchange as I rewrap my angry flesh.

After a sigh, she leans against the counter. "It might be hard for you to hear, but she cares for him. And given the smitten way he tends to her, I'd say he cares for her, too. She's growing up."

A sensation like I've never known catches fire at the base of my ribs. My sister is too young for what Aunt Judy is describing, isn't she? A sudden image of her riding atop my shoulders with braided pigtails and a toothless grin plays like a short film in my mind.

"She's not allowed to date." This is the first time I've spoken these words, but they feel right. Needed, even.

She hikes a groomed eyebrow at me. "As I recall, your parents allowed *you* to date at sixteen."

"That's different, I was a . . ." I rake my good hand through my hair. *Why is it a thousand degrees in this house?* I cross the room to the thermostat and hit the down arrow. Repeatedly.

"A what? A boy?" she finishes with a laugh. "Afraid you're going to need a better argument than that, sweetheart. Tyler's a good kid from a solid family, but you already know that. Gabby could do far worse for a first boyfriend." Aunt Judy says this as if that's what he is now—a boyfriend. Sweat prickles the back of my neck.

"The two of them have been hard at work on a project during their free time at camp, a curriculum to assist Tyler's mom in teaching an ASL class in early fall."

I try not to act as bothered as I feel by this. "Where?"

"I'm not sure on the location, but I do know they're hoping to advertise it at the church."

The big grin on Aunt Judy's face when she says this is not surprising. She believes church is the solution to every ailment we face in life, while I tend to believe the church is the reason my parents are dead and my sister is deaf.

"I'll talk it over with her once she's back home," I amend civilly, knowing full well that Gabby is smart enough to recognize that her summer camp schedule is far from real life. While she may be enjoying a world of freedom in the woods with new friends now, her fall is full. Especially with the classes she's hoping to take for dual-enrollment credits toward college. I'm not sure assisting with an ASL class will be a priority. "Between her schooling, her online therapy, doctor appointments, tutoring sessions, and her church commitments, her fall schedule is pretty packed."

Aunt Judy nods, but it's the kind of nod that could fill a couple paragraphs if her brain were to dump all the words she's not speaking onto a page. I bend my arm at the elbow, hoping to appease some of the pressure in my palm. And if I'm honest, the pressure building under my aunt's gaze, too.

"Your sister is doing remarkably well, August." She smiles, and the crinkles at the corners of her brown eyes remind me of my dad. "To see her thriving again—laughing, teasing, acting like a boy-crazy teenager without limitation or insecurity was . . . well, it was good for my heart. And more importantly, I believe it's been good for Gabby's heart."

I say nothing to this because I sense there's more to it. She's already thanked me for letting Gabby attend, already told me about the boy who's wiggled his way past friendship territory, so what is—

"I pride myself on keeping confidences, and you know more than anyone how precious Gabby is to me, so please know I only share this with you because I know how much you dislike being caught off-guard."

I hold my breath, braced for the words I've feared most since the day I became Gabby's legal guardian.

"Gabby doesn't feel you can provide what she needs as a growing young woman."

"Gabby's asked if she can move in with me."

"Gabby sees through all your false pretenses and is ashamed of you."

"Gabby deserves more than you can give her."

Aunt Judy shifts her stance but holds her gaze steady. "Your sister told me that because of these weeks at camp and the community she's building, she's considering applying to the private all-deaf college that sponsored the camp. She's asked me to help her with looking into scholarships, as the tuition is pricey." She rubs her lips together. "But the good news is, Radiance University is only a six-hour drive from here, and she'll likely know a few—"

I shake my head. The conversation regarding Tyler might have caught me off-guard, but this? This is a different kind of blow altogether, one that threatens to take me out at my knees.

"Deaf college?" I ask in a tone that's teetering too close to a line I've never allowed myself to cross. "She doesn't need to go to an all-deaf anything. She has hearing aids, and when she wears them, they work perfectly fine."

"That may be true for now, but think about the future, August, and what the doctor told us. I think this summer has helped her discover just how important shared community is with peers who are dealing with similar challenges. It wouldn't surprise me at all if God plans to use her hardship for something that will eventually bless a whole lot of people."

Blindsided by this announcement, I can say nothing. Do nothing. None of this is the plan. Gabby is going to complete her associate's degree by the end of her senior year through the local community college and then go into elementary education right here at Sonoma State University so she can stay at home. Save money. She's great with kids—excellent, in fact. Teaching is what she's wanted to do since the year my parents adopted her from Colombia.

"If it's the tuition you're concerned about, there are scholarships and grants out there, we just have to find them." She gentles her voice, and I know whatever comes next will be about money. I'm not wrong. "I have a little investment account I've put aside. I'll talk to Jeff. I'm sure he'll be happy to donate a set amount toward Gabby's tuition."

"While that's very generous, I think we might be getting too far ahead of ourselves here." I laugh, though there is little I find humorous. "Gabby and I have been talking about her future plans for well over a year now. I've helped with her transcripts and met with guidance counselors to look over her schedule for the online college classes she's adding this fall. The admin has assured me she'll have every accommodation she needs. She doesn't need an all-deaf college to become a grade school teacher."

"Why do you think she's become so passionate about learning ASL this past year?" Aunt Judy doesn't wait for my answer. "Because she refuses to fear the future, whatever it may bring."

I study my work boots for several long seconds. "If Gabby attends a school for the deaf, what's to stop her from becoming isolated by her impairment instead of learning how to integrate with the hearing world?"

"All she's done is integrate. She was even willing to drill a hole in her head to please you, August. But the cochlear implant wasn't the answer. And the aids are only a short-term solution."

"There are new developments happening in medical technology all the time," I counter, taking care not to say more. It's neither the time nor place to go into the experimental procedures I've researched like an after-hours job. She'd never understand the submission process for such things, much less the upfront medical costs required. Aunt Judy might be a woman of faith, but she accepted my sister's prognosis at face value before I'd even signed Gabby out of the hospital.

It's been a long time since we've tapped into this recycled conversation, and to be honest, I don't think either of us are up for it. At least, that's what I'm banking on.

"You heard Doctor Radcliff the same as I did, August," Aunt Judy says gently. "Her prognosis is degenerative. Outside of a miracle, it won't improve. Her only option is adaptability. Right now she can still hear with her hearing aids, but we have to be realistic. Neither of us knows how long that will last. Until then, I believe her time is best spent preparing for a future without sound."

My gut roils. "He's only one opinion."

"He was your *fourth* opinion—all of which were nearly verbatim." Her eyes mist with passion as she closes in and touches my cheek the way she did when I was a young boy. Her musky perfume sticks in my nostrils. "I know it's hard. But you need to learn to accept where she's at. If not for your own sake, then for hers."

When I don't respond, she pats my cheek and moves to the dining room to swipe her purse off the table. She pulls out a colorful brochure and places it on the table next to the fudge. All I see are the words: *Radiance University*.

She pauses in front of me again. "It's noble, what you've sacrificed in order to care for her needs. You've honored your parents by how you've provided for their daughter, but they couldn't know when they wrote their will just how different Gabby's life would be at the time of their death." I stare at the brochure featuring several happy, smiling young adults on the cover. "It might be time you take a baby step back and allow her to speak for herself." She grips my shoulder, squeezes. "In the meantime, I'm praying for you both. I'll never stop."

She doesn't wait for me to speak again. She simply slides her purse strap over her shoulder and lets herself out, leaving the brochure for an alternate life and an alternate future behind.

Voice Memo

Gabby Tate

2 months, 3 weeks, 4 days after the accident

Hello?

I guess it's strange to say hello to myself. I've never done this before. Obviously. Weird, it really is dictating everything I say just like the nurse said it would. And wow, it's adding punctuation, too? Okay, so I guess this is a pretty cool app. Anyway, I don't really know what all I'm supposed to be recording. She said I should treat these memos like a diary since I can't write anything down with my arm still in a sling.

Still, this is really awkward.

Maybe I'll just give an update. Um. I still can't hear anything at all with my right ear and only random lower pitches in my left. The sound kind of makes me feel sick sometimes, like I'm on one of those teeter-totters Dad and I used to play on in the summers at the park around the corner.

It's weird to talk about him like he's not here. I wonder if it ever won't be weird.

August moved into our house. His stuff was here when I came home from the rehab place with Aunt Judy. He's been sleeping in the room across the hall from mine. It was his bedroom a long time ago, when I was like . . . um . . . seven or eight, maybe? But it's been Mom's study ever since, even though I never saw her studying much of anything in there except for her Bible. We used to laugh about how that room was mostly used to collect items that didn't belong anywhere else in the house. I hope August doesn't feel that way about it now, but even if he did, I'm sure he wouldn't tell me.

It's strange how you can live in the same house with someone and not really know them. I feel like it's that way with my brother. I always thought he was so cool when I was young. I loved seeing him on holidays and on our family vacations, but I don't remember the everyday version of him anymore. I don't know the food he likes or the movies he watches or how he likes to spend his free time, other than at the beach surfing, which he hasn't done yet even though I told him he doesn't have to babysit me. I'm now fourteen and a half. Mom and Dad let me stay on my own all the time.

I tried to talk to him again the other night about what happened when I woke up after the accident. But every time I try, it's like he disappears somewhere inside his head. I know I'm the one with all the ear trouble right now, but I swear it's like he can't hear me when I talk about this.

I overheard him discussing something with Aunt Judy three nights ago. Maybe not overheard as much as spied on them. There are certain words I can pick up, and body language is pretty easy to read when you start paying attention. He looked upset when he said my name, and I watched two deep creases form between my aunt's eyebrows. They went back and forth for a long time until August finally turned away and Aunt Judy cried. I hate that I'm the reason they're both so upset. I wish Mom were here to fix it. She always knew what to say.

I don't know how to end this thing, so I guess that's it for today.

7

Sophie

For a woman who once sang, danced, and acted her heart out on stage for hundreds—even thousands—of people, it's strange how different reading for an audience of one can feel. Even with my eyes focused on the digital manuscript I've been narrating from August's iPad, it's impossible to ignore the way he studies me through a layer of soundproof glass like I'm a rare exhibit at a national museum. Despite my limited research on *best practices for audiobook narrators*, the whole vulnerability factor of reading while an incredibly attractive producer scrutinizes your every spoken word was conveniently left out of my findings.

As soon as I finish reading the last sentence of chapter six, I raise my hand, indicating my desire for a break. The heat index inside this recording booth requires a reprieve at least every two to three hours. To be fair, the booth was a comfortable temperature when I first arrived, but as the hours ticked on, my internal thermostat crept up. During our setup, August had kindly explained that the reasoning behind no air vents in the booth has to do with the sensitivity of the microphone, which means the only way to effectively cool the space down is to open the door and filter the studio's air conditioning inside whenever we're not recording. It's for this reason I will not be wearing denim in the foreseeable future. Nor will I be wearing my hair down. It's currently secured into the updo I perfected in the seventh grade after watching Rory wield a BIC pen like a magical hair wand on *Gilmore Girls*.

When August nods in acknowledgment of my raised hand, I ask, "Do you mind if we take ten before we finish the last two chapters for today?" I pinch the fabric directly below the scooped neckline of my cotton tee in hopes of creating a breeze. Parched, I reach for my water bottle only to remember I drained my honey lemon tea during my last break.

"Certainly." August's voice comes through the speakers of the sound booth, and I feel the vibration of it buzz through me. "I need to run up to the house for a minute. Do you need a refill? Tea again?"

"Yes, please." Even though what I'd really love is an ice-cold slushy. Why, oh why does ice have to be so terrible on the vocal cords? "Thank you."

"You're making great time. If you continue at this pace, we should finish ahead of schedule."

"Fabulous." I take his approval to heart, enjoying the easy communication between us today. From the moment I arrived this morning, August has been nothing but accommodating, often anticipating my needs before I voice them aloud. Whatever awkwardness was present during our first meeting hasn't made an appearance today.

The obvious reason is Phantom's absence, I suppose, but it's hard not to wonder if it could also be related to the friendly texts we exchanged over the weekend. After the unpleasant shift I'd worked in the tasting room Saturday night, I'd escaped to the quiet of the pool house only to discover another text from August.

August:

Good luck on your reading marathon tonight. I won't be keeping pace with you, but I'll cheer from the sidelines.

And for reasons I can't explain, it was exactly what I needed in that moment. A distraction. A reminder that I wasn't as alone as I felt. And from that point on, I kept him apprised of my progress. I texted him an emoji summary of each chapter, to which he cheered me on in similar fashion.

I bite back a grin, thinking of the ridiculousness of it all. How when I reached chapter thirty-nine and sent him a broken heart and at least a dozen cry-face emojis, he sent back a Band-Aid and an ice cream cone.

I stand from the stool where I've been perched for hours, and as soon as I step into the short hallway and feel the cool whisper of air across my sweat-damp skin, my brain reboots. With my empty water bottle in hand, I round the corner to where August sits at his soundboard.

He looks up at my approach. "I still can't believe you managed to read that entire book in less than two days."

"I think I did Mrs. Deitz's third grade class proud."

"You earned your superstar button for sure," he says through slightly upturned lips. He begins to roll back in his chair when I hear a thud, followed by a sharp hiss. Immediately, my attention goes to his bandage-wrapped left hand. The same bandage he explained away earlier with the casual mention of a "yardwork incident" when I asked him what happened.

I'm no medical expert here, but I'd say between the excruciating look on his face and the unholy amount of gauze I saw piled in the restroom sink earlier, his little yardwork incident was more serious than he let on.

"August?" I step a little closer, noting the flush of his cheeks for the first time since I stepped out of the booth. "Are you okay?"

"I'm fine," he manages through clenched teeth. "I just need to pop another Tylenol." He blows out a hard breath. "I'll bring you back some tea."

With disbelieving eyes, I watch as he recovers his zip-up sweatshirt from the back of his chair and tries to pull it on—to no avail, seeing as he can't seem to get his bandaged hand through the left sleeve.

Before I can dull my reaction, I audibly gasp at the sight of his fingers. They're not okay. And neither is the man those fingers are connected to. Upon closer inspection, I see that August is not only flushed, but his forehead is glistening with sweat. There's also a patchy rash spreading outside the boundary lines of his bandage.

And yet, he's still working hard to pull on a jacket before he opens the door to a ninety-five degree summer day.

"August, I don't think you're okay." *Understatement.*

"Can't say this is my preferred way to wear a sweatshirt," he deadpans while the left sleeve swings behind his back. Okay, so his sarcasm is still intact. That has to count for something, right?

I set my tumbler on his desk and retrieve the dangling sleeve for him. "Do you often wear sweatshirts in the middle of summer?"

He eyes me as if searching for a hidden meaning in my question, which concerns me almost as much as his choice in attire.

I try a different approach. "Do you feel chilled?"

"It's the air conditioning," he says automatically. "It's colder than usual in here today."

His gaze tracks mine as I confirm that the thermostat on the wall reflects a perfectly comfortable seventy-two degrees.

"August," I say with caution, "I think you might have a fever."

He scrunches his forehead, which causes a bead of sweat to stray from the corner of his right eyebrow down his cheek. "Doubtful. I haven't had a fever since before my tonsils came out when I was eleven."

"May I?" I lift the back of my hand to touch the forehead of a man I've known for less than two business days.

"Sophie, I don't have a fever, I—"

I flinch at the searing heat radiating from him and then immediately drop my gaze to his bare arm. Up close, the trailing rash looks even more menacing, and in an instant I recall where I've seen something similar. A couple years back, while on the set of *Matilda*, our prop director stepped through an old windowpane during the intermission set change. A few of our bigger guys carried her to a restroom, where we removed the glass and cleaned and bandaged her wound. But within forty-eight hours, she was admitted to the hospital with a critical staph infection. My stomach sours at the memory of the show's director sharing the news about her grueling recovery.

"You need to get to a hospital," I say without preamble.

"I'll be fine after I take some Tylenol. My last dose wore off a couple hours ago."

"You see all this redness here?" I point to the rash crawling up his wrist. "There's a serious infection that can cause this. It could be why you have a fever, too, and why your fingers look like Ball Park hotdogs."

He angles his head. "That's a little dramatic."

I try not to recoil at his word choice, one of my father's favorites for me. That and *attention-seeker*. "Not as dramatic as losing your fingers will be if we don't get you to a hospital soon." I assess his half-dressed state and sweaty forehead for a second time and realize he is in no shape to drive himself anywhere. "I can drive you to the ER unless you have someone else who can get here quickly."

He slow blinks. Twice. "Tell you what, how 'bout we reevaluate all this after we finish up your session in the booth. That should give the Tylenol some time to kick in."

Something hot and irrational begins to build in the base of my belly. "No."

"No?" He wipes a hand on his clammy forehead.

"No. There's no way I'm going back in that booth with you out here looking like . . . like that." I point to his hand and then to his face. "I can drive you, or I can call 9-1-1 and get a paramedic out here to drive you. Your choice."

This seems to shake him out of whatever fever stupor he's living in. "Fine." He huffs. "I'll drive—"

"No, you won't." I cut him off. "I'm sorry to be so blunt, but you look like you've been hungover for three days." I glance around his desk. "Now, do you have your wallet on you? Your phone? Anything else you might need?"

He studies me with an incredulity that leaves me ninety-nine percent certain he's about to tell me to go home and never come back.

"Top drawer, left-hand side for the wallet," he all but sighs. "Phone's in my back pocket."

"Perfect." I collect his wallet for him and then assist with his sweatshirt dilemma, tucking it over his left shoulder before I race back to the sound booth for my backpack. It's only after I lock the studio door behind us and we're walking down his driveway that I remember my mode of transportation parked on the curb.

He stops short, slowly dragging his gaze from the street back to me. "Either my fever has reached the hallucination level, or that Escalade is being swallowed by a giant bottle of wine."

It's my turn to wince as I walk him down the remainder of the driveway to the passenger side. "Unfortunately, it's not your fever."

If I were to rate August's pain-free acting abilities from the time he climbed into the Escalade—or the *Wine-Calade*, as he deemed it—to when he asked me to dig through his wallet for his license at the check-in station, I'd give his performance a solid 8.5 out of 10. It's not until I had to help him fill out his paperwork because he couldn't even grip the clipboard that I saw the first real cracks in his armor.

He might have been able to deflect his escalating pain on the drive over with sarcastic jabs about my vehicle, but there is only so long a person can keep up the all-is-well ruse while infection invades their body. Outside of the one-word answers he gave me for the questionnaire, his brand of quiet is the kind rooted in deep concentration. Even now, as the nurse calls him back, he struggles to stand from the waiting room chair. His jaw is clenched so tightly I worry his molars might fuse together.

"Mr. Tate?" The young nurse calls out again as she lifts up on her tiptoes to sweep the continent of people between her and the empty corner where we've set up camp. I wave at her to catch her eye. The last thing August needs is to be marked as a no-show and passed up for a runny nose and cough combination.

Once he finally gets upright, August sways on his feet, and I quickly grab his right elbow to stabilize him.

"I got you," I say, gripping a forearm that is no stranger to a weight set. "We're almost there."

He blinks down at me. "We haven't moved."

"Quite astute of you, yes." I smile up at him. "Just a second."

He grunts as I reach behind us with lightning-quick reflexes for the sweatshirt he shrugged off earlier along with the backpack that holds his wallet and the majority of my earthly possessions. And then I re-hook my arm through his and lead the way toward a nurse that looks like she's young enough to be here on a high school field trip.

August's breathing is labored as we trek across a room that might as well be the Great Valley in *The Land Before Time*. When we finally reach our destination, I've prepped my face with a reassuring smile in order to minimize whatever awkwardness August might feel when I say good-bye and pass him off to the nurse. According to the cheap clock over the doorway, I have little more than an hour before it's time to jump on my first girls-night-in video chat with Dana. We've finally found a time that works for us both to stream *Gilmore Girls* and spend the evening pretending we don't live three thousand miles away from one another. I've missed those nights beyond what I knew was even possible.

Only, when August's gaze skips back to mine, it's not embarrassment that pinches the corners of his eyes. It's something else. Something I can feel more than I can name—because I've been where he is now. Not in an ER with an infected cut on my hand, but having to face something hard and uncertain all on my own. Before I met Dana. Before I understood what a gift it is to have a true friend.

My chest pulls taut at the sobering realization that he'll be alone for whatever's going to happen to him beyond these doors.

"Are you August Tate?" the young woman in powder-pink nursing scrubs asks as she glances up from her clipboard.

He gives a short verbal confirmation.

"Alright," she says, before a distinct look of alarm crosses her features as she takes him in. "Actually, let me call Bruce for a—"

She's mid-sentence when a man in navy scrubs appears with a wheelchair. An obvious pro at his job, he has August squared away in the seat in record time. And before I can think to utter a word, the brakes are released and August is being wheeled through the automatic doors that lead into the part of the hospital reserved for patients and their loved ones.

I don't know what I was expecting to happen at this point—a good-bye hug? A three-point wish-you-well speech? A tip for being his rideshare driver? But as the double doors swish closed behind him, I remember his sweatshirt draped over my arm, which suddenly feels like the most critical thing in the world to return to him. I stride ahead for the doors where Nurse Hadley is still posted with her clipboard. With any luck, she'll be able to get it to him. Instead, she simply waves her badge over the security box on the wall. The doors swoosh open.

"You change your mind?" She smiles. "Go on ahead. Bruce will get you a family pass so you can stay as long as you want." She doesn't bother to wait for a response before she announces the next name on her list.

A thousand thoughts ping against my skull, most of which are a variation of *You are a stranger. Don't you dare try to pass as his family when you've only known him for—*

And then I'm racing to catch them.

Bruce, a nurse of maybe forty with dark skin and even darker eyes, barely twists his neck in the direction of my pattering feet, as if he was expecting me. Perhaps my I-could-be-family vibes are stronger than I thought. I glance at August, who looks as if he's losing a battle against consciousness. The groan that passes through his lips as the wheelchair jostles his body is unlike any sound I've heard him make so far. My empathy twists into a knot.

"Will he be okay?" I whisper to Bruce, who drives the wheelchair with impressive speed. But Bruce has other questions on his mind.

"Do you know when he last ate or drank something?"

We take a sharp left, where Bruce flashes his badge at another automatic door and our surroundings instantly change to the fast-paced environment of an emergency room. Nurses and doctors cross paths, and machines beep and whiz from every direction.

Bruce rotates enough to hike an eyebrow, and it's only then that I remember he's still waiting for my answer.

"Oh, um . . ." I think back to our car ride, and then before that to the recording studio. There was an open energy drink on his desk when I arrived at nine, but I don't remember him taking a sip of anything after my first break. And there was no sign of food to be found. But I don't want to guess wrong and put August at risk. "I don't think he's had anything since around ten this morning."

"Any allergies?"

"None that he knows of." It's the same answer August gave me in the waiting room an hour ago. "And he's only had one surgery—a tonsillectomy when he was eleven. No complications to anesthesia."

"What about pain medication? When did he last take something today?"

I recall what August told the first triage nurse at the check-in desk. "He had a dose of Tylenol when he woke around six this morning. But nothing since."

Bruce nods as if we're equals in this real-life episode of *Grey's Anatomy* when the real truth is that only one of us is authorized to discuss August's medical history. The other is a big fat fraud.

As soon as Bruce throws back the curtain of a tiny exam room with space enough for one bed and one chair, all five of my senses slap me in the face at once. *What am I doing back here? I barely even know this guy.*

"I'll get a quick check of his vitals for Dr. Rock, and then I can get you checked in as well, Mrs.—"

"Sophie." I interrupt using my best stage smile, hoping it will ward off any follow-up questions about my non-relation to August.

At the sound of my name, the patient in question lifts his fever-glazed eyes to mine. There's a small wrinkle in his brow, as if he's as confused by my presence as I am, and I offer him a little wave that I hope translates to *I'm so sorry for invading your privacy* and also, *I don't want you to be alone.* The moment is short-lived as Bruce steps between us to help August onto the bed.

"August," Bruce says in an authoritative tone. "Can you manage getting a gown on without assistance?"

August lifts his chin an inch and gives him a look that would cripple a lesser man.

"No," he hisses through gritted teeth.

"Then do I have your consent to assist you?"

When August confirms, I start toward the curtain, poised to walk out, when Bruce stops me. "Would you mind holding that gown open for me, Sophie?" He gestures to the limp strip of fabric at the foot of the bed. And then to August he says, "We'll try and make this as pain-free as possible."

When Bruce works to stretch the fabric of August's T-shirt wide enough for his swollen arm to fit through, we hear a labored "Just . . . cut it off."

Bruce wastes no time with this request. He cuts a long slit in both sleeves and then one straight line from the neck down to the waist. The shocking flash of August's toned chest steals the breath straight out of me, and I quickly hold up the printed gown like a shield until Bruce's adept hands take it from me and finish the job.

Within three minutes of Dr. Rock's examination of August's infected palm, the term *cellulitis* is spoken multiple times to Bruce, followed by the phrases *wound flush* and *IV antibiotics.* None of which sound great. Unfortunately, I'm not wrong about that.

The following hour or so is a blur of adrenaline and anguish—and I'm not even the one who had to endure it. Sometime during the flush-out portion of August's treatment plan, I reached for his right hand and held on tight as he hissed in pain. I couldn't say if it lasted two minutes or two hours, but even if I live to be a hundred, it would be too soon to see a repeat of that procedure.

Bruce was just setting August up with his IV meds when I stepped out to get the cup of ice he requested. And to take a breather from the intensity of the emergency room drama. Truth is, I've been around enough realistic-looking medical props in theater not to flinch at the sight of blood or gore, but watching someone writhe in pain when all you can do is hold their hand and tell them they're going to be okay takes a toll on a person.

As soon as I escape into the quiet to locate the ice machine, my nerves take a collective sigh. Hospital cup in hand, I flatten my back against the wall and feel the cold cinder blocks calm me from the outside in. *He's going to be fine. Everything is fine.*

I breathe in through my nose and out through my mouth and repeat the words several times over in my head before I'm able to fill the insulated cup with ice. I've just turned toward the hallway that leads to August's temporary quarters when my phone rings.

And it's only then I remember.

Dana.

I scramble to maneuver the cup from my dominant hand so I can answer before it goes to voicemail. "Hello?"

"Hey, girl." Her face fills my screen. Her hair is in a high pony-tail, and I recognize the bright coral top she's wearing because I have the same one. We bought matching jammies last summer that read: *Vacay in my pjs.* "You ready? I want to hear all about your first day! I totally splurged and bought the expensive root beer you like for my float tonight and even made our favorite snack mix to celebrate." She lifts a bowl of assorted savory and sweet treats and shakes it. "And before you ask, no. I did not buy pickle ice cream—"

"Oh, Dana, I'm so sorry," I whisper as I tuck myself into the small alcove near the ice machine. "But I'm not at home right now. There was a bit of an emergency."

"Emergency?" She leans closer to her laptop screen, eyes going wide. "Where are you?"

"The hospital."

"*What?*" she yells, and I hear the snack bowl she just showed me clunk down hard onto the coffee table I bought at a flea market. "Why? Are you hurt? Sick? Did something—"

"It's not me," I amend quickly. "I drove a friend here." Did holding someone's hand during an agonizing procedure qualify as a friendship? "He has a pretty serious infection in his palm from an untreated cut, so I offered to take him in."

She blinks. Stares. And blinks again. "Wait, does this *friend* also happen to be Hot Producer Guy with the naturally beach-blond hair and sultry blue eyes?"

I nod, half regretting my description of August to her last week even though it all still holds one hundred percent true. Though, to be fair, *hot* and *sultry* were her word choices, not mine. Still, August and I are coworkers. And even if this job is only meant as a place-holder for the next few months, he is more than his pretty head of hair and ridiculous set of sea-blue eyes. He's a professional. I make a mental note to speak about him as such from now on—even if the only one I speak to is my best friend.

"He's on meds now and is already doing better. I don't think I'll be here too much longer, but I'm not sure how he's getting home yet. He mentioned he has a ride coming, but so far I haven't seen anyone. Can I text you when I leave? Maybe we'll still have a little time before you have to get to sleep."

There's a slight wiggle to her eyebrows as she says, "You're there with him alone? Just the two of you?"

"We're in a public hospital, inside a tiny space with a curtain for a door," I confirm. "If I had to guess, there are likely a thousand people somewhere within the vicinity of this building right now."

"Still," she says with a dreamy sigh. "That sounds more romantic than the last date I was on."

"Let me assure you, this is no date." I laugh. "August is connected to a drip line and is wearing an open-backed hospital gown."

She does a little hop on the sofa and squeals. "Giiiirrrl, did you peek?"

"Oh my gosh, Dana. *Stop.*" I hit the volume button on the side of the phone until her voice is nearly muted. "And *no*, I did not." At least, I didn't try to. She's still laughing. "Okay, okay, I should probably jump off and bring him back his water cup. But I'm sorry this wasn't what either of us planned tonight. You forgive me?"

She gives me her best contemplative face. "Send me a pic of him in that gown and I'll forgive you."

I roll my eyes. "Don't hold your breath on that. I'll text you later. Love you."

My finger hovers over the red disconnect icon when she nods and says, "You're a super good friend, Soph. He's lucky to have you."

Her words whittle their way from my ears to my heart. And even though I know there is nothing intimate going on between August and me, the slight flutter in my chest is as unexpected as it is curious. I stare down at the darkened phone in my left hand and then to the hospital cup cradled in the nook of my right arm and resolve to help August secure a ride home from the hospital as soon as possible.

Once I'm in front of the curtain blocking me from August's room, I pull on a pleasant expression and clear my throat. "Knock, knock."

"Come in," he replies in an almost whimsical sounding voice I don't recognize.

When I enter the familiar space again, Dr. Rock is with him, standing at the computer.

She twists around, her expression kind and open. "Oh good, I was hoping I'd get a word with you. It's Sophie, isn't it?"

I nod and then slowly look at the man lounging on his hospital bed as if reclined on a beach chair at some exotic resort and not in a hectic emergency room. Why on earth is he grinning like that? And what exactly has he told her about me? Then again, what does he really even know about me? That I own a cat he despises? That I can speak Woodland Creature on demand? Or perhaps the most curious truth of the day, that we've been coworkers for all of seven hours.

"I just told August that he owes you a steak dinner." She leans in my direction and stage whispers, "Or at the least something expensive that requires a reservation and a fancy dress."

This clears nothing up.

But then Mr. Relaxation himself chimes in. "Doc says you saved my life."

"Oh, no." I balk and shake my head. "All I did was—"

"Convince him to come in when he'd convinced himself he'd be fine to wait it out at home with a couple of Tylenols?" Dr. Rock concludes. "Cellulitis is a serious infection, and if left unattended, it can easily turn septic. He's lucky he has someone like you in his life."

Hearing a similar sentiment from Dana was one thing, but hearing it from a doctor on August's behalf is more than a little awkward. Despite what the visitor sticker on my shirt declares, I'm not actually a part of his life. It only takes a second for me to dig out the improv skills and apply humor. "Honestly"—I lift my chin in August's direction—"he's just lucky he came willingly."

His laugh is as uninhibited as it is contagious, and even Dr. Rock chuckles at the two of us. I study the drip line in August's arm, and it's only then that I realize there are two bags of fluid being pumped into him through his IV. One is the antibiotics he needs; the other must be whatever is making him smile as if his usual frown is a farfetched concept.

"Somehow I doubt that an unconscious male is the strangest cargo that SUV has transported," he says. "It looks like hotel art on wheels."

"I wish I could say it's the drugs talking," I tell the doctor, "but he isn't wrong. My brother designed the advertisement wrap so . . ." I shrug like, *What more can I say?*

"You two are officially my favorite people on this floor today." Dr. Rock beams at us both before dropping back into her professional voice. "I sent in the prescription for oral antibiotics to your pharmacy, August." She then points to the fuller of the two IV bags. "As soon as your antibiotic drip is finished, Bruce will be back in to explain the protocol for your at-home wound care."

"What's that?" I ask.

"August will need to have his wound cleaned and bandaged at least once a day, preferably twice." Once again, she looks at me as if my connection to her patient is something it's not. "Don't worry, Bruce can show you all the tricks. But considering you watched the whole procedure earlier, I'm guessing you're not the squeamish type." She pats August on the leg. "Once again, you should consider yourself lucky. Not everybody has someone at home who is capable or willing to assist."

Thankfully, when the inevitable awkward pause at her assumption crash lands in the center of the exam room, August is with it enough to come to the rescue.

"What's the alternative?" he asks in a curious tone.

"That would depend on your insurance. But likely a daily visit to your local urgent care or possibly home health care."

"Wow," August says under his breath. "That would be unfortunate."

"Exactly," Dr. Rock says as she pulls off her gloves, tosses them in the receptacle, and moves to exit through the curtain. As she pulls it open, she winks in my direction. "Which is why I highly recommend you make that fancy dinner reservation for when all this is over. Take care, you two. And thanks for the laughs."

When the curtain swishes closed behind her and we're alone, I feel August's gaze return to me, but I'm not quite brave enough to look at him yet. If he unnerved me this morning when there was a shield of glass between us at the studio, then I don't have the right vocabulary for whatever his gaze is doing to me now.

"You stayed," August says in a tone I don't recognize. It's gentle and light and full of an emotion that sounds a whole lot like gratitude.

"It seemed like you could use the company."

A beat passes before he says, "Or maybe you were just hoping to see me in this sweet minidress."

I bite my bottom lip at that. "I've been meaning to tell you that those faded blue and yellow stars do a lot for your complexion."

"Do you think Bruce will notice if I wear it home?"

"Honestly, I don't think Bruce misses much of anything around here."

"True." August chuckles. "But I suppose the same could be said for you. I'm not sure how many people would be observant enough to spot my symptoms as warning signs for infection the way you did."

Something like awe laces his words, and when I look up, he points to the chair beside his bed. I sit without hesitation and then wonder how it is I feel so at ease with August when that's rarely the case with any man I encounter. Even those I'm related to.

My knee brushes the edge of the mattress where he rubs the thin blanket stretched over his legs between his index finger and thumb. It's the same hand I held while August blanched white and fought to stay conscious.

"I hope this goes without saying, but I don't expect you to help me with this after I'm home." He lifts his left arm where the IV is flowing into his bandaged hand and wrist. "Wound care is not a part of your narration package at the studio. I made a stupid decision, and now I have to pay for it. I'll figure it out."

I can tell he's trying to minimize the situation. But having filled out August's medical questionnaire for him, I know too much. The self-employment insurance he carries is for major medical only. None of this is covered. I'd guess daily wound care isn't either. Knowing the balance in my own bank account at the moment, I'd be freaking out if the situation were reversed.

"Is there someone who lives close by who could help? A friend? A neighbor, maybe?"

"Not really," he says tiredly. "Gabby won't be back home for two weeks."

Gabby? August lives with a woman? How had I missed that?

"Is she . . . on a trip or something?"

He takes a sip of his water and nods in confirmation.

I try to play off my disappointment at the thought of a woman in his life. Usually I'm pretty good at picking up on that vibe. "If you don't mind me asking, how long have the two of you been together?"

August lowers his jug of ice water, and I watch as his lips curve north. "Guess that depends on how you define *together*. Technically speaking, she's been an important part of my life for a little over a decade, but I only moved in two years ago."

"A decade?" Shock spikes my volume. "Were you like, high school sweethearts or something?"

He barks out a laugh. "Try brother and sister."

An icy hot sensation muffles my hearing. "What?"

"Gabby's sixteen. She's my sister."

"Oh. *Oh.*" Even for a professional actress, I know my *oh* does not sound nearly as casual as I intend. "You live with your teenage sister—well, that's fun."

"It's something for sure." His eyelids grow heavy, but his grin continues to hold a tender component I don't want to walk away from. "She'll like you."

A flutter spasms in my lower abdomen at his soft, unhindered words. "Why do you say that?"

"Because you're both . . ." His breathing slows. "Spunky."

My mouth falls open. "Spunky?" I snicker, as this is not a word I often hear, and yet I kind of love it. Even if August is too intoxicated to remember saying it tomorrow.

Eyes closed, he nods. "I can be stubborn."

"You don't say," I tease.

"See?" A lopsided smile fills his face. "*Spunky.* And still you managed to get me here somehow. Not a small feat."

"Guess you're not the only one who can be stubborn at times."

He's quiet for a moment before he peeks at me with one eye. "You should go home, Sophie."

"What?"

"I'm a big boy," he says on the tail end of a yawn. "I'll call a rideshare once I'm discharged. I'm good now, thank you."

"Are you firing me as your chauffeur? I can assure you I've never had a single ticket or accident." Of course, I don't tell him I took off driving for the last eight years.

"No, I'm giving you back your night." Eyes closed again, he makes an exaggerated shooing motion with his bandaged hand. It's utterly ridiculous. "Now go. I'll see you tomorrow at the studio. Unless you decide to quit after today. Completely understandable."

I rub the chill from my arms and then spot his sweatshirt hanging on a hook by the curtain. I pull it on and hunker back down into the seat. "What if I enjoy hospitals?"

"Liar," he says. "Nobody enjoys hospitals."

"You definitely seem to be enjoying yourself."

"For the moment," he says almost incoherently. "But I'm not usually the patient. It's much harder to be the one in your seat."

I scrunch my eyebrows in, wondering at such a statement. But then I feel something in the pocket of his zip-up sweatshirt. Something small and crinkly. I pull it out and then have to bite back my gasp. In my palm lies a yellow star shape cut out of construction paper. *Superstar Reader* is written across the front in black Sharpie with one point pricked through by a safety pin.

He made me a badge.

I look from the fragile paper star in my hand to the sleeping man in the bed and decide right then that I don't care how long it takes the drip line to empty or for Bruce to bring his discharge papers. Something tells me August could use the rest.

And inexplicably, I want to be the one here when he wakes up.

I slip the star into the back pocket of my purse to keep it from tearing, text Dana an update and a plan to reschedule soon, and watch a self-proclaimed stubborn stranger sleep.

I don't know how conscious he is when he slides his free arm over the top of the blanket to where my hand rests, but when his warm skin covers mine, my heart feels a bit like that fragile paper star in the pocket of my purse.

And for the first time since meeting August, I think I might be in real trouble.

Voice Memo

Gabby Tate

3 months, 3 weeks, 5 days after the accident

I haven't done one of these in a few weeks. Mostly because there hasn't been much of anything new to tell, but after last night, I figured I should probably update you. Or I guess, update me? I don't know. I'm pretty tired.

I had to wake August up in the middle of the night. It took me a couple of hard shakes to get him to respond, but when he did, he grabbed at his chest like he was ninety-six and not just twenty-six. If I hadn't been in so much pain, I'm sure I would have laughed.

My left ear had started ringing sometime after dinner last night. I didn't say anything to August then because I figured it would go away on its own. It usually does. It got a little better when I laid down, but then it woke me up out of my dream, and it was a good dream, too. I dreamed I was with Mom and Dad and that they had come home for a visit. I kept asking them to stay, but they just kept telling me they loved me. Anyway, the pain in my ear finally woke me up. It felt like a knife jabbing over and over into my skull. I'm not sure if I was crying from that or from the dream.

August must have been able to tell something was really wrong with me because I've never seen him move so fast. He almost forgot his shoes in the house! We drove to the emergency room, and thankfully they got me in to see a doctor right away. We were there most of the night, running tests and pulling up my medical file to add notes for when I see my doctor tomorrow afternoon. The pain finally did fade like the nurse promised, but when I saw the ER doctor say the word *surgery* to my brother, I almost cried again. I asked him about it later, and he told me not to worry and that

103

we'd have to see what my doctor says. I tried to act brave, but the truth is I don't want another surgery. I'm beginning to really hate hospitals as much as August does. On the way home, he took me to get a cookie pizza, and I swear I've never tasted anything so good in all my life. I saved the leftovers for breakfast.

I prayed that God would help me remember what He did for me after the accident. How when I was scared, He took away my fear. I asked Him to do that again. I don't want another surgery, but I do know I can trust Him. So that's what I'm going to do.

8

August

It's been thirteen days since I woke up holding Sophie's hand at the hospital. Thirteen days of her showing up at my studio prepared to nurse a wound she didn't cause. And thirteen days since a secondary infection took me by surprise.

My symptoms started off small at first—a shiver at the briefest touch of our hands, a twinge at the sound of her voice in my headphones, an ache at the end of every work session after she says, "Good-bye until tomorrow."

Only every tomorrow feels like a fever dream I don't want to wake from.

I know the prognosis should scare me—terrify me, even. I promised myself I wouldn't let this happen again. I swore it. The last time I cared about a woman, my whole world came crashing down. And yet nothing about this, about *her*, feels like a repeat of Vanessa.

And yet I've been wrong before.

"There you go, Mr. Tate," Sophie says as she lowers my freshly bandaged hand to the gray sofa cushion wedged between us. We learned quickly that the studio bathroom isn't large enough for two people plus a medical supply kit, and given that Sophie is a coworker, it hasn't felt appropriate to invite her inside my house alone.

"From everything Bruce explained about the stages of healing, I think you're ahead of schedule. You've been a superstar patient."

While Sophie turns to sort the remaining supplies, I clear my throat and debate for the thousandth time if I should capitalize on the moment and make good on that dinner date Dr. Rock suggested in the ER.

I flex my healing hand for courage. No pain. I open my mouth, the words on the tip of my tongue, when she flips around with a huge grin on her face. "I think it's time I give you this. You've earned it."

She holds out a yellow paper star with the words *Superstar Patient* written on the front in black, bold letters, complete with a safety pin through one of the points. At first, I'm speechless, but then I see the badge she's pinned to her own shirt.

The badge I'd made and figured I'd lost in the unexpected shuffle to the hospital.

She must read the unspoken questions on my face.

"I found it in the pocket of your sweatshirt that night in the hospital. Hope I was right in assuming it was meant for me? I've been saving it for just the right moment." She touches her wrinkled star. "Thank you for this, by the way. I'll wear it with pride."

I blink, nod. "You're welcome."

She holds up my badge. "May I do the honors? I'm not sure your hand has graduated to safety-pin dexterity quite yet."

I try to laugh, but my throat dries out as soon as she touches my chest and tugs at my shirt. "First you bandage me like a pro, and now you're coming at me with a needle. I think you're more medically inclined that you realized."

"'Fraid the closest I've come to nursing was playing Florence Nightingale in a musical several years back."

"A musical," I muse, hoping her fingers linger longer than necessary.

She pats the badge on my chest and pulls her hand away. "Yep. I actually majored in musical theater."

"I'd guessed you were a singer."

"Yeah?" She laughs me off as if I'm joking. "How's that?"

"Because I've heard your voice."

She pulls a goofy face. "I'm pretty sure I'd remember breaking into song in front of you, August."

I fixate on her perfect lips as she says my name. "It's in the way you speak—your pitch control and clarity, your resonance and range. You also have a reverence for enunciation and tone I've rarely heard in my field. It's hardly a perfect science, but in the same way a coach can recognize a trained athlete by the muscle groups they've built, a trained ear can recognize a professionally trained voice."

Her amusement slips into a stunned expression I've only seen her wear a handful of times. "You're completely serious."

"I rarely joke about what I hear in my sound booth." I pause, wondering how far I should take this. "If I had to guess, I'd say you're a mezzo-soprano with a sweet spot similar to Adele's range—A4–E5."

Sophie's jaw slacks. "How can you possibly know that when you've only heard me read fantasy fiction?"

I shrug again. "Am I wrong?"

Slowly, she shakes her head back and forth, but it's the way her eyes shimmer and her words fall hoarse that makes me realize I should have stopped while I was ahead. *"What are you?"*

The question strikes me in the hollow of my throat. "I'm a sound engineer."

"What else?"

I'm not sure if it's the question she asks or the expectation behind it that sends my mind swirling down a funnel of no return. Without warning, I'm back to the conversation I overheard between my parents after they listened to me play an entire song from the radio on our old, out-of-tune piano stored in the garage. I hadn't missed a note. I was seven years old.

"*But how, Brian?*" Mom whispered. "*Tell me how that's possible when he's never taken a single piano lesson? Neither you or I can sing, much less play an instrument.*"

"*I dunno,*" Dad said in that bewildered way of his. "*Perhaps God's given him a special ear for music.*"

Mom's laugh-cry was muffled then, and when I peeked around the corner into the kitchen, I watched their embrace, Dad's arms tightly secured around her back. "*Do you think he could be some sort of prodigy? He's constantly drumming on every surface—chairs, countertops, windowsills. Even my leg when we all sit together at church. It's like there's always a song playing in his head. I thought it was just a boy thing, but maybe it's—*"

"*It's not for us to determine, Sara. We can hire a music teacher and get an assessment. But even if he is . . . special, fixating on a singular gifting is not our job. Our job is to help him mature into a man of character.*"

"August?" Sophie's voice slingshots me back to the present, where concern has crimped her brow. I blink and work to smile normally.

This isn't where I wanted our conversation to land before Sophie takes the booth for our next session. I was thinking more along the lines of discussing the possibility of a nice restaurant in Napa where the two of us could—

Sophie stands abruptly from the sofa and moves to assess the framed pictures of artists I've worked with in the past. She sweeps her pointer finger through the air as if she's puzzling something out. "You're a sound engineer now, but you worked as a music producer in LA."

"That's right," I say carefully.

And then she rotates to the assortment of guitars hanging on the opposite wall near the keyboard and synth pads in the corner. "At first I thought these instruments were here for aesthetic reasons." She slowly turns in my direction. "But you can play all of these, can't you?"

I hesitate. "Yes."

I watch a switch flip on inside her at my answer. "Does that mean you compose?"

"No." It's not a lie, but it's not exactly the truth, either. She didn't ask if I *have ever* composed, but if I compose. As in present tense. And that answer is accurate.

Somehow, she doesn't appear deterred by my short response.

"May I?" She points to my 914ce Builder's Edition Grand Auditorium acoustic guitar. It's my second favorite Taylor.

"You play?"

"Only good enough for a campfire setting."

I chuckle at that but stop laughing when she whips out her cell phone and does a quick tune using an app. After securing the strap around her neck, she faces away from me and strums a chord.

"What chord am I playing?" she asks.

Tiny pinpricks of sweat break out under my arms. I don't care much for this game, but I keep my voice light and unassuming. "How would I know? I can't see your hands."

She glances at me over her shoulder and narrows her eyes in a *don't-toy-with-me* kind of way. She strums another chord. "What about this one?"

"Sophie, I think this party trick of yours might need some work."

She stops the resonance of sound with her palm and twists to face me.

This time, when our gazes collide, I wonder if this is how it happens. How a man lost at sea finally surrenders to the siren's call. Sophie is beautiful and generous and filled with the kind of magnetic goodness I'd do almost anything to stay close to. But it's the admiration in her eyes that feels altogether unsettling.

Vanessa never looked at me like that.

With her, every step of our relationship was a premeditated equation. She knew all there was to know about me before I ever laid eyes on her that first time. She knew I traveled with a band who sang about Jesus on stage and lived like they knew nothing about Him as soon as they stepped off it. When she found me, I was days away from throwing in the towel and going home with my tail tucked between my legs. My parents had never been on board with LA. My mom hadn't felt a peace about the band I produced for, even from the start. Vanessa had come along at just the right moment, stroking my ego with a dream job I couldn't say no to. And just like that, I'd become the ace up her sleeve.

There was nothing she denied me as long as it meant I remained at her studio, and eventually, at her home. I certainly wasn't the first man under her employ to fall prey to her snare of chart-topping clientele, massive bonus checks, and the high-roller lifestyle I'd been convinced I wanted.

Until I wanted none of it.

Until the shame of my recklessness had become like barbed wire around my neck.

Is that why I was so drawn to Sophie? Because everything about her felt like the opposite of everything about me?

My breath shallows at the crackling silence between us now, and I'm acutely aware of every curve my guitar hugs on Sophie's figure. I'm so aware, in fact, that I'm waiting for her fingers to strum again and force me to answer when instead she closes her eyes and belts out a vocal run that causes every hair on my arms to stand and salute. My imagination hadn't done her singing voice justice. It's spectacular. Mesmerizing, even. Her vibrato, her control, her rising crescendo when she hits the high note and simultaneously forces the air from my lungs. With expert skill, she eases back the reins and opens her eyes.

"D-sharp," I say breathlessly.

Gazes locked, she sings another.

"G."

She launches into several scale sequences, and I answer them all without hesitation. She confirms my responses one by one as she plucks the corresponding notes on my Taylor.

A tiny curve lifts the corner of her lips. "Why, August Tate, you have perfect pitch."

My nod is honest, yet subdued.

"You're the real party trick," she says with far too much pleasure.

"Actually, I'm just a career nerd who prefers to stay behind the scenes."

She tilts her head in observation. "I've befriended a lot of stay-behind-the-scenes types over the years, and do you know what most of them have in common?"

"I'm sure you're about to enlighten me."

"Secrets." She shrugs, but there is zero nonchalance about it. "Secret hopes, secret dreams, secret pasts."

"Interesting," I say, tapping my chin. "Especially since I don't recall you volunteering much in the way of personal information over the last two weeks, either. I think you might need to expand your theory."

If she's surprised by my bluntness, her expression doesn't show it. She walks toward the sofa, and my gaze climbs the length of her lean, shapely legs to where her elbows rest on the body of my guitar. She's so close when she stops that if I didn't tip my chin, I'd be smacked in the face by my Taylor's ebony bridge.

"You want to know one of my secrets, August?"

I swallow. "I would."

"I've always been envious of people with perfect pitch. Do you know how rare that is?" She doesn't wait for my response. "One in ten thousand."

"And your voice is one in ten million," I say evenly, though my pulse is erratic. "It's exquisite."

She blinks down at me, the teasing in her gaze cleared by the time she manages to speak. "Thank you, August. That means . . . a lot. It's been a while since I've sang in front of anyone, much less someone with your skillset."

I want to understand what she means by *a while*. Actually, I want to ask a hundred follow-up questions starting with, *Why are you reading books when you should be performing on a stage?* But before I can utter a word, Sophie has already turned back to the wall to hang up the guitar, and when she faces me again, it's clear the spell has been broken. It's also clear she broke it on purpose.

She picks up her work backpack near my sound table. "I have a shift at the winery this evening, so we should probably get started. There are some grueling, emotional scenes on the agenda today." She sighs dramatically. "Chapter thirty-nine." She clutches at her heart, which just so happens to be located directly under the badge I made her.

Before my mind even has a chance to fully reroute, she's already hoofing it to the sound booth. Sophie may not be a behind-the-scenes type like me, but I have no doubt she has secrets, too. None as terrible as my own, I'm sure, but secrets nonetheless.

Despite the quick mood shift, Sophie's performance in the booth is unmatched. Of the handful of completed projects voiced by the other narrators I've produced up to this point, it's difficult not to compare the difference in talent level. There is such emotional tension in every scene Sophie reads that I find myself sitting on the edge of my seat as I follow along with her on my own iPad. In today's four-hour session, she's stopped three times—all of which were her asking to reread a section because she thought she could do it better a second time. She rarely skips or mispronounces a word or even has a tickle in her throat. She's disciplined to drink her hot lemon tea even though I know it must be stifling in there. She's the true prodigy among us.

It's difficult not to let my eyes drift from the words on the screen I'm supposed to be following, but her animated storytelling could be a main attraction. I'd certainly buy a ticket. Even now, her ponytail swishes violently as she reads the end of a battle scene I can see perfectly in my mind. I would have cared far more about my English classes if I'd known fiction could read like this.

"'Rayun! No!'" Sophie screams in character. "'No, no, no! Please, don't do this. You have to wake up—you hear me? You are not allowed to die. We've fought too hard together for you to leave me now.'" Sophie wails into her microphone and soon real tears streak her cheeks. I'm not going to lie, even with her earlier warning, I did *not* see the death of such a beloved character coming. Sophie's voice cracks with raw emotion, and to my surprise, I have to blink away the heat building behind my eyes. "'I'll take you to the healer. You just have to stay alive until I can—'"

At the tap on my shoulder, I nearly jump out of my skin.

Gabby's face is angled as she leans against my desk. She's waving and speaking, and for a moment I'm so disoriented by the sound of Sophie's grief in my ears that I can't tell if my sister's presence is real or imagined. The instant I tug off my headphones, the world around me slowly returns, and with it, my bearings.

"G-Gabby," I stutter. "You're here? You're home?"

"Surprise!" My sister's easy grin is familiar, and yet she looks different somehow—more mature, more like a woman than a teenager. How is that even possible in only four weeks' time? It must be the new way she's styling her hair.

I stand and throw my arms around her in an embrace that hides little and holds nothing back. I pick her up as she squeals and squirms, and I know she's equal parts delighted and mortified by me. And I hope that never changes. It took us close to a year to get comfortable with physical affection after living apart for so long, but not anymore. Not after all we've been through together.

Gabby's home. Gabby's safe. Gabby's here.

And I've missed her. More than I dared to admit to myself.

When she pulls back an instant later, I spot the tiny hardware inside her ears and wonder how often she wore her aids during camp. I want to ask, but I won't. Questions about her customized bilateral routing of signal—BiCROS—hearing aids is one of the quickest ways to kill a good mood. But this tiny transmitter and amplifier system is the best solution we have as of right now. I sold my favorite guitar to afford them, and I'd do it again to be able to communicate with her.

For now, the technology allows Gabby's dead ear—her right—to pick up sound through the transmitter and send a signal to the active hearing aid on her left. Even with extensive hearing loss on that side due to trauma, the system helps balance the sound she can hear, much like a regular hearing aid. It's been deemed a miracle for some, and for others, like Gabby, the adjustments are ever-changing due to her degenerative condition. Noisy rooms and environments frustrate her to no end, as does trying to localize sound. But it's something. And until I can afford something better, something more permanent, this *something* is better than nothing.

"Is Aunt Judy in the house?" I ask.

Gabby shakes her head and signs at the same time she speaks. Another surprise. She's tried this in the past, and from what her ASL tutor and speech therapist have explained, the two languages are quite different, each with their own rules, patterns, and grammar codes. It's often been too frustrating for her to keep it up for long, but I'm struck by how quickly her hands are moving when she says, "Aunt Judy didn't take me home, a friend did." She raises up on her toes and claps her hands. "Do you have plans for dinner tonight? Because we stopped at the grocery store on our way home. I took a cooking class at camp and learned a new recipe. I can't wait to make it for us!"

She signs whatever menu item she's referring to, but I have no clue what it is. Her speed is nearly triple what it was before she left, and I make the sign for her to slow down. In the early days of Gabby's recovery from the accident, before we knew if she'd have any hearing in her left ear at all, the doctors had encouraged Aunt Judy and me to take some online ASL classes in order to motivate Gabby to learn. Turns out, Gabby didn't need much in the way of motivation. I only managed to learn the basics before the swelling in Gabby's head went down enough for her to test slightly above profound loss in her left ear.

"What's that sign?" I ask, but before Gabby can respond, she catches sight of the woman engrossed in an epic performance in my booth. Though neither of us can hear what Sophie is saying into the mic from this side of the glass, it's obvious she's continued on with the scene—which looks quite distressing. *Did Rayun make it to the healer in time?*

Did I seriously just wonder about the fate of a fictional character?

Gabby swivels back to me, and her rapid-fire questions knock me back a step. "Why is there a woman crying in your booth? What is she saying? Does she need help?"

I raise both hands in an attempt to bring calm, but then her focus moves to my bandage. Her eyes go wide as she grabs my arm and assesses me accusingly. An entirely new set of questions begins. At the time of my injury, it seemed unnecessary to recount the whole medical drama over text. Especially when our texting sessions were often sporadic and limited.

I'm regretting that decision now.

"What happened to your hand?" she demands.

"It's no big deal. Just a cut that got infected. I saw a doctor and got on some antibiotics. My friend's been helping me with fresh bandages."

"How did it happen?"

I grip the back of my neck.

"August?"

"I was fixing the roof of Mom's greenhouse."

"The roof?!" She glowers at me with the look of offended teenage girls everywhere. "Remember how you gave me that whole big speech at camp drop-off about not taking any unnecessary risks? And then you go and get on a roof?"

I feel a swift kick of guilt as her accusation lands.

"You should have texted me," she says, crossing her arms.

"I didn't want to worry you."

She rolls her eyes. There is no need for interpretation there.

I press my right fist to my chest and rub in a clockwise circle. *Sorry.* That is one sign I know well. I used it a lot in the early days. *Sorry,* but you can't go surfing with your friends this weekend. Too risky. *Sorry,* but turning up your music that loud can damage your remaining hearing. *Sorry,* but Aunt Judy isn't your legal guardian. I am.

"I'm sorry," I say. "But I'm good now. I promise."

She drops her arms and then gestures to the booth again, where Sophie has balled up a tissue in her hand and is currently blotting her eyes. I have no clue how she hasn't seen us out here. A testament to her professional focus, I suppose.

"So?" Gabby asks. "Who is she?"

"Her name is Sophie," I explain. "She's an actress Chip hired to narrate audiobooks for his publisher. She's been coming to the studio for the last few weeks. The scene she's reading is sad."

Her gaze shifts left to right. "Does that mean Chip's your boss now?"

I scratch the back of my neck. "In a way, I guess. I signed a contract to produce ten audiobooks for Fog Harbor, with an option for more."

Her eyebrows spike in an expression I've seen many times. "And Sophie works here with you every day?"

"Most days."

She peers at me as if she's working out a calculation, then rotates toward the glass that separates the studio from the booth. Only it's empty.

"Hello." Sophie appears around the corner and gives us both a little wave. Her cheeks are splotchy, and her eyes still hold the hint of tears, but her smile is heartfelt if not a little curious, too.

My sister's countenance changes in an instant.

"Hello," she says perkily as she stretches out her hand. "I'm Gabby, August's favorite little sister."

It's also her favorite little joke.

Sophie extends her hand to Gabby and introduces herself, as well, though I can tell she's trying to place the unique tone she hears in Gabby's voice. Though my sister's been speaking English since she was adopted at six, the trauma she suffered to her head and eardrums in the accident has slightly altered the way she speaks. She graduated from physical and cognitive therapies not long after the first year, but Gabby will remain in speech therapy for the foreseeable future.

If only there was a specialized therapy for her hearing prognosis, too.

Gabby turns to me and signs, *Wow! She's very beautiful.*

I give a slight shake of my head to deter her from going any further with this game she loves.

But in true Gabby style, she is not easily put off. She counters with a simple sign I'm sure is the equivalent to me being the same no-fun brother she left a month ago, followed by an eye roll.

I am not amused.

When I finally look over at Sophie, her gaze is pinging back and forth between us, her eyes round and on alert. I may have left out a few things when I mentioned my sister to her.

"I'm sorry," I say. "My sister seems to have left her manners at camp."

"I have great manners," Gabby retorts. "My brother said you're an actress. Did you come from Hollywood? Because you are super, super pretty."

"Oh, thank you." Sophie laughs and touches a hand to her chest. "I think you're really pretty, too." She glances at me. "As for Hollywood . . ." She shakes her head.

"What?" Gabby asks, focusing hard on Sophie's face. Unfinished sentences can be difficult, especially when the speaker's head is turned. Gabby uses several senses to reach the accuracy she has with her aids—lipreading being a key player.

"Um, I . . ." Sophie starts, obviously flustered by how to finish. "I'm sorry. Am I doing something wrong?"

Gabby looks at me and signs that she doesn't know what she's saying.

I place a gentle hand on Sophie's back. "It's best to use complete sentences. Gabby's aids pick up a lot, but certain tones are more difficult than others. She also lipreads."

"Oh, okay, sure," Sophie says, bewildered. "I've never . . . I mean, I wish I would have learned more than the alphabet in ASL."

Gabby smiles patiently. "If you ever decide to learn, you should teach my brother." She winks. "He basically only knows how to ask where the bathroom is and how to tell me to stop being annoying."

It's my turn to roll my eyes, but Sophie laughs. And I can tell Gabby enjoys that very much.

"What were you saying about Hollywood?" Gabby asks.

This time, I watch as Sophie readies herself to answer. "I've never acted in a movie, but I have been in a few musicals."

"She's been on Broadway," I add proudly.

Sophie looks surprised at my knowledge of this, and it's then I remember it was Chip who told me this information, not Sophie herself.

"Broadway? I love theater!" my sister erupts. "I'm hoping I can join a drama club with a few of my friends from church," Gabby says with a glance back at me.

Oh, good. More things to be involved in at church.

"That's sounds wonderful!" Sophie replies with an enthusiasm I don't share for multiple reasons. The biggest having to do with a certain friend we haven't yet discussed in context. "I actually got started with acting at a small drama club not too far from here."

"Can you stay for dinner?" Gabby asks abruptly. "I'm making homemade fettuccine Alfredo. August says I'm almost as good of a cook as our mother, and she was fantastic—right, August?" Then to me Gabby says, "Can Sophie stay for dinner? Please?"

Though I'd imagined asking Sophie to dinner many times over the last few days, this wasn't what I'd had in mind.

"That's okay, really." Sophie waves her hand dismissively. "I'm sure you two have a lot to catch up on."

"Most of what I have to catch Gabby up on involves you." My honesty is almost as unexpected as the way Sophie's gaze locks on mine. "If you're available, we'd love to invite you to have dinner with us tonight."

9

Sophie

Am I available for dinner tonight? No. But do I want to be available? So much.

Of all the nights to have a shift in the tasting room, why does it have to be tonight?

Truth is, it's been a long time since I've eaten dinner away from the winery. Most nights I end up eating in the pool house while Phantom circles my feet. It's not until right now that I realize how nice sharing a meal with someone else would be—two someones, in this case. Going from a communal living environment in New York City where I slept, ate, worked, played, and memorized lines with an entire cast to living alone with my cat has been far lonelier than I thought possible.

"Your dinner sounds delicious," I tell Gabby apologetically, making sure to look at her when I speak. I'm still not sure what she can or can't hear, but I want to learn. "And I appreciate your offer so much." I swallow against the growing lump in my throat. "But I'm scheduled to work a shift tonight."

"I missed that," Gabby says as she signs to her brother.

"Sophie has to work tonight," August confirms.

Gabby looks around. "But I thought you worked here? With my brother?"

"I do," I say, "but I also work for my brother." Admitting that out loud splinters my pride.

"Then maybe you should call him and ask for the night off?" Gabby places her palms together like the prayer hands emoji. "Please?"

If only. "My brother is not . . ."

"What?" Gabby asks, focusing on my lips.

I chide myself for letting yet another sentence run away from me.

"Sorry," I say, looking at her now. "My brother isn't nice like yours."

Gabby points at August. "You think *he's* nice?"

August stuffs his hands into his pockets and glances at the ceiling. "You're so hilarious."

Gabby beams at him self-indulgently, and something in their exchange makes me want to better understand their dynamic. Why does Gabby live with him? Where are their parents? I think back through our morning conversations when I changed his bandage—how I purposefully steered us toward light and easy discussions. August had seemed more than willing to wade in the shallows with me.

We talked about his surfing hobby and how much I was gonna miss NYC in the fall. We spoke about our favorite comfort foods, movies we rewatched annually, and the book series I wished I could read for the first time—a question only relating to me as August was still warming up to fiction. I didn't ask him about his family simply because I didn't want to reciprocate. The information I provided him during our morning chats was generic—mostly history about the winery that could easily be found on any search engine online.

And then, today, I'd gone and cracked the code on his secret prodigy genius.

Even now, as my mind flashes back to the way he looked at me when I sang those runs, I feel the faintest fluttering in my chest. *He's only a friend*, I'm quick to remind myself. In a way, I suppose August is also a colleague. The last thing I need is to read into something just because I'm desperate for companionship.

"Another time, then," August says, but I don't miss the disappointment I hear in his tone or the disappointment I feel. "Don't let Gabby's glowing review of me fool you. She loves boring nights at home with her big brother."

But Gabby doesn't comment on her brother's teasing jab. Her eyes are too honed on me. On second thought, I'm not totally sure she heard him at all. The mystery surrounding her hearing continues to grow.

"I'm sorry," I offer her again. "I'd be happy to talk theater with you any time I'm here."

She gives me a smile that makes me wish I could give her something more than a declined invitation to a dinner she's obviously excited to share.

"I'll walk you out, Sophie." It's not the first time August has escorted me down the driveway to say good-bye; it's just the first time he's announced it. Perhaps because we both know there's more to say to each other than a simple "See you tomorrow."

I collect my stuff from the booth and tell Gabby it was lovely to meet her.

A few minutes later as I walk down the driveway with August toward the Wine-Calade, I admit, "I feel bad I had to say no."

"Don't be. She just had a month of playtime at camp. She'll be fine."

I stop at the curb and look up at him, shielding my eyes from the blazing sun over the tree line separating his house from the neighbors. There are so many things I want to ask, but I'm still not sure how or even if he wants me to.

"You can ask," he prompts gently. "To be fair, I should have told you before today. I owe you that much."

"You don't owe me anything."

He raises his bandaged hand. "I think you're forgetting the last thirteen days."

I give an uncomfortable laugh. "I just mean, I want to respect your personal life."

He looks down at his feet, and for several seconds, I wonder if I've given him the out he needs and if I should just say good-bye now and be on my way. Whatever we've shared in these last two weeks has been fun and unexpected and maybe even the perfect kind of distraction—at least for me. But there is obviously so much we don't know about each other. And maybe it's better it stays that way. Maybe—

"Our parents died two years ago in a train accident overseas," he begins. "They adopted Gabby at the age of six from Colombia when I was a senior in high school. She was traveling with them on that train, and she suffered a head trauma that resulted in unilateral hearing loss. Her cochlear nerve was completely severed in her right ear, and there's only a trace amount of residual hearing in her left, depending on the frequency. Her condition is . . . unstable. Our parents named me her legal guardian, and I moved back as soon as she was out of the hospital."

For the second time today, my eyes grow misty. Only this time it isn't due to fiction. It's real. And it's beyond heartbreaking.

I search his face, trying to process the crushing words he's just spoken, and failing to come up with any of my own. Perhaps there are no words for this at all.

"It's quite the conversation killer, isn't it?" he teases darkly.

"August." I close my eyes, swallow. "I don't know what to say."

"That's perfect."

"What?" I glance up at him again, confused. "What's perfect?"

"That you don't know. Nobody does. Heck, I don't even know what to say about it half the time, and it's my life. My story." He combs his good hand through his hair, making a mess of the golden waves. I want to reach up and fix it. But really, I want to fix so much more than that for him. And for his precious sister, too.

I take out my phone then, trying not to think about the man who will answer on the other end, or any future consequences of asking him for a favor now. Instead, I'm thinking only of a sixteen-year-old girl who shares the same passion I once did at her age and the small gift I can offer her by showing up to a dinner party she's invited me to.

"What are you doing?" August asks as I tap Jasper's contact.

"Calling my brother."

"Sophie, no. You really don't have to—"

"Hello?" The female voice on the other end of the line surprises me.

"Hello? Is . . . is Jasper there?"

"Hi, Sophie. This is Natalie." Strange as it is that I don't recognize my own sister-in-law's voice, I can't remember the last time we spoke on the phone.

"Oh, hey. Um, I had a question for him. About tonight."

"Jasper just stepped out for a minute. Is it something I can answer for you?" The surrealness of this interaction isn't lost on me. Nobody speaks for Jasper, least of all Natalie, who up until recently rarely spoke at all. Especially where I'm concerned.

"Maybe? I'm in Petaluma right now, about to head back for my shift later this evening, but some friends have invited me over for dinner. I was wondering if I might be able to rearrange my work schedule and trade tonight's shift for a double tomorrow. I just needed to ask if I could keep the Escalade tonight and get the name of whoever's scheduled so I can see about a switch."

She's quiet for a second. "I'll take it for you."

I squint into the sun and then look at the pavement, trying to orient myself. "You'll take what?"

"Your shift. I owe you a favor, and I have some inventory that needs doing, so I don't mind keeping an eye on the counter if we get busy. Fridays can be hit or miss when there are no private events going on."

I open my mouth twice before I finally get a word out. "Thank you, Natalie. I . . . I really appreciate that."

"No problem. And next time, you can bypass your brother and call me directly. He hates messing with scheduling details. I'll send you my phone number."

Not quite trusting my strike of good fortune, I thank her again and hang up.

August eyes me. "You didn't have to do that."

I slip my phone into my back pocket. "You're right, but I wanted to."

The inside of August's house is not at all what I expect. There is nothing about it that says "bachelor raising his younger sister." Instead, the white brick rancher is cozy and well loved, furnished in soft neutrals with eye-catching pops of color and patterns in throw pillows, rugs, and wall art. It's homey and comfortable, and I can't help but feel a distinct family vibe as soon as I cross over the threshold. And that's when it hits me.

"Was this your—" I swallow as he takes my backpack from me and sets it on the long wooden bench across the wall of the entry-way—"your parents' house?"

He dips his chin. "My parents purchased it when I was in third grade. It was an eyesore back then; worst house in the neighborhood by far. But my mom had vision and patience, and since my dad had worked in construction since high school, he did all the renovations on the weekends." He looks around. "They spent the better part of two decades taking on projects little by little as they had money and time. They never planned to live anywhere else."

"They did a beautiful job." It's an impossible thing to say without the bittersweet aftertaste that follows, but it's true. The open floor plan is bright and airy, and I'm certain there were several walls torn down to make it so. From the wide-plank flooring to the unique lighting fixtures in every room to the gorgeous fireplace with the exposed wood mantel, it's easy to imagine their vision for this home. It's also easy to see why August's studio was so well executed. He obviously inherited his father's construction skills. "It's a lovely home."

August clears his throat and hitches a thumb to the left side of the house toward a hallway. "I should probably let our chef know she'll be cooking for three after all. Feel free to wander."

"That's a pretty brave offer," I tease. "What if I'm a snoop?"

"If you are, would you mind keeping an eye out for two missing hairbrushes, a handful of spoons, and about a dozen single socks looking for their mate?"

I laugh. "Will do."

August starts toward the hallway but then stops and turns back. "Actually, if you wouldn't mind keeping your exploration clear of the door at the end of the hallway, I'd appreciate it." I can tell he's trying to keep his tone light, and yet, the ache in my belly grows at the possibilities that lay beyond that doorway. And the grief attached to them all.

"Of course."

When he disappears around the corner, I take the opportunity to study the pictures on the mantel. There are five in total. One of a beautiful couple wearing early nineties wedding attire gazing at each other over a three-tiered cake with white lattice icing. The next is a young picture of August—gap-toothed grin, sitting on a stool with a guitar that looks twice the size of him. There's no denying he was an adorable kid. The next is a picture of his high school graduation. Gabby's in this one. She's holding her mom's hand, but she's looking up to her big brother with so much admiration I can almost feel the warmth of it through the glass. There's a picture of Gabby dressed up as Snow White, standing on a tiny stage with her mouth and arms open wide. She's definitely younger here—maybe eleven or twelve? It's hard to say, but it's clear by her expression how much she loves this moment in time. I wonder how her hearing loss has affected her love of theater, and more importantly, how much her life has changed because of it. Not only has Gabby lost her parents, but she's also lost a critical part of herself, as well.

When I move to peer into the frame of the last picture, my breath stills. It's August and Gabby on a sandy beach with their father between them. All three are dressed in wet suits, and all three are hugging a surfboard. Their hair is windblown, and their smiles are huge. I wonder if their mom is the one behind the camera.

I also wonder how soon after this image was taken that their world changed forever.

"You're back!" Gabby's voice announces into the room.

I spin around. I wasn't being polite earlier when I said Gabby was beautiful—if anything, beautiful is an understatement. Her rich, Colombian skin tone is honeyed in color, and her eyes are a striking molten chocolate. But it's her hair that must be the envy of all her girlfriends. Thick, dark waves hang down to the center of her back.

I make sure to face her directly when I ask if I can help with dinner preparation.

"Do you like to cook, too?" she asks.

"A little. But I like to plate food even more," I admit. "Does that count?"

August follows her into the room and laughs at my admission, but it's clear by Gabby's expression that my answer didn't fully compute. "Do you mean you like to set the table?"

"No." I shake my head and try again. "I've worked in a few restaurants over the years. I love the art of plating the food before serving it to customers." I do a poor job of demonstrating the motions and wish I had taken ASL in school instead of the second language I chose that I haven't used once in my adult life.

"Oh," Gabby says, understanding this time. "Then you can plate our food when dinner is ready. Maybe you can teach me, too?" She turns to August and asks him to cut some fresh oregano and basil from the garden.

"You have an herb garden?" I wonder aloud.

"We have a greenhouse," Gabby replies. "*If* it's still standing after August's fall, that is."

August glances at the ceiling, and I do my best not to look at his bandaged hand.

"Our mom loved to garden and cook," she continues. "She taught us both."

126

"Who's the better cook between the two of you?" I ask, leaning my back against the sofa.

Both siblings point to themselves.

"Right." I laugh. "Got it."

"Maybe Sophie should be our judge?" Gabby offers.

"You're the only one cooking tonight," August says.

"That just means she'll have to come back when it's your night." She looks to me. "He's a messy cook."

August hitches his thumb to his sister. "And she over seasons everything."

Gabby slaps a hand to her chest as if she's been struck, and then promptly signs something to him that's incredibly animated.

"You know I didn't catch any of that," he deadpans.

"And whose problem is that?" She smirks before she moseys her way into the kitchen, where she begins unloading the three bags of groceries sitting on the counter. She tosses a jar of sun-dried tomatoes to August, and without any further instruction, he opens it and sets it next to her on the counter.

I watch their lively dynamic and wonder if it's always been like this between them—easy and comfortable. I can't imagine having a sibling I could joke with, let alone cook and eat a meal with without it feeling like a punishment. I wonder what their relationship was like prior to the accident and how it's changed since.

The thought replays a scene from two weeks ago in my mind: a sleepy August with an IV in his arm, telling me it's much harder to be the one in the seat *next* to the hospital bed.

How many times has August sat in that bedside chair?

My heart is heavy in pondering when August asks if I want to venture to the greenhouse with him.

As we head into the backyard, I confess that I can't identify many of the herbs without their labels, and August confesses that he doesn't know the difference between red and white wine food pairings. We agree that both these confessions can be easily remedied with time and experience. Two things I find myself hoping for more of when it comes to August Tate.

Over the next hour or so, the house is filled with delectable aromas as we're all put to work by Chef Gabby. She makes homemade fettuccine noodles while August and I chop, mince, and grate. But most of all, we laugh as she regales us with the hilarious mishaps from her weeks at summer camp. I'm not sure if I've wiped more tears from laughter at her irreverent expressions or from the potent white onion I was directed to dice earlier. But even as she entertained us with stories of teenage drama, she managed to concoct a glorious cream sauce with fresh herbs and veggies and enough Parmesan to make me grateful I'm not lactose intolerant.

Once everything is ready, Gabby asks me to show her how I'd plate each item on tonight's menu if this were a fancy restaurant. She focuses on my hands as I drizzle olive oil onto the rim of the porcelain plate and arrange the fresh herbs and then the food in each quadrant the way I was shown when I was around her age.

"You made it look so pretty," Gabby says.

"Not too pretty to eat, I hope," I say, spooning a bit of the cream sauce onto the steamed broccoli.

I feel a tap on my shoulder and realize my mistake. I'm standing on her bad side and was speaking to the plate, not to her. At the greenhouse, August informed me how her aids weren't a perfect science and how female voices can be especially difficult for her to detect without line of sight due to the particulars of her hearing loss.

"Sorry," I say and then immediately repeat my earlier comment to her.

"No way," Gabby counters. "I think we should *only* eat pretty food."

Which makes us all laugh as we carry the plates to the table.

We're a little over halfway through our delicious meal—Gabby on one side of the table while August and I sit across from her—when her phone begins to flash and vibrate next to her water glass. And it's not the only thing that lights up. Gabby's entire face breaks into a huge, giddy grin, and I don't have to wonder long about the person who's calling.

It's one hundred percent a boy she's crushing on. Chances are good it's the Tyler guy she mentioned at least a dozen times during dinner prep.

She answers the phone, and I feel August go still beside me.

"Hi," she says, grinning from ear to ear.

I pause my fork, waiting to hear his reply. But none comes. At least not that I can hear. Gabby laughs at the screen she's holding and nods.

"Oh my gosh, really? It's what we hoped would happen!"

August leans over. "She uses a special video app that provides real time captioning and can pair directly into her hearing aids. As long as she's wearing them." He says this last part under his breath.

After Gabby carries on for another minute or so, smiling and giggling without a care in the world, August sets his fork on his plate and stares at his sister pointedly. But Gabby pays no mind to him at all, not even when her brother goes uncomfortably quiet beside me.

"Do you know who she's talking to?" I whisper.

"I believe I do," he says flatly.

Gabby laughs into the screen again. "I will, I promise." She looks at her watch. "Um, maybe in an hour or so? We're still eating dinner, and we have a guest over." She lowers her phone momentarily and flashes me a quick grin, which I return, despite the frosty presence to my left.

Once she resumes wrapping up her conversation, I glance at August expectantly.

"I'm guessing it's Tyler." He says this as if he's just spoken the name of a wanted criminal.

"Are they dating?"

I see him flinch at the same time Gabby hangs up and places her phone on the table beside her plate. Either she's choosing not to notice her brother's recent rigor mortis, or she's happily oblivious.

I'm going with option two.

"Tyler says hi," she announces to us both.

"Oh? Hi back." I make sure my face reflects only nonjudgmental curiosity when I ask, "Did you meet him at camp?"

She shakes her head. "No, I met him here. We were introduced a little over a year ago by his mom. She's my ASL and speech tutor. He just called to tell me the best news!"

She's practically levitating out of her seat with excitement. But still, August remains mute, contemplative. I encourage her to continue with her story even though what I really want is to elbow her brother in the ribs and tell him to snap out it.

"So," Gabby says conversationally, "while we were at camp, the two of us began to dream up ways we could bring some of the more immersive ASL teaching methods we experienced this summer into the greater community. Tyler called his mom to ask if she'd be willing to teach a class if we agreed to help out as mentors. She was pretty excited about it and called Pastor Kreissig, who just told her we can announce it at church *this* Sunday!" Gabby pinches her lips closed and does a little jig that's impossibly cute. "Tyler's working on a save-the-date handout for anyone who's interested, since the class won't begin until September." She presses her hands to her pinked cheeks. "It's just so neat to see everything coming together like we imagined it—the location, the time, and now a huge amount of exposure on a main stage in the community. That's, like, seventeen hundred people if you add up both services." Her eyes go wide, but I don't see even the slightest hint of nerves. This girl would do amazingly well on a stage, no doubt. "Tyler and I need to work on our announcement script tonight since we only have tomorrow to practice our blocking."

"Blocking?" I question. "Are you doing a skit?"

"More like a sixty second commercial. We just need to make sure we get it right." She swivels her gaze to August, and I watch her deflate as soon as she registers his unenthusiastic response. "You'll be there, won't you, August? I've never been on stage at church before."

He takes a deep breath, and when he speaks, his voice is softer than I expect. "I thought we agreed before you left for camp that you wouldn't take on any new commitments without checking with me first."

Despite what I'd consider to be a nonconfrontational tone, she bristles. "I told you about it in my texts."

"No," August says matter-of-factly. "You told me you were enjoying camp and making friends and hoping to do more with them when you came home. It was Aunt Judy who told me you were making specific plans to start a class." He waits a beat and picks up his ice water. "And that wasn't all she told me."

I see the instant Gabby's mood switches from offense to defense. "Are you talking about Tyler?"

August pushes his plate away. "You tell me."

"Um . . ." I look between the two of them and stand to clear the dishes. "I should go so that you two can—"

"No." They both say in unison. "*Stay.*"

Awkwardly, I sit back down.

"What do you want me to tell you?" Gabby asks her brother with a shrug. "That we have feelings for each other? That he makes me happy? That he's the kindest, most caring person I've ever known?"

I see August wince, and then I get it. He's never done this before. This girl-talk session is brand-new territory for him. Empathy strums my ribcage like a stringed instrument.

"Was Tyler the friend who gave you a ride home from camp?" August asks.

"Yes, Aunt Judy said it was fine. Why should she have to drive two hours out of her way when Tyler lives five minutes from here—"

"Because that was our arrangement, Gabby. Aunt Judy is not the one responsible for you, I am. You should have talked to me first, and you know it."

I cringe inwardly. This is not going to end well.

"You mean like how you told me about the infected cut on your hand?" Gabby gestures to his bandage. *Touché.* She definitely scored a point there.

"I apologized for that, which I've yet to hear from you." He sits back, crosses his arms over his chest. "You're too young to have a boyfriend."

She jerks her head back as if she's been slapped. "I'm *too young* or *too deaf*?" Tears flood her eyes. "Or maybe Tyler's the one who's too deaf?"

August closes his eyes, rolls his neck. "Gabby—"

"No, don't tell me I'm being overdramatic. You know as well as I do that if Tyler was *hearing*, this conversation would be very different."

I expect August to defend himself, but he says nothing as Gabby pushes away from the table and rushes down the hallway. A second later, a door slams.

August sighs and drops his face into his non-bandaged palm. "I'm sorry, Sophie. Battle of the Siblings was not on the agenda for tonight." He threads his fingers through his hair, and for a minute, I can't do anything but stare. Not because I'm offended or uncomfortable, but because I've rarely witnessed such a passionate debate between two people who love each other like they do.

"This is new." He huffs a breath. "The boy stuff, I mean." Music blares at a volume that causes August to shake his head. "I thought I had a lot more time."

I try to suppress my surprise. "How long did you think you had?"

"Two, three years? Maybe post-college if I was really lucky?" He glances up at me, and his expression is so innocent I feel a momentary pinch of guilt for having to be the bearer of bad news.

"What?" he asks. "What's that look?"

I proceed with caution. "I'm just wondering if that's how it was for you?"

He's quiet, and I know the answer before he opens his mouth. "No, but I made a lot of stupid mistakes I don't want her to make. More than that, I don't want her to get hurt."

"That's understandable," I say. "But from the sound of it, they've been good friends for a while now. And they seem to share some big common interests." I stop myself from saying more. I haven't parented anyone, and I don't even have a sibling I can use in an example. So instead, I ask more questions. "What can you tell me about Tyler? Do you think he's a good kid?"

"Technically, he's not a kid. He's eighteen."

"Okay," I say. "And what's he like? Is he respectful?"

August contemplates his answer for a minute. "I suppose. He always comes to the door when he picks Gabby up for church—looks me in the eye, shakes my hand, that kind of thing. He graduated in May, summa cum laude, though from what I understand, he's taking a gap year to help his parents with a new business endeavor." He looks down at his hands. "His family's been good to Gabby, his mom especially. Although . . ." He pauses for a long moment.

"What?" I press.

"We have different perspectives." He takes a deep breath before continuing. "Tyler's dad was born deaf in both ears, and so was Tyler. They waited until he was old enough to decide if he wanted a cochlear implant." August shakes his head, sighs. "I guess he didn't. So instead he signs, reads lips, and sometimes uses his voice, although according to Gabby, it's not his preference."

I let his explanation sink in before I dare to ask another question. "Do you think there's any truth to what Gabby said about you having more of an issue with her dating Tyler because of his impairment than someone who can hear?"

He studies my face for several heartbeats before I hear the tension release in his exhale. "I wish I could say it didn't bother me. And yes, I'm fully aware of how awful that makes me sound, but nothing about Gabby's situation is black-and-white. I'd be lying if I said their relationship doesn't concern me—especially in regard to her future. A relationship between them adds another layer of complication to an already complicated situation."

I nod, appreciating his honesty more than I can say, and then nudge his shoulder. "So what happens next?"

"I wait until it's safe to approach her door and hope she doesn't throw a shoe at my head?" His right dimple winks at me, and it's so endearing I can't help but reach out for his bandaged hand on the table. I give his fingers a companionable squeeze.

"You're a good brother, August."

He studies our joined hands. "I try, but I fail a lot. As you witnessed here tonight."

"That's what she'll remember most," I say quietly.

"What?" He chuckles. "That I fail a lot?"

"No." I meet his gaze and think of all the moments I could have used a big brother like him when I was growing up. "That you never stopped trying."

Voice Memo

Gabby Tate

5 months, 3 weeks, 1 day after the accident

I met with my new ASL tutor/speech therapist today. Honestly, it was one of the best days I've had in a long time. The nurse at my audiologist's office told my brother about her, and I'm so glad he agreed for us to meet. And it's so crazy that her home office is only a few blocks from our house!

She has a super fun personality, and she seemed impressed with what I've learned online so far. As soon as my brother walked out of the room, she asked me how I was liking my new hearing aids. I told her the truth. That I don't like them much at all. I told her how everybody still sounds like an alien and how my left ear rings constantly. She seemed to really care about my answers, like she wants to help me, even though she has two fully working ears herself. Later on she told me that her son and her husband are both deaf. I've never met anyone who can't hear anything at all. Although, I suppose that could be my story someday.

Before I left her office, I saw a flyer on her bulletin board about an ASL interpretation ministry at the big church on the other side of town. When I asked her about it, it took all my strength not to start crying. She probably thought I was getting emotional due to the story she told me about becoming an interpreter so that her husband could attend services with her. But really, I was thinking about the last time I went to the little church I grew up in. August and I went together a few weeks ago at Aunt Judy's request because she insisted we thank all the people who brought us dinners and sent cards and flowers.

But neither of us were prepared for how hard it would be. So many people came up to us after the service, hugging us and telling us how much they miss Mom and Dad and how sorry they are for our loss. It was the funeral all over again. August didn't leave my side the entire time, even though I could tell he couldn't wait to go home. But all the "we're praying for you and your brother" conversations wasn't the hardest part for me. The hardest part was seeing the seats my parents used to sit in every Sunday filled by people who weren't my mom and dad.

August and I didn't talk on the drive home that day. And even once we parked in the driveway, August went straight to the garage to get his tool belt so he could go fix something that probably didn't even need fixing. I headed straight for my parents' bedroom where I wrapped my mom's wedding quilt around me and then tucked myself into their closet, careful to slide the mirrored door all the way closed before I touched the box I promised not to open without my brother.

I wish he would tell me why he's so upset over Pastor Bedi's letter. Maybe then I could understand why he refuses to go near this box, or our parents' room, for that matter. Sometimes my brother treats me like I'm eight and not nearly fifteen. I pray he'll change his mind about the box soon.

I also pray he'll change his mind about attending church and come with me to this new one.

10

August

If not for the guilt-induced compromise I made with Gabby after our argument on Friday night, I never could have imagined walking into the megachurch where my sister spends the majority of her free time. And if not for said compromise, I would have timed my arrival to be well after the threat of small talk in the lobby was over and the song service had ended. But today, I remind myself, is about supporting my sister. Which is the only reason I'm here five minutes early. That, and the chance to have a little chat with Tyler, man to man.

While I've dropped her off here dozens of times to meet up with her tutor and, eventually, her friends from the youth group, I've never attended a full service. It's been a sore spot in our relationship to be sure—one I've tried to smooth over as gently as possible. But despite my efforts, she still doesn't understand my reasonings. And honestly, that's probably for the best. Gabby deserves the comfort she's found in her faith, even if comfort is the last thing I feel when I walk through the large lobby.

My first real observation of note is the vast difference between this church and the small neighborhood chapel Gabby and I grew up attending with our parents. For that, at least, I'm grateful.

If this church was a video game, I passed the first level with bonus points when I scored a parking spot that wasn't a fifteen-minute hike to the front doors. Level two is to dodge every welcome greeter posted outside the sanctuary doors with breath mints and bulletins. This challenge takes a bit more strategy, but as soon as I see an older gentleman get caught in a conversation about his grandkids, I make my move, undetected. Level three *should* be fairly straightforward: find a seat near the back where I can avoid being asked to fill out one of those visitor information cards advertised all over the lobby like it's Times Square.

The visitor marketing campaign looks to be an exchange program of sorts, the card for a free gift located at one of the kiosks near the cafe. But not even the coolest free pen or plastic water bottle in the world is enough to convince me to take a second glance at that card. Perhaps if the incentivized gift was an indefinite no-small-talk pass, the number of responses would be infinitely larger.

I'm side-shuffling down a row near the back of the sanctuary, in search of the perfect seat for invisibility, when I spot a face through the massive crowd that must be a doppelgänger. Because there is simply no other explanation for why Sophie Wilder would be in this room, much less for why she would be speaking to a young woman near the stage who resembles my sister.

"You have got to be kidding me," I mutter.

"If you're in a hurry, you can go right on ahead and pass me, mister," quips the white-haired woman blocking the middle of my row with her walker. "I know where I'm going, I just don't know how many more times the good Lord is gonna make me waddle these aisles before I get there."

"Oh, sorry." I hold up my hands. "My comment wasn't meant for you."

She looks around before quirking a barely-there eyebrow at me. "You lonely, son?"

I nearly choke. "What?"

"People talk to themselves more when they're lonely. It's a fact." She scans the large auditorium. "Just ask any widow and widower in here, they'll tell ya."

Okay, so maybe it's not only small talk I'd like to avoid. "I, uh, I'm sure you're correct."

Still hunched over her walker, she gives me a once over. When a flicker of awareness crosses her face, I grow even more uncomfortable. "You a member at this church?"

I want to lie. I want to lie so badly that my tongue is already forming the word *yes*. "No, ma'am."

With a nod, she braces one age-spotted hand on the handle of her walker and then pulls out a wad of colorful flyers from her front basket. She thrusts them at my chest. "There's a blue newcomer's card in that mess somewhere. Make sure you fill it out." She winks. "They'll give you a free pen."

Level three: failed.

"Thanks." I pull the blue card out of her stack and then glance up to see the instant Gabby and Sophie find me. They wave for me to join them up front, where they have apparently secured some seats. *Wonderful.*

"Those your friends up there?"

"It appears so," I say flatly.

"Then here, you'll need these, too." She reaches back down into her basket again to hand me a tiny package I recognize immediately. "Disposable earplugs," she clarifies. "They're a great-grandmother's best friend." The irony in this day has reached an all-time high.

With that, she turns and plants herself on the chair with a huff that sounds like the deflation of a bike tire. "What's your name, son?"

"August."

She sticks out her hand, and I lean down to shake it from where I'm still standing in the center of this row. "I'm Bonnie Brewer. I sit here every Sunday so I can get to my handicap spot in the parking lot before some teenager trying to get their Holy Hamburger from In-N-Out can mow me down first." She chuckles and coughs. "Enjoy the service."

And with that, she starts flipping through her deconstructed bulletin again.

"Thanks," I say. "You too, Mrs. Brewer."

As I turn to exit, making my way around knees and over purses and bags and coffee cups, I hear Bonnie's craggy voice call out after me, "Don't be a stranger!"

I head to the front of the auditorium, where Sophie is chatting with a young couple in the seats in front of her. But Gabby waves at me, Tyler by her side.

"Hey, man. Thanks for coming this morning," Tyler says with a too-eager grin. It's remarkable how clearly he speaks—even without the help of aids or a cochlear implant. Was that a testament to his mother being a speech therapist? I'm sure it couldn't hurt. From what I've researched on the subject, early intervention is highly recommended.

Gabby stands comfortably by his side when she reaches for my arm. "I'm so happy you're here."

I nod, feeling the need to unbutton my shirt collar at the sight of them standing so close. How had I been so blind to miss the forming attachment between them? "I was hoping to catch you two before you left the driveway this morning." I make sure to look Tyler in the eye, wondering if he'll be able to lip-read what I've just said. Gabby has bragged many times about this superpower of his. No time like the present to put it to the test.

He dips his chin in acknowledgment. "Sorry I missed you. I came to the door, but Gabby said you were in the shower. We were hoping to get here in plenty of time to rehearse."

I'm about to respond when Gabby interrupts.

"What?" she asks Tyler, obviously having missed the start of this exchange. She touches her left ear, and I know the large crowd is making it difficult for her to differentiate our voices from the background noises. I need to see if I can adjust the controls on her app this week. When it works, it's much more convenient than having to wait for an appointment with her audiologist.

Instead of repeating himself vocally, Tyler signs in ASL to Gabby. She nods and responds in kind. I watch, feeling more like a third wheel than I have since my awkward middle school days.

Is that . . . is that how Gabby feels in conversations with hearing people?

"Yes," Gabby vocalizes, and it takes me a moment to realize that she's responding to the conversation she's having with Tyler. Then she turns to me. "Our announcement went super well during first service. Pastor Kreissig says we're welcome on this stage any time. We'll be on right after the worship band finishes. We attended first service already, so we'll probably stay backstage, which is why there are just two seats up here for you and Sophie."

At the sound of her name, Sophie twists in my direction, and for an instant, I forget how much I dreaded coming this morning. I don't ever get to see Sophie on the weekends—and I can't ignore the way my pulse doubles its cadence at the thought of more time with her. Her dress is a soft pink that ties at the waist and grazes the tops of her sandaled feet. She's styled her long hair down today, the ends curling several inches below her shoulders. I note the tiny trail of freckles along her cheekbones and the way she radiates sunshine when she smiles at me.

"Hey," she says, her eyes twinkling bright, "I was hoping you weren't going to make me sit alone up here."

"I didn't realize you would be here," I answer honestly.

"Your sister invited me. That's okay with you, right?"

I catch Gabby's mischievous grin as she trails Tyler backstage. I can't interpret everything she signs, but the gist of it is clear enough. She texted Sophie last night. Probably hijacked my phone in my sleep to do it, too.

You're welcome, she signs just as she disappears behind the stage curtain.

I clear my throat and focus once again on Sophie. "Of course it's fine. Do you . . . enjoy sitting this close to a stage?"

"I don't mind it," she says, taking her seat and prompting me to do the same. "Your sister was the one who saved them for us."

Naturally. Only Gabby would choose to sit in the second row of a church that seats more than a couple thousand. Next time I negotiate a deal with her, I'll need to be much clearer on the terms I'm agreeing to.

Sophie's leg starts to bounce beside mine as she cranes her neck to look around. "This is not at all what I expected when your sister invited me to her *church*." She laughs. "I've performed in theaters a quarter of this size."

"What were you expecting?" I ask, grateful for such a beautiful distraction in a place where I definitely need distracting.

"Something . . . I don't know. Less modern, I guess." Sophie shrugs and rubs her palms down the fabric of her dress. "I haven't been inside a church since before my Gigi died—and that was only sporadic. And it was nothing like this. But I've missed going, more than I realized." She touches her chest softly. "*Oh,* that reminds me." She bends to slip a familiar blue flyer from her purse. "A nice guy in the lobby told me that if I fill this out they'll give me a free gift."

I give myself extra points for holding back a groan. Instead, I circle back to one of the few personal things she's volunteered about her childhood.

"Does that mean you didn't grow up attending church?"

"Hardly." She pulls a face. "My father is the reason my Gigi could only take me with her on occasion. Mostly when he was out of town on business. He forbade it."

"Forbade?" I repeat. "That sounds a bit—"

"Medieval?" She nods. "It is. He thinks all this is foolish. 'Dramatic sensationalism,' he'd call it. Gigi's convictions infuriated my father, and like always, my mom was caught in the crossfire. Their religious differences nearly cost my parents the winery. It was a mess. Still is, I suppose." She sighs as if she hasn't just lifted the lid on Pandora's box. I have no less than a dozen questions drumming against my skull, waiting to be asked. If church is what it took for Sophie to open up, then I'll count today as a win. "But despite all that,

I believed what my Gigi taught me about God and sin and eternal life, even if I haven't always followed it as closely as I should." She touches the dainty gold cross around her neck. "This was hers. It was the one thing I rescued from her estate without asking permission."

From my periphery, I see the band step onto the stage, adjust their in-ear monitors, and ready their instruments.

"What about you?" she asks. "Did you grow up going to this church with your family? Gabby seems so comfortable here." Her smile is so sincere and harmless, and yet her words tear at a scar I'd rather leave closed.

"Not this church, no, but—"

Before I can finish, the lights drop suddenly, and the first few strums on an acoustic guitar are played.

Sophie startles beside me and grips my arm. "Ooh, what's happening?"

Dread settles in my lower belly. "It's the—"

"Good morning, Seaside Community Fellowship! Will you please stand with me and pray as we enter into a time of praise." The worship leader is fairly nondescript in his trendy blue jeans, button-up shirt, and brown leather boots, but Sophie looks from him to me and whispers, "This feels like a concert."

I want to agree with her, but commenting at all will make me feel even more like a fraud than I already do. I have no right to be the spokesperson of an organization I've avoided for years.

Her eyebrows jump as an upbeat song begins to play, and I can't ignore the unique chord progression as the entire congregation begins to clap and sing. Except for the two of us in the second row. But likely for two totally different reasons: Sophie doesn't know these songs; and I simply can't stand to sing them anymore.

Unlike Sophie, my entire upbringing was guided by my parents' faith in God. Even before I could read the Bible for myself, my parents had told me the stories using picture books and other illustrations from around the house. Once, my mother got extra creative and tried to show me the parting of the Red Sea using gelatin mix and food dye. It didn't really work, but I also never forgot it.

It's difficult to tune the band out when you're so close to the stage you can see the untied shoe of the bass player and fixate on the way the keyboardist misses every fourth chord in the chorus. Why isn't she hitting the E-flat? But it's easier for me to focus on all these superficial things than what's happening beside me as Sophie begins to participate by singing the lyrics to the third song. This one's slower and less musically advanced than the others. It's also one of the songs we sang at my parents' joint funeral after their bodies were recovered and flown home from India.

Sophie's ethereal voice is nearly enough to still the quake behind my ribcage. But not quite. Because every stanza she sings exposes the chasm between God's mercy and my inexcusable failures.

Finally, the song is over, and we're being asked to greet our neighbors and take a seat.

"That was incredible," Sophie whispers. "Does this happen every Sunday?"

I nod once, hoping to dismiss the role of church advocate she's wrongly appointed me. That job is better suited for someone like Bonnie Brewer, who is smartly seated a hundred rows back.

"Morning, friends," the man I believe to be Pastor Kreissig says. "What an awesome day to be in the house of the Lord, amen?"

"Amen!" congregants around us shout.

"Before we open God's Word to the Gospel of Matthew, I want to invite a few specials guests to join me on stage. If you've been around Seaside for any length of time, you've probably interacted with the Pimentel family at some point. Whether they're passing out communion trays, directing our holiday children's productions, or spearheading our interpretation ministry for the deaf and hard of hearing, they are almost always around. You may remember the successful fundraiser they testified about right here last spring for the purchase of that old theater on Ramsey Street?" A few people in the audience cheer. "Well, today they're back with an important message. I hope you'll be as moved by their invitation as I am."

Sophie straightens next to me and clasps her hands under her chin as the lights go dim. "This is it."

When the spotlight comes up on Gabby, I can't help but hold my breath at the sight of my sister alone on that stage. She's strolling in silence when she lifts her head and sees someone in the distance—Tyler. She waves him over and the two immediately launch into a full-blown conversation in ASL. They're going back and forth for quite some time while the audience watches on without interpretation. I'm able to catch every fifth or sixth sign, maybe, but between their speed and their angle on stage, it's nearly impossible to comprehend much at all.

As soon as the spotlight on them clicks off, they freeze in position, while another one blinks on and illuminates Tyler's mom, Portia Pimentel.

She signs as she speaks. "How many of you have been on the outside of a conversation you couldn't understand no matter how much you wanted to? How did it make you feel? Frustrated? Left out? Isolated?"

Beside me, Sophie gasps and immediately shrinks in her seat.

"What are you doing?" I bend and whisper.

She points to the stage discreetly. "Portia is Tyler's mom?"

I nod. "You know her?"

She makes a small, indeterminable sound in the back of her throat.

". . . for many deaf and hard of hearing people, what you just saw on this stage is a reenactment of what they deal with on a daily basis, only in reverse. Without a hearing interpreter trained in ASL to help bridge the gap between the hearing and the non-hearing, our worlds remain segregated. Our conversations remain isolated. And for so many wonderful deaf and hard of hearing members in our community, that means they may never know the saving love and grace of the gospel," Portia says with fervor. "In fact, studies show that ninety-eight percent of the deaf and hard-of-hearing community has never been shown the story of Jesus in their native, visual language of ASL. As the wife of a deaf husband and mother of a deaf son who both use ASL as their primary form of communication, we are passionate about helping our hard-of-hearing friends find hope in a lonely world. We are a family committed to the outreach of inclusive communication." Portia smiles broadly. "Which is why we're starting an ASL class at our community theater in September. If you're interested in learning more about the needs and benefits of interpretation and this beautiful visual language, then please meet us at the kiosk right after the service. And now, let's add some interpretation to Tyler and Gabby's conversation."

The spotlight on the teens flicks on again, and the two start over. Portia interprets for both teens, and the audience responds almost immediately by laughing in all the right places. Gabby is telling Tyler a hilarious story about a summer camp prank gone awry while Tyler adds his own commentary to the mix. The church is roaring, which easily proves Portia's point. I have zero doubt there will be a long line at her kiosk today. I also have no doubt that Gabby will be the most zealous recruiter among them.

The three receive a standing ovation when they take a bow and are joined once again by Pastor Kreissig, who does a final push for the ASL classes at the Twilight Theater. And then I see the exact moment when Portia pauses at Sophie's presence in the audience. There's a story there for sure. If we weren't so close to the front, I'd ask Sophie about it right now. But instead, we're asked to settle in for the next thirty-eight minutes while Pastor Kreissig walks us through the parable of the lost sheep.

Growing up, this parable was akin to a bedtime story. There's hardly a fresh take left when it comes to a Good Shepherd who leaves behind the ninety-nine to chase after the one, and yet I'm growing increasingly more agitated the longer this manipulative tale draws out.

My parents died chasing after the elusive one.

A little over two and a half years ago, a regular, everyday couple from Petaluma, California, were moved by a missionary's Power-Point talk at their church exposing a need in rural India where school buildings were in high demand and skilled construction workers were few. They asked if I'd go with them, encouraging me to spend some intentional time with my teenage sister and serve "the least of these" together, the way we'd done in years past as a family of four. For a myriad of reasons, I turned them down and wished them well on their adventure, never knowing how many times I'd replay that decision in the days, weeks, months, years to come.

Never knowing how deep of a hole regret could dig.

They left home as soon as Gabby completed her eighth grade year, in hopes the trip would grow my sister's faith and teach her how everyday people can make an extraordinary difference in the world. Yet there was nothing extraordinary about the deaths my parents died in an overcrowded train car that slid off the tracks or the trauma that will haunt my sister forever.

People often comment on my sister's remarkable resilience, on her unwavering courage and selfless love for others amidst her own painful past. And it's true. All of it and then some. My sister has long been the bravest person I know. But it's the faith she claims as the source of such strength that I can no longer pretend to share. Not even for her.

Sophie shifts to lean forward in her seat, her gaze hyper-focused on Pastor Kreissig as he goes in for the kill shot. "If you identify with the lost sheep I've just described, please believe there is no place too far, too hopeless, too dark, too sinful, too apathetic, too unreachable for your Good Shepard to find you. He's already called you chosen; the question is, will you choose Him?"

I watch a lone tear slide down Sophie's cheek and stain the soft pink fabric of her dress as she follows the prompts to bow her head and close her eyes. And it's in those quiet, isolating moments that follow, when she raises her hand to go up for prayer, that I realize how truly alone I really am.

11

Sophie

I'm on my feet as soon as the service ends, making my way to the prayer corner Pastor Kreissig pointed out at the close of his sermon. A kind lady in a floral top and white cropped pants is there to greet me, clasping my hands and asking if I'd like prayer for anything specific. "I don't really know," I admit. "I've never asked for prayer before, but there's been a lot of big changes in my life lately, and I think I've been a wandering sheep for a while now. And I don't want to be one anymore."

"Oh, sweetheart," she assures me through a teary smile. "That's one of the best prayers we can ever pray."

The kind woman—Alisha—asks me several questions and genuinely seems to care about my answers. Soon, we've bowed our heads in prayer, and I feel an unmistakable sense of rightness. The kind that seems to echo through my heart with a sense of belonging I've always been searching for.

I've come close to finding it in theater and maybe even with certain friend groups. But today felt like a reminder of something I've only ever grazed the surface of. It felt like a homecoming.

After we say *amen*, Alisha reminds me to drop my information card off at the welcome kiosk and proceeds to give me a big hug. "You weren't here by accident today, Sophie. God has a plan for your life."

It's perhaps one of the most beautiful sentiments a stranger has ever spoken to me. As I slowly walk back to the second row to collect my things in a rapidly emptying auditorium, I'm surprised to find August waiting at the end of the main aisle near the back, my purse and phone in his possession.

I make my way to him.

"Hey." I smile, marveling at the swell of happiness I feel at the sight of him.

"Hey." He barely meets my gaze as he hands me my belongings. "You okay?"

"Better than okay. Today was . . ." I bite my bottom lip, trying to find the words. "Exactly what I needed. It felt like Pastor Kreissig was speaking directly to me." I laugh, though it feels more like an outburst of delight. "I'm so glad your sister invited me. I can't wait to come back again next week."

After a beat of silence, he says, "I'm happy for you."

He moves to open the lobby doors, but I grasp for his elbow and pull him back. "Wait, do you know where Gabby is? I want to tell her what an awesome job she did today."

His heated gaze studies the place my fingers hold, rising slowly up the length of my forearm. And something about the familiarity of our closeness triggers a muscle memory response I wasn't sure existed before now. On instinct, I reach for his left wrist and gently rotate it the same way I've done a dozen times in order to assess the injury on his palm. When he flinches at my touch, I note the crease in his brow. "You're not in any new pain, are you?" I trace the edge of his bandage with my fingertip, pressing the pinked skin for any hidden signs of infection. But everything appears to be healthy. Healing.

"I'm fine, Sophie." He closes his fist and drops it to his side. "Gabby went this way."

Before I can ask anything further, he's pushing open the lobby door, waiting for me to follow. A cacophony of voices hum in the large, open space, and I wonder how difficult this environment must be on Gabby's ears. On anyone with impaired hearing, for that matter.

For as many people who have vacated the sanctuary after the service, it's clear the majority of them haven't made it out to the parking lot. They're talking, laughing, sipping on coffees, making lunch plans with friends. And a few mingle around the kiosk where Gabby and Tyler are handing out sign-up sheets and answering questions.

And where Portia Pimentel is staring directly at me, the same way she did when she was on stage earlier.

My knees go a bit rubbery.

Whatever illusion I was under to hope she may have forgotten my face—much less the mortifying moment of me fleeing her theater last month without explanation—dies the instant recognition shines from her gaze. As she steps away from the kiosk, I'm braced for the worst. Even if Portia is the type of person who can overlook a grown woman using her wine wallpapered SUV as a getaway car, it's clear from her first word that this will be no simple reintroduction.

"Sophie," Portia calls to my shame. "What a small world. I had no idea that the *Sophie* Gabby's told me about was you."

"Yes, um." I half laugh, half cringe. "Small world."

"I was hoping our paths would cross again."

Confused, I rub my lips together, the need to apologize for my awkward disappearing act as strong as the espresso wafting through the cafe. But I'm not quite sure how to bring it up when she's smiling at me like she's legitimately happy to see me again.

August glances between us. "How is it you two know each other?"

Here we go, I think, cringing inwardly as I wait for her to spill my secret.

"I met Sophie a few weeks ago." Portia's attention steadies on me. "She's the most experienced actress we've had inside our little theater to date."

August rotates to face me. "I thought you said you haven't acted since New York."

"I haven't," I confirm, while pinpricks of perspiration break out on the back of my neck. "But I . . . I . . ."

Portia touches my arm as if to pause whatever pitiful excuse I'm about to offer. "We're hopeful she'll audition for one of our shows some day." She gives me a knowing smile, and relief floods my system. "In the meantime, I'm thrilled you've become friends with the Tates." She presses a hand to her chest. "Gabby's been a precious gift to our family this last year, and I'm thrilled she's so excited about helping with this class in the fall. It's nothing short of miraculous how quickly she's picked up ASL since she began tutoring with me. Her passion certainly goes beyond her own needs." Portia regards Gabby's big brother then, her face softening. "I hope you'll consider joining us, too, August. I know you hold a foundational understanding of ASL, but being able to practice new signs and vocabulary at home will expedite your learning, as well as Gabby's. And since your sister is volunteering so much of her time, I'll insist on waiving your class fees and materials costs."

I'm expecting August to jump at this unique opportunity with a resounding *yes*; after all, what isn't there to love about Portia's generous offer? But instead, he simply shifts his weight from one foot to the other. "I'm afraid Tuesday evenings aren't good for me, sorry."

I nearly object at such a flippant response because one, what the heck does "not good for me" mean? And two, he's the boss of his own schedule, and I simply can't imagine him not being able to take two hours a week for something so important to his sister. I glance over Portia's head, grateful that Gabby is busy having a conversation with an elderly woman pushing a walker where she can't overhear her brother's reply.

"Could I get some information on the class?" I ask. "I'd love to learn."

"Oh, absolutely." She beams. "Here's the initial sign-up info." She hands me an orange flyer. "And registration can be done online through our website. Oh, and I can take that visitor card you're holding. Do you know which gift you'd like?" She moves to the other side of the kiosk. "Looks like we're out of the water bottles here, but I do have a Seaside Fellowship pen and a Bible plan journal."

"Oh, great, thanks." In truth, I've never even heard of a Bible plan journal, but it sounds nice.

"I've loved this tool for my daily reading. I use it often." She hands it to me, and I flip through it, noting the date and Scripture reference near the top of each page.

Over the years I've read some portions of the Bible, and I know most of the key stories, but I've never studied it. If I'm being honest, I don't really know how.

"What would you say to a coffee date sometime?" Portia asks. "I'd love to hear more about your experience in theater arts."

Surprisingly, I don't feel a twinge of panic at her request. I feel . . . hopeful. "I'd love to go to coffee with you."

"Here's my number." She writes on the back of my ASL class flyer. "My schedule is pretty flexible now that the Summer Showcase is over and we're heading into fall."

"Sophie!" I spin at the sound of her voice, and then Gabby is all but leaping toward me. She throws her arms around me in a hug that feels as if we've known each other for much longer than a day. She pulls back and looks at the journal and flyer in my hand. "Are you gonna come to our class?"

She watches my lips.

"I'd like to, yes. I loved everything about this morning. Thank you for inviting me. I needed this today." Gabby beams at my praise, and I gently squeeze her arms. "Also, you and Tyler did an incredible job—I was so, so proud of you."

"She's a natural on stage," Portia agrees, rubbing a maternal hand over Gabby's back.

The three of us fall into an easy conversation about stage presence and future opportunities for exposure and promotion of their class in the community, but when I turn to ask August a question, he's no longer standing behind me. He doesn't appear to be anywhere.

The lobby is nearly empty now. The only people remaining are wearing lanyards or participating in clean-up activities.

"August said to tell you good-bye," Gabby says quietly.

"He did? When?" I can't keep the disappointment from my voice. "I wouldn't have kept talking if I'd known he needed to leave."

Truthfully, I was hoping we might go do something together afterward. Grab some lunch, talk through the service, take another step forward in our growing friendship. But Gabby's expression tells me there's something I'm missing.

"It's not you," she says. "August . . . well, this isn't really his scene."

"Ah." It's clicking into place now. "Because small talk makes him uncomfortable." He's mentioned this to me a time or two. Or twenty.

She seems to consider me for a moment, and I'm just about to repeat myself, when she says, "Actually, *all* of it makes him uncomfortable."

"All of what?"

"Anything having to do with his faith in God. It's been that way since the accident."

Sorry I missed you when you left this morning. You doing okay? I'm headed home now if you want to call. I'll be around all day. 😊

By the time I've parked back at the winery, thoughts of August make up roughly ninety-two percent of my brain—many of them pertaining to what his sister told me after church. *"It's been that way since the accident."*

What did that mean? And what did God and the church have to do with his parents' accident? Isn't faith what people turn to most amid a crisis?

The minute I think it, a grainy, recycled image of the wine cellar downloads into my brain without permission. I shut it out immediately. Whatever August is going through now is far worse than anything done to me.

But as I walk the path to the pool house, I imagine how different my life might be today if I'd grown up hearing sermons like the one preached this morning, or if I'd sang songs about a God whose love is unconditional and full of mercy. How different things would be if my home had been a place where competition and comparison hadn't led the way . . . or where love hadn't been as easily won as it was lost.

How far my family has strayed from the legacy Gigi had prayed for. I touch the cross at the base of my neck.

After Gigi's first husband died in his early thirties, leaving her with a child to support, she came up with a plan to harvest the small crop of grapes on the hillside of her property. It was a last-ditch effort seeing as she was months away from losing her farm altogether. After dozens of wine critics turned their nose up at her request for a tasting, one lone soul had finally agreed: a fellow widower who was as impressed with my grandma's tenacity as he was with her wine making. Eventually, she married Christopher Bentley, and between the two of them, they planted, harvested, bottled, marketed, and sold their wine to local vendors, stores, and restaurants for more than thirty years, until the day Papa passed quietly in his sleep.

The winery that started as a dream seeded in desperation had flourished into a profitable business with a reputable name, which is why Gigi put conditions on the inheritance she passed down to her daughter in her trust—a sore spot with my father, to be sure. I was too young to remember the specifics of all the disagreements between Gigi and my dad, but it was clear there was no love lost between the two of them when she died. His final protest against her removing his name from her beneficiaries and excluding him from the board of trustees was his boycott of her funeral.

It was my nine-year-old hand that rubbed my mother's back as she wept and tossed white roses onto Gigi's grave. I'd also asked the preacher to sing her favorite song: "His Eye Is on the Sparrow."

Shortly after Gigi was gone, I began to dread Sundays at the winery. As kids, Jasper and I were usually tasked with things like restocking inventory, cycling the service laundry, pressure-washing mossy pathways, and attending the weekly business meeting disguised as a family meal. When it came to the game of winning our father's favor, I was rarely, if ever, the victor.

Thankful those days are over, I'm already planning to get in my comfys and open this journal as soon as I'm in the pool house—

"Sophie."

At the sound of my name, I stop mid-stride to find my sister-in-law gliding across the back patio of what was once my childhood home—minus the latest renovations. Her ombre wrap dress ripples in the breeze, drawing my full attention.

"Hey," I reply, trying to sound casual even though I've never felt casual around Natalie a day in my life. "How are you?"

She grips the railing, facing the glorious view of the vineyard and rolling hills beyond me. She leans in and pitches her voice low. "Your parents are here. They got in last night. Your mom said she's been trying to get ahold of you all morning. I figured you'd like a heads-up before lunch."

A brick of nerves lands hard in the pit of my belly. My parents are here? Now? Four weeks ago I felt ready for this. I'd had an entire day of travel to mentally prepare for conversations long overdue. But today? I lift my phone and see that, sure enough, it's still set on Do Not Disturb. I panic scroll through my missed notifications. My mom has called three times and texted twice. And even though my nerves have just been set on fire, I notice the one notification that isn't there.

"Do I have time to run to the pool house and—"

The back door opens behind Natalie, and my words freeze.

"Natalie? Have you heard from So—*Oh.*" My mother spots me and lightly touches her fingertips to her lips. "Sophie." She blinks rapidly. "You're home."

For the briefest moment, it's as if I can see Gigi staring back at me through my mother's eyes, and I feel the most overwhelming urge to break into a run and throw my arms around her neck. To tell her I've missed her. To tell her I love her. To tell her why I had to leave home all those years ago even after she begged me to stay.

But then my mother blinks, and the spell is broken. Outward displays of affection are simply not the Wilder way. And my mother is nothing if not a model of proper behavior.

With practiced elegance, Anita Wilder crosses the patio dressed in white tailored pants and a pearl-buttoned summer cardigan. She waits for me to climb the steps and move toward her. Her eyes glitter as she assesses me, and I hold my breath when she reaches out to smooth a lock of my hair and tuck it behind my ear.

"Hi, Mom," I say around the growing lump in my throat.

"That color of pink has always suited your complexion well," she says before moving on to straighten the neckline of my sundress. When her fingers pause their compulsive fixing, I *feel* rather than see the moment she registers her mother's cross pendant around my neck. But in typical Anita Wilder fashion, she avoids the potential confrontation and simply doesn't ask the question that glows from her eyes.

"Did you have a nice cruise?" I ask dutifully.

The smile she offers is fragile but genuine. "The Mediterranean is always beautiful this time of year, although our schedule wasn't conducive to a lot of sightseeing."

Meaning my father kept them moving at a brisk pace.

"But your father enjoyed himself. He was quite the networker." She gives a halfhearted chuckle. "So much for semi-retirement." She looks over her shoulder at Natalie. "What are we gonna do with these men of ours, Natalie?" Mom shakes her head good-naturedly. "It's all work and no play with them. It's why your father insisted upon lunch today despite our jetlagged state. But your father wanted to share the potential contacts he made with your brother while they were still fresh in his mind."

Never mind the daughter he hasn't seen in nearly three years; it was business that brought him to the house today.

Natalie glances between us. "We should probably head inside. Looks like lunch is ready."

I furrow my brow, wondering if Jasper arranged for one of the chefs to come in on their day off and cook. But once I step inside to the dining room, I discover that lunch has actually been provided by a popular Asian bistro in midtown. My father's favorite. I don't think I've ever seen so many sushi rolls in one place.

My brother pats my father's shoulder twice with the hand not gripping a glass of amber liquid and lends him one of his most congenial smiles. The two laugh in the way only rich men sharing a cocktail at noon can laugh, and my feet pause there. Just a few steps behind my father's turned back.

When Jasper's gaze finally flicks to me, the energy in the room changes course.

My father, Ronald Wilder, is slow to face me, and I feel every milli-second of his rotation as if he's tied a tourniquet around my chest.

"Hello, Dad. It's good to see you again."

"Sophie, my prodigal daughter returned," my father says by way of greeting, lifting his glass ever so slightly before taking a sip. For a man who claims to despise all organized religion, as well as those who take part in it, he seems to pay no mind to the irony behind his biblical reference. "Your mother was worried you'd miss Sunday lunch when she couldn't get ahold of you, but I assured her you'd come back. Same as I did when you left home the first time."

"And here she arrived right on time," my mom interjects peace-ably, briefly touching my back before handing me a plate. She does the same for my father, my brother, and Natalie. The four of us shuffle toward the buffet and fill our plates before we take a seat around the table. All the while, I'm rehashing in my mind the con-versations I've shared with Dana over the years regarding healthy boundaries and productive communication tools. We spent many evenings psychoanalyzing our dysfunctional family dynamics and sharing our secret hurts, fears, and hopes.

I am not the same helpless girl I was at sixteen. I have no reason to cower. My viewpoints are valid, and my voice is strong. I am strong.

These are the phrases I repeat in my head, the same ones I know Dana would coach me to repeat if she were with me now.

We sit at the grand dining table meant for a family three times our size, and I'm more than a little surprised to see my brother sitting at the head of the table. I realize this is no longer my parents' primary residence, and that technically it's Jasper who oversees the operation of the winery now, but I hadn't expected the transfer of power to be so . . . complete.

My mother, with her single roll and quarter cup of cucumber salad, glances around the table. "This is nice, isn't it? All of us together again for a summer lunch at the winery." Either everyone is too busy dunking their sushi in soy sauce to respond, or there are differing opinions on the matter. "Sophie, Natalie tells me what a help you've been to her in the tasting room these last few weeks."

"Oh," I say. "Well, that's nice of her." I spare a glance at Natalie, who only has a bowl of fried rice in front of her and appears to be more interested in counting each grain of rice with her chopsticks than eating. "Thank you, Natalie." She nods once at my sentiment. It's better than nothing, I suppose.

"Have you had a chance to catch up with any old friends? When you weren't in the pool house this morning, I'd wondered if you'd met someone for breakfast." I'm not sure which friends my mother might be referring to, as anyone I was acquainted with in high school moved on long ago. But technically speaking, she was on the right track.

"I *was* with friends, but I've only met them recently," I begin, and my pulse doubles. It's not until the words are halfway out of my mouth that I realize I'm fully committed. "I spent the morning with them at church, actually."

"Church?" This, from my father.

My mother's carefully selected piece of sushi slips from her chopsticks and splashes into her soy sauce dish. Natalie rushes to hand her a second napkin. And then a third. All eyes settle on me.

"Yes," I answer. "It was a beautiful service. I really enjoyed it."

"So you've traded in acting for organized religion?" my father asks dryly. "I'd assumed your blunder on Broadway might have curbed your affinity for living in a fairy-tale world."

Shame pricks my cheeks at his mention of my screw-up on stage last February, and I catch my brother's smirk as he takes a sip of his cocktail. Up until this moment, I'd figured the only thing my father knew about my homecoming was what I'd written in my email—that I needed a change of scenery and was hoping to secure a job at the winery until I could get back on my feet financially. But "Blunder on Broadway" was the title an online theater critic gave to my performance—or lack thereof. Which means my father must have seen it. Read it. Maybe even watched a clip of it.

The thought makes my appetite die.

Before I have a chance to recalibrate from my mortification, my father says, "You may have rejected my advice at eighteen, Sophie, but perhaps you should rethink it now, considering your less-than-desirable circumstances living as a squatter in the family's pool house." He lets his words hover for a good four seconds before he continues. "The only way to get ahead in this world is to pay your dues the way your brother has done here for over a decade now. He's sacrificed momentary enjoyment for hard work, even when that work went unnoticed and underappreciated." He lifts an eyebrow and then tips his head in Jasper's direction. "If you play your cards right, you might just be able to work yourself into a managerial role under your brother's tutelage and establish a reputable career." He grips his son's shoulder, and I note the pride in my mother's eyes. Interestingly enough, Natalie's expression isn't as easy to read.

"I don't believe," Jasper says with a wry tone, "that she has much spare time for my tutelage, Dad."

"And why's that?" my father asks after another large helping of spicy tuna. "I was under the impression she was only working part-time."

"Here, yes," Jasper supplies. "But if her daily sign-out of the Escalade is any indication, I'd guess she's secured other employment."

"Jasper," Natalie chides softly. "It's none of our business how she spends her free time. She's a grown adult."

Jasper's expression lifts in amusement as he silently circles a finger around the rim of his glass and cuts his gaze to his wife. "I'd say it's my business when she's using one of the vehicles in our fleet to drive herself there."

"You told me I could check out a car whenever I needed to as long as one was available."

"I suppose I did," Jasper says easily enough. "Although, at the time, I hadn't realized just how often that would be."

My mother's gaze skirts to me, but she remains quiet.

"Did you take on a second job?" My father's accusing tone dries out my throat.

I try to draw from the confidence I once summoned on stage, but no matter how hard I try, I cannot pull on a character quickly enough to protect myself. I can only be me. "Yes, I've signed a contract at a recording studio in Petaluma."

"Oh, are you singing, dear?" my mother asks with something akin to nostalgia in her voice. "Are you recording music?"

"No," I say feebly, "I'm voice acting—narrating audiobooks for a reputable publishing house."

For the longest time, nobody speaks. Not one person.

Until my father breaks the silence. "You're reading books." He stares a hole through me. "What kind of adult job is that?"

"Ronald," my mother says cautiously, "if it's something she enjoys, then maybe—"

"Then maybe what, Anita?" He balls up his napkin and tosses it on his plate. "She's embarrassed us from a distance, so why not allow her to do the same while she's living off of our blood, sweat, and tears? Unbelievable."

He's still bemoaning my shortcomings as he leaves the table, but I can't hear him. Not over the vivid memory that confiscates my mind and holds me captive:

Dad, with his back turned, talking to the sheriff on the phone three months after the incident in the cellar. *"I understand, Sheriff, and we value the time and resources your men have put into this."* Pause. *"No, no, moving to a private investigation won't be necessary. As embarrassing as it is to admit, I've had some doubts regarding the accuracy of Sophie's story for some time now."* Pause. *"Right, right. Exactly. She's always been a bit of an attention-seeker, overly dramatic. You know the type."* Pause. Laugh. *"Good to know I'm not the only one. Thanks again."*

12

August

I tried.

Even with my lingering unease after the church service yesterday, I tried to be the open-minded, accommodating big brother Gabby wanted me to be. When she asked if she could help Tyler's family with their renovations at the Twilight Theater, I agreed. By the sound of it, there were plenty of projects to last through the end of the year, and according to Gabby, the Pimentels had even offered to pay her an hourly wage for her time. And considering I wasn't keen on her working a real job during the school year, it seemed a fair compromise.

But that was all before my discovery this morning.

For the most part, I do my best to avoid going into Gabby's bathroom. For one, it's usually a disaster of lotions and potions I want no part of, and for two, I have my own facilities on the opposite side of the house. But after squeezing the last drop of toothpaste from its tube last night, it was time for me to hit up the stockpile Gabby hoards in her vanity this morning.

That's where I found her hearing aids.

At first I couldn't make sense of why they'd be snapped into their protective case and shoved to the bottom of a drawer filled with extra toiletries. Until I did. Until the revelation ripped the tenuous seam I'd haphazardly mended after yesterday's service wide open. It wasn't the expensive price tag or even the threat to the delicate technology that had my blood pumping hot as I gripped them in my fist.

It was the fear it triggered inside me.

Between Aunt Judy's push for a deaf college and Gabby's infatuation with her new deaf boyfriend and her ever-increasing involvement within the deaf community . . . I could almost feel her slipping away from me, losing hope in the whispered vow I made to her after the accident. *I will find a way to fix this, Gabby. I swear it.*

Once again, I was failing her.

Worse, I was failing our parents.

To an outsider, Gabby's steady acceptance of her limitation was courageous. Admirable, even. But I knew differently. I knew that with a single phone call to Dr. Johnston's office, her degenerative prognosis could be erased!—the hearing in her left ear saved!—if only I had the resources.

Now, more than an hour after the discovery, my hand still shakes as I jam my dad's drill bit into the sheetrock of my studio wall, resolved to fix the sagging corner shelf and the impossible financial situation I'm in. Not for the first time, I consider the ramifications of taking on a second mortgage. Maybe it's time I finally have a chat with Chip's finance guy in Sacramento.

I'm testing out the shelf when the studio door opens and closes softly behind me.

I twist on my haunches, grateful for the positive distraction of Sophie's arrival to offset my inner dialogue, when all she offers is a muffled "Hey, August" before she disappears around the corner without another word.

I've never claimed to be an expert on women, but clearly something's not right here.

Sophie is usually a sunbeam of happiness when she enters the studio. I don't think there's been a single morning when she hasn't initiated at least ten minutes of warm-up talking at my soundboard before traipsing back to the booth. It's only in the lack that I realize how much I've come to rely on her charisma to set the mood of my whole day.

As soon as I'm up on my feet, I banish all thoughts of unworn hearing aids and medical expenses to focus solely on Sophie's melancholy movements through the glass that separates us. Everything she does in the recording booth—from unzipping her backpack, to setting her iPad on the stand, to adjusting her stool, to sipping on her tumbler of lemon-ginger tea—looks strained and somber. She stares off into space as she gathers her thick hair atop her head, allowing the strays to cascade down her back. When she secures her headphones and moves her pink lips close to the mic, I study them for a beat too long before placing on my own headphones and pressing the intercom button. "Morning." I narrow my gaze on the dark shadows under her eyes. "You doing alright?"

Her gaze is fleeting, but she offers me a thumbs-up regardless. "I'm okay . . . just ready to get rolling."

I'm struggling to place her expression when I realize *that's the problem.* In all our time together, she's never looked so . . . unexpressive. I tap my iPad screen and jump to where we left off last Friday, only to read my notes and grimace at the poor timing.

Tentatively, I engage the two-way Talk button again. "So, unfortunately, we're gonna need to roll back to the scene break in chapter thirty-nine. The mic picked up the tissue you used to wipe your cheeks, so we'll need to rerecord that section."

When she blinks and looks up at me, I feel a distinct tug in the upper left quadrant of my chest. "I don't think I can do that scene today." She swallows and rubs her lips. "Do you mind if we skip it for now and come back later?"

Her request is spoken with such tenderness that I have the urge to tell her she never has to read that scene again if she doesn't want to, but it's the *why* that has me wanting to break through this window and beg her to trust me with what's really going on.

But instead, I simply say, "Sure, we can start at forty, as long as you feel ready to—"

"I'm ready."

Even though the resolve in her voice is trimmed in professionalism, the last thing I want to do is give her a countdown. But I do it anyway. Because whatever's going on with her, it's not something she's chosen to share with me. And I can respect that. Or at least, I can try to respect that.

I cue the recording chime in her ear, but as soon as she reads the chapter title, I know this session is going to be a bust. Her voice is as flat and lifeless as her eyes. Two words that should never be associated with Sophie Wilder.

The main character in the scene Sophie's narrating is currently making battle plans against the heinous beasts who left her mate, Rayun, for dead, and yet Sophie might as well be reading one of my textbooks on sound engineering.

I could engage the Talk button and attempt to coach her through the technical issues . . . but instead, I remove my headphones and push away from my soundboard. I have no plan when I round the corner to the booth and open the door, but I hope she'll invite me in. Not only inside this tiny room, but into whatever's going on with her today.

I lean against the doorjamb without a word, taking in the sight of her linen overalls and pale yellow tank top, when her eyes finally snag up to mine.

"August?" She startles. "What are you—"

"I thought maybe you could use a break," I say without preamble. "Figured I might take one with you. If you don't mind the company, that is."

Immediately, her bottom lip begins to quiver, and then she's up on her feet, turning her back to stare at the wall. "I'm sorry, I know that take was terrible. I'll get myself sorted, I promise. I can be a professional. I just . . . I need a minute."

For a woman who literally held my hand while I was on the verge of passing out in an emergency room, one would think I'd know how to be a comfort to her in this moment. But I'm at a loss. I don't know what my role is here, or maybe I *do* know it, and that's the problem. Too many lines have been blurred when it comes to Sophie to know which one I'm supposed to stand behind now.

I have a brief flashback to yesterday, to my last impression of a smiling Sophie at the kiosk with Portia. Did something happen after I left? Something with her family? I still knew so little about her life at the winery.

"Take all the time you need," I start. "I know we haven't known each other long, Sophie, but if . . . if you want to talk, I'm here."

As soon as she rotates to face me, I know I've screwed up. And, thanks to the accompanying bolt of lightning that zaps through my core, I don't have to wonder *how* for longer than an exhale.

Sophie texted me after church yesterday, and I'd been too busy sulking around the house to call her back.

I bite back a groan. "I, uh, I never called you back yesterday."

"That's not why I'm upset," she says with a kindness I don't deserve. "I'm sure you were busy, and it was only optional—the calling me back part, I mean." She rubs her lips together, and I worry it's to keep her watering eyes from spilling over. "I only texted to check in on you. It felt strange not to say good-bye after sitting together. That's all." When she tries to smile, I want to ram my own fist into my jaw. Had Sophie checked on me while something in her own world was breaking?

Wow. What a guy, August. Way to go.

"I didn't say good-bye because I didn't want to interrupt your conversation with Portia." It's a lame excuse, and she knows it. "I'm sorry."

"You don't owe me an apology."

"You're right, I owe you more than that. You've been a friend to me from day one, and if I'm honest, I haven't quite figured out how to reciprocate that. I have one close friend and only a handful of acquaintances, most of whom I keep at arm's length. I'm far from a natural when it comes to people—not the way you are, anyway. I don't trust easily." I pause the fire hose of honesty only long enough to cycle a breath before launching in again. "So maybe if you can tell me what's bothering you, it will give me the opportunity to redeem myself from being a complete jack wagon."

This brings a smile to her face. A real one. It's so striking I commit it to memory and then save it to my favorites album.

She takes in a deep breath, then exhales. "My parents showed up at the winery yesterday after an extended trip away. I hadn't seen my mom in close to a year and my dad in nearly three."

I work to keep my face neutral. "I'm guessing it didn't go well?"

"Worse than any of my roleplays with Dana before I left New York."

"Who's Dana?"

"She's my . . ." She thinks, then gives a shrug. "She's the equivalent of your Chip to me, I guess."

I chuckle. "Got it."

"When I left home at eighteen, it wasn't on good terms. My father wanted a specific future for me, one that followed in his and my older brother's footsteps, despite me being born with the complete opposite personality for such a career. I was set to go to Stanford, his alma mater, where I could be molded into the type of respectable daughter he could find pride in. That was the plan, anyway. And then . . ." She pauses, swallows. "Something happened when I was sixteen that caused me to take a hard look at my future. I was struggling and alone, and the only thing I had to look forward to was this drama camp I begged my mom to let me attend the following summer." She looks at the wall, at the window, at the iPad, and then finally at me. "That's when theater became more than something I wished I could do and became something I decided I would do. I researched schools and knew I'd do whatever it took to get accepted into NYU's Tisch School of the Arts, like many of my favorite actors. The application process was rigorous and stressful, but I did it, all on my own." The pride in her voice is almost enough to drown out the catch I hear at the end of her statement.

"Your parents weren't supportive?"

She shakes her head. "They didn't know until I left the acceptance letter on my father's desk." She sighs. "He tore it up and gave me an ultimatum. I either decline the offer and all that goes along with it—including my desire to be a glorified showgirl—"

"A glorified showgirl? Is that actually what he said?" It's difficult to keep my frustration at bay as I watch the flash of pain in her eyes before she continues.

"Or I leave without his support—financial or otherwise. That was eight years ago, and not much has changed. Yesterday's lunch notwithstanding."

Still propped against the doorjamb, I shove my hands in my pockets. "What about your mom?"

This takes Sophie a bit longer to answer. "I think my mom is a good person with a good heart." She nods almost as if trying to convince herself that this is true. "But she's been under my father's thumb for nearly forty years, and she rarely, if ever, goes against him, which means our relationship has suffered a great deal since I left." I think she's finished when she says, "They're embarrassed of me." She swallows. "Of my decisions and my failures. And now this—working as a voice actress, reading books." She holds out her hands as if to indicate the studio. "I know I shouldn't care what they think—I mean, I've lived on my own for years now. But my dad insists I should be working to build a *real career* at the winery, and I simply can't imagine staying in a place that's only ever made me feel worthless." She groans and tips her head back to stare up at the ceiling. "So tell me why I laid awake half the night replaying his words over and over?"

"Easy," I say without hesitation. "Because we never stop wanting our parents' approval."

When her eyes snap to mine, her expression is stricken. "Oh, August." She covers her mouth. "I'm so sorry. This entire conversation is so insensitive of me. I shouldn't be complaining about my parents when—"

"No, it's okay. I'm saying I can relate to that struggle."

Her next words marinate for several slow seconds before she speaks again. "I was under the impression your family was super close before the accident."

My reply takes equally as long to formulate. "My parents raised us to be a close family, and we were." *Until I ruined everything and cut them off for a woman they warned me against.* "But it's difficult to stay as connected when you're separated by distance."

Her chin bobs in slow motion, as if she's trying to decode what I haven't said. "Does going to church remind you of them? Is that why you left without saying anything yesterday?"

My lips part, but no sounds follow. This is not a conversation I have often—and certainly not a conversation I've had with anyone outside a select few.

Sophie takes a step around the recording stool, watching me, and I don't know how this conversation got flipped around so quickly, but her eyes are clear while mine feel . . . hot. "In a way, yes. It's complicated."

"I'm sure it is." She inches her way closer, so close I can see each of her perfect eyelashes as she blinks. "Gabby mentioned it's not a comfortable place for you. And yet you still went yesterday. For her." She appraises me. "I think that says a lot about you."

Yeah, it says I'm a fraud.

I only have to look as far as my sister to see that. Her increasing faith since the accident has only shed light on my decreasing attachment to anything I once held true. In the days following her recovery, Gabby wouldn't stop talking about those hazy moments between the train crash and when she blacked out and woke in a hospital halfway around the world. But unlike her, all I wanted was to never talk about it again.

"I suppose we all find comfort in different ways," I try. "Gabby found it in her faith and in her church, and apparently also in some dude named Tyler."

Sophie chuckles at this, and a thrill zings through me at the musicality of it. "And what about you? What brings you comfort right now?"

In a space this tight, there is no place to look other than at her, which makes my omission of the first thing that comes to mind ten times harder than it needs to be. "Surfing."

She makes a contemplative sound. "I've always wanted to learn to surf. Maybe you can give me some pointers one day?"

I swallow. Just the thought of Sophie in a wet suit on a board next to me in the ocean blurs another line. But before I can summon a reply, my phone flashes and vibrates in my pocket. Gabby changed my ring settings to a visual alert notification like hers over the weekend, and I'm far from used to it.

It's Chip.

I show Sophie the screen before I answer, and she blinks up at me with curious eyes.

I have to look away before I accept the call. "Hey, Chip."

"Hey there, does Sophie happen to be at the studio with you right now?"

I spare a glance in her direction. "Affirmative."

"If I'm not interrupting a session, would you mind putting this call on speaker where she can hear?"

I pull it from my ear and tap the Speaker icon, moving a step closer. "We're both here, Chip. Go ahead."

"Great. First off, Sophie?"

"Yes?"

"Not only did Allie love the sample clip August sent over of your first few chapters, but after I shared them with our executive team, your name came up during our last meeting. In short, I have a business proposal for you and August both. Something I think will cater to each of your talents nicely."

Her eyes look from me to the phone. I shrug as if to say this is all new to me, too.

"Full-scale, multimedia productions have become popular in the last couple years, especially around the holidays. Think 1960s radio shows with foley artists doing sound effects and multiple narrators. We just contracted one of our top authors for an original Christmas romance script that will be marketed in a limited-time promotion as a free download with any one of the audiobook subscription services we'll be offering our readers starting November first. We've also just secured a multi-award–winning voice actor as the male counterpart, but our female lead fell through due to a timing conflict. The long and short of it is that we'd love for you to consider playing the female roles for this production."

"Really?" Sophie asks, as if she truly doesn't know how lucky they are to have her talent in their arsenal. "I listened to a couple of those productions last Christmas with my roommate. I'd be honored to be involved with one."

Pride like I haven't felt in some time swells in my chest for the woman standing less than a foot away from me. I *knew* she was something special, and even though I have nothing to do with her talent or this offer, I want it for her. I want everything for her.

". . . you in, too, August?"

"What's that? I think I missed something," I say, even though I feel Sophie eyeing me.

"Are you good with being our resident foley artist for sound effects? We'll need an original music score for our intro and outro, as well."

Dread pools in my core at this request. I haven't created anything original since the accident, and Chip knows it. Sound effects are one thing, but a score is something else entirely.

"You know how I am, Chip," I say without meeting Sophie's eyes, mostly because I don't want my answer to sway hers in any way. "I'd like to read over the details before committing."

"Yup, I'll be sending them over to you both soon, but I think you'll be pleased with the compensation plan. There's a generous signing advance, plus a percentage on each subscription sold for the duration of the promotion period. Based on the data we've run so far, we have every reason to believe this type of project will do quite well for everyone involved."

"Do you have a production timeline in mind?"

"Once we finish editing the script, you should have two to three weeks to finish it. We'll need it back by the beginning of October."

Two to three weeks is not a lot of time considering the other contracts I'm producing or in light of my responsibilities to Gabby once the school year begins. But I simply say, "Great. We'll both circle back with you soon."

"Awesome," Chip says. "Keep up the good work, you two. With your dedication to quality, your future possibilities are endless. You're an audio dream team in the making."

"Thanks, Chip," Sophie chirps. "Talk to you soon!"

I end the call, but something isn't sitting right, and I can't quite put my finger on it.

"You don't want to do it, do you?" There's no judgment in her voice, just curiosity.

"I didn't say that."

"Your face is saying it," she challenges. "Expression is like fifty percent of communication, August."

"I'm pretty sure that number is closer to ninety percent in your case."

She tilts her head and scrutinizes me with a look that ignites an urge to reach out and pull her close. Instead, I stuff my hands in my pockets.

"I don't want to push you into saying yes, but this kind of promo deal has the potential for a lot of visibility, especially around the time of year when every red-blooded American woman is looking for a heartfelt holiday romance. I think it could be a huge opportunity for us both, which is why I'll help you however I can—errands, carpool drives, Gabby's homework, whatever."

"You already work two jobs."

"So do you." She crosses her arms and smirks in a way that causes me to fixate on the perfect pout of her lips. "You heard Chip. We're an audio dream team."

Why does that phrase trigger a mini avalanche inside my chest every time I hear it?

I study her, needing to say something I'm sure I'll regret the second it's out. "Chip's wrong, Sophie. Your talent doesn't need to be *teamed up* with anyone to be exceptional. And I can assure you, this opportunity has next to nothing to do with me. There are producers just like me with studios better than mine all over this state." Though the very thought of her sitting in a booth while some other dude memorizes her every microexpression makes me want to run my fist through this drywall.

"August—"

"I'm serious," I continue. "Whatever comes up, be it now or in the future, I never want you to miss out on an opportunity, even if it means I can't be involved in it with you."

Her nod comes slowly, but I see the sparkle of resilience return to her eyes. "But you're still going to look over the contract, right?"

"Yes."

"And you'll let me help with Gabby if you need an extra hand?"

I pause, and she raises an eyebrow.

"If you insist."

"I do." She smiles at me like I'm the one offering to do something kind when it's actually the other way around. *Again.* She glances at the clock. "I'm good now—to record, I mean. Thanks for giving me a minute to be unprofessional."

She moves to take her seat at the stool again, but I catch her wrist. It happens so quickly that neither of us seems to understand how it happened, even though it's my hand that's out of line and won't let go.

"What you said before, about me not returning your call yesterday," I say quietly. "It wasn't optional. That was me being an idiot instead of being a friend. It won't happen again. I promise."

She acknowledges my words with the slightest of nods. "Thank you." She drops her gaze to my hand. "And I promise to keep Unprofessional Sophie and all her personal drama out of the booth from now on."

"So where can I see her?"

"What?"

I rub my thumb along her delicate wrist bone and watch the pulse point in her neck flutter. "I was hoping to ask Unprofessional Sophie to join me for a thank-you dinner in her honor. What do you think she'll say?"

The playful way she bites her bottom lip makes me hyper-focused on her next words. "She'll tell you to ask her again the second she's out of this booth."

"I'll do that."

That evening, as I pretend to review the Christmas contract Chip sent over from the comfort of my living room sofa, I'm actually spying on the flirty teenagers sitting at my dining room table, eating pizza and "going over curriculum notes" for the introductory ASL class next week. And wonder of wonders: Gabby's hearing aids have magically returned to her ears. She, of course, is none the wiser to my knowledge of her master scam, but I refuse to die on that hill. I'd rather climb a new one. And with the help of this contract, that epic hike might be happening sooner than I'd dared to hope.

My phone flashes bright with an incoming text, and I smile as soon as I read the sender's name.

> **Sophie:**
> So . . . will I be working with a random producer in a random studio next week or will I be decking the halls with you?

> I'm reading the contract over now but keep getting distracted. Chaperoning.

> **Sophie:**
> ?

I snap a covert photo of Gabby and Tyler and send it.

> **Sophie:**
> Ah, they are the sweetest!

> On second thought, I think you might be better off working with a random producer.

Sophie:

> (😵) You can't tell me you're not impressed with this comp plan! The earning potential could be huge for us both. Also, here's my availability to help with rides for Gabby in September if you find yourself double-booked.

She sends over a calendar she's made on a spreadsheet app, showing the dates and times she'll have the Escalade at her disposal for the next month, as well as her work schedule. I can't help but note her availability next weekend. Partly because she's circled it three times in red. I smile at the not-so-subtle hint.

> Am I safe to assume next Saturday night is open for me to take After-Hours Sophie to dinner?

Sophie:

> What if I told you that's my monthly date night with Phantom?

> Then I'd tell you my previous offer has been revoked due to irreconcilable differences.

Sophie:

> Your cat prejudices are not charming, August. I WILL change your mind about him. Mark my words.

I smile at her cheekiness.

> Are you working at the winery now?

Sophie:

> Yeah. It's a slow shift, though. Mondays usually are.

She sends a selfie, only she's cross-eyed and standing with her back to a counter of wine racks. I shouldn't be nearly as charmed by it as I am.

> Might want to take it easy on the wine tonight, looks like it's affecting your vision.

She sends another picture of her pretending to sing into a mop handle, and it's so ridiculous, I laugh. It's only then I notice Gabby and Tyler's eyes have shifted from each other to me. No idea how long they've been watching me smile at my phone like a goon, but I'm immediately self-conscious.

They give each other a knowing look, and then Gabby finger-spells Sophie's name. I watch the silent shake of Tyler's shoulders. *Ha ha, yeah, so funny.*

I set the phone down and work to concentrate on the contract details in front of me. Sophie isn't wrong about the deal points—between the higher rate and the projected promotional subscription commissions, there's some potentially life-changing money to be made if all goes well. And I know exactly whose life it should change.

I glance up at the table again and watch my sister copy a sign Tyler is teaching her, and I feel the familiar stab of guilt at all she's lost. And all that I haven't been able to fix for her. *Yet.*

After she was denied eligibility for a cochlear implant last summer due to nerve damage, I'd gone on a deep dive in search for alternative answers. Whenever Gabby slept, I would be out here on my laptop. Researching. Bookmarking. Submitting requests to otolaryngologist specialists, asking them to consider reviewing Gabby's unique case.

Fourteen never replied.

Eight sent auto rejection emails.

And one responded with a secure link to submit Gabby's medical file through a confidential portal for official review.

I exit Chip's attachment and click into the digital folder in my inbox.

Dear Mr. Tate,

Thank you for submitting your request through our secured medical portal. After careful examination of Gabriella Tate's case by our trained staff, we've determined her eligibility to participate in the next steps of our experimental procedure (please see attached waivers for detailed liabilities and explanations) to restore hearing after traumatic nerve damage.

Due to the high demand of this advanced, groundbreaking surgery, our next available appointment to meet with the surgeon would be in the December/January timeframe. As mentioned in our extensive terms and conditions policy, we require a 50 percent deposit at the set appointment time. Please refer to the cost breakdown and payment plan attached to this email, and call our office at your earliest convenience to schedule her appointment.

Kindest regards,

Julie Lox
Medical Administrative Staff

Doctor Susan Johnston
Otolaryngology MD

Refiner's Pediatrics
San Francisco, CA

I open the secure attachment for what is likely the tenth time since I received the email at the start of June. No big surprise that the cost breakdown looks the same—an exorbitant, untouchable figure no insurance coverage plan will even look at due to the key word: *experimental.* And up until now, I've had no way to even imagine covering the deposit, much less the proposed post-surgery payment plan.

Until this multimedia Christmas production.

After a second scan through the proposed contract from Chip, I don't care how creatively numb I feel regarding writing an original score. I send back an affirmative reply and then pick up my phone to text the talent.

> Looks like the dream team will be fa-la-la-ing together come September.

Voice Memo

Gabby Tate
6 months after the accident

Tyler is picking me up for church tomorrow! Tyler!!!

Technically, Tyler and I are only seventeen months apart—I did the math. And when I think about the majority of couples in the world, that really isn't much of an age gap. Of course, we're not an actual couple. We're just friends, but I'm only a couple weeks away from fifteen now, and who knows what might happen in the future? I like him so, so much.

When we met three months ago during one of my tutoring sessions in his mom's office, I seriously thought he was one of the cutest boys I've ever seen in real life. But the thing about Tyler is, he's also one of the nicest people, too. He was bringing his mom a mug of hot tea because she was recovering from a sore throat. She didn't even ask him to, either. He just did it for her on his own! Tyler is always helping somebody. He volunteers after church every Sunday to put away chairs and help with cleanup. I started staying after, too. Tyler has introduced me to so many friends. Most of them know at least a little ASL, but he's also crazy good at lipreading. I hope I can do that someday, too. I really love this church. I wish August will come with me someday. I'm still praying about that.

Tomorrow morning Portia has to be at the church super early because of the Christmas production, so she asked August if Tyler could pick me up and take me to the first service so I could help with greeting. I was freaking out inside when he said yes. Maybe I should pray that those twelve minutes to church feel like an hour.

Christmas is only two weeks away. August keeps asking me what I'd like to do, but I don't really know. It's hard to think about having Christmas without Mom and Dad. I asked him to bring down the plastic tub of holiday stuff from the attic, and he did. But I haven't been ready to open it yet. Maybe this is how August feels about the box in my parents' closet. It's hard to open something you know will make you sad. For now, we just have a Christmas tree with a string of colored lights on it.

Aunt Judy always says grief is complicated. I'm sure she's right about that; she's a lot smarter than me. But sometimes I think grief is pretty simple. Right now it looks like an unopened tub of Christmas decorations sitting on the floor of my bedroom.

13

Sophie

I exhale an uneven breath as I approach the ornate doors of the Twilight Theater for the second time in as many months. Never in a hundred years did I think I'd return. Granted, the feat feels a tiny bit easier considering Portia's graciousness and the fact that this is an introductory ASL class I'm attending and not an audition.

As soon as I step into the lobby, I shoot a reply back to Gabby.

I'm here.

Unlike the first time I visited, I'm struck not only by the nostalgic interior of a theater rich in history and charm, but also by the freshly painted walls in the lobby. Gabby and her crew have been hard at work. I detect where the cracks along the baseboard have been caulked and where dated light fixtures have been upgraded.

I meander a bit farther to the center of the lobby, where I focus on the inky-black domed ceiling. There's a smattering of painted metallic stars in the center—no doubt the namesake for this gorgeous theater—but as I ponder the impossible darkness after all the ambient light has been blotted out during the live shows, a chill skitters my spine.

Footsteps approach from behind, and I swivel to find Gabby. She smiles and signs hello to me in ASL. I sign back, proud of myself for learning a few basics on my own.

She gives me a hug as if she's known me for years.

"Good job," she exclaims, and when we break apart, I notice her hearing aids more than usual due to the double Dutch braids she's wearing tonight—an adorable style on her. Though I've seen her aids dozens of times, I've never seen them so exposed. The technology is fascinating. They're so small, and the wires are nearly invisible to my naked eye.

She picks up on my focal point, and I immediately want to apologize for staring.

"Thing One and Thing Two are getting a bit more attention than usual today," Gabby says without any sense of self-consciousness.

"I'm sorry. I shouldn't stare, I'm just fascinated by how they work and . . ."

"And what?" she teases. "It's okay, Sophie, I'm not easily offended. You can ask me anything."

"I thought you couldn't hear out of your right ear but you still wear an aid in that one?"

She nods as if she's answered this many times before. "Right, because even though I'm profoundly deaf in the right, these aids use the vibrations inside of my skull to transmit sound to my partially hearing ear." She shrugs, and the action is so authentically teenage girl that I can't help but smile. It's weird to think I was her age only a decade ago. "My brother explains the science part a lot better, but in echoey spaces like the auditorium we'll be in tonight, they make it easier for me to localize sound and pick up on specific conversations."

I'm still stunned by their size. They're a fraction of the size I remember my Gigi's being when I was her age. "Are they comfortable?"

She pauses before answering this time. "They're okay. Sometimes the distortion can be really annoying, and I get headaches if I wear them too long, but it's the tinnitus that makes me feel . . ." She purses her lips. "Like I want to rip my ears off."

"Tinnitus." I scrunch my eyebrows, trying to place the word. "That's the high-pitched ringing sound?"

"For hours and hours," she confirms and then says, "But I can be a better help to Portia tonight if I keep them in. I'm not as skilled of a lip-reader as Tyler yet, and even if I was, it becomes really difficult when there are multiple speakers interacting at once. I can help Portia with interpretation when I have them in, although the acoustics in the room still cause me to miss things. But that's why we're here, right? To promote the many benefits of interpreters."

"Right." I recall the interpreters I've watched during second service on Sunday mornings. When Portia first started the ministry at Seaside so her husband could attend, she was the only interpreter. Now, there are four on rotation.

Gabby links her arm through mine and tugs me deeper into the lobby. My pulse kicks a little harder in my chest. I can tell my brain I'm only here to attend a class, but my body knows exactly where I am. I've simply been inside too many auditoriums for me to pretend otherwise.

"If it wasn't for my brother," Gabby continues with ease, "I probably would have ditched my aids altogether after camp, though."

The mention of August sends a rush of warmth through me. "Why if not for your brother?"

"Because he doesn't want to accept that I'll be deaf forever."

This draws me up short. "What do you mean?"

Her hesitation is the first time I've felt her hold back, and I don't know if it's her brother she's protecting or herself. "My condition is degenerative. It's why my aids don't work as well now as they did when August first bought them for me." She rubs her lips together. "August still hopes I can be *fixed* someday—that my life will be better if I can go back to hearing and communicating the way I used to."

I flinch at her use of the word *fixed*, and it takes me a second to recalibrate my thoughts. "And what do you hope for?"

"Peace." Her voice holds so much honesty, I don't dare take a breath. "I should have died two years ago in the same accident that killed my parents, but I'm still here. I don't understand why things happened the way they did, but I trust that God has a plan. My mom raised me to believe He works in every circumstance in our lives. Even the hardest ones."

The way she speaks about God, with such confidence, reminds me of what August said about Gabby finding comfort in her faith. And I understand it now. Because her words have brought me comfort, too.

Behind us, I hear several more people enter the theater. By the way they're conversing back and forth, I know they're hearing attendees. As I follow Gabby through the auditorium, she boldly greets each guest with a smile and a wave, being sure to thank them for coming.

Meanwhile, butterflies hatch in my gut at the smell of polished wood and velvet seat cushions.

"So glad you made it, Sophie," Portia says, greeting me as Gabby points out our saved seats facing the front of center stage. While Portia asks questions about my day, the sight of the stage behind her is distracting at best. "I was hoping to talk with you about something after the meeting tonight. Do you have a few minutes to spare?"

And then the butterflies hatch in full. With as much as I appreciate Portia's kindness to me, I've feared being asked to do more at the theater outside these Tuesday night classes. For one, my commitments at the studio and the winery simply won't allow it. And for two, I'm not ready. No matter how badly I want to be, the panicked hum in my limbs warns me otherwise.

"Sure, I can stay after class for a few minutes."

"Great." Portia squeezes my arm lightly before she makes her way to the stage. There are maybe forty-ish people in attendance tonight, and from the look that passes between my seatmate and her boyfriend, I can see how delighted they are by the turnout.

Tyler signs something to her and then points to me.

I lean in. "What did he say?"

"He says we'll have to start thinking of some good name ideas for you."

"Name ideas?"

"Yes. Your ASL sign name. Only a deaf person can give you one."

"Really?" The thought brightens my mood considerably. "That's really neat."

Portia takes the stage then. She reintroduces herself to the room using both English and ASL. It's intimidating to watch how quickly her hands move, but also inspiring. The more I see of this beautiful language, the more I want to understand it. Unlike the last time I saw Portia address an audience from a stage, this time she introduces her husband, Nick, to the group. Nick stands, turns, and waves.

We all wave back.

"Nick is the best man I know, which is why I was the one to propose marriage to him first because I didn't want him to get away," Portia says in a somewhat mischievous tone.

Nick, still standing, signs something back, and I notice the way he uses his entire body in his response—his shoulders play as active a role as his facial expressions. I don't need to understand everything he's saying to understand he has a funny sense of humor like his wife. Gabby belly-laughs beside me, and so do a few others in the room. And I'm desperate to know what he's said.

Portia is laughing as she tries to deliver her husband's reply. "Nick says, 'Oh, no, you don't. That's not how it happened at all. The only reason she asked first is because her mouth moves three times quicker than my hands. I was already on bended knee, holding out the ring to her, and she stole my next line like a diva.'"

The rest of the room erupts into laughter, and it's incredible how the atmosphere relaxes. As stage actors, we're shown techniques to warm up an audience, but this is next level. In a single interaction, this couple has bridged two worlds, and I'd bet there's not a soul in this room who doesn't look at ASL like the incredible gift it is.

With the attention squarely focused on the stage, Portia shares a brief overview on the history of ASL and how this special language has played both a personal and a professional role in her life as a certified ASL interpreter, tutor, and speech therapist. Her vision to integrate the hearing and non-hearing communities in our area is commendable, and I find that as she shares, I'm overcome with a desire to know more. Like how this old theater plays a part in her family's life. How did Twilight Theater come to be purchased by them?

We spend the rest of the class discussing the layout of the months ahead, the workbooks and curriculum for purchase, the at-home videos we'll need to watch and practice each week, and our overall commitment to learning. It's a lot, but it's right. I know it is.

When Portia mentions the option of memorizing a weekly Bible verse in ASL before the start of class each week, I watch her find me in the crowd. Perhaps she's remembering our brief conversation about the Bible journal we share. I'll be happy to tell her I've been tracking my progress with the plan in the mornings.

As the meeting winds down and eventually wraps up, I make my way to Portia, who is surrounded by attendees. When the last person finally steps away, she rotates to face me.

"Great job tonight," I say. "You're really inspiring."

"I believe I said the same thing about your résumé the first time we met."

I feel my calm slip and my nerves return, but then she reaches for my hand. "I've been thinking about that coffee date we talked about."

"Oh yeah?" I release the anxious breath I've been holding. Committing to coffee is an easy yes.

"Yeah," she continues, "only I'm wondering what you might think of doing something a bit more routine, like meeting for an hour or so before class on Tuesdays to talk through what we're reading and discovering in the Bible since we're following the same plan. Could you do that?"

"Absolutely. I'd love to." I'm equal parts flattered and thrilled by her suggestion. "Thank you."

She drops her voice to a whisper. "What do you think about inviting Gabby to join us? I know she has an aunt who sees her every couple of weeks, but I lost my mom when I was an older teen, and I know how valuable a consistent female influence is at her age." I nod emphatically, and she smiles and touches my arm. "Great. And for the record, Sophie, I don't think you're in the Tates' lives by accident."

A tiny thrill climbs my spine as the sentiment takes root. I think about what Gabby said earlier—how she trusts God is at work in every circumstance. How she believes He has a plan even in the hard times. The thought is so remarkable I can't help but try it on for size myself.

Could God's plan be at work in my life at this very minute? The question is almost dizzying as I process the untimely ending of my stage career, my move back to California, my narration gig at the studio, and even my friendship with the Tates. With one in particular.

A thought that leaves a smile on my face for the entirety of my drive home.

14

Sophie

August is on his way to the winery.

I'm heading to meet him at the front of the main house in my three-inch wedge sandals and white halter dress when I suddenly remember the denim jacket I forgot in the tasting room. We closed early today due to the private event Jasper is hosting this evening, an event he's booked for the first Saturday night of every month under the name *Art and Social Club*. Personally, I couldn't care less what he calls it—I'm just grateful for the night off. And bonus, I didn't even have to ask for it. Natalie had simply texted to let me know Jasper had hired a separate crew for these "club" nights, to which I responded with an enthusiastic thumbs-up.

If the plans I'd made for tonight's dinner out with August were close by, I'd forgo a jacket, seeing as this September evening is almost warm enough to break a sweat. But the bay is always chillier—especially after the sun goes down.

I pause where the walking path forks, contemplating the lesser of two evils: being frozen on the beach or potentially interrupting my brother's monthly snobbery club. But when I glance at my watch and then into the picture window of the tasting room, there's no indication that anyone's inside. It's still early. A few minutes to five. Yet, despite the *Closed for a Private Event* sign on the door, the hairs on the back of my neck stand at attention. Even after months of being back, there's not a day I don't think about the consequences of entering a dark tasting room alone after hours.

It's fine, I coach myself. *There's still plenty of daylight outside. I'll be in and out in a blink.*

I don't give myself another option as I dash up the walk, enter my employee code into the security box, and prop the door open with the stopper. I slip inside the empty dining room and make a hard right toward the bar to retrieve my coat from the staff closet. I stop short when I see my brother's back arched over an open laptop on the bar's counter. His shirt sleeves are rolled up to his elbows, and two wireless earbuds are shoved into his ears.

". . . not good enough," he says in a firm tone, and it's only then I realize he's on a phone call. The black iPhone lies face up on the bar top, next to his computer. "If you want to get paid, you'll get it right."

From here, I can barely make out the images on his screen but it looks as if there are a couple of paintings he's studying closely. Is he adding to his art collection?

I know I should leave before he catches my silhouette in the reflection of his screen, but my feet remain planted. My heart stutters an erratic, nonsensical beat because something feels off, and I want to understand why.

Jasper slaps the counter with his open palm, and my adrenaline spikes. "We set up in an hour, Andre. There's no time for second thoughts—"

I don't hear what's next because the pocket of my dress begins to vibrate. *My phone.* August must be calling. No, August must be here.

Using the "soft feet" technique I learned from my first choreographer, I flee the room, jacketless, fervently hoping that my brother's earbuds are turned up loud enough to block the sound of the door closing behind me.

For more reasons than I care to explain—not including my current mad dash out of the tasting room—I want to keep August far away from the messiest parts of my life. At the top of that list: my brother. When I couldn't talk August out of picking me up for dinner tonight, I decided I'd simply play the part of goalie instead. I'd meet him out front and fight to preserve the few untainted impressions of my Gigi's legacy.

I race across the path and up the steps to the main house, where I swipe two bottles of wine from the staff kitchen, then burst out the side door into the small parking lot. I'm just in time to spot him heading up the front walk, holding a large bouquet of flowers.

"Hey," I call out to him, breathless.

He spins around in a circle, tracking me as I jog in my wedged sandals to his midnight-blue sedan. "Oh? Hello." Confusion crimps his brow as he gestures toward the house with the bouquet. "You know, when I told you I would pick you up tonight, it included a walk to your front door like any respectable gentleman would—"

"That's okay," I quip while moving to his trunk and cradling our house red and white in my arms. "Because I'm already here. See? I saved you a trip." I flash him a grin.

"Uh, yes. I do see." He tilts his head and narrows his eyes on the wine bottles. "Although I'm starting to wonder if we might have different definitions of a thank-you dinner."

"No, no." I shake my head. "These are just for you. To try at home. We give them out to all our VIP tourists."

He looks from me to the estate and then back again. "When did I have a VIP tour?"

"You haven't yet. But you will. Just not tonight."

"So that's, like, what? Conciliatory wine?"

"Exactly." I smile.

He bobs his chin once, yet I can tell he understands nothing. Not that I can blame him. All I know is that I want to get out of here—*and fast.* I'm still not totally sure my brother didn't spot me spying on him. And I'd rather not find out while in August's company.

"Shall we go?" I ask in my most Positive Polly voice.

He presses a button on his key fob and pops his trunk, where he helps me secure the bottles before assisting me into the passenger seat. When he hands me the sweet bouquet of mixed wildflowers, I wish I could risk running back inside to put them in water.

"Thank you for the flowers, August. They're beautiful."

"You're welcome."

I'm reaching for the seatbelt when he asks, "Who's that on the porch?"

I nearly lose control of my bladder before I confirm it's only Natalie. She offers me a tenuous smile and a quick wave. I wave back. This has become our new normal since the Sunday brunch with my parents. We've upgraded to in-laws who smile and wave. I don't even care if it's probably out of pity. It's nice.

"My sister-in-law, Natalie."

"And will a formal introduction be included in my future VIP tour?"

I laugh. "Potentially."

The second he pulls out of the driveway, my entire body sags in relief. We made it, I think, and without a run-in with Jasper. I'm on the tail end of a deep exhale when I spot August's large water thermos in the cup holder.

"Mind if I pop the lid off your thermos and use it as a flower vase?"

"Be my guest."

Once my flowers are properly hydrated, August rotates his head, eyeing me with great suspicion. "How long are we supposed to pretend that wasn't weird back there?"

"Back where?"

"Sophie." He deadpans. "I feel like I'm driving a getaway car."

I laugh, although his words land a little too close to home. I touch his forearm. "Sorry. I'm just really excited to be going to dinner with you tonight."

This, at least, causes the corners of his lips to tick north. "About that, would you care to provide me with the address of where you made our reservations?"

"I didn't make a reservation."

"What?" The car swerves. "Please tell me you're joking."

I say nothing.

"Sophie, I know you haven't been back in the area for long, but there is next to a zero percent chance we'll be able to walk into any restaurant around here on a Saturday without a reservation."

"Which is exactly why I'd hoped we could go somewhere not around here. Is that okay with you?"

"Of course." He glances my way. "I told you I'd take you anywhere you wanted to go." The tension in his shoulders relaxes. "Where do you have in mind?"

"Bodega Bay."

He whips his head toward me. "Bodega Bay?"

"Yeah, why? Is that too far?" In reality it's only a thirty-minute drive to the west, but by the baffled look on August's face, my suggestion seems outrageous.

"No, no. It's not too far," he says. "It's just . . . Why *that* beach?"

"Because it's one of the last places I remember being truly happy before I moved away. I went there right after I found out I got accepted to NYU." The night before I told my parents.

August remains contemplative as he steers us onto the highway, and I wish I could read his mind.

"I'm guessing you've been there before?" I pry.

"Many times. It's where my dad taught me to surf."

My jaw slacks. Of all the beaches in the area, I go and choose the worst one for him. "Oh. August. We can totally go somewhere else, there are so many other—"

He moves his hand to my arm, and my skin sings at his touch. "No, it's only good memories for me there, too. It's still where I go to surf, any time I can."

I set my free hand atop his. "Okay, then, as long as you're sure."

"I am. Although . . ." A line of concern marks his brow. "What about food? The area isn't known for its fancy dining."

"No, but it *is* known for fresh fish tacos and chips and salsa, and in my opinion, that beats caviar and escargot any night of the week." I wiggle my eyebrows at him. "Plus, we can get it to go."

15

August

The taunting aroma of the hot, deep-fried tortilla chips and fresh tacos Sophie left me to babysit while she *runs a quick errand* is quite possibly the biggest test of my willpower to date. She's been inside the tiny pink-and-white striped building on the side of the road for four minutes now. Not that I'm counting.

Only, I most definitely am.

When she finally emerges, she's carrying a giant bag of multi-colored saltwater taffy. Her white dress billows around her shapely legs as she jogs back to the car, and it's only then that my gnawing physical hunger makes room for a different kind of desire. One that's sure to put my current willpower test to shame if she keeps smiling at me like that.

"That was almost a tragedy," she says as she pops into the car and buckles up again. "They normally close at five, but an employee happened to be there doing inventory so he made an exception for me."

"Oh, I'm sure he did," I say wryly.

"What is *that* supposed to mean?"

I make a show of looking her over before I reverse onto the street again. "I mean, no red-blooded male would have sent you away."

She laughs like I'm making a joke, but I'm not. First of all, I'm too hungry to joke. Second of all, there is nothing laughable about the level of Sophie's attractiveness.

"Well, all that matters is that we now have a beach-worthy dessert. Oh, wait. I think I learned that word."

"Learned what word?" I ask absentmindedly as I park much closer than my usual spot, seeing as we're not here to surf. Thankfully, I have a blanket in the back that can work for this spontaneous beach picnic. I've already spied a spot with little wind interference due to the sand berms.

But Sophie's in another world. She's too busy forming her fingers into . . . *Ah.* She taps the circle part of two ASL Ds together.

"*Dessert!*" she exclaims with pride. "I remembered because it's like two big bellies bumping together. That was in the basics bonus lesson I took online this week—although, honestly, I think I'd use that sign more than *water.*"

Despite my increasing hunger pangs, I laugh. But when I collect our food bags from the back seat, I inform Sophie that if I don't eat within the next five minutes, she'll need to learn an allotment of new signs, likely those having to do with my untimely death.

She gets out of the car.

There are less than half a dozen cars parked in the small lot behind us, which accounts for the kiteboarders I see on the open water and the older couple tossing a Frisbee into the surf for their golden retriever, as well as a group of teens circling the tide pools on the outskirts of what we can see from the blanket I've spread out for us, where it looks like we've just opened a Mexican restaurant. In addition to the chips, salsa, queso, and guacamole containers, we also have a platter of fish tacos at our disposal.

It's after my second helping that the dip in my blood sugar levels finally evens out. And it dawns on me then that Sophie hasn't said a word since we tapped our respective tacos together in bon appetit fashion and turned our attention to the ocean.

"You've gone quiet," I venture.

"That's because I'm eating." Her reply is simple, yet I don't completely trust it.

In general, the women I've shared a meal with in the past have been disgruntled by my lack of communication during a meal. So this is unchartered water.

"You don't like to talk when you eat?" If this is a test, I don't want to screw it up.

She dabs the corners of her mouth with a napkin. "Sometimes, I guess. But I enjoy savoring the flavors of a good meal. And right now, that good meal is a taco on the beach with a friend." With a satisfied-sounding sigh, she sets her to-go box on the blanket and takes a slow sip of her bottled water. I try not to stare at the curve of her collarbones or the sweet angles of her face in the waning sunlight. I fail.

"This is a perfect evening, August. Thank you for inviting me."

There's not a trace of irony to be found in her statement as she looks from the surf to me, and yet I'm still stuck on the fact that she could have chosen anywhere—any highbrow establishment in any of the affluent cities surrounding us—and she chose this. A quiet evening on a beach as personal to me as my adolescence, eating tacos out of a to-go box.

Sophie Wilder might be the most marriageable woman on the planet.

I blink hard. *Did I really just think that?*

I wipe my mouth with a napkin before setting the remains of my dinner aside. "If anybody is getting thanked tonight, it's you—seeing as you likely saved my hand."

Sophie turns her twinkly eyes on me, and my heart thuds hard in my chest. "It would have been a shame to lose it. It's such a nice hand." Though her tone holds the remnant of a tease, the light, familiar way her fingers graze my healing scar is anything but laughable. "I hope you'll think twice about climbing on top of greenhouses in the future, or at least, if you do, make sure to implement the buddy system."

"The buddy system?" I quirk an eyebrow at her. "Not sure I'm familiar with that terminology in construction."

"Well, you should be." She tucks her legs and leans toward me. "Because the buddy system can be used anywhere, in nearly any situation." Her confidence is captivating. "Let's take the greenhouse scenario, for example. One buddy would climb onto the damaged roof while wearing a rope that's attached to the other buddy, who will remain on the ground. Like a safety net of sorts. They'd simply stay connected until the job is done."

"Ah, I see." It's an effort to dull the amusement in my voice. "And in this case, the buddy on the ground would be . . ."

"Me." She flattens a hand to her chest.

"And if I was sliding down the corrugated roof—"

"You mean hypothetically?" she teases.

"Yes, if I was hypothetically sliding off the roof, then your plan down below would be to . . . ?"

This stumps her for a second, and I can tell she's spotting the holes in her logic. "I'd hold on to the rope."

"And do what with it? Lasso me to the tallest tree before I hit the ground?"

When she breaks into a full-bellied laugh, I listen as the tempting sound of her voice swirls and harmonizes with the rumble of the tide. It feels every bit like the start of a symphony. And for the first time in so long, I allow myself to compose it in my mind, adding in the percussion, and the high notes of a flute, and the low resonance of a cello—

At her light touch on my arm, the growing orchestra in my head fades.

"Where did you go, August?"

I blink and try to form a coherent response. "Nowhere. I'm here, with you."

To my relief, her expression gentles. "Then can I ask you something I've been wondering about?"

"Of course."

"Why don't you attend the ASL classes on Tuesday nights?"

I probably should have anticipated this question. It's only right she'd be curious, but my answer isn't quick or uncomplicated. "What do you say we clean up and resume this conversation on the beach?"

"Yes, please." I help her to her feet as she says, "Make sure you grab our taffy when you put the blanket away."

As I give her a salute, I notice the shiver she tries to hide, only I know it will be even windier near the water. Back at the car, I find a navy zip-up in the back seat. I give it a quick sniff test before I toss it over my arm, stash the blanket, and collect her bag of colorful taffy as instructed.

"I thought you could also use this." I hold out the jacket to her.

"Ah, thank you." She wastes no time putting it on and zipping it up to her throat. As distracting as she is in a dress, the sight of her in my sweatshirt is a different kind of distraction. "I'd planned to grab something warm before we left, but . . ." She trails off. "I ran out of time."

We leave our shoes at the bottom of the trail and exchange a few pleasantries about the stunning rock formations close to the shore and then about the backdrop of a golden horizon. And then it's time for me to answer Sophie's questions about my relationship with ASL and the deaf community.

"It's not ASL I have an issue with," I say, watching the moving shadow of the taffy bag in my right hand along the sand. "I think it's an incredible resource with incredible benefits for those who need it—both inside and outside the hard-of-hearing world."

"Okay," she says patiently. "So what is it, then?"

I pause, as there are few times I've spoken this out loud, and even fewer people I've trusted enough to speak it to. I'm either shamed for my viewpoint or misunderstood. Both are equally unmotivating when it comes to opening a future dialogue.

"I don't want Gabby to stop hoping for a cure."

I'm not sure what Sophie was expecting me to say, but her sudden stillness catches me off guard. "A cure for her deafness? I didn't think . . ." She hesitates for a moment. "I didn't realize that was even a possibility."

"Most medical professionals would say it's not." I think of the many doctors we've seen, of the scans, tests, reports, trials, ear molds, therapies, and medical opinions we've pursued. I think of the long days following the accident, of waiting for news on Gabby's condition, realizing that nothing about our lives would ever be the same again. "But because the type of head trauma Gabby endured isn't textbook, it makes her case unique. There aren't many options left to pursue, but there's one that has the potential to restore the limited hearing that remains in her left ear."

"Really? That's sounds . . . incredible." Sophie's footsteps in the sand slow, and she twists her face to the amber horizon. The golden hue washes over her skin, glittering in her eyes, and rendering me momentarily speechless. "What does your sister think about all that?"

I hesitate. "She doesn't know. Not yet, anyway. I don't want to get her hopes up until I can secure the appointment with the surgeon. She's had too many ups and downs and false hopes to contend with. I won't do that to her again, not until everything has been cleared."

Her brows pull together. "What's involved in setting the appointment?"

I must hesitate for longer than Sophie finds comfortable. "I'm sorry if that was too presumptuous. You don't have to answer that."

Only, I want to answer it. Outside of Aunt Judy, the only other person I've spoken to regarding my sister's medical needs is Chip, and even with him, I've been guarded and reluctant to share the intimate details of our situation. But with Sophie, guarded is the last thing I want to be.

"Money." The simple admission humbles me to my core. My parents entrusted me to take care of Gabby. They entrusted me to provide for her when and if they no longer could. I won't fail at that—not the way I failed them while they were still alive.

"What about medical insurance—isn't she covered?"

"Not for this."

Sophie's appalled gasp is more endearing than she could possibly know. "Why not?"

"It's too new," I say simply. "Insurance approval takes time. I was told it could be years, and by then her degenerative condition will likely be too advanced for this operation."

We're silent for several minutes as we walk the length of the beach. Our footsteps leave behind a trail of unspoken thoughts as the waves grow testier. The dimming skyline reflects the tension out at sea, leaving behind a smear of crimson.

"Can I ask you something that could be borderline offensive?"

I nod.

"Was there any . . ." She hesitates, as if struggling to come up with the remainder of that sentence. "Did you parents leave you and your sister any kind of inheritance?"

"The house," I say plainly. "Which is still a few years from being paid off, but it's an asset nonetheless. My folks were wise with the money they made. They lived frugally and saved where they could, but they weren't wealthy by any stretch. My father had a small life insurance policy due to his career in construction. It paid out just enough to cover their funeral costs and roughly half of Gabby's initial surgery and hospital bills until we could get on a payment plan and apply for her social security. The rest, well . . ." I hesitate at the vulnerability of my next confession. "My career in LA was lucrative enough to be a supplemental source of income for the first year or so while I worked to grow my business here. But it's been slow, even with the studio musicians I produce for each month."

Sophie stops, disregarding the creeping tide that nips at our toes in the chilly surf. "Your entire world changed in a blink."

I say nothing to this, but she isn't wrong.

"And you came back here, even though you had an entire life in LA, a successful career you loved, industry connections." I can see her mind puzzling it out. "Did you ever consider moving Gabby to you?"

"No." I shove my hands into my pockets and remember one of the final arguments I had with Vanessa about this very subject after Gabby was finally stable enough for me to make the phone call I'd been dreading. *But why would you need to move back home, August?*

Why can't she just move here with us?" Vanessa whined when I told her Gabby's prognosis. *"My house is plenty big for the short term, and once she heals, we can put her in private school—maybe one of those boarding schools for people with disabilities."* I'd stared at my phone then, hearing my father's predictions about a woman I never should have dated to begin with. It's what finally gave me the courage to end it.

I chose my wants and desires over my family once; I would never make that mistake again.

"This is Gabby's home," I continue, blinking away the image of my ex-girlfriend and the baggage she represents. "The last thing she needed was another huge change after so much had been taken from her. She has friends here, a school, a church, a home she's spent the formative years of her life in, and an aunt who plans weekend stays with her whenever possible. I couldn't ask her to leave all that."

"She's lucky to have you as her big brother, August."

Her statement is an emotion-packed punch to my gut. How badly I want that to be true, how badly I want to believe Gabby won't grow up to resent me, the way I fear she might. Especially considering I turned Aunt Judy down when she offered to take my place and shoulder the responsibility of guardianship shortly after the accident.

"I hope she'll feel that way one day."

"I have no doubt she feels it even now." The conviction in her voice tugs at my curiosity. "She might do her teenage angst stuff from time to time, but it's obvious how much she respects you."

I thank her and then silently study her profile as we begin to walk along the surf again. "What's your relationship with your brother like?"

She makes a sound between a laugh and a sigh. "Nonexistent."

Given the tense dynamics she's described in conversations about her childhood and recent interactions with her family, that isn't hard to imagine.

"He's five years older than me, but our age gap is the least of our differences." She shrugs and kicks at the water. "Where my dad is hardheaded and chauvinistic, Jasper is something altogether different."

The odd note in her tone spikes my concern. "How so?"

"He's hard to explain." She sighs. "The majority of people who know him see Jasper as this celebrated business tycoon—all winsome smiles and networking events and pats on the back. He has friends who own private yachts and collect fine art, and he sends my parents on extravagant trips to extravagant destinations in his place. But it's like I get this completely different version of him that nobody else seems to see. It used to make me feel crazy sometimes." She shakes her head dismissively.

"What version is he with you?"

"Detached, yet somehow always in control."

I know the personality type she's describing well. I lived in a Hollywood mansion with it for nearly eighteen months before my eyes were finally opened in the wake of tragedy. I touch her arm, and she pauses in the surf. "And he lives at the winery with you?"

"Technically, I live in *his* pool house—the one he built to go with his new pool and spa area currently under construction. Thankfully, he put Natalie over my work schedule so our interactions at the winery are limited. But without his signature at the end of my six-month commitment in December, I'll be forced to leave the winery with nothing more than the debt I came with."

Sophie fills me in on the details of her Gigi's trust, about the conditions surrounding the biannual payout, and how she's eager to have enough funds to be fully independent and out from under her brother's thumb.

I'm about to ask her more of what she envisions for her future, but Sophie seems to have other plans. She makes a move for the bag of saltwater taffy and steals it from my grasp.

"Bet I can guess your favorite taffy flavor," she teases as she takes a step backward in the wet sand.

"Doubt it." I try to swipe the bag back, but soon she's splashing away in the surf as if we're engaged in a child's game of tag.

At first, I keep my steps light, seeing as I have exactly one change of pants, but then Sophie picks up speed and I have no choice but to do the same. Every few strides I hear the faint echo of her laugh, and it propels me forward. All too soon my pants are soggy.

She's fast, much faster than I would have suspected given her attire, but still, the advantage is mine. I know this beach like I know my childhood home. She's about to run into the rocks that lead to the tide pools—it's impassable with bare feet.

"Give them up! You're out of beach," I holler into the wind.

"Never," she calls back with slightly less enthusiasm as she faces down the path of agony.

I cringe as she starts across the sharp, coral-like rock formations jutting up from the sand. I stop where I am because I don't want to push her any further. I don't want her to get hurt. And she will. I've had my fair share of scrapes and cuts on these rocks as a boy. Just the thought of her in pain makes my abdomen burn something fierce.

"Sophie," I warn again as she takes another hesitant step. "Fine, you win." I relent and hold up my hands. "I'm implementing the buddy system."

She stops, turns. "What did you say?"

"I'm implementing the buddy system. You said it works in every circumstance, so let's put it to the test. Right here, right now."

"Okay." Even in shadow, I can see the illumination of her smile. "And how do you propose we go about it when I'm here and you're there?"

I glance around the beach for some inspiration, only to give up and follow the prompt of my instinct—which in all likelihood will be as ridiculous in practice as it is in my head considering my *buddy* is a professional actress. I squat low and attempt a pantomime in my half-soaked pants. I pretend to grip a rope from the sand and tie one end around my waist while I lasso the other end for a good five seconds in the air as if I'm an experienced cattle farmer from the Midwest. Once I've finally built enough imaginary momentum, I toss it out to Sophie.

And when I do, she's ready.

She's fully in character when she secures the taffy bag between her teeth so she can catch the lasso with her hands and shimmy it up her legs, over her hips, and around the small of her waist.

When her eyes meet mine, she gives me a thumbs-up, a response I interpret to mean she's ready to be reeled in.

The whole thing is completely ludicrous, and yet, it's everything I didn't know I needed. *She's* everything I didn't know I needed.

Inch by inch, I tug the invisible rope toward me, careful not to rush her over the rough terrain. Every successful step decreases the tension trapped in my lungs.

And then, finally, she's standing in front of me, wearing my old sweatshirt with a bag of taffy dangling at her side. The wind at her back tugs at her braids and creates a wispy halo effect around her face. Her eyes gleam with a look that signals an emotion I wish I knew how to hold on to for the rest of my life.

"You're a pretty good actor, August Tate."

I don't want to act with you is what I'm desperate to admit as my gaze lingers with hers and the air between us thins.

So much of my current reality has been built on the pretense that I know what I'm doing—how to raise a teenager, how to run a household, how to start a business, how to reconcile my anger, how to grieve the parents I wounded.

How to not kiss my coworker and risk the last functioning piece of my heart.

But as I stare at the inviting lips on a face I've memorized through the safety of a glass wall over the last two months, I want to risk it. For her. For me.

For the possibility of something I didn't even know I could hope for, much less find.

I touch her waist, pull her close, and watch her eyelids shutter closed in anticipation, and then I—

Her palm flattens on the center of my chest and instead of feeling the warm brush of her lips, I feel the space her gentle push creates between us. Confusion knits my brow until I see a flash of panic tinge her expression. And then it's gone in a blink.

"You never let me guess your favorite taffy flavor," she says a bit unsteadily as she reaches into her bag and pulls out an orange-and-white piece of taffy. "Is it creamsicle?" It's as if she's suddenly become a character in a play and not the woman I've been pining after since we met.

"Sophie." I want to rein her back in, ask her to explain what's going on inside her head, but she's already slipped out of my reach. "Did I do something wrong?"

"Or maybe," she continues on without acknowledgment, "you don't much like the combo flavors. Give me a hint?" She speaks as if we've been transported back to ten minutes ago when we were still playing cat-and-mouse on the beach. And maybe that's where she wants to be, but I'm still here. Still hoping she'll let me in. Still hoping she won't push me away.

"Please don't say its root beer. That's the worst flavor. Well, maybe not as bad as lime. That one smells like bathroom cleaner."

"It's blue," I say with some reluctance.

"*Blue* is technically not a flavor, but I'll allow it. Its given name is actually blue raspberry." She sifts through her taffy bag while I search for clues as to what changed. To how I read her so wrong.

"Here it is," she says, plucking it out. "One blue raspberry with your name on it." She sets it into my open palm, her act dropping away long enough for me to hear the answer to my unasked question. "I'm grateful for your friendship, August. I hope you know how much it means to me."

As I watch her retreating down the beach under a September moon, I close my fingers around the taffy, knowing that one piece of Sophie will never be enough to satisfy.

16

Sophie

*S*hould I have let him kiss me?

This is the question I've asked myself a thousand times since the night August fake-lassoed me off the tide pools. And it's the same question I'm still asking, more than two weeks later, even while I banter with another man about the correct usage of the term *mistletoe* in August's studio.

Elliot Sanderson, the award-winning voice actor and my official male counterpart in *Mistletoe Matrimony*, a Fog Harbor Audio original, showed up three days ago with a marked-up script in hand. The first day was spent discussing production notes with our executive producer, who also happens to be the man whose lips I've daydreamed about each and every time I've sat in this booth.

Which is pretty much the only perk since starting this project.

"*Cut.*" August's voice breaks into our headphones.

Elliot halts mid-sentence and, not for the first time, peers over his right shoulder at said executive producer. I shrink in my seat. *Not again,* I think.

"Your pace on that punchline is too sluggish," August asserts.

Elliot, a twenty-something dark academia type, pulls his trendy reading glasses from his face, which I interpret to be the equivalent of a cowboy's hand on his holster. "So first, you accuse me of jumping her line, and now I'm too sluggish?"

August stares him down through the glass. "That's correct."

Seemingly exasperated from all the starts and stops, Elliot looks to me for backup, only August isn't wrong in his assessment. Despite his less-than-tactful delivery method, August sees what I've been trying to overcompensate for. The chemistry between Elliot and me is all kinds of off. Which means the timing and delivery of our dialogue is off, too.

Elliot has tried to blame the awkward flow on the script, but I think the script is exactly as it should be: funny, romantic, and full of holiday hijinks. And while the man-child sitting opposite me may have a trained voice with solid inflection and tone, his execution falls flat on every page. A critique August has made more than once in the last two hours.

"I'm reading these lines exactly as they're written," Elliot argues. "What more do you want from me?"

"Believability," August counters coolly.

I groan.

"You're saying *I'm not believable*?" Elliot's chilly laugh echoes in the tiny space we share. "I have almost a decade of experience in voice acting—I've worked with Pixar and Disney!" He locks eyes with me then, as if to ask, *Is this guy for real?* Only, August Tate might be the realest person I've ever known. A fact I've been failing to edit from my heart since the moment I rejected him on that beach. And for all the moments since, when he's given me space as if that's what I want when all I really want is to protect us both from the heartache of starting something we can't finish.

August can't leave California, and I have no desire to stay in a place that has more bad memories than good. I don't wish to stay at the winery a day longer than absolutely necessary. Which is why I've been job hunting again. Not for another fill-in job, but one that will use my background in the arts.

I've applied to several school districts and theater programs across the nation. Perhaps if I can't act on stage, it might be time for me to teach others how to.

"Show me you actually care about what you're saying *to her*." August delivers the challenge from the opposite side of the glass. "Because right now you sound like you're delivering these lines to a random stranger in the produce section. *Not* like someone you have a vested interest in. *Not* like someone you've been pining after since you first met."

Despite the clammy atmosphere inside this closet-like space, goosebumps race down my arms at his words. It's impossible not to recall the imprinted memory of August with the ocean at his back—the way his eyes studied my mouth, the way his voice grew husky with want, the way he leaned in—

"Fine," Elliot spats. "You think you can do it better? Be my guest." He jerks his arms wide open as if he's just pushed all his chips to the center of the poker table and expects his opponent to fold in intimidation. But I know August well enough to know there's no way he'll back down. Not now.

The instant his gaze finds mine, I feel it bubble up inside me all over again: the hope, the want, the desperation. He gives me a nod, and instinctively, I interpret his unasked question.

And then, August begins to read into his two-way mic.

"'You ever wonder why the most iconic representatives for love during the romance holidays could star in a *True Crimes* plot?'" August asks in a voice that is both a hundred percent him and a hundred percent the sarcastic groomsman he's reading for.

"'Are you trying to get on my nerves, Blake? If so, it's working. I don't have time for your cynical trivia today,'" I say with the impatient tone of Noelle Barnes, the renowned wedding coordinator who must rely on her best friend's kid brother after she returns to her hometown, tasked with coordinating her most extravagant Christmas Eve wedding yet. "'But I would very much appreciate if you would apply all that mental energy of yours to the task at hand. Our bride's mother will be here in less than an hour to approve what

I've done here, and there are still at least a dozen mistletoe left to hang in the reception hall.'"

Blake—August—replies with perfect timing. "'Think about it, Noelle. Cupid carries a weapon that would be borderline illegal in most states, and mistletoe is poisonous when ingested . . . so tell me why anybody would want these things on display during a wedding ceremony? You should be more concerned about this.'"

"'What I'm concerned about,'" I say tersely, "'is creating the kissable environment my paying bride and groom have requested for their reception hall.'"

August waits a beat, then two, and when I glance up from the iPad to catch his eye through the window, he reads, "'If any man needs the permission of a dead, poisonous shrub to kiss the woman he loves, he shouldn't be allowed to marry her in the first place.'"

"'It's not about permission, Blake,'" I—I mean my character says a bit shakily. "'It's about the romance.'"

"'No, it's about canned commercialism. Romance is spontaneous and desperate and all-consuming. It simultaneously hollows you out and fills you up. And it always, *always* leaves you wanting more. Another glance. Another touch. Another chance to share the same time and space with the one person you can't seem to live without no matter how much you've tried.'"

Though I've heard Elliot deliver these same lines at least three times now, none of them have been spoken with this much conviction. None of them have caused my stomach to clench and somersault. None of them have been anywhere close to this . . . *believable*.

August holds my gaze through the glass, and I wish for the thousandth time since that night on the beach that I could break through this barrier and pretend that kissing him wouldn't be the most reckless thing I could do. August has lost too much for me to suggest something casual between us. Three months isn't long enough for what I know I could feel for him. For what I feel for him even now.

And by the avalanche that crumbles inside my chest every time he looks at me, I know he must feel it, too.

This wordless exchange rebels against the careful boundaries we've been operating in for weeks. Since the moment I placed that saltwater taffy in the palm of his hand, the two of us have remained in an emotional quarantine.

The sound of Elliot kicking back his recording stool nearly jolts me from my own, and I watch August's shoulders stiffen and tense.

"I don't know what's going on here"—Elliot looks between the two of us—"but I have three other productions waiting on me to respond. I'm not about to waste my time or my talent where it's not appreciated."

Before either of us can think to argue, Elliot has yanked the booth door open and is marching through the studio toward the exit. At the hard slam of the door, the walls shudder, causing one of August's framed awards to crash to the floor.

When he makes no effort to go after the guy, I watch and wait for the consequences of Elliot's desertion to fully register on August's face.

And . . . there it is.

This isn't good. We're already behind schedule. And based on the way August has yet to give me a straight answer regarding the music he's supposed to be composing for the project, we're likely further behind than I even realize.

I step into the hallway and round the corner to where August hunches over his soundboard, head in his hands, fingers threaded through his butterscotch waves. I drink in the sight of him. And then I chastise myself for doing so.

Put him first, Sophie. This isn't about you or your feelings.

"I'm going to have to call Chip," he confesses in a volume that tells me he's tracked my presence. "He'll need to send over a replacement ASAP or . . ."

Or we won't make the October 1st deadline.

I narrow my eyes in thought. If I was a casting director for this project, I wouldn't want another professional like Elliot. Not after hearing what this scene could sound like; not after hearing August read it. An idea forms quickly, snapping together like a 3-D puzzle in my mind.

"What if we already have a replacement?"

He lifts his head and gives me a side-eye that makes me want to reach out and tame his crazy surfer hair. I restrain myself.

"You could do it," I say easily.

He laughs without humor. "No way."

"*Yes* way. You have a great speaking voice, and your delivery was a thousand times stronger than Elliot's." I push what looks to be two manuals about the science of sound to the back of his desk and then plop myself down across from him. His gaze drifts to my crossed legs before he leans back in his chair and presses the heels of his hands into his eye sockets.

"That's not exactly a compliment. I've had better chemistry with a block of cheese than what was happening between the two of you in that booth."

"My point exactly." I swing my foot until the toe of my sandal connects with his knee. "You and I already know each other."

"I'm not an actor."

"You don't need to be. This part might as well be written for you. Blake is sarcastic and intelligent and a bit of a moody smart aleck."

August lowers his hands and hikes a brow at me in challenge.

Not to mention thoughtful and kind and incredibly attractive is what I finish in my head silently. "Don't act like you don't know it's true."

"So then what?" He stares at me incredulously. "You're suggesting I just call Chip and tell him I'm the new Blake? You forget he's known me since we were fifteen. He knows all my hidden talents, and acting isn't one of them."

"So don't call him—not yet. Wait and send him a sample clip from whatever we manage to record today and then offer to save him the money of finding a local voice actor by playing the part yourself. Maybe you can even negotiate a higher rate as they'll be saving whatever money they were paying Elliot, right?" I pause, studying the crease between his brows. "It's more money that can go toward Gabby's procedure."

This is the moment his expression slips from incredulity to possibility. "And what happens if I ruin the whole performance because

I don't have a clue what I'm doing? I don't want to be the reason this project fails. There's a reason people audition for things like this."

I push myself off his desk and plant my feet on the ground in front of him. I expect him to roll backward at my nearness, seeing as he's offered me a wide berth since the beach, but he holds steady. Watching. Waiting.

"I know theater, August. It was my whole life for close to a decade. If I didn't think you could do this, I would say so. But you've had this script for weeks now. You've been taking production notes, figuring out sound effects, and composing the theme music. At this point, you know it better than any potential hire sitting in an audition queue ever could." My pulse picks up speed as he stares at me with none of the filters he's been using these past few weeks. "And you know me," I say softly. "And together . . . together, we're believable."

August is locked inside his head for so long I'm certain he's about to give me a list of every reason why he thinks this idea is terrible. "I'll give it two hours. If we can't get a decent cut for Chip by the time you leave today, then I'll call him and tell him he needs to find us a new hero."

I nod in agreement, although I know I've already found him.

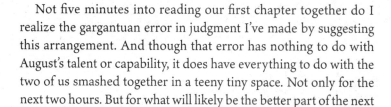

Not five minutes into reading our first chapter together do I realize the gargantuan error in judgment I've made by suggesting this arrangement. And though that error has nothing to do with August's talent or capability, it does have everything to do with the two of us smashed together in a teeny tiny space. Not only for the next two hours. But for what will likely be the better part of the next two weeks after edits and polishing.

When August exits the booth to adjust something on the soundboard, I close my eyes and try to recall what Bible passage I've been studying with Portia and Gabby in our time before ASL class. I'm pretty sure it has something to do with the mind—on thinking good thoughts? Or was it noble thoughts? Lovely thoughts? Boring thoughts? At the moment, the last one feels the safest. Maybe if I could imagine August as a sniveling, dark academia type like Elliot, I'd be able to fight my attraction for him. I'm a good enough actress to pull off narrating this script *and* visualizing August as an overgrown Harry Potter, right?

"Okay, sorry," he says, strolling back inside and closing the door. "It's weird being on this side of the glass." He sits on the stool across from me, and our knees bump, shooting a jolt of electricity up my spine. What is wrong with me? I've been in far more up-close-and-personal scenarios than this with my onstage counterparts. I've danced, embraced, and sang directly into the faces of my pretend Romeos without feeling half of what one look from August makes me feel. So why can't I shake this?

The answer comes swiftly: because this isn't pretend.

He adjusts his microphone and wakes his iPad screen. "Before we start again, do you have any critiques for me?"

I shake my head dumbly.

He looks doubtful. "Sophie, if this arrangement is going to work, you have to be honest with me."

I can't be honest with you, August, that's the problem. "I will be." I nod overenthusiastically. "You're doing great."

"Let the record show, this is a continent away from my comfort zone," he says with a sort of kiddish frown that makes my insides constrict.

When he scrolls to find his place on the digital script, I squint, trying to visualize what he'd look like in a pair of obnoxious nerd glasses. Only that doesn't work. Because on August, those glasses would make him look like a sexy scholar.

He preemptively hands me my water bottle. "We're already rolling. Your lines are first. You ready?"

I take a big swig of the lukewarm lemon water I prepared this morning and lie through my teeth. "Absolutely."

The next seventy-four minutes are some sort of twisted math problem. August bumps my knee accidentally seven times. He smiles three times during our back-and-forth banter. And he actually winks at me once, after I miss my cue and have to restart a paragraph because I was too busy watching him read.

This might be the longest two weeks of my life to date.

As soon as Blake and Noelle are forced together at the fictional wedding venue, working to reconcile their differing personalities and opinions with the job at hand, I'm completely absorbed in the plot again, and with these characters and their specific goals and challenges. Their banter is lively and addicting and laugh-out-loud funny at times, and nearly every page has at least one stand-out quip that makes my lips quirk into a grin. It's what I'm focused on more than anything else right now—the disconnection of the here and now.

Only it doesn't work, because no matter how invested I am in this script, I can't forget what August shared with me on the beach that night. I can't unhear his dedication to his family. I can't unlearn the kind of son, brother, or man he is. Or how I've rarely met his equal.

My mind snaps to attention when August finishes a paragraph of narrative and jumps into his next line of dialogue.

"'What on earth is this giant bubble maker thing for?'" August, as Blake, asks as he riffles through Noelle's inventory of wedding supplies without permission. "'Wait, is this for some kind of circus-themed wedding? Do you break out a red-and-white striped tent and spin cotton candy for that one? Gotta say, I think that's an improvement on this mistletoe-obsessed thing you have going on inside here.'"

"'That's not a bubble maker, it's a snow machine,'" I say as Noelle. "'It's actually the highest-rated model on the market today.'"

"'That might be the most embarrassing thing you've said yet.'"

"'It is not. That happens to be my secret weapon for creating my signature winter wonderlands,'" she says defensively. "'It only takes soap, and it comes with a remote start.'"

"'Nope. I was wrong,'" Blake deadpans. "'That right there is the most embarrassing thing you've ever said. How 'bout we take that same remote and skip this conversation back a few so you have time to reassess your freaky devotion to a glorified soap belcher, huh?'" August raises his hand as if he's about to engage said remote. "'Ready, set, go.'"

A tickle of hysteria crawls up my throat as soon as he speaks his final word, and soon my girlish giggle turns into a full-bodied guffaw.

"I'm s-s-s-orry," I say, trying to get ahold of myself. "Just a sec."

When I hear the low rumble of his laugh and see the bounce of his shoulders, any ground I've gained is gone. It's all over now. My dignity, my professionalism, my hope of finishing out this chapter within the next fifteen minutes before I have to head back to the winery for work.

"And here I thought you were supposed to be the professional," August jests, still laughing. "You'd never get away with that during a live performance."

"Guess it's a good thing I don't plan to ever be on stage again, then, huh?" It's meant as a joke, one that should be easily bypassed by the next clever turn of phrase, but his pause is too long and his eyes are too focused, and suddenly, the humor in the air is charged by something new. Something tangible and raw and real.

Too real.

The seconds tick by like minutes, and the ache in my throat expands to my chest.

"What happened in New York, Sophie?"

Everything in me wants to divert us back to the script, back to the flirty fun of our characters, but how can I do that to him when he's shared things with me that are ten times more personal than what I've shared with him?

"I bombed a pretty big performance on opening night, and there was simply no coming back from it."

"Bombed how?"

I blink, swallow, and feel the sweat gather at the nape of my neck as I glance over his shoulder at the closed door behind him. August must sense my growing need for air, because without taking his eyes off me, he reaches back for the door handle and breaks the seal, popping it open. The rush of AC offers my claustrophobia immediate relief.

"According to industry reviews and the official statement from my director, I had a 'nervous breakdown on stage due to a panic disorder I failed to disclose to my director or fellow cast members before opening night.'" I'd memorized the quote, though every time I think it, the twist in my gut tightens. "Thankfully, my understudy was prepared. They closed the curtain, helped me off stage, and my understudy stepped in and saved the show. There are even rumors her performance will be up for a Tony Award." I don't want to be a poor sport, so I keep my grin in place. "It's hard"—*impossible*—"to come back from a failure like that in my industry. I was labeled a liability overnight and couldn't even get a first audition, much less a paying role for months afterward. I moved back to California because I was out of options and time . . . and money."

That's a lot to process, but I can tell by August's expression that he's trying. "Had that ever happened to you before? The panic attack, I mean?"

Few in my life have bothered to ask such a question; fewer still have been close enough to know the truth. I rub my hands down my bare thighs and grip my knees for something solid to hold on to. I blow out a breath, reliving the moment that triggered the end of my professional acting career. "I had a scare the night before the show opened."

But just as August's shoulders tense, Gabby peeks her head through the open door, and I jump. She immediately apologizes, using both her voice and her hands.

"Sorry, sorry!" She grimaces. "I was so happy to see the Escalade was still here after Portia dropped me off. She says hi, by the way."

It's a tough mental transition, but I do my best to smile as I stand to embrace her. I make sure to pull back all the way before I start to speak again. "We were just finishing up in here."

Gabby repositions herself, her eyes widening as she takes in her brother. "Are you both recording in here? At the same time?"

August stands, which shrinks the already too-small room. "We're working on a Christmas project."

Gabby signs *Christmas*, and I nod and repeat the sign.

"Like the Christmas movies I watch on TV?" she clarifies. "The romance ones?"

Heat warms my cheeks as I avoid eye contact with her brother. Three is definitely a crowd in this booth. "There is some romance in this story, yes."

Her gaze bounces between us.

Gabby has many qualities, but subtlety is not one of them.

She taps her chin and grins. "I think you need some Christmas inspiration for your studio, August."

"No." August both vocalizes *and* aggressively signs the word. "Don't even think about decorating in here."

Gabby's expression says this idea is well past the thinking stage and fully in the add-to-cart stage.

I exhale a weary breath and pick up my purse and water bottle, then give Gabby a gentle arm squeeze and tell her I'll see her at church on Sunday.

She signs that she'll save me a seat, and I answer back without having to think through my reply.

She cheers. "You're doing so good! Isn't she doing good, August? Portia says Sophie's her most dedicated student in class."

August gives his sister a distracted nod as he eyes me, and I can tell he's waiting to walk me to my car so he can ask more about New York. Only I don't think I'm strong enough to handle giving him more, not with how intently he's watching me. Not when New York barely scratches the surface of what happened only a handful of miles from where I stand.

Dana is the only soul I've trusted that particular tale to—or rather, she's the only soul who believes me.

So before August can make a break from his sister to walk me to my car, I tell them I'm running late for work and take the coward's way out.

Voice Memo

Gabby Tate

9 months, 1 week, 3 days after the accident

Today is my ninth Gotcha Day.

I decided not to remind August about it. It's not like it's my birthday or a federal holiday or anything, and I guess I just don't want him to feel bad that he's not Mom.

I woke up thinking about how she always made this day feel special, though. Every year was a little different, but it always started with the same tradition. First, she'd pull me out of school for the day and make me a huge pancake breakfast with fresh blueberries and a candle sticking in the center of the stack. She'd tell me to think of a happy memory from the previous year before I blew it out.

And then while we ate, she'd tell me the same story about the night she asked August his thoughts about becoming a summer host family through a church program that connect orphaned children with forever families. She was worried August might feel slighted since it was his senior year of high school. She knew that hosting a younger child might change some of the plans they made with him.

But as Mom told it, August turned the conversation around completely and asked her what she knew about the child they'd be hosting. She pulled up the email from the program director at church and showed him my picture on her computer—big cheesy grin, no front teeth, frizzy, out-of-control hair.

Mom said August studied the screen for a whole minute without saying a word. And then, when he finally spoke, the first thing he said was, "What's keeping us from being her forever family?"

Mom said that was the moment she stopped praying about being my host family and started praying about being my forever family.

I suppose in a way, August chose me even before my parents did. I've always—

"Gabby? You awake? I have breakfast on the table for you."

Oh, hang on.

Okay, I'm back. That was August.

He made me a stack of blueberry pancakes, and he even remembered the candle. Next year's happy memory won't be hard to come up with.

17

August

Few things cause me to forget myself the way music can. From my earliest memories of sitting at that old upright piano in my parents' garage, to working on a client's album for sixteen hours straight . . . time seems to suspend altogether when I'm composing. And for the first time in years, exercising the muscle memory of creation doesn't feel stiff or forced. It feels natural. Which is why I'm struggling to reorient myself when I stop the recording of my latest attempt at the score for *Mistletoe Matrimony* to find the many texts awaiting me—starting at 12:13 p.m.

The current time: 4:04 p.m.

12:13

Sophie:

> Hey, I just finished up inventory with my sister-in-law, but there's a bit of a vehicle issue. Both Escalades are out for the evening. I'm currently trying to locate the keys for the utility van. If I find them, are you still good with me coming out tonight? I'm hoping we can finish things up.

12:15

Gabby:

School is letting out early today because of the coming storm. I guess it's supposed to get bad. Can you come get me?

12:26

Gabby:

Okay, I'm guessing you're recording or something so I just called Tyler. You good if I go to his house? Yes, his mom will be home with us the whole time. And no, we won't do anything stupid. And yes, I'll be home before dinner.

12:29

Gabby:

Hello?

12:30

Missed call from Gabby.

12:31

Missed call from Gabby.

12:44

Gabby:

This is a perfect example of how nice it would be to get my license. Instead, I'm still at school like a loser waiting to give Tyler an answer on if he can pick me up or not.

12:46

Gabby:

And now it's raining. I'm going with Tyler. Portia said I can stay through dinner.

3:19

Sophie:

> FINALLY found the stupid keys for this van! I'm not sure what's worse—driving the Wine-Calade or this van that looks like it belongs to a seriel killer.

Sophie:

> Just saw the storm alert out your way. Please don't think about climbing onto any rooftops until a certified buddy is there to secure you with a rope. Be there in twenty-ish.

My brain short-circuits at all that I've missed in the last few hours, but I quickly deduce my first priority of business and scramble to video call Gabby. No answer. Instead she fires back an immediate text.

Gabby:

> Sorry, Gabby can't come to the phone right now because you left her to drown outside a locked school building alone. Please try your call again later.

I groan and close my eyes.

> I'm sorry. I was working on a music project and my phone was set to DND.

Gabby:

> And I was trying to get ahold of my only emergency contact in the area . . . and he didn't answer.

This I feel deep in my gut.

She's right to be mad. I'm an idiot for putting my phone on DND when I'm somebody's sole guardian. Such a rookie mistake for being two years in. I make the fix to my phone setting immediately, allowing two contacts the ability to break through my sacred focus mode: Gabby and Sophie.

I stare at the second name for longer than I should, considering the friend zone she put me in weeks ago.

I text my sister again.

> Your brother says he's VERY sorry for missing your texts and calls. He promises to do his best to never let that happen again and hopes you can forgive him?

An entire minute goes by before Gabby responds.

Gabby:

> That depends. Do you promise to keep ALL the Christmas decorations I put up in your studio until your project with Sophie is finished?

I groan again. This time for a very different reason.

I glance around at the "festive surprise" Gabby created in my studio last night after I went to bed. Her little holiday prank consisted of Christmas throw pillows tossed on the sofa, a cotton ball–like substance adorning my shelves and windowsills, and every remaining available surface overwhelmed with miniature fir trees, snow globes, or something plaid and ridiculous. But the worst of it is—

Gabby:

> And that means you'll keep the mistletoe in the sound booth, too.

I grit my teeth. Before I got lost in my music time warp, I'd planned on taking it all down before Sophie arrived this afternoon—starting with the hideous plastic mistletoe sprig my parents used to hang above their bedroom door every holiday season since I was a boy.

I release a heavy sigh.

> Fine. But you will be on clean-up duty as soon as my project is finished.

Gabby:

Gabby the Elf agrees to that.

So I'm forgiven?

Gabby:

If Christ can forgive you, then I guess I can, too.

Despite myself, I smile at her wit.

Gabby:

Also, will you show me the music you've been working on sometime?

I read the sentence over twice and have to swallow against the thickening in my throat. Outside from sharing the same parents, music was once the strongest bond we shared, a tie that kept us connected during the years we lived apart. I would send her early tracks of songs I'd yet to master, and she would provide feedback sure to make me laugh.

It's been a long time since she's asked to hear anything of mine—longer still since I wrote anything new, I suppose—and I want to give that to her. I want to give her so much more than that. Hopefully, after this project, that will be a reality.

Anytime.

Just then, the studio door bursts open with gusto, revealing a windblown, rain-speckled Sophie on the threshold looking like she just walked here from the winery. Anything not nailed down scatters from my desk and cyclones in the center of the studio. Sophie's hair whips in every direction. By the time I pull her inside and shut the door behind her, her thin sweater has slipped off her shoulders, exposing a lace-trimmed tank I can't blink away fast enough.

Without warning, she flips her head upside down and rakes her fingers through the tangled mass of chestnut locks.

"It is *insane* outside," she says from behind the curtain of hair. "Pretty sure I could have brought Phantom with me under our natural disaster clause. I was almost tornadoed to Oz."

"Didn't realize tornado could be used as a verb."

Still upside down, she twists her neck to peek up at me through one eye. "It's a new world, August. Anything can be made into a verb." She flings upright, and I'm momentarily paralyzed by whatever spell she's just cast. My throat feels like it's actively trying to swallow a handful of sand. Seemingly oblivious to her magical powers, Sophie glances out the window in the direction of the house. "Wait—is Gabby home? I hope she's not out in this. The sky was nearly black behind me. I think it's gonna pour soon."

The concern in her voice is both endearing and irritating. Endearing that she'd think of Gabby so quickly after arriving and irritating that I all but forgot I even had a sister.

"She's actually staying at Portia's for dinner. I'll grab her after the storm blows over." It's still easier for me to pretend Portia is the reason for Gabby's request and not a certain boy who can't take his eyes off her whenever she's near.

Sophie laughs. "Ah, so she's hanging out with Tyler tonight."

"I'm told he's present, yes."

She rolls her eyes, which makes me smile.

"That boy is such a sweetheart to her. Do you know that every Tuesday night he buys her a root beer and a bag of peanut M&Ms from the vending machine and has it waiting for her on her seat? Not even you can deny that they're adorable together."

"They're too young is what they are." I cross my arms over my chest. "Adolescent hormones are hardly a case for long-term compatibility."

She frowns. "Well, hello, Mr. Cynical. It sounds like Blake is rubbing off on you."

"Blake who?"

She gives me eyes that call into question my mental acumen.

Oh, right. *Blake.* From the script. "Forgive me if I don't use fictional characters as references in my daily conversations."

She tosses her backpack on the sofa. "You're forgiven." And then she freezes, her eyes scanning the room in slow motion. "Um, why does it look like Christmas threw up in here?"

"Because it did," I say flatly. "Gabby the Elf decided my studio needed an aesthetic change after I went to bed last night. Apparently, she also read the script." I reach for the marked-up paper copy I keep on my desk.

Sophie presses her lips together and picks up a glittery battery-operated candle with the words *Sweater Weather* scrolled across the center in red-and-black plaid. "But where did it all come from?"

I stuff my hands into my jean pockets and shift on my feet. "From our mom's holiday tub in the attic. She loved Christmas."

Immediately, her grin sobers, and I rush in to fill the void as there's nothing quite like killing the mood with dead parents at Christmastime. "It's fine."

"How did you and Gabby spend your last two Christmases?" she asks softly.

"Uh . . ." It's an effort to reroute my thoughts. "The first we spent at home. It was . . . quiet. I tried to make it special, but I'm not sure I succeeded. We were both pretty shell-shocked still." I clear my throat. "The second we spent at Aunt Judy's house."

Sophie picks up an angel figurine from the shelf I built and turns it in her hand. "Does Gabby usually decorate?"

I frown, trying to recall. "I remember bringing the box down last year, but I can't remember if she put anything out."

Sophie makes a contemplative sound. "I wonder if seeing these decorations up is a comfort to her." She touches the tiny gold cross she wears around her neck. "It's fascinating how much sentimentality a tradition or item can hold."

Unbidden, a list of the many holiday traditions my parents kept over the years scrolls through my mind. The candlelight services. The pjs on Christmas Eve. The Christmas story in the morning. The best homemade cinnamon rolls and fresh-squeezed orange juice for breakfast. The round-robin present opening. Dad's intermission for a second pour of coffee. Mom's famous molasses cookie drop-offs to neighbors and friends.

I tug at the back of my neck. "And here I thought she did all this as a prank."

She touches my arm. "Maybe it's a bit of both. Pranking her big brother and a safe space to create some needed nostalgia."

In moments like this, it's hard not to openly stare at Sophie. I never would have made that connection, not in a hundred years. And at the same time, I'm grateful she did. I'm even more grateful that Gabby has Sophie in her life.

The thought rubs against a raw nerve as I watch her handle several more decorations with care. Despite my resolve to be her friend and nothing more since that night on the beach, it has not become easier with time. If anything, time has worked against me. Her commitment to this project and to my sister has only exacerbated the fissure in my chest.

Sophie places a set of silver bells on the table next to the sofa and then begins to make her way to the sound booth. "I guess we should probably get moving if we're going to meet today's quota before we pick up Gabby."

I don't know if her *we* in that sentence is intentional or accidental. Either way, it registers with far more meaning than I should allow.

She's halfway down the short hall when a sudden onslaught of rain beats against the window in the studio. She jumps, hand clutched to her heart.

"Looks like the storm is here."

A loud crack and pop coming from the direction of the neighbor's tree line causes her to twist back a second time. With winds this strong, I know there'll be more branches to follow. I wouldn't be surprised if they litter the entire driveway. We're no strangers to wind damage in these parts. I'm thankful I parked in the garage.

Concern etches Sophie's features. "Are we safe in here with it like this outside? It sounds terrible."

"Yes, those branches snap easily," I assure her. "You won't hear any of it in the booth though. It's too insulated." I made sure to use premium-grade material when I built the studio for this very reason. I also made sure to use the best storm surge protection on the market today for my soundboard. Even still, my fingers twitch to confirm that every cord and knob is in place as she settles herself on the opposite side of the glass.

As soon as I slip on my headphones, I hear her voice. "August?"

I press the two-way talk button. "Yeah?" I lift my eyes from the controls and see her pointing above the mic at the plastic shrub.

"Looks like the booth was visited by Gabby the Elf, too."

Heat climbs my neck. "I noticed that."

"It's pretty clever, considering the title of the script," she says, even though the title is the last thing I'm thinking about with Sophie perched beneath it.

"Also," she continues, "the iPad charger isn't here, and mine is almost dead."

"Oh, right. I used it at the keyboard earlier. I'll grab it."

I pull off my headphones and stride to the far side of the studio where my keyboard sits, then drop to my knees to unplug the charger from the wall. With my arm outstretched and my fingers fumbling for the block, the power suddenly cuts off.

Blind and disoriented, I attempt to stand, forgetting that my two-hundred-pound studio keyboard hovers directly above me. At the hard bang, a choice word slips out, and I rub at the bump forming on the crown of my head. I crawl my way out and am struck by the utter darkness when there's no daylight streaming through the window. The deafening soundtrack of pelting rain against glass is almost as disconcerting as the power outage. I feel for the phone in my pocket, then remember I left it next to the soundboard.

It's not until I'm working to navigate around the shadows that I realize what I don't hear in the mix of rain and wind.

Sophie. Why hasn't she come out?

A cold sensation creeps up my spine as I stumble down the hall, thankful my sister didn't line the floor with my mother's nutcracker collection, and slide my hand down the textured wall until I reach the doorjamb of the soundproof room. I grip the handle and push inside.

The tiny space is void of light; an entirely new level of darkness and disorientation.

"Sophie, you alright?"

When the only response I hear is the sound of rapid, erratic breaths, my pulse accelerates.

"Sophie?" Despite the unexplainable sense of urgency I feel, I soften my voice. "Where are you?"

"August." The strained, choked sound of my name sends a flash of fear through my core.

Something's very wrong. The revelation nearly swallows me whole as I struggle to move through the darkness until I reach the cool metal of the empty recording stool. Did she fall? Did she hit her head? "Talk to me, sweetheart. Where are you?"

"H-h-here," she says through short, sharp pants.

Carefully, I lower to my knees to crawl along the floor. I don't want to hurt her, but I can sense her panic even from a distance. The instant my fingers brush the hem of her long sweater, I'm reaching for her and pulling her limp body into mine.

I rub my palms along her shuddering back.

"You're okay," I whisper in her ear, willing myself to believe it as truth. "You're okay, Sophie. I'm here now, and I'm not going to let you go. Breathe with me." I take in a long slow inhale. She tries to follow, but her struggle for air is gut-wrenching. "You're doing great," I say calmly. "Let's try it again. Good. Nice and slow." Chest to chest, we breathe together. Again and again until I feel some of the rigidity in her body begin to relax.

It's only then that her arms tighten around me. She holds on like I might disappear, and something inside me breaks at the thought. Her breaths are still too shallow to be okay, and I know with unshakable conviction that I need to get her out of this room. Out of this darkness.

I cradle the back of her head as my lips skim her temple. "Do you have your phone on you?"

She shakes her head no. "In . . . my . . . backpack."

It's what I figured. "I'm gonna help you stand, and then we're going to walk down the hall together, okay? Do you remember the candle you found next to the sofa? We'll turn it on."

She nods into my shirt, and I count to three and pull her to her feet, making sure to keep a strong hold on her waist.

She's far from stable, but I'm encouraged when she puts one foot in front of the other. It's progress.

"Here we go." I feel for the sofa and ease her onto it as I fumble for that flameless holiday candle. If it works, I'll tell Gabby she can keep this Christmas decor up for the rest of the year if she wants to. I click the button on the bottom, and the room illuminates with a golden hue.

I've never been so thankful for a candle in all my life.

I pull the piano bench directly in front of Sophie and set the light there. I want to get it as close to her as humanly possible.

Outside, the wind and rain battle for attention, but inside, the only sounds I'm focused on are the slowing exhales of the woman nestled beside me. Panic attacks are not my area of expertise. I don't know what is helpful or harmful in situations like this, but much like the candle I set before her a moment ago, I want to be as close to Sophie as humanly possible.

I open my arms to her in silent invitation, and without speaking a word, she curls into me. I don't know how long we stay huddled together in the stormy dark, or when she finally feels safe enough to drift off to sleep, but I do know that whatever past experience brought Sophie to the panicked state I found her in is far more significant than she's let on.

And I hold her all the closer for it.

18

Sophie

Did I leave the light on in the tasting room?

I'm half a key-turn away from getting out of the February cold and curling up with Pretty Little Liars while binge-eating my feelings on all the food Mom never lets me eat when she's home, when I see the stupid light in my periphery. As if Kiersten getting the stomach flu and cutting our sleepover short wasn't bad enough, now I get to walk across the property in the rainy dark without a coat. Unless I wait until morning? The thought is so tempting I nearly give in. But ultimately, I don't need to give my dad one more reason to think I'm too irresponsible to get my driver's license next week.

I drop my backpack on the porch and march down the path, braced against the frigid wind. The four-digit code on the tasting room door was recently changed, but I have it memorized, so I punch it in quickly. But as soon as I'm inside, heading for the main switch, the hairs on the back of my neck stand at attention.

I hear voices. Multiple. Male.

Get out. Get out. Get out. The words slam into my skull, and I have no intention of ignoring them. I spin for the exit, frantic to get back to my house, lock the door, and dial 9-1-1.

But I never get that chance.

A meaty, gloved hand shoots out from behind me and presses hard against my mouth. I can't scream. I can't breathe. I thrash and fight and hear my captor arguing with someone about what to do with me.

I wasn't part of their plan.

I twist, gaining enough leverage to elbow my attacker in the ribs, hoping the blow will give me a chance to break away, but it only angers him more, and soon my vision spots and my limbs grow heavy and weak.

I'm going to suffocate.

I'm going to die.

The second voice grows closer now. When the brute behind me smashes my cheek onto the cool bar top, I catch a glimpse of the masked man before he pats me down in search of my phone. He won't find it. It's still in my backpack on the front porch.

I'm pulled up by my hair and commanded to walk, keep my head down, keep my mouth shut. If I obey I won't get hurt.

My assailant's monstrous body brushes against my back as we take the stairs to the cellar one at a time. Sickness sloshes in my belly. What are they going to do to me?

His fingers dig under my collarbone like a hook, and even though my mouth is free, I'm too afraid to cry out. Even if I did, who would hear me? My parents are out of town for the weekend, Jasper is away at college, and there are no employees expected till Monday morning.

For a moment, I wonder if I can pull off a maneuver like the kind I've watched in movies, where the lead actress distracts her offender and then dodges his attempts at recapture. But this staircase is steep and narrow, and even if I could make it to the top without him catching me, his accomplice is still looming somewhere above us, waiting.

So I take a different approach.

"P-please," I stammer. "Please let me go. I won't say anything. I swear. You can take whatever you want if you just—"

"Shut up." He squeezes my bones until I wince, but I don't shut up. I can't.

"*Please don't hurt me,*" I try again. "*I'm—*"

"*I said shut up!*" A hot jolt of pain zings through my spine as I fall to my knees in front of the cellar's entrance, panting hard.

The thick redwood door is a recent addition of my father's, as is the security feature on the outside to keep my dad's most prized and valuable possessions from walking out unattended from their locked display cases. The man behind me enters the code without hesitation.

The locks release.

"*Get up.*"

I struggle to engage my feet beneath me, and he pulls my hair until I'm standing. I cry out, and it's then I note the wet warmth between my legs, soaking through my pants.

He still has a hold of my ponytail when he whispers into my ear, "*Scream all you want down here,* Principessa. *Nobody will hear you.*"

He shoves me inside my family's cellar, where I stumble onto shattered glass. The shards slice through the denim covering my knees. But at the sound of the automatic door closing behind me, I spin to find the retreating back of my captor.

"*Wait, please,*" I sob. "*Please don't leave me down here.*"

The tomb seals and locks me in from the outside. And then the power is cut. The security lights flicker off, and soon I'm plunged into a darkness so thick it seems to seep into my soul.

I scream for help until my voice is raw. And then until I have no voice left at all.

Someone is singing. No, someone is humming.

A smooth, melodic baritone taps on the walls of my subconscious, coaxing my eyes open as I work to make sense of the world around me. My head is propped on a throw pillow, my legs curled into the back cushions of a couch, and my spine is being played like piano keys by fingers that don't belong to me.

Shadows flicker on the ceiling from a light source I can't see from my current angle. And it's then I remember. The storm. The power outage. The panic.

August.

Groggily, I sit upright, my head throbbing something fierce at the sudden change in orientation.

"Easy there," August says, steadying my arm.

I twist on the cushion until my feet are firmly planted on the floor, hoping to simultaneously ground myself and delay the mortification sure to come. It's already seeping in. I slap my hands over my face and groan.

"I'm so embarrassed. You must think I'm a total freak—and maybe that's exactly what I am. But I'm also horrified that you—"

"*Sophie.*" The pained way he says my name cuts off my words. I don't want to look at him, but it's clear that's exactly what he wants from me when he reaches for my hand and gives it a gentle squeeze. "You're safe. That's the only thing I care about. The only thing that matters."

Time slows again as his words burrow into my heart, and even though it's difficult to look him in the eye, I do.

"I owe you an explanation," I say.

"No, sweetheart," he counters as he runs his thumb along the back of my hand. "You don't owe me anything you're not ready to give."

The threat of overexposure is a current that runs through each of my limbs, my core, my heart. And I'm certain that if August were anyone else, I would take the out he's so graciously offered and push this decade-old trauma down deep where it belongs.

Until the next time it surfaces, that is. This thought is immediately followed by another. *Haven't my captors stolen enough from me?*

The answer resounds inside my head as I study the patience etched in August's expression. I drop my gaze to our joined hands, drawing from his strength as I open my mouth to tell a story that sounds like fiction but is as real as the scar tissue on my knees.

On the tail end of a long exhale, I do my best to summarize the nightmare I've failed to outrun for the last ten years.

"When I was sixteen, I was in the wrong place at the wrong time. . . ." I begin.

August stills beside me as I describe the details of that fateful night. The light in the tasting room. The masked men. The broken glass. The dark cellar. The locked door.

I don't know how long it takes me to tell it, but when I finally come up for air, August's voice sounds almost robotic when he asks, "How long were you down there?"

"Close to forty hours. From Saturday night to Monday morning, when Maria, our cleaner, found me. I was . . . disoriented and pretty dehydrated." I think of the blue Gatorade Maria retrieved from her son's sports bag in her trunk. How she forced me to drink while I tried to recount the details of what happened.

A muscle in his jaw jumps. "And where were your parents?"

"Laguna Beach. They always take their anniversary trip in February since business is slow."

When he says nothing to this, I tell him about the open investigation with the sheriff's department, and about the statements I gave and the suspects they interrogated, and how ultimately, nothing ever came of any of it.

Except, of course, my crippling anxiety of being trapped in the dark, and my father's belief that I staged the whole thing for the sake of attention. *"As embarrassing as it is to admit, Detective, I've had my doubts regarding the accuracy of Sophie's story for some time now. She's always been a bit of an attention seeker, a drama queen. You know the type."*

It's *this*, the part of the story that haunts me the most, that I can't ever seem to admit out loud. Not to August; not even to Dana.

Still, I'm not too blind to see how if not for overhearing that phone call six months into the investigation, I never would have found the courage to pursue the arts and apply to a college three thousand miles away from home. I never would have learned the power of the stage, or how to become someone else anytime I needed to escape myself.

I side-eye August on the sofa, wondering what must be going

through his brain as I watch the steady tick of his jaw. But the longer he waits to speak, the more I want to fill the silence.

"I'm okay now. I mean, it's been ten years. And honestly, it could have been so much worse—"

"Don't do that. *Please*, don't minimize this." He pushes forward on the sofa, unclasping our hands to grip his head. "You are not okay; none of this is okay." When he unclenches his hair, all I want to do is smooth it back into place. "I had an hour to prepare for whatever scenario you might share with me once you woke. I promised myself that whatever it was, I'd be ready to hear it, to support you through it." He twists his neck in my direction, eyes trained on my face. "But what I can't understand is why nobody checked on you? You were *sixteen*—why did your parents think it was okay for you to not answer your phone for a day and a half? Dehydration is no joke!"

"You're . . . angry." It's a curious, almost hesitant observation.

"Of course *I'm angry*." He shakes his head, stands, begins to pace. "I've never heard of an investigation being called off when there's a minor involved! You were attacked, Sophie. There had to be evidence. Fingerprints? Tire tracks? Surveillance footage? *Something!* How would they know the door codes unless it was an inside job?" He throws up his hands. "It doesn't make sense."

"I know," I say, feeling myself shrink back with every doubt he brings to the surface. "They wore gloves, and my parents didn't have security cameras at that point."

"What about the staff?" he presses. "Were they all called in for questioning?"

I nod. "They were released."

"And the weird accent you heard? Did you tell them about that? Could you identify it if you heard it again? Did they even have you talk with a—"

"I told the police everything I could remember, August," I cut in with a calm I don't feel. "Everything I told you."

"And when they failed to do their job, your parents didn't push back?"

"The department said they ran out of resources."

"They . . . they *ran out of resources*?" August repeats in a lethal tone. "How could any parent be satisfied with that?"

"Because *they didn't believe me*! That's how!"

At my outburst, my eyes round in horror. If there is anything more mortifying than admitting you weren't loved or protected by the two people who should have loved and protected you most . . . I don't know it. The confession sets my cheeks ablaze, the heat searing into my palms as I cover my face.

"It's fine," I lie, hoping to ward him off.

Instead, it brings him close. So close I don't have to part my fingers to know he's crouched directly in front of me.

"It's not fine," he says with a tenderness that pricks my eyes. "I can't even imagine how that must have hurt you."

I say nothing.

"Sophie. Look at me, *please*."

It takes everything in me to grant his request.

"I believe you," he says. "I. Believe. You."

Three words that simultaneously reopen and heal a wound he didn't cause.

My bottom lip begins to quiver. "I overheard my father on the phone with the detective. He thinks I fabricated the story and staged the evidence—everything from the clipped circuit board to the broken glass in the cellar to locking myself inside only a few hours before our housekeeper found me. The only thing that could have proved how long I was in there was my dehydration, but I never went to the doctor. Maria, like most of our staff, was afraid of my father and the ramifications of crossing him. She insisted I eat, drink, and shower before my parents came home. By the time they saw me, their doubts about my story were already starting to creep in. My father turned down the option of funding a private investigation."

Still balancing on the balls of his feet in front of me, he cups my face in his hands. "I'm so, so sorry."

Tears slip from the corners of my eyes. "You did nothing wrong."

"Neither did you."

The hot coil in my chest begins to unravel as his eyes search my face, and I know without a fraction of doubt that he was right before. That I'm safe here. That I'm safe with him.

It's been more than ten years since the nights I spent trapped in that cellar. Ten years since I hummed Gigi's favorite hymn in the darkness to block out the fear. Ten years since I began to question if I would ever experience the kind of affection August has shown me over the last few months.

He's only a fraction of a breath away, but in this moment it feels too far.

When I flatten my palm to his chest, I don't use it to push him away like I did on the beach. This time, I use it to grip the fabric of his shirt front and pull him close. So close that when I brush my lips against his, I feel his body tense and his breath pause. For all of three seconds, the kiss I've imagined a hundred times over is dreamlike in its execution. Warm and soft and achingly sweet . . .

And then it's over.

August loses his center of gravity and topples to the side, catching himself with one hand as his backside hits the floor.

His face looks almost as stunned as mine feels. Did I really just kiss him? And on the same night I spilled my guts about my childhood trauma? Wow, how beautifully romantic of me. But before I can utter a word of apology, he makes a miraculous recovery, wasting no time in reclaiming my mouth.

Within two heartbeats, it's clear this kiss is not some pity-driven momentary lapse in judgment. Rather, August kisses me the way I imagine he'd compose an original song. Like he's searching for each right note in a melody only he can hear. I've performed on dozens of stages in my short career as an actress, but no music has ever caused my lips to hum like this. Or my heart to sing.

We may not know what comes next for us, but I do know I never want this song to end.

19

August

The only problem with kissing Sophie Wilder is that I never want to *stop* kissing her.

Even after the storm dies down and it's safe enough to trek to the house via the garage, returning to those lips remains a top priority.

It ranks right below locating my dad's old generator.

As soon as I plug in the extension cord to power the kitchen lights and the refrigerator, Sophie does a little dance that does nothing to decrease my desire to kiss her senseless for a second time. But after glimpsing the fallen tree limbs carpeting the driveway from the front windows, my mind pulls in an entirely new direction. If the roads are even half as bad as the driveway, it's likely I'll be exercising a hefty dose of self-control for the remainder of our evening together.

Starting now.

I reach for the utility flashlight I brought in from the garage. "You okay if I take a look around outside?"

She looks from the darkened back patio doors to me. "Sure you

236

don't want to take a buddy with you?" She winks. "Might be a good time to put our system to the test."

I step toward her, zeroing in on a pout I hope to get better acquainted with. "I'd much rather my buddy stay inside where its safe." I touch her chin before I turn for the front door.

"Then I'll make us a snack dinner for when you're back."

I twist back. "A what dinner?"

"Fancier folks might call it a charcuterie board, but Dana and I always called them snack dinners when we lived together in New York." She shrugs. "It's easier to say and less pretentious."

I make a mental note to ask her more about New York when I return. Truth is, there's a lot I'd like to discuss with her when I return. And by the way she eyes me, she knows it, too.

"Call it whatever you want," I tease, "as long as *snack* doesn't indicate portion size. Because if that's the case, you should know I'm all-you-can-eat-buffet-level hungry."

"Don't worry." She laughs and turns toward the pantry door. "I'll take good care of you."

I tell myself it's just an expression, that she doesn't mean it literally. But just the possibility of having Sophie in my corner long after our audio projects conclude is a hope that feels too good to be true.

And yet I want it to be true.

I want her to be mine.

By the time I finish my patrol around the property and check in on Norma, our widowed neighbor to the right, Sophie is waiting for me at the table.

There's a battery-operated candle in the center, as well as a cutting board topped with an assortment of fruit, cheese, cold meats, pickles, trail mix, veggies, and several varieties of crackers from the pantry. The presentation alone is a ten out of ten. Yet another way she's gifted.

I also note the presence of two familiar bottles of wine on the table from a local vineyard that still owes me a VIP tour.

"I thought tonight would be as good a time as any to explain red and white wine pairings to you." She points to the Snow White and Little Mermaid mini juice glasses on the table. "Also, I couldn't find your stemware, so I improvised. Those are both yours, by the way. Ariel for the cabernet and Snow White for the Chardonnay."

"Wow, I haven't seen those for a while." I laugh as a memory comes flooding in. "We went to Disneyland for Gabby's eighth birthday, and she begged our mom to buy her the entire Disney princess plastic juice cup collection from the gift shop. The crazy girl refused to drink out of anything else for an entire year."

"Well, they're the perfect size for a tasting."

"Where's yours?" I ask, lifting Ariel's contents to my nose for closer inspection. "I know for a fact we have at least six others stored in the same place you found these."

"I'm good. Besides, I still have to drive back."

"About that." I set Ariel down. "I can't let you drive home tonight. Half the county is off grid, and there are tree limbs everywhere. It's not safe."

She stares at me unblinking with an expression I'm not sure how to interpret. "So you're suggesting *what* exactly?"

"That you stay here with me."

"Uh . . . I . . ." At her rounding eyes, I hear how suggestive that must have sounded to her.

"Oh, no. That's not what I . . ." I hold up a hand. "I already called Gabby, and she's offered you her bed, along with the use of whatever things you might need. She'll be staying in Portia's guest room for the night."

"Okay, thank you," Sophie says with a slight nod of her head. "There's been a lot to process in the course of a single evening."

I reach out to clasp her hand. "Maybe we can process it together over this stellar snack dinner and Disney princess wine tasting?"

Her ready smile is the only answer I need.

For the most part, our conversation stays light while Sophie tries—and fails—to refine my palate in a single evening. Although

I finish my cartoon tumbler of the red wine, which paired nicely with the meat, cheese, and dark chocolate, I cannot stand the white. Sophie might be able to taste the apple, vanilla, and hints of butterscotch hidden away in this prize-winning bottle. But to me it tastes the way Gabby's nail polish remover smells.

Sophie scooches Snow White toward herself and then takes a sip. "I'll keep working on you."

"I hope you will," I say, noting the perfect segue into our next conversation and my sudden onslaught of nerves. As soon as her eyes meet mine, I begin. "I can count on three fingers the positive things that have come out of the two hardest years of my life." I pause before I raise the first finger. "Gabby's survival." I unfold the next. "Chip bribing me to let a stranger record a demo in my studio." And then a third finger. "And this afternoon. With you."

Her blush is soft, yet immediate. "Our kiss?"

"That was so much more than a kiss for me, Sophie." It's perhaps the most transparent thing I've admitted to her so far, but it's true.

"I feel the same." She reaches for my hand. "Which is why I was afraid to let it happen. I knew we wouldn't be able to go backward once we went there." She tilts her head to the side, examining me as I give her the space to say whatever she needs to, even though a low-level panic begins to brew somewhere behind my ribcage. "I never planned to stay in California, August. I may not know what's next for me career-wise, but the one thing I was adamant about was leaving as soon as I had enough money to pay my debts and start over somewhere new. Somewhere with fewer bad memories and unsupportive family members." She stares at her plate of half-eaten fruit and cheese. "After that night on the beach with you, I applied for several teaching and directing positions around the country that would utilize my theater degree and give me a way out of this state, but every time an interview has popped up in my inbox . . . I've declined it." She traces the scar on my upturned palm. "Because you're not there."

"So stay." I close my hand around hers, desperate to hold on to her for as long as I possibly can. "I know it's selfish of me to ask that of you, especially considering that the sacrifice isn't mutual."

"It's not selfish," she counters. "I get it. Your whole world is here. You have your sister and Chip and this beautiful home you grew up in. Not to mention your studio and a wonderfully supportive church."

I don't correct her on the last one. "You have many of those same things, too, now. And more."

Gabby has told me how Sophie goes early to the ASL classes every week to meet with her and Portia. And even though I'd like to drop-kick Sophie's father into next week after the trauma she endured as a teenager, I want to believe that not all the Wilders are bad apples. How could they be when Sophie is full of such goodness and love?

Then again, if someone were to examine the character of my parents and sister, there's no chance mine would measure up. In the Tate family, there is only one bad apple.

Her sweet contemplation pulls me back to the here and now.

"I know neither of us can predict the future. I know that better than most," I admit. "But I think we owe it to whatever this is between us to give it a real chance, to give *us* a real chance." I bring her hand to my mouth, kiss the back of it. "Maybe it's time we created some good memories for you in California . . . if you're willing to try?"

Her smile wobbles as she says, "I'm willing as long as you're in them."

I cup my hand to the back of her neck, bridge the gap across the table, and kiss her. Again and again and again.

One new memory at a time.

20

Sophie

The power came on at 5:41 a.m. this morning. I only know because of the multicolored string lights lining the perimeter of Gabby's room. The assault on my eyes felt like I'd been tossed into a giant bag of glow-in-the-dark party sticks. By the time I stumbled from her bed and stepped around several piles of clothes, shoes, makeup, and books to find the correct outlet, I gave up hope of going back to sleep.

Instead, I set my sights on something equally gratifying: breakfast.

I take a few minutes for a mini refresh in the bathroom across the hall, deciding to remain in the strawberry sleep pants I borrowed from Gabby. It's too early for yesterday's denim. As my fingers make quick work of braiding my hair, I replay the late-night conversations I had with August on the sofa while sharing the last of the chocolate I'd found.

Tiptoeing past August's door and into the Tates' adorable farm-style kitchen, I make myself at home, pulling out a cold carton of eggs from the fridge as well as an impressive selection of fresh veggies—spinach, onion, bell peppers, broccoli, asparagus. I'd never guess a bachelor and a teenager lived here.

I sigh with relief when I find a container of feta in the side drawer of the fridge. No decent egg scramble is complete without it.

The Tates' pantry, like their cupboards and cabinets, is well stocked and organized. I can't help but think it's likely due to their mother's touch. I wonder how many mornings she stood where I am now, cooking for the same family members I've come to care so much for over the past few months.

I've just begun sautéing the veggies when a throat clears to my right. I glance at the pass-through that separates the dining area from the kitchen to find August. Clad in a pair of navy jogging pants and a white tee, he props a shoulder against the wall and drags his sleepy gaze from my bare feet to my braided hair.

"Guess this answers my question," August says in a gravelly voice I'll encourage him to reproduce when he reads as *Blake* later. Audiobook fans everywhere will thank me.

Despite his disarming charm, I nod. "Oh yes, the power came back on early this morning."

"No," he says, pushing off the wall and stalking toward me. "My question was more along the lines of you still being here when I woke up."

I blush as he slips his arms around me from behind and plants a soft kiss at my temple. "Good morning, Sophie."

My entire body short-circuits at his nearness, forcing my eyelids to shutter closed only to remember the gas stove I'm cooking on a second later.

I nudge him back with my elbow. "You're a fire hazard."

"Mmm." He nuzzles his stubbly chin into the crook of my neck, and I squirm and giggle and make a halfhearted attempt at escape. "I can handle that."

And it's somewhere between this playfulness and the real conversations we shared last night that I realize I've never known this.

Onstage crushes, sure. Short-term relationships with surface-level expectations and commitments? Also, yes. But this? Never. The magnitude of all that's taken place over the last twenty-four hours registers high on the scale of unbelievable. And yet, the longer August holds me in his arms, the more comfortable and real the idea of us becomes.

"Whatever you have going on in that pan smells incredible." His voice is a low rumble against my ear. "How can I help?"

It takes a moment for my brain to switch from conserve power mode to full functional use again.

"Coffee?" I suggest. "I'd planned on making some before you woke up, but that high-tech machine is not my speed."

He chuckles. "It's easier than it looks. Promise."

"Says the guy with three advanced-level sound engineering textbooks on his desk."

He side-eyes me as he opens a cupboard for the espresso beans. "Those are really fascinating reads."

"O-k-a-y, sure," I say, thinking of the fantasy reads I have on my nightstand at the pool house.

While August fiddles with his fancy machine, I toast two sourdough English muffins and finish up the scramble. I've just set our plates on the table, along with butter and raspberry jam, when I hear my phone alerting me to an incoming video call.

I quickly grab it off the counter, prepared to shoot Dana a text to say I'll call her later this afternoon as I have a lot to fill her in on. Only it's not Dana. It's Gabby.

August hands me my cup of decaf just as I answer his sister's call.

"Hey, Gabs," I say to the screen. "Oh, and hello Tyler."

The two teenagers press in together and wave. They're outside somewhere—a yard? A driveway?

August pops his head over my shoulder, and I don't miss the way Gabby's smiling eyes ping-pong between us. "So, let me get this straight," he says in a teasing tone. "I text to say good morning and ask when you want a ride home, and you respond by video calling Sophie? How does that work?"

Tyler chuckles at this, and I wonder if he's reading the live transcript on the screen or lipreading. It's hard to tell.

Gabby swivels the phone to herself, and I can't quite tell if she's wearing her aids or not. "Sophie answers every time I call her." Gabby smirks. "And she's way prettier on camera."

"Can't argue with that." Without warning, he leans in and plants a kiss on my cheek.

And when he does, Gabby comes undone.

"*Wait*, are you serious right now?" She squeals and jumps. "Are you guys together? Like *together*, together?"

I eye August like, *Did you really just do that?* And also like, *You have no clue what you're in for now.*

"Well, at the moment we're together trying to enjoy a peaceful breakfast—"

"It was the mistletoe I put in the booth, wasn't it?" She jumps again, and it's all I can do to keep my lips from turning up. She'll be picking out bridesmaid dresses in no time.

Is that where this is going?

"No," August says pointedly. "It was not the mistletoe."

But Gabby is too busy holding a side conversation offscreen to pay attention to her brother.

"Gabby," August says. When she doesn't answer, he tries again. "*Gabby.*"

With her profile still turned to the camera, it's clear she's concentrating on something—or *someone*. It's also clear she's not wearing her aids. She nods and gives a thumbs-up.

She turns her lively expression back to us. "Are you cool if I stay a bit and help Tyler clear some of the branches from his neighbor's driveway? The roads are still a mess here—there's even a house across the street that had a tree crush their back fence." Gabby flings the camera to show Tyler walking to the house next door wearing work gloves with a leaf blower strapped to his back.

One thing's for sure, there is no way August can deny the kindness Gabby's boyfriend possesses. They are well matched.

But when I glance up at August, I don't find the same easy demeanor as before. "Where are your aids, Gabs?"

Gabby looks momentarily stricken. "Inside."

"Inside where?" he presses.

"My . . . backpack. I can't wear them around all this clean-up noise. And I haven't missed anything you've said, right? This new transcript app works great."

I don't miss the disappointment in his voice when he answers with "I'll pick you up around noon."

She nods, but her smile is half-mast. "Will you still be there, Sophie?"

"Yes," I say. "We have a full day of recording to finish in the studio. I'll come with August."

"Okay, see ya. Bye!"

As we end the call and move to sit at the table, August is subdued. And even though he compliments my scramble and tells me his plan to clear his neighbor's driveway before we start our recording session today, his mind is somewhere else entirely.

I set down my fork and watch him. "You're upset."

"Her aids aren't in her backpack," he says without preamble.

It takes me a second to catch on. "Then where are they?"

"Probably in the same place she's been hiding them every time she plans to be away from home—from me, specifically. In the bottom drawer of her bathroom vanity." He blows out a long breath. "That was the first time I've asked her about it directly."

"Why do you think she'd lie to you?"

"Why does anybody lie?" he asks, staring off momentarily. "Because they're more afraid to face the truth than the consequences of being caught."

I'm about to comment on this when my phone vibrates between us on the table.

Natalie.

I silence it, not wanting to cut this conversation short with August when I'm certain she's only calling to confirm she got my message last night and fed Phantom this morning.

When she immediately calls back, August stands and clears our plates. "Go ahead and take that. I'm gonna head next door. Feel free to come by afterward. Norma loves company."

"Sure," I say. "I'll see you in a minute."

The instant he leaves through the garage door, I answer Natalie's call.

"Good morning, Nat—"

"Did you take the utility van to Petaluma last night?"

"What?" I'm startled by her abrupt tone.

"The white utility van Jasper keeps locked in the single car garage."

"Um, yes. The Escalades were both out on tour drop-offs when I needed to leave for the studio, so I—"

"He's on his way there."

"Where?" I ask as icy fingers walk my spine.

"To wherever you parked the van. He went to use it this morning, and when it wasn't there, he tracked it. Where did you even find the keys?"

On rubbery legs, I move across the living room to the front door. "They were inside the van—tucked into the visor." I spent a good thirty minutes searching the garage and the house before recalling a random memory of Jasper before he left for college in a shiny new Corvette. He'd popped his visor and managed to shoot his keyring directly onto his pointer finger.

"I don't understand why he's coming," I say. "I can drive it back as soon as the roads clear up. Most of them aren't even passable yet. The storm was brutal last night."

I step out onto the front porch, shielding my eyes from the sun as I spot the van in question across the street. I'd parked under a tree, not wanting to take up August's entire driveway. But the closer I get to it, the more my dread solidifies. Especially when I see the fallen branches. I blink at them in disbelief.

"He won't give up," Natalie says a bit breathlessly. "Here's what you're going to do. When he gets there, just hand him the keys and tell him you didn't know the van was off-limits. Tell him you thought it was a part of the fleet, and it won't happen again. *Do not argue with him, just—*"

"Um . . . Natalie?" I clutch the phone to my ear and stare incredulously at the giant dent in the van's roof and the way the side wall looks as if it's been beaten by the world's largest baseball bat. On repeat. At eighty miles an hour. "The van is . . . it's damaged. Dented from the storm."

My sister-in-law goes quiet. "How bad is it?"

As I walk around to the back, any optimism I hold for its repair plummets. The back doors are warped to the point they won't fully open or latch closed. "Bad. Possibly even totaled."

I hear her take a deep breath. "Tell Jasper you called me and that I'm already working on an insurance claim. Don't ask questions, and don't—"

But her words are drowned out by the distorted sound of a loud engine coming up behind me on the side of the road. The sun's glare on the front windshield of the shiny silver Mercedes SUV is too intense to see the driver, but the man who thrusts open the passenger door is, without a doubt, my brother.

"He's here," I whisper into the phone receiver before I end the call.

When he stalks toward me, there's a gleam in his eye that pulls at every childhood insecurity. Of all things for me to be wearing, these strawberry-patterned pajama pants are certainly not adding to my confidence. I throw a glance in the direction of Norma's driveway, but I don't see August anywhere. A part of me is relieved he won't be a witness to this, while another part—the fearful part—wants to scream his name. Especially when Jasper circles the van with the stealth of a predator.

"I just saw the damage a few minutes ago. I'm so sorry this happened." I try to remember what Natalie told me to say, but the words are frozen in an unreachable capsule. "If I'd known the storm was going to be this bad, I'd have—"

"You would have what?" he prompts. "You wouldn't have stolen the van parked in my locked garage?" His gaze chills me through as he pulls out his phone and holds it in one hand. "You realize that

247

with a single phone call to the police I could have you arrested for grand theft auto on the spot. Due to its value, that would be a felony and a minimum five years in jail."

"A *felony*?" I all but choke. "I'm not a criminal, Jasper. I'm your sister."

He steps in close, his expensive cologne churning my stomach as his voice dips low. "I knew it was a mistake to listen to Mom's bleeding heart and let you come back when you've never been anything but a drain on this family." He points to the dented van. "How exactly are you planning to fix this?"

Though his words slice deep, I refuse to give him the cowardly reaction he desires from me. "I just hung up with Natalie. She's confident she can sort this all out with insurance."

"No." His eyes darken as he takes my measure. "Insurance won't be paying a dime toward the repairs for this vehicle. You will be."

Confused, I look from the van back to him, calculating the possible deductible. It couldn't be more than a thousand dollars, right? "But if it's totaled—"

"Then it will come out of your trust payout." He studies the van. "Between the customizations and inflation markups, you should plan on roughly six figures."

My jaw slacks at the idea of handing over the majority of the payout to my wealthy brother. "But I can't afford that."

His patronizing expression twists into a dare. "Would you rather I send you packing and deny you a payout altogether? Because that can be arranged. It's your choice."

I've tiptoed around my brother's entitlement for years, scared to speak my mind, scared of what he'd tell my parents, scared of the grudges he'd hold or the repercussions he'd set in motion. But staying scared has never gotten me anywhere.

I ball my fists at my side.

"Why do you hate me so much?" The question rips from my throat with such force my vision blurs.

He stares at me without any trace of emotion until I see him peer beyond me. In a matter of two seconds, his countenance morphs into the Jasper I've only observed from a distance. And in one more second, I understand why.

"Sophie?"

I feel August's comforting hand on my shoulder before he angles his body between me and my brother.

"Is there a problem here?" August asks in a tone I've never heard him use.

"None at all." My brother's ability to switch moods is impressive, I'll give him that. He sticks out his hand to my boyfriend, and after a beat of hesitation, August accepts it. "I'm Jasper. Sophie's brother. And you must be the award-winning August Tate I've read so much about."

Acid rises in my throat. He's read about him—how? I've never used his full name, much less the address of the studio. *Tracked*, I think. Natalie had used the word *tracked* when she called.

"I've looked you up," Jasper says, hands in his pockets, smile on his face. "You've worked with some impressive artists."

August's stony expression is immovable. "What brings you out today?" But with a single twist of his head, he answers his own question. I feel him tense the moment he sees the extensive damage.

"Nothing to concern yourself with. Just a misunderstanding," my brother says with an easy smile. "I'll take those keys and leave you to your day, Sophie."

The level of crazy I feel—from one to ten—is an eleven. I've never been able to understand how he can keep up the front of being a likable, decent human being when I know him as anything but.

I pull the keys from my pocket and hand them over.

Jasper tips his head and moves to the driver's side door. The metal-on-metal screech it makes sends an involuntary shiver through my torso. "Come by the winery anytime, August. I'll make sure you get the VIP treatment."

August nods as my brother closes the door and starts up the engine. His hold on me tightens incrementally.

It's not until Jasper pulls away from the curb, followed closely by the large Mercedes, that the face of the driver comes into focus.

Clinton. The pretentious stockbroker from the tasting room.

He has the audacity to wink at me before driving away.

The instant they are out of sight, August wraps his arms around me in a hug that seems to embrace every horrible truth. He kisses the top of my head, my temple. "Are you okay?"

I nod into his chest. "I am now."

"Norma baked me cookies as a thank you for blowing off her driveway. I didn't see the Mercedes SUV until I came back out."

I want to tell him it's okay. But it's not. There is nothing okay about my brother.

"Don't let him in your head," August says firmly, pulling back enough to look me in the eyes.

"What do you mean?"

"I know his type of manipulation."

Curiosity burdens my brow. "How?"

"I knew someone just like him. My ex-boss and girlfriend of nearly two years in LA." His lips pull into something like a grimace. "Vanessa. She was a real piece of work. At first, I didn't see it. Or maybe I just didn't want to see it, but eventually, her narcissism became too obvious to ignore. I regret not walking away sooner." He pulls me close again, and it feels as if he needs me as much as I need him in this moment. "I regret a lot of things about that time."

We stay that way for several minutes, hugging in a contented, comforting silence. There will be plenty of time for me to ask more about Vanessa, just like there will be plenty of time for him to ask more about my brother. But for now, I have more pressing issues to address.

"After this, my transportation privileges will be over," I say with certainty. "Which means I'll need to find another way to get here." I ponder the little savings I've been able to put away after paying Dana back what I owed her for past rent and incidentals. And then I try not to think about what I will owe my brother if the van is totaled. If the majority of my trust payout is wiped, then my dependence on my audio contract has drastically increased.

"You can use my car."

"What? No." Immediately, I break our embrace. "That's not happening."

"Yes, it is. I have my dad's Bronco in the garage. It just had a tune-up. Your weekly commute is ten times what mine is."

"What about when Gabby drives? I know she loves that Bronco. She's mentioned it to me several times. Isn't she going to be learning soon?" I'd wondered this before, as Gabby is technically six months past the legal driving age in the state of California.

But August gives a single shake of his head. "It's not an option."

I want to ask him why not, but this is neither the time nor place for this conversation. Despite the start of a new relationship, the aftermath of a storm, a little sister who is hiding her hearing aids, and a bully brother who just threatened my entire financial future, we still have an audiobook to finish the raw recording of by the end of the week. From there, August will still have all the sound effects and original intros and outros to add and polish.

I take his hand and point us in the direction of the studio. I need to get my head in the game. I also need to put this conversation about my future transportation to rest. "I'll figure out a plan later."

He tugs me to a stop outside his studio door. "Sophie, I want you to take my car for however long you need it. Last night you agreed to adjust your future plans for my sake, so please, allow me this."

I glance up at him, remembering the first day we met on this little stoop outside his studio, never knowing all that would come. How can I deny him anything when he's looking at me like that? So I don't deny him; I simply rise up on my toes and accept his generosity.

Voice Memo

Gabby Tate

12 months, 1 day after the accident

August went surfing without me again.

I know it's probably not fair of me to be so angry about this, but I am angry. First of all, August knows how much I miss surfing, and second of all, the doctor never said I shouldn't surf, he just said it might not be the best thing for me considering my ears. It's the same reason he wants me to wait on my driver's permit. But you know what? I'm tired of considering my ears. Sometimes it feels like my ears are the only thing anybody wants to consider about me anymore. Except for Tyler.

How is it my deaf friend is the one person in my life who treats me like there's nothing wrong with me?

Okay, fine. None of this is the real reason I'm so angry with August.

The online grief therapist Aunt Judy set me up with suggested I try to talk to my brother again about the events I remember about the accident, and since yesterday was the one-year anniversary of their deaths, I figured a little hope might do us both some good. But every time I even hint at what happened to me after the crash, August finds a way to change the subject. He must think I'm too dumb to notice when he does this, but I notice a whole lot more than he realizes. Tyler says observation can be a superpower. I think he's right.

Finally, I straight up asked August why he always changes the subject whenever I talk about the day of the accident. And you know what he said? He said it's because he doesn't want to encourage my belief in something that never happened. Something he calls "a figment of my imagination."

I was so furious I went to bed without dinner.

21

August

> I'm hoping you went to bed hours ago like a sane person, but I wanted you to be the first to know that the mastered copy of *Mistletoe Matrimony* has officially been sent off to Chip.

Sophie:

> Congratulations!!!

> To you, too. Let's hope it pays off in every way possible.

Sophie:

> It will! I've been praying it does something incredible for us both. I mean, think how excited Chip was after he heard the sample of you reading as Blake!

> Don't remind me. If he calls me August the Narrator one more time . . .

Sophie:

😋Well, he's right to think it's going to do well. You did a fantastic job!

Learned from the best.

Sophie:

🙂So . . . do I finally get to hear the score you composed?

Depends.

Sophie:

On what?

If you wanna play hookie with me in the morning. Figure we could both use a day off.

Sophie:

Do I get to know where this celebratory hookie morning is taking place? A girl needs to know how to dress for such an occasion.

Wear your swimsuit under something warm. I should have everything else you'll need.

Sophie:

My swimsuit? It's October!

You'll be fine, I promise. Can you be ready by 5? We need to get an early start. I'll pick you up.

Sophie:

As in 4.5 hours from now?

Affirmative. Sweet dreams.

Sophie:

They will be. 🤍

I pick Sophie up in my dad's Bronco right on time, and she's both ready and waiting as soon as I pull up to the winery. It's the second time I've been here that I haven't made it past the driveway. For scorekeeping purposes, I'm now zero for two on that VIP tour Sophie promised.

"I adore the retro interior of this Bronco—it's super cool. I can see why you and Gabby love it so much." She sweeps a hand across the dashboard. "I bet you have a lot of great memories in here."

"I do." My headlights slash through the early morning darkness. "I was a freshman in high school when he made a trade for it. He built a deck for a guy at his church. He always wanted a vehicle with a rack to make the surfboards easier to transport."

She clasps her hands at her chest and does a little hop in her seat. "Please tell me surfing is the reason behind your wet suit and the boards strapped to the roof?"

I flash her a grin as I pull onto the deserted highway. "Figured it was time I took my girlfriend out for her first lesson."

"Yes!" She pumps her fists in the air. "I was hoping that was your plan. I'm also hoping we can enjoy the drive while listening to a newly composed soundtrack. Hint hint." She wiggles her eyebrows. "Let's hear it. You promised me."

"Unfortunately, my dad never installed a sound system, so I have nothing to play it on in here."

She eyes me suspiciously. "Does that mean you have the file on your phone?"

I wait a beat before answering. "Affirmative."

She immediately reaches for the bag at her feet and plucks out her earbuds. "I've come prepared."

With some reluctance, I hand her my phone and give her the passcode, and then walk her through how to find the audio file. In seconds, Sophie's earphones are connected.

She taps Play and almost immediately pulls one earbud out. "*This.*

This is the song you were humming when I woke up after my . . ." She swallows. "After the power went out in the studio."

Now it's my turn to be surprised. "You remember that?"

She nods. "I do. I loved it then, and I love it even more now with all the instruments you've added. It's a perfect culmination of the storyline, too. A little angsty, a little cutesy, a little Christmas-y, and definitely romantic. It's perfect for the book."

"Thank you," I say, genuinely overcome by her affirming response. "I rewrote the entire melody line in my head that day while you slept in my arms."

She plugs her earbuds in again and starts it over from the top. The song itself is only a minute and forty-two seconds, but Sophie plays it on repeat for the remainder of the drive to the beach. And I can't help but fall all the harder for her because of it.

When I finally pull up to the curb of Doran Beach—a spectacular spot for a first surfing lesson located in Bodega Bay—Sophie leans over the console and plants a kiss on my cheek. "Did you know my super hot surfer boyfriend is a musical prodigy who also narrates and produces audiobooks?"

I'm smiling as I capture her brazen smile with a kiss of my own. Already, the early morning wake-up call feels worth it.

We unpack the Bronco as the sunrise begins to peek out from behind the mountains. Coming up with surfing gear for Sophie wasn't an issue in the slightest. I used to joke that my parents' garage could double as a small surf shop. That's what happens when an entire family adopts the same hobby. There's a pinch in my chest when I recall how easily Gabby agreed to loan Sophie her wet suit for today when I haven't allowed her a day out on the water since the accident.

"Are you sure this thing is rated for a beginner?" Sophie asks, scrutinizing the board I've just leaned against the Bronco.

The board I brought for Sophie is an eight-foot soft top, ideal for her height, weight, and lack of experience.

"Positive." I hold out Gabby's wet suit to her and launch into best practices for getting into a wet suit for the first time. Surprisingly, she doesn't seem fazed by my cautionary instructions.

Instead, she takes the garment from me and steps around to the back of the Bronco to disrobe from her sweats and hoodie. The instant I see the red flash of her bathing suit, I turn around. "If you even knew how many times I've had to change in and out of regency ballgowns while under the duress of a corset backstage, you wouldn't question my ability to handle a bit of neoprene."

After a couple minutes of fidgeting in the sand, Sophie tells me she's done. And I'm not the least bit astonished by how good she looks in surfing gear.

I show her how to carry her board down to the water, as my arms and back are loaded. And much like with her wet suit, she handles it like a champ. The temperature of the water on her bare feet, however, she struggles with a bit more.

"How are you standing in this without flinching?" she asks as she dances in the tide on her tiptoes. "I forgot how cold the Pacific is."

I belt out a laugh and secure the leash to her ankle. "It's fifty-eight degrees. Give yourself a minute. You'll adjust."

"Pretty sure this will still feel frigid to me in an hour."

"Look." I point behind us at the sunrise yawing awake, reflecting off the open water. If anything, the coming light will warm her, which will help distract from her chilled extremities.

And just like I thought, she seems to forget all about her discomfort and focuses instead on the addictive beauty of the ocean at sunrise. There's nothing like it in all the world.

Sophie's mesmerized by the sherbet-colored sky, and in turn, I'm mesmerized by her. The only thing better than enjoying a sunrise on the beach alone is having someone I care for enjoy it with me. *Not just someone*, I think. *Sophie*.

"There's nothing random." Her words are so hushed they're nearly lost to the rhythmic hum of the waves beyond.

"What?" I ask, coming up beside her in the surf, board tucked under one arm while I secure the other around her waist.

"I'm just thinking how none of this is by chance." The awe in her voice is unmistakable, and I have enough self-awareness to know she's not speaking about us, not directly anyway. The expression she wears now is one I, too, have worn dozens of times while standing on this side of the open water. There's something about the vastness of the ocean that beckons to something deep within.

"All of this—the sun, the ocean, those birds in the sky, every creature in the sea . . . *you and me.*" She takes in a deep breath, then slowly releases it with her face tilted toward the sky. "I was just chatting with Portia and Gabby about that last Tuesday." Her smile is huge when she declares, "Nothing is ever random. God has a plan for everything, and we're all a part of it." She fills her lungs with the salty air. "There is nothing outside His redemption because redemption is His plan. I think that's one of the most comforting things about having a relationship with God."

Unbidden, several Scriptures I memorized long ago chase across my mind, reinforcing Sophie's claims as truth. Yet my chest burns with a familiar discomfort. I remember what it was like to feel that way about the things of God. To look at creation with wonder and awe, to see myself as part of God's divine master plan. But that was two dead parents and one injured sister ago. And no matter how my views may change or shift, I'd never get a second chance to make things right with the two people who fought the hardest for me. I'd never get the chance to tell them I was wrong.

Where's the redemption in that?

"You were right." Sophie nudges me. "My feet don't hurt now that they're numb." Her delight over this revelation pulls me out of my spiral. "So what do we do now?"

This, at least, is an answer that requires no amount of self-reflection. "Now, we learn to surf."

For the next couple hours, I teach Sophie the proper way to pop up and balance while still on the sand before we progress to the water and learn paddle techniques, along with how to adjust her position on the board. I also show her how to bail. It will be a while until she's ready for the final step in the four-part cycle of paddle, adjust, chase, surf. She's fallen off her board dozens of times by this point, and though her arms visibly shake with signs of fatigue, she continues to climb back on. Again and again. I keep waiting for her to call it a day as her arms are likely leaden weights by this point, but unlike other first-timers I've been around, Sophie doesn't seem defeated by her slow progress; she seems all the more determined by it. And my admiration and respect for her grows with each wave she balances on.

"You should surf, August," she calls out as we paddle toward each other in the shallows. She's lying prostrate on her board, her cupped hands treading at half speed through the open water. "I can hang out on the beach and wait for you."

I've been straddling my board, using it more as a floating device today than anything else so I can be close when she needs me.

"I'm good," I say. "I'm happy to go at your speed."

"I don't want you to miss out. All you've done is watch me get on my board and then promptly fall off." She offers me a tired grin. "I'll be happy to watch you while I take a rest in the sunshine."

When she shakes her wave-beaten head, I can't imagine that lopsided bun will be easy to untangle once we're out of the water. Yet even so, Sophie is the only person I know who can still look radiant after succumbing to dozens of wipeouts.

"Nobody's a natural on their first or even their tenth time out—and if you hear otherwise, they're lying. You did great." I hook my foot under her board and draw her in close. The waves and weather really are perfect today. "How about I help you get settled on the beach, and then if you're really sure you're okay with me going out—"

"I'm sure. Although . . ." She shoots me a withering look. "I'll be honest with you, I don't know if I'm gonna have enough muscle left to walk back to the Bronco when it's time."

"Then you can borrow my muscle." It's only after I say it that I realize how cheesy it sounds, but Sophie isn't looking at me like I've just said the world's dumbest pickup line. She's looking at me the way I hope I'm looking at her. Like she's mine. Like we belong together.

Once we wash up on shore, I reach for Sophie's board and disconnect the leash from her ankle, gladly taking on the extra burden so she can wobble up to dry land. I set my own board aside near our pile of belongings and watch her plop onto a beach towel with the boneless *thwunk* of exhausted surfers everywhere.

I plant a quick kiss on the top of her head and tell her I won't be long out there.

"Take your time," she says. "I was thinking about calling Dana since it's nearly ten her time." Sophie collects her phone. "I bet she's just eating breakfast right about now."

I turn toward my board. "Have a good time."

"Wait, wait!" Sophie calls after me, making a halfhearted attempt to swipe for my leg even though I'm out of reach at this point. "You should meet her first. She's my family—the chosen kind."

"Sure." I plunk down on the beach towel beside her while she taps on her phone. I've heard a fair amount of stories about Dana, but I'm unprepared when she answers the video call with giant foam curlers in her hair while eating what looks like leftover chow mein from a to-go container.

"Hey—" Dana stops mid-bite, eyes rounding.

"Morning," Sophie chirps as she swivels the camera to include me. I wave idiotically.

"Hey there," I say awkwardly.

"August just gave me my first surfing lesson this morning, and I wanted him to meet you before he goes back out."

Dana puts her chopsticks down and moves a hand to the curler bobbing near to her ear. "Hello, August." And then, "Please tell your girlfriend how much I appreciate her giving me a heads-up prior to this phone call so I could make myself presentable."

I laugh. "Will do."

Sophie rolls onto her belly. "Consider this payback for all the times you let Jason into our apartment while I was nap-drooling on the sofa."

"Fair enough. In that case . . ." She takes a huge bite of her congealed noodles and grins.

I laugh at their friendly banter. It's good to see this side of Sophie. She's told me how much Dana did for her after she lost her income and needed a job. It reminds me of what Chip did for me after the accident.

I participate in a polite Q&A session directed by Dana, even though I'm certain she knows far more answers than she lets on. Even after I say good-bye and start for my board, I can still hear the women chatting.

"So I don't think it's any coincidence that you called this morning because I just read a very inspiring post from one of our favorite traveling theater companies."

"Oh really?" Sophie asks. "Wait, why are you doing that weird eyebrow thing?"

"How 'bout I just forward you the post and you can read it for yourself. Just remember, we only live once and these types of opportunities are not offered every day. Plus, I'm your best friend. Part of my job is to push you to do things you're not comfortable with for the greater good."

As I grab for my surfboard, I hear Sophie say, "And who, exactly, is the greater good in this case?"

I'm too far to hear how Dana replies, but Sophie's laugh rings out loud and clear.

I chuckle at their funny antics as I step into the ocean, making a mental note to ask her about it after my run. All too soon, I've lost myself to the pull of the ocean and the progression of the waves.

I'm not sure how long I stayed out, but when I get back to Sophie's beach towel, she's off the phone and munching on a protein bar. The autumn sunshine bathes her in a golden hue, and if I wasn't dripping with saltwater, I'd be grabbing for my phone to snap her picture, crazy beach hair and all.

"You're an even better surfer than you look, August Tate," she says.

I quirk an eyebrow and then pat my face dry with a towel. "Not sure if I should take that as a compliment?"

"You definitely should."

As I settle in beside her, I tap the lopsided cinnamon roll atop her head. "I think it's gonna take a bit of work to untangle this top knot of yours."

"I know. But sadly, I don't know if my arms will be up for such a task for some time. Might be next week before my muscles stop shaking."

"Do you have a brush with you?"

"Of course." She points to the bag at her feet. "I always keep one in my bag."

"Care if I give it a go?"

"As long as you know it's an enter-at-your-own-risk situation."

With a groan, she sits up while I collect her bag and carefully pick my way around clean clothes, a collection of snacks and gum, a few pieces of makeup, earbuds, and a wallet, and ah, *bingo*. A hairbrush.

Brush in hand, I move to sit behind her, rising up on my knees. "So, I've never actually done this before."

"You've never brushed someone's hair before?" She tilts her chin up with a smirk. "Is that the secret to keeping your hair looking all mussed and sultry?"

"You think my hair looks *sultry*?"

"Don't even try to pretend you don't have sultry surfer hair. It's part of your aesthetic."

"Also didn't know I had an aesthetic."

"You absolutely do. Yours is moody musician with sultry surfer hair meets secret musical prodigy and snarky holiday romance narrator."

"So just your typical average Joe."

She laughs as I reach for the hair tie on top of her head that is somehow binding this wet nest together. I tug strand after strand to try and make sense of—

"You'll never get it out if you treat my head like a fine French pastry, August. You'll just end up making more of a mess. Secure a finger under the tie and then just yank it out."

I cringe. "That sounds incredibly painful."

"Welcome to pretty much everything in the female world."

I try my best to untangle it my way, but eventually, I'm forced to adopt Sophie's methodology.

"How did the rest of your call with Dana go?" I ask. "It sounded lively, to say the least. I like her, by the way. She's exactly what I pictured from your descriptions."

"She likes you, too. And she totally picked up on your aesthetic." Sophie scoops sand with her hand and lets it slip through her fingers. "Um, let's see, the rest of our call was . . . interesting."

"How so?" I ask, brushing from the bottom of her hair and moving upward. Inch by tangled inch.

She draws her knees up and wraps her arms around them. "You remember what I told you about how I froze on stage during opening night and how the director had to call in my understudy?"

"Yes," I hedge, though there is little more I know about that night.

"Dana was with me on stage that night. But she was also with me when my breakdown began the night before. Super long story short, everything I'd worked hard to stuff down over the past ten years chose the worst moment to fight back."

I continue to brush out the snarls. "We're gonna be here a while, so if you don't mind, I'd like to hear the long version, please."

She chuckles at this and then reaches back to squeeze my knee. "So tech week is brutal in the world of live theater. Lots of stress, short fuses, dramatic exits . . . you get the picture. Right before we ended our last dress rehearsal, an argument broke out between the cast members, creating all sorts of extra chaos while the theater was closing down for the night. I'd just exited the auditorium doors when I realized I'd forgotten my phone backstage. I called out to my friends to wait up, but when I tried to open the door, it was already locked, so I had to run to the opposite side of the theater to try one of the side doors. I got in and was relieved to find the safety lights still on inside the auditorium. I figured I'd be okay. But as soon as I stepped behind the backstage curtain, every light in the building powered off. It was the same kind of blackness as the cellar and . . . I freaked."

The idea of Sophie having to relive that moment makes me

physically ill. "Were you able to call your friends once you found your phone?"

"Backstage is always so crowded with props and sets, and with no lights, my phone was impossible to find. At first I called out for help, hoping someone would come looking for me. But in the chaos of the evening, most of them hadn't realized I stepped away. Except for Dana. She's the one who eventually figured it out and came looking for me. She found me but . . . I was pretty shaken up by then." She releases a deep exhale. "No matter what I tried to tell myself, it was as if I was reliving the attack and those dark hours in the cellar all over again."

It's impossible not to recall my recent experience of finding Sophie in the dark. I was terrified. "Was that when you told Dana what happened to you?"

"No," she says, laughing humorlessly. "I was too busy lying to myself, too busy thinking that I could just power through it. Despite all Dana did for me that night, making me tea and readying a bath, my nerves were shot. Too shot to fall asleep. I should have told my director I wasn't okay as soon as the morning came, but instead, I faked my way through hair and makeup and even my vocal warm-ups. But the instant that spotlight came on, it was like every cell in my body rebelled against me. When I opened my mouth to sing, no voice came out. It was just . . . gone." She takes a moment to scoop up another handful of sand and watch it slip through her fingers. "Honestly, my director had every right to be upset. Same with the audience. I didn't tell Dana about the cellar until after the press hit and I knew the damage to my reputation was irreversible. And even then, I couldn't bring myself to share everything."

"I'm sorry that happened to you," I say.

"Me too," she says. "Although, I think I have a better understanding of why it did."

I tug the last of her knots free and marvel at the way her hair stretches to the center of her back. I move to settle beside her again on the towel.

She turns to face me. "Dana thinks the reason behind all this happening the way it did is so I can have some kind of epic professional comeback that will relaunch my career and my confidence." She stares out at the ocean. "She thinks I'll regret not pursuing auditions and opportunities that arise because I never know which one might lead to an extraordinary career breakthrough."

My chest tightens. "And what do you think?"

She chews on her bottom lip. "It's possible, I suppose. I do think I've regained some stage confidence since working with you in the studio, but I also think telling you what happened when I was sixteen shifted something inside me." She picks up my hand. "You were the first person I've ever told the full story to, August. I always worried that if I admitted what I heard my father say to the detective about me that day that it would somehow make it . . . true."

"Sophie." I lift my hand to rub my thumb along her jaw. "What you heard that day couldn't be further from the truth."

Sophie squints at me with one eye, her freshly brushed hair blowing over one shoulder and sticking to the wet suit. "I decided to test it out again, like a working theory of sorts. So I told the whole story to Portia last Tuesday night before our ASL class. Your sister was there, too." She pauses as if waiting for me to interject, but I'm too stunned to say a word. "I've come to trust and care for them both, and I wanted them to know me. To *really* know me. I'm tired of keeping secrets that have only made me feel shame and fear."

I adjust my position in the sand, sitting up a bit straighter, my pulse a hard knock in my chest. Still, I can't quite find adequate words. Maybe because I truly have none to offer.

She beams when she adds, "Afterward, I felt brave. Strong. Free, even." Her eyes turn watery. "They helped me see the truth: I'm not the same girl who was locked in that cellar at sixteen. I'm not forgotten or unloved or uncared for." Tears glitter in her eyes.

This, I finally have a response to. My lips part to say, *I love you, Sophie,* when she hits me with, "No matter what my circumstance, no matter how cold my brother is or how undermining my father is or how passive my mother is, I *know* God loves me. Not only because my Gigi believed it for me. But because I finally believe it for myself."

My chest spasms as a tiny fracture begins at the base of my ribs, spidering its way through every rung. At first the pain is tolerable. A pinch. A stab. But soon enough, the pain spreads. And with every intake of breath, it intensifies, sharpening to the point it's nearly all-consuming.

Tell her now, I think. I should tell her the things I've never admitted out loud to anyone. The things I've been too ashamed might be true. The things I'm too afraid are already true.

She angles her head. "What are you thinking, August?"

That if I can't accept my own shame, how can I possibly ask you to accept it?

I swallow the words and give her a different truth instead.

"That I'm proud of you. You deserve to feel loved."

Voice Memo

Gabby Tate

14 months, 2 weeks, 6 days after the accident

When I got home from school today, I was missing my dad so much. Some days it's easy to recognize the thing that makes me sad. Other days it just feels like a pressure in my chest that doesn't go away until after I let myself cry.

As soon as August dropped me off at the house on his way to run errands, I made a snack and went into the garage.

When I miss my mom and need to feel close to her, I wrap the wedding quilt at the end of their bed around me like I'm inside a cocoon. Her smell comforts me like nothing else. But when it's my dad I'm missing, all I want to do is sit inside the Bronco. I have so many memories of being with him in that car. We drove to the ocean together so many times for a day of surfing and ice cream and tide pool combing.

Today, the tears came as soon as I saw the hole for the radio. My dad didn't have a sound system in either of his vehicles. Not in his beat-up construction truck or in the Bronco he restored. A few weeks before we left for India, I teased him about not getting it fixed since he'd literally fixed everything else. But he told me it was because the silence reminded him to pray. I guess he used to think he didn't have enough time for prayer when he first became a Christian, but then once he started adding up all the time he spent driving during the week, he realized he had plenty.

When I asked him what he prayed for most, he said us—me and August. My stomach hurt when he said my brother's name that day because I knew my parents worried about him. I'd overheard their hushed conversations in the kitchen more times than they knew about. I don't know when August stopped working for the band he originally left home for, but I do know he went to work for some rich lady named Vanessa. I think she's the real reason my brother stopped coming home for weekend visits, and I have a feeling she's also the reason August told my mom he wasn't coming to India with us.

On the last drive I took with my dad before we left for India, I asked if we could pray together on our way back from surfing. We prayed for my brother.

So today, I prayed for him again.

22

Sophie

After the first November ASL class ends, I follow Portia through the auditorium for some private talk time at her request. It isn't unusual for her to inquire about Gabby's well-being from time to time. Her maternal heart stretches further than a mother analyzing her son's girlfriend. She often remarks on how grateful she is that Gabby has another consistent adult in her life outside of her older brother, who, unfortunately, has chosen to make himself scarce in communities like this one.

The same way he does with church on Sunday mornings, despite my numerous invitations for him to join us. In response, he always has a ready excuse: helping Chip move apartment complexes in San Francisco, raking Norma's yard, winterizing the greenhouse, catching up with an old LA client for brunch on their way through town, and, of course, work at the studio.

Last weekend, I finally asked if there was a specific reason why he didn't want to attend service with us. But once again, August evaded giving me a clear answer, claiming he was "happy you and my sister enjoy going." And though he didn't say as much, I got the distinct impression he was hoping his response would put the matter to rest. As if my current Sunday morning routine of sitting next to Gabby and Tyler in the ASL section and taking notes on the sermon should be enough to satisfy me indefinitely. Only, I know it won't be. While I have zero room to complain regarding how often we see each other during the week, I feel his absence acutely every time I walk into Seaside Fellowship without him.

I make my way to Portia, who's carrying a music stand backstage. Though my situational awareness grows as I climb the steps to meet her, my anxiety neutralizes as soon as she flips the switch to illuminate props, sets, and lighting rigs. It's strange to think how this backstage world was once more familiar to me than the tiny apartment I shared in New York with Dana. I run my fingers over the texture of a felt hat with a feather sticking out of the brim. I pick it up and barely stop myself from trying it on. Maybe Dana's right. Maybe I miss this more than I've allowed myself to realize.

"It was a great class tonight," I tell Portia. "I took so many notes in the margin of my book that I don't know how I'm going to read my microscopic handwriting. But the grammar rules of ASL are so fascinating."

Portia smiles and leans against the backdrop of a massive sunflower with a country road winding up a crown of mountains in the distance. "I wish all my students were as enthusiastic about learning a new language as you. You must have been a superstar student in school."

I laugh. "I certainly was *not* a superstar student." That title only ever belonged to Jasper. I set the hat down and move to grip the king's scepter, the one with the large amber gem attached to the end. "Whenever learning felt like school, I hated it. But when I finally had the chance to learn about the things I was truly fascinated by— something in my head worked differently. It's the reason I was able to major in theater arts."

"Because theater made your soul sing like nothing else," she coos in such a gentle, knowing way that I turn to face her.

"Yes." I swallow back unexpected emotion. "I suppose that's exactly how I felt."

"And how do you feel about it now?"

I study the scepter in my hand, recalling the email I received today courtesy of Dana's meddling. Not only did she find an old audition video of mine on her phone from a time when I asked her for feedback, but she actually submitted it to the traveling theater company we'd dreamed of touring with one day . . . without my knowledge or consent. But according to their reply email, they absolutely loved it. They sent me an invite to schedule a live, online callback. Dana received one, too.

"Promise me you'll at least schedule the callback, Sophie. Do it for us. For all the years we dreamed of taking a show on the road together and seeing the country. This could be our chance," she begged as soon as I called her asking why I was getting feedback on an audition I hadn't even submitted.

After much back and forth, I promised her I would at least try. It was the least I could do after all she's been willing to do for me.

"I can't say for sure," I respond to Portia, "but I can say there's been a lot of wonderful changes in my life since the last time I performed on a live stage." For what might be the first time since my move to California, I don't cringe at the thought of that horrible opening night or the failure I was so ashamed to face. I was so certain this season of my life would be the worst in my existence, and yet it's far from it. God provided me with a job I love, gave me a welcoming church home, expanded my community, and brought me friends who feel closer than family.

And then, there's August. My heart kick-starts even now at the thought of him.

Portia's curious gaze twinkles. "I've been praying God would bring you some much needed restoration in this area of your life."

"You mean, in *theater*?"

She nods.

I open my mouth to thank her, but before I can, she holds up a finger. She might be a full head shorter than me, but Portia is no pushover. "Don't thank me quite yet. I do have selfish motives at work." I laugh at her honesty. "When we won the bid on this historical theater, Nick and I had to address the immediate needs first: plumbing issues in the ladies' restroom, the leaky roof, safety code violations, etc. We were able to put on a couple dinner shows, which helped bring in enough revenue to take care of those pressing needs and gain some exposure in our local community." She shifts her stance and brings her hands up to her chest. "But my dream, long before there was ever a theater available to bid on, was to someday direct a live, onstage production with both deaf and hearing actors. Nick and I feel called to bridge the gap wherever God leads and to do our part to further the representation of our beloved friends in the deaf community. Creating a deaf-friendly theater isn't a small undertaking, but we feel it's time we take the next steps forward. And we'd like you to pray about being involved with us. Perhaps as our musical director."

My jaw hinges open. But once again, she holds up her hand to stop me from speaking.

"I've Googled you, Sophie. I've watched your published auditions, and I've seen you act and sing on stage. I wasn't wrong about you. You'd be an incredible asset to any production team no matter what role you took on. God's given you a tremendous voice, and I think His plans reach beyond the limits of acting on a stage."

I blink back tears. "I . . . wow. Thank you. I don't even know what to say to all that."

"You don't need to say anything. Deaf theaters are rare and often difficult and expensive to facilitate, which is one of the reasons there are only a handful of them in the nation. But their existence is what gives us hope and inspiration to try."

I sit on a rolling staircase, a bit shell-shocked that this is coming on the very same day as Dana's email plea for me to *please use this link to schedule your live callback audition* for the sake of a "dream opportunity" she's told me very little about.

"Will you tell me how they work?" I ask Portia.

The sparkle in her eyes intensifies. "We'd select a show that can fairly represent deaf actors—who will play deaf characters on stage using American Sign Language—and hearing actors who will use spoken or sung English during the performance. The goal is to create a cohesive, innovative experience that would once again bridge the deaf and hearing communities. Theater, much like books and music and art, has always been about connecting audiences through the magic of storytelling. And we want the voice of *this* theater to be inclusive enough so that the stories shared here can be understood by everyone."

"That's a beautiful vision."

"It is beautiful, yes—" she sighs warily—"but I'd like you to spend some time in prayer before you give me an answer. I'll be honest with you; this dream of ours won't be able to pay you what your expertise deserves, not at first. And while it's fun to dream and discuss show possibilities, there will be a lot of research and planning that will have to come first." She gestures around to the backstage. "For starters, we'll need to make this area accessible for a deaf actor. The lighting isn't conducive to communicate with ASL so we may need to research specialty headlamps so signing hands have the visibility they need to be seen. And then there's safety concerns that will need to be addressed, as well as finding the right LED screen for the supertitles that will be projected above the stage to interpret for both the hearing and deaf audience members. And then," she says, taking a huge breath, "we'll need to find and secure an ASL theater interpreter willing to take on a show."

I nod, thinking back on a few weeks ago when Portia had mentioned different types of interpreter needs in ASL. I'd been shocked to learn that a live theater interpreter requires no less than seven years of training and experience. Apparently, it's an extremely rare talent to find. From the short video clips she's shown us in class, it's also a physically and mentally taxing profession. Even still, I could imagine how rewarding such an investment would be to the Pimentels' overall vision.

"I'm guessing you'll need to raise quite a bit of funds for all that," I venture.

"We will," she agrees. "We've just started brainstorming."

"What are your top ideas so far?"

"Perhaps another dinner show or something similar to what we did this summer with the one-act plays. Whatever we do, it's important we make it as accessible as we can to both the hearing and the deaf in our community. I'd love to run a private audition for a handful of one-act entrants willing to work with partners—an actor and an ASL proficient interpreter. I was thinking I could advertise it to all my students and drama teams so we could get a good variety of comedy, singing, dialogue, and skits."

"That's brilliant, Portia." And just like that, my mind begins to whirl. "What about a winter showcase?" My eye catches on the fake Christmas tree in the corner. "We could plan it for December. That way we could have an inspirational theme behind it all since people tend to be a bit more generous and open to community gatherings around the holidays. Maybe we could even find a way to announce the fundraiser at church?"

"See?" She smiles. "You're already an asset to this theater." A worry line creases her brow. "But do you really think we could pull it off that soon? We'd only have six, seven weeks max and you already work two jobs and have a boyfriend who I hear is rather fond of you—"

"I can make it work." There is no possible way I'd miss it. Portia has fast become an incredible blessing in my life, and more than that, she and her family are a blessing to so many in this community—especially to a teenage girl I've grown to love like a sister.

With a promise to pray about everything else she mentioned, I hug her good-bye and begin my chilly trek to where I parked August's car. Only when I get there, I'm not alone.

"Hi," Gabby says with a wave. "Would you mind taking me home? I know it's out of your way, but I was hoping we could talk."

I don't even have to consider my answer. "Absolutely. Did you let Portia know you didn't need a ride tonight?"

When she assures me she did, I unlock the car and engage the seat warmers. Temperatures are only in the low-fifties, but after such a long summer of sunshine and warmth, I'm definitely feeling the change in seasons.

As I pull onto the main street, I mentally prepare for a Tyler-dominated conversation, when she hits me with "Did Portia tell you about her dream for a deaf theater?"

I hesitate, not knowing how to respond at first. Portia didn't specify confidentiality during our backstage conversation, but—

"It's not a secret," Gabby confirms quickly. "I helped her brainstorm some fundraiser ideas a few nights ago, and she mentioned she was going to talk to you." I see her bite her lip nervously out of the corner of my eye. "I've been hoping she'll choose to do another one-act showcase."

I breathe a little easier and nod. Perhaps the reason Portia took me backstage was more about her asking me to consider a future at the theater. "It sounds like you'll get your wish. We're going to shoot for a winter showcase in December."

"Really?" Gabby clasps her hands under her chin, and I can tell by her quick response time while in the shadows in her brother's car that her aids must still be in from class. "I know there are some incredibly talented actors in the community, but . . . but I want to audition."

"Then you should," I say automatically. I saw the girl on a live stage, and she was absolutely wonderful. "What do you want to do?"

"I want to do a dramatic retelling of something I experienced—using ASL." She pauses again, causing me to spare another glance in her direction. "And I'd like you to be my voice."

"You'd like me to . . . *be your voice*?" I nearly swerve out of my lane.

I can see her nod out of the corner of my eye, and I feel the same type of pressure building in my chest as I did that first morning in church listening to the parable of the lost sheep.

"I want you to be my hearing partner, to voice my story in English, while I tell it in ASL."

I wait till after I turn onto her street so I can swallow down the lump in my throat before I answer. "I'd be honored."

"Thank you," she says, right before I see her knee begin to bounce.

"Also, I have these . . . um . . . voice recordings things. They're kind of like a spoken journal, I guess. In the beginning, the doctors weren't sure how much the swelling in my brain would affect me long-term or what I'd be able to remember. They weren't sure if my hearing would return or not at that point. And since my right arm was broken, one of the nurses suggested I use this voice memo app and start recording what I could remember about the accident—or anything for that matter—just in case I needed it." She fidgets in her seat. "The memos transcribe what I say, so it's kind of like writing, but much faster and with better grammar. Plus, it kept my voice active when I couldn't do much else."

Compassion and sadness grip me so hard at her pronouncement. Picturing vibrant, gregarious, wise-beyond-her-years Gabby suffering in a hospital bed after the loss of her parents makes it difficult to take a full breath.

"Sounds like cool technology. What did you talk about in the memos?"

"Random stuff at first, things that happened once I was back home when August came to live with me. I figured I'd stop recording at some point and switch to a real journal, but I never have. It's sort of a habit now, something I look forward to doing when I have a minute alone and just want to decompress." She clears her throat. "I was hoping to send a few of them to you—the memos, I mean. Most of them are under five minutes, so they shouldn't take a lot of time to listen to, but there's one I recorded that's pretty important to me. I describe what happened after the accident. I'd like to see if I can make it into a monologue script for stage. If you think I can, I was hoping you might help me write it in a way that could work well for ASL and for English."

I'm pulling into the Tates' driveway now and doing my best to keep my many conflicting emotions at bay as I shift the car into Park. I reach for her hand across the center console. "Of course, Gabby. I'll help with anything you need."

There are tears in her voice as she holds on to me. "Really?"

"Absolutely."

She nods. "I'll send a few of them over to you tonight, then."

"I'm looking forward to it."

Suddenly, her grip tightens as we see her brother open the front door and head for the driveway toward us. "But you can't tell August."

I'm so stunned by her panicked plea that my face has no time to apply a play-it-cool expression.

"But why?"

"Please, Sophie," she repeats as August approaches the driver's side. "Don't tell him about the voice memos or the showcase. I need to do this on my own, in my own way and time." She stares at me straight on. "Promise?"

"Okay, yes," I assure her. "I promise."

After a brief squeeze, she pops open her door and races down the driveway toward the house, not bothering with more than a quick hello to August.

Despite the chilly air outside, I roll down my window to greet him, but he's too busy tracking his sister's sprint inside.

"What was all that about?" he asks.

I have no answer to offer because I, too, am clueless.

His brow dips into a V. "I thought Portia was taking her home tonight."

"Uh, she was, but Gabby asked if I could give her a ride instead."

"Why?"

I pinch my lips closed in what is likely the most suspicious improv gesture on the planet.

"Ah," he says with a level of amusement that surprises me. "I get it. Girl talk." He taps the top of the window frame. "Or probably more specifically, boy talk."

"Yep." The *P* pops on the word. "You guessed it."

My nod is as exaggerated as they come.

But then his pleasant expression shifts to mortification. "Wait, she wasn't asking you about . . . something physical, right?" He grips the back of his head. "Did she tell you they were—"

And then it clicks. "Oh, no! No, no! Gosh, no. They've only just had their first kiss."

"*What*?!" he all but howls through the darkened neighborhood. "They've kissed?"

"*August*," I chide. "Shhh!"

"When did *that* happen?" he whisper-shouts.

"Last week, on their group date when they went to that drive-in movie with closed captioning. She video-called me later that night to tell me."

His eyes double in size. "And you didn't think that was information I should know? Why am I just now hearing about this?"

"Stand down, big brother. If you keep looking like a deranged meerkat every time something new comes up, she'll never tell you anything." I reach out the car window and pat his shadowed cheek. I quite like his nine o'clock shadow. "It was only a little peck on the lips. It was actually super sweet, and kind of an accident."

He squints his eyes at me. "Sorry, sweetheart, but there are no accidental kisses when it comes to teenage boys. I should know, I used to be one."

"No really, it was," I chuckle. "They were sitting in the back of the pickup truck, sharing a pack of gummy worms, and there was this double worm so Gabby suggested—"

"Nope. N-o-p-e." He shakes his head. "I need this story to end right now."

I laugh in full. "Fine. But other than that, they're both being incredibly respectful of the physical boundaries you and the Pimentels have set for them."

He releases a long exhale.

I pat my open window frame until he shrinks down enough to plant his elbows inside. "You're really cute, you know that?"

"No," he huffs. "But I do know why my dad went gray so young."

"I think you'll be a super sexy silver fox whenever that day comes." What I don't say is that I hope I'm here to see it.

It's these unprompted thoughts that make me question my promise to Dana. Even scheduling a callback seems ludicrous when I can't imagine leaving him. Not with how my feelings for him have grown.

And yet, lately, I've wondered if those feelings are still mutual.

There are moments, much like this one, when August's gaze seems to spell out the same three words that burn inside my own chest for him. But instead of speaking out the declaration I long to hear most, August will always find a way to break the connection. A deliberate distraction. A change of subject. A physical separation.

Tonight, he does all three.

When he straightens and crosses his arms over his chest, I can't even pretend not to feel rejection's sting. "Is your brother still out of town?"

I sigh. "You really want to discuss my brother?"

"No, but can you blame me if I sleep better at night when I know he's not around?"

Confusing as this man is to me at times, a tiny vibration purrs in my chest at his protective tone. August's Jasper-radar flipped on the day he came to collect the van, and it hasn't turned off since. Thankfully, my brother's been out of town for nearly a week, reducing the usual tension around the winery to nonexistent. Other than the estimate he invoiced me for his van repairs, that is. Natalie says she'll keep working on him to make an insurance claim, but so far, it hasn't happened yet.

Due to my brother's absenece, my father hasn't come around much, and my mother has popped in for "brunch with her girls" twice. And while our conversations are never more than surface-deep, I can be thankful there's no contention between us.

"He's still gone," I confirm to August.

"Good." He nods. "It will be a relief when you're out of there."

I study his face in the moonlight, wishing he'd say more, wishing he'd tell me where he sees this going. Wishing for a commitment outside the ambiguous terms we agreed to when he'd asked me to "give this thing between us a try."

Only now I'm way past try. *But where is he?*

"I've been praying something amazing will happen with *Mistletoe*

Matrimony so I can afford to move out and find something a bit closer to . . ."—you and Gabby—"all my activities in town."

"That would be nice." August squeezes my shoulder reassuringly and nods. It's the closest he's come to affirming my prayers. "Text me when you're home, okay?"

"I always do."

He leans through the open window and presses a kiss to my lips. I cherish every heartbeat we share until he pulls away and says good-bye. I'm so lost in thought after I leave his driveway that I startle when I hear the chime of Gabby's voice memos download-ing to my phone.

By the time I pull into the reserved parking space on the east side of the winery, I've listened to half the memos Gabby sent me through the Bluetooth connection in August's car. No matter the memo, her voice always stirs something inside me. A giggle, a swoon, a tear or two, a desire to reach through the recording and pull her close. She's just begun to share the details of the day her family loaded into a train car to visit a village they hadn't originally planned on when I see an all-too-familiar silver Mercedes G-Wagon parked in the main lot in front of the estate.

Why on earth would Clinton be here at this hour?

Did my brother get home from his trip ahead of schedule? Are they having a drink? I suppose it's possible. It's not like I know anything about my brother's social habits.

Still, I can't ignore the red-flag feeling in my gut that something is off. Just as I think it, I see Clinton stroll out the front door, car-rying a small black duffle bag in his hand. Even though I'm mostly sheltered from his view, I slink all the way down in my seat, feeling the hammer of my heartbeat against my ribs. I spare a single glance to see if he's noticed August's sedan, but if he has, he's paying it no mind as he climbs into the driver's seat of his fancy high-roller SUV.

Even after I hear the roar of his obnoxious engine, I stay put, trying to make sense of his presence. Several scenarios play out in my active imagination at once, but before I give myself over to any one assumption, I need to find Natalie.

I speed-walk down the path that runs between the house and the tasting room in search of her when a faint meow pulls my attention to the pool area.

Natalie's there, in all her grace and elegance, strolling through the gated spa oasis on this cold November night in a plum-colored tracksuit with gold reflective stripes on each pant leg. Phantom is following her like he's a well-trained puppy and not a socially anxious stray who hates the water. *Or so I thought.*

In the aqua hue of the pool lights, I watch as he jumps onto the chaise lounge next to where my sister-in-law pushes up her pant legs and carefully sits on the edge of the Jacuzzi.

"Natalie?"

Her back is to me when I enter, but she's either wearing earbuds or she can't hear me over the bubbling spa. On closer inspection, she appears to be typing something on her phone.

The outside air is cold, and my sweatshirt is hardly thick enough to ward off the chill, but I slip through the pool gate anyway, marveling at the luxuriousness of it all from the inside. As if he's suddenly on security duty for the winery, my cat alerts Natalie to my presence.

"Is this where I accuse you of catnapping?" It's a lame joke, I know.

Natalie stares at me as if she's unsure of her defense. "I only let him out because he cries every time I pass the pool house door. I can't bear it." As if on cue, Phantom drags his fluffy tail along her back. Little manipulator. "I worried he'd try to jump the fence the first time I brought him in with me, but he doesn't seem to mind being near the water."

I chuckle at that. "I think it's you he likes."

She pets his back. "He's sweet. I always wanted a cat."

I stop myself from asking why she doesn't have one. I know the answer. Speaking of which. "Did, uh, did Jasper get back from his trip early?"

She looks at me oddly. "No, why?"

I open my mouth to answer her, only to realize I have no clue what I'm answering. I saw Clinton walk out the front door. *The front door.* He wasn't sneaking around or even trying to be discreet. He had to have been invited inside, right? And if Jasper's still gone, the only possible person who would have been with him inside the house was . . . Natalie.

I don't want to believe the obvious conclusion my brain is creating, but the circumstantial evidence is not looking good. Then again, accusing my sister-in-law of having an affair with my brother's friend after we've only recently found some common ground will likely kill whatever relationship we've gained. No, I need to tread carefully. If she trusts me, she'll confide in me. And if she confides in me, then maybe I can help her. Or at least point her in the right direction.

I glance down at her track pants that are currently rolled up to her knees. Certainly not the kind of wardrobe one might wear while having an illicit affair, right?

"Want to join me? The water's nice, even if the company is so-so."

I study her curiously. "Was that a joke?"

She laughs without humor. "If you have to ask, it probably doesn't qualify."

She pats the heated tile beside her, and I notice the washed-out tint of her skin and the shadowy half-moons under her eyes. Both have become more pronounced over the last few weeks.

I slip off my shoes and socks and roll up my jeans. And then I lift up a silent prayer for help with this conversation as I take a seat and lower my legs into the Jacuzzi. She's right; the warm water feels heavenly as I swish my cold feet back and forth.

"There are towels warming in the wicker armoire over there for afterward," she adds.

"I bet you'll be thrilled to have your pool house back after I leave."

She lifts her dainty feet out of the water for all of two seconds before dunking them in again. "Actually, it's been nice sharing the property with another female." It takes me a moment to recognize the subtle compliment she's just paid me. "Although, it feels like

282

you're hardly around much anymore. You have a fuller social life than I did back in high school."

"I don't think that's possible. You were Miss Popularity in high school," I say, recalling the prom queen herself. "A trendsetter, too. Did you know that when you left for senior prom in that white glitter dress, I tried to replicate it using my mom's favorite white linens?"

She whips her head in my direction. "You did not."

"Unfortunately, I did. I sprayed them with fabric glue, then sprinkled them with all the iridescent craft glitter I could find in our art closet."

"Did it work?"

"Sure, if you count *work* to mean something that resembled a wingless fairy wearing a toga that was obviously still a fitted sheet." I shake my head. "That's the night I gave up my dreams in fashion design."

Her laugh is so unexpected, I jump a little, which causes her to laugh all the more. And soon, I'm laughing with her. The more we fight for control, the more we continue to erupt.

"I haven't laughed like that in . . ." Her words trail off as she swipes a finger under her eyes. "A really long time."

"Eighth-grade Sophie would have been thrilled to be your comic relief. Honestly, she would have been thrilled just to sit in the same room as you." The words come out before I can properly calculate how pathetic they sound.

Her smile dips half a degree, and her tone sobers. "I thought I knew everything when I was eighteen—and whatever I didn't know, I relied on Jasper to fill in the blanks for me."

I try to laugh this off, but there's little humor to be found when it comes to my childhood. "Let me guess, he told you I was a drama queen and that you should stay clear of me?"

She doesn't need to confirm my suspicion with a verbal reply. Her eyes say it all.

I clear my throat. "Well, I won't pretend I didn't have a flair for the dramatic. But I certainly never wanted to be in the spotlight in this home."

She rubs her lips together. "So where do you go when you're not here? I mean, outside of your boyfriend's studio. Unless that's the only place you go."

I shake my head at her implication. "On Tuesday nights I go to the Twilight Theater. I'm taking an American Sign Language class with some friends from church."

Clearly, she wasn't expecting this. She starts to ask several different questions at once only to land on "Why?"

"The short answer? August's sister lost her hearing a couple years ago, and I want to support her as best I can. The longer answer is a bit more involved." One I'm still figuring out, in fact. "But ultimately, I've loved being part of such a beautiful community. And since I'm being honest, I'm going to be praying about making a more permanent commitment there in the future."

She studies me, her expression too mixed for me to read. "It's real then? The whole church stuff you mentioned at family brunch that day? That wasn't just to get a rise out of your folks?"

"It's real," I say simply.

Natalie blinks, and I swear I see tears in her eyes before she looks up at the full moon. "I don't think I'd ever be welcome in a church."

"Why do you say that?"

"I've made a lot of poor choices I can't ever take back."

Her words double-tap against my heart. "So have I."

"Not like me," she retorts. "I'm pretty sure my heart is half rotted from the things I've done."

I lean back onto my palms. "Not even the most perfect person on earth is perfect enough to save themselves. That's the irony of grace. We all need a savior, and yet none of us can ever earn what He's already given to us for free." I keep my focus on the moon, even as I feel hers shift to me. I don't add more.

I think of the many Tuesday evenings before class when Portia's only answer to my questions about the Bible were to point me to Scriptures where I could find the truth I sought. At first it frustrated me, especially when some of the verses didn't seem as black-and-white as I wanted them to be. But Portia's job wasn't to supply me with her opinions. Rather, it was to point me back to the God who promises to meet me exactly where I am and love me unconditionally.

Natalie zips up her sweatshirt. "I haven't been sleeping well for a while now. There's been a lot on my mind."

I lean in, hoping she'll confide more, but she stays quiet.

"Want to talk about it?"

She looks at me, considering. "Can I take a raincheck on that offer?"

"Of course," I say. "In the meantime, I'll be praying for you."

This time, when her eyes fill with tears, she simply says, "Thank you."

Voice Memo

Gabby Tate

16 months, 3 weeks, 3 days after the accident

Tonight was my youth group's outdoor praise and worship night. It's fall, which is usually my favorite weather as far as temperature goes, but as the lead guitarist began to strum and sing on stage, the sky grew dark, and in less than a minute, it started to rain.

My friends started shrieking and laughing and pulling their sweatshirt hoods up over their heads, but none of them left to find shelter. They all just kept singing and clapping as the rain soaked them through. But I couldn't stay.

I didn't know Tyler followed me to the big oak tree at the far end of the church property, but when I turned around, he was there. He asked me if I was okay, and all I could do was run into his arms.

I think it must have been the mix of music and rain that brought the memory of my parents back to me so strongly. It poured the night before the accident. It wasn't like any kind of rain I'd ever seen—more like an up-ended river pouring out of the sky.

We'd been gathered together under a shelter with open walls and a metal roof, sharing about the day's events the same way we'd done all week. I'd spent most of my time playing games with the little children while Mom served their mothers and Dad framed the buildings that would soon become educational centers. We'd been told June was the start of India's monsoon season, but we'd yet to see it in action for ourselves. As soon as it started, Pastor Bedi tried to dismiss our team back to our sleeping quarters, but none of us were ready to leave.

One of the guys picked up his guitar, and even though we couldn't hear a single chord he played, we lifted our voices above the sound of the storm and sang with our whole hearts. At one point, my chest felt overfilled, like a balloon ready to pop. The sensation was so crazy that I stopped singing to look around and see if anybody else felt it. But instead, I saw my parents. Even though the rain had blown through the open walls and soaked their clothes all the way through, their arms were stretched to the heavens and they looked . . . well, they looked joyful.

That's how I remember them. Not the perfect beach day pictures that were shown in a slideshow at their funerals, with Mom's hair all pretty and Dad in a shirt that wasn't stained or ripped from work. But like this. Like two people who didn't let a storm keep them from worshiping God.

23

August

I see my ransom note worked as planned." Chip's tone borders on cocky when he stands to greet me from the corner booth of Golden Gate Subs and Sandwiches.

He texted me a pin to this hole-in-the-wall deli yesterday, along with the ransom-style instructions that if I wanted the current metrics on *Mistletoe Matrimony*'s performance, then I shouldn't be late. And seeing as that bonus is the only thing keeping me from scheduling Gabby's consultation with the surgeon, I didn't balk at the demand. The multimedia audiobook went live on Fog Harbor's website November first, a little more than two weeks ago now.

"Withholding payment for work rendered is a crime in the state of California, Chip." My joke sounds drier than I intend, but I'm using all my willpower to keep the coiling tension from leaking out. My two-year search might be over in a matter of minutes.

He chuckles and slaps me on the back before we take our seats on opposite sides of the booth. He slides a plate with a hot pastrami sandwich on rye toward me, complete with an extra dill pickle spear. I'd ask how he knows my lunch order, but my sandwich preference ranks low on the scale of weird facts we've retained about each other over the years. The pros and cons of meeting your best friend at fifteen.

It's been at least a month since I helped Chip move apartment complexes, and though it's hardly the longest gap we've had between our in-person meet-ups, a lot has transpired since the day he convinced me that audiobook production could be a viable side hustle. He wasn't wrong. So far, the paychecks have been decent and far more consistent than the work I was picking up on my own.

"You want the good news or the bad news first?" Chip asks after swallowing a huge bite of his French dip.

I narrow my eyes. "If you made me drive all the way here so you could tell me the audiobook was a huge flop, then–"

"Good or bad," he repeats with a jester's grin.

"Bad."

"Ya know, I was really hoping Sophie would change that pessimistic outlook of yours."

"She's my girlfriend, not a miracle worker."

Chip laughs. "I suppose the fact that she even agreed to be your girlfriend in the first place is miracle enough."

"I won't argue with that." Chip doesn't need to tell me what I already know: I could never deserve Sophie. Not in a hundred lifetimes. Not with a thousand of her journaled prayers for me. I push my plate away, leaving only a quarter of a spear of pickle and a smear of Dijon mustard behind.

I stare him down and throw out the scenario I've feared most. "Is Fog Harbor Audio pulling the plug?" I know firsthand how brutal the first six months of any new business venture can be, including the make-or-break financial pressures. And if the sales and downloads haven't met Fog Harbor's expectations, it'd make the most sense for them to cut their losses as early as possible.

He gives a firm shake of his head. "No plug-pulling here. But I do think you should know that the whole of publishing slows down this time of year, which will affect contract negotiations between authors and narrators and will ultimately bring in less raw audio to master and produce until roughly mid-January."

The pastrami I ingested turns to granite in the pit of my stomach. Guess I shouldn't have been so quick to cross studio musician work off my schedule.

"But the good news is, you won't need those audio contracts during this holiday season because you are . . . hang on." He holds up a finger. "Let me get the wording exactly right." He picks up his phone and scrolls for what feels like twenty years. "'The sexiest voice in entertainment since the Hemsworth brothers.'"

I stare at him as if he's lost his mind.

"You've become a viral sensation, August. *You.*" He slaps the table and gut laughs. "I knew Sophie's talent would secure a loyal following, but nobody expected the frenzied manhunt your voice would cause in the audiobook community. Also, you might want to think about locking down your old social media accounts."

I can't possibly lower my eyebrows any further. "Explain all the words you're saying right now."

"Let's just say it's not only the audio excerpts of *Mistletoe Matrimony* floating around the socials that have quadrupled our downloads in the last week." He pauses with a look of intrigue I want to douse with a cup of ice water. "Your face was polled and voted on as the character inspiration for Blake on the author's fan page and now, well, it's become a whole thing."

I'm waiting for Chip to break character or at least throw in a well-timed "*Dude, I'm just messing with you, relax,*" but he keeps right on talking.

"Before I left the office, our marketing manager pulled me aside and told me that if this keeps up, it will be, and I quote, 'Our most lucrative marketing campaign to date.'"

The earth must orbit around the sun forty times before I can find my voice. "This isn't a joke?"

"I never joke about book sales."

"That's . . . this is . . ." I fist my hair. "This is all completely insane."

"Yes," Chip agrees readily. "It is. But so are the mad subscription bonus checks you and Sophie will make at the end of the month. I'm basically Santa in this moment."

Now *this* shakes me out of my stupor. "We made our bonuses?"

He waves a hand in front of my face. "Did you not hear a word I said? This thing is unstoppable. There's already a hashtag: Augie." When I say nothing to this nonsense word, he rolls his eyes and follows up with, "Your couple name. August plus Sophie." His smile spreads as wide as I've ever seen it. "I hope you're both up for what's to come because these readers are going to demand more multimedia originals starring the two of you, and probably some livestreams from your studio as well. Thankfully, we already have some new scripts in the works—every major holiday plus one for the pumpkin spice season." He laughs. "Plus, I think there are some real opportunities coming your way as far as original soundtracks go. I'll say more when I know more, but trust me. The right people are talking about you." He beams. "It's crazy how things have a way of working out sometimes."

I slump against the booth and fight to process what he just told me. My brain spins and spins until all I can get out is "You swear on our friendship you're not messing with me?"

"August, I'm in the business of fiction, and not even I could make this up."

It's right then that the dam I've been fighting to hold back—since the night my aunt called with news that my only living family member was currently being airlifted to a medical research hospital in Mumbai—breaks. Two years of feeling utterly helpless in the face of so much despair whooshes out of me at once. I fall forward and catch my head in my hands, shoving the heels of my palms into my eyes. *Breathe. Breathe. Breathe.* The muscles in my back and shoulders constrict, as if they're not sure how to let go of the stress they've been carrying for so long.

Not here, I think. *Not now.*

But grief has little respect for privacy. It doesn't care that I'm in the middle of a deli in San Francisco. Heat builds behind my eyes and burns in my chest. *Could this really be the moment I've been wait-ing for? The moment I can finally crawl out of the dark pit and finally atone for my mistakes?*

I'm so deep in my head when Chip speaks that his voice offers an emergency portal back to the present. I take it gratefully and scrub my hands over my damp eyes.

"You needed that, the bonus check," he says knowingly. "It's for something important, isn't it?"

Where I've given Chip limited access to these types of inquiries in the past due to my revulsion to pity, I can't now. How could I, when the only reason I'm here is because of him?

"It's for Gabby." I blow out a deep breath, lift my head, and slowly fill him in on the experimental surgery I've been researching for the better part of the past eighteen months. I tell him how it's been proven to work for cases similar to my sister's. I tell him about the denial from insurance and the upfront costs in order to schedule the procedure after she has a consult with the surgeon.

Chip says nothing for several long seconds, and it's not until I hear the break in his voice that I realize the reason. "I wish you would have told me about this sooner."

"It wasn't your problem to fix."

There is no humor in his laugh. "And moving my fourteen-inch memory foam mattress down four flights of stairs last month wasn't your problem either, but you did it anyway. Because that's what friends do for each other. They show up when you need them."

"You got me the work and paid me better than you promised. You've done plenty for me."

He lifts his empty water glass, swishes the remaining ice cubes several times. Sets it down. And then does it all again, two more times. When he finally leaves it on the table, he asks, "Have you opened the box yet?"

His question couldn't have been more alarming than if he'd stabbed me in the neck with his fork.

I don't answer, which of course is answer enough.

He threads his fingers on the table. "This surgery might fix your sister's hearing, but you know it won't fix everything. It can't."

"My sister is my primary responsibility. I'm her—"

"Legal guardian? Yes, I know. I was there, remember? I answered your phone in the hospital for you when the attorney called."

I bob my chin once. How could I forget? I was practically as catatonic as my sister in that moment.

He lowers his voice. "Listen, I may not know what it's like to be somebody's guardian, but I do know what it's like to watch the people I care for grieve." I know he's referencing a world much wider than the one I live in with Gabby. "The ones who suffer most are the ones who refuse to examine the source of their pain."

I study my hands, wishing for the life of me that I could have held all this in a few more minutes until I made it out to the car.

He releases a breath, and with it, I feel him throw me a bone I'm not too proud to take.

"How are things with Sophie?"

"Better than I deserve," I say honestly. "She's home with Gabby now. They're working on some big project for a class they take together."

Chip's deflated optimism is slowly refilling. "I figured they'd get along well."

"I'm pretty sure if you asked my sister, she'd choose Sophie ten out of ten times over me."

"Smart girl."

We both chuckle at that.

"So what's your next move?" he asks. "As far as the surgery goes."

"I make the call to the surgeon's office and set up Gabby's consultation." I glance at my watch—only a quarter after three. "Which I plan to do today."

Chip nods. "You've both waited a long time for this."

"Actually, Gabby doesn't know yet."

Chip's eyebrows take on a life of their own. "As in, she doesn't know about the bonus or the surgery?"

"Either." I drum my fingers on the table. "I should probably think of a good way to tell her tonight."

Chip raises his hands. "Don't look at me. Allie says I'm terrible at reading what women want." He shrugs. "I can only assume that includes teenagers, as well."

I smirk. "Do you always talk about such personal matters with your authors, or is that exclusive to Allie?"

"No, yes. I don't know." He shrugs. "It's more that we both tend to work odd hours . . . or we used to, anyway. Things are different now."

"Different how?"

Chip suddenly looks as if he's more interested in the construction of this booth than having this conversation, but after everything I just divulged, it's only fair.

"Marketing's been working on a big collaboration between Allie and Bo Jensen and—" Chip stops as if realizing who he's talking to. "He's a—"

"I know who Bo Jensen is." I may not be a reader myself, but I see that dude's books everywhere. Gabby even has a few on her bookshelf. "His novels are massive."

As if this comment is somehow a personal affront, Chip stretches his neck. "Actually, they're about average size for an epic fantasy."

"Oh, o-o-okay," I draw out. "And this collaboration's a problem because . . . ?"

"Never said it was a problem. They're just pretty focused. On each other. And the booklover's cruise they'll be featured at together next summer."

"I'm sorry, did you just say *a booklover's cruise*? As in a cruise where people sit around and read books together? Sounds thrilling." I tip my head back and pretend to snore.

He presses his palms to the table and begins to exit the booth. "Perhaps I'll let marketing know that the sexiest voice in entertainment has graciously offered to create an ad—pro bono—for said cruise for all the wonderful things Fog Harbor has done for him."

I give a short laugh as he waits for me to scoot out from the entrapment of this booth.

Once I'm freed, we make our way to the parking lot, and Chip's gaze falls to his loafers before we go our separate ways. "All jokes aside, I hope you know I only want the best for you and your sister."

"I do," I say. "I also know I couldn't have done any of this without your help. You're a good friend, Chip."

His nod is slow but sincere as he stuffs his hands into the pockets of his chinos. "Keep me updated."

"Will do."

He's already turned to walk back to his office when I call after him. "You have to keep me updated, too, ya know?"

He swivels his neck with a questioning eyebrow.

"On the other collaboration. For the record, I don't think Bo Jensen and his beefy books have anything on you," I reply.

His only response is an eye roll and a two-finger salute.

I tuck into my car, grateful for the solitude.

I suppose a civilized person would have waited until they were home to make the phone call they've imagined making since the audiologist first spoke the words *"I'm afraid her condition is degenerative. You'll need to make the necessary adjustments to her daily life as we work to test her for hearing aids. Of course, they will likely be a temporary solution."*

No, *civilized* is far from what I feel when I click into the email I've read a dozen times and tap on the contact number near the bottom and place the call. I breathe in the mix of relief and triumph as the medical admin searches for the surgeon's next available consultation date, but it's the sense of absolution I'm still waiting on as I make my way to my sister's favorite bakery to pick up the sugar supply a celebration like this demands.

24

Sophie

On the same day I listened to the last voice memo Gabby sent me, I received a callback from the casting director Dana's been in contact with in LA, asking me to fly down for a final reading. Six months ago, I would have jumped at the opportunity, no questions asked. But six months ago I didn't know just how full my life could be, or how badly I would want to stay in California.

Which is why I've struggled to reconcile Gabby's powerful testimony with August's reluctance to speak with me about the accident at all. It's not as if he hasn't had the opportunity or time . . . we've been with each other daily for months now. It's this brutal truth that has brought more uncertainty about our current standing than my willingness to let go of a lifelong dream.

The juxtaposition is happening again in real time as Gabby prints out a copy of what we've been working on together all afternoon for her part in the showcase: stage sketches, prop brainstorms, a basic one-act play template in English, and a dramatic narrative outline for ASL.

Technically, Gabby has everything she needs to take her raw voice memo of that inexplicable event and mold it into something ready for the stage. But I can't let her do that. Not yet anyway.

I crouch down beside her as she uses a neon yellow highlighter to indicate the key sentences she wants us to rework into our two scripts—hers and mine. And though I've heard this story spoken by her own voice, reading her words on paper now makes the impact all the more real. I can only imagine what it will do to a captive live audience.

I still her arm with my hand, and she glances my way. "This is the reason you have so much peace about your hearing loss, isn't it?" I touch my own ear. "And about your parents." My gaze drifts to their picture on her nightstand. It's of the three of them at a beach—all in swimwear, giant ice cream cones in their hands with the surf behind them. They're a beautiful family, despite the one not pictured.

It takes Gabby a second to process what she's read on my lips seeing as she's opted not to wear her hearing aids today. "I do have peace."

I reposition myself on her rug directly in front of her. "I'm proud of you for being so brave."

She signs *God* in ASL, and I know there is nothing flippant or cliché about it. How could there be after everything she's suffered and endured? After everything she's experienced?

I tap on the paper and make sure I speak clearly even though my voice breaks. "You have a powerful testimony."

"I've been praying God will use it," she says.

"He already has." I place a hand over my heart.

She fiddles with the highlighter. "I'm a little worried about how some people might respond. . . ."

I wait for her to speak again, but when she doesn't, I touch her shoulder to draw her attention back.

"Are you afraid they won't believe you?"

When she confirms my suspicion with a nod, a knot of fear roots in my belly. I can only hope "some people" doesn't refer to a man we both love and care for deeply. Despite my unanswered questions, she's held me to my promise not to share any of this with August, saying she has a plan and that she's praying God will answer it in the right time.

I have no choice but to trust her.

I also know I do have a choice when it comes to having a different conversation with her brother. One I've been putting off out of fear. But I know it needs to take place tonight.

Gabby and I spend the next hour syncing up lines and phrasing that can work for both scripts while trying to keep the storyline pure and the facts undoctored. It's a challenge, but the results have been beautiful so far. The best thing about dramatic narratives is how they aim to enhance an original storyline by bringing it to life through visual and emotional cues.

As soon as I hear the front door unlock and open, a sensor triggers a light on Gabby's ceiling that blinks on and off three times.

She looks at me. "August's home."

The swoop in my abdomen is equal parts anticipation and nerves.

I listen for a moment, waiting for him to call out for us. He doesn't. *Odd.* But even still, Gabby begins her cleanup of our afternoon's work, and I watch her slide her hearing aids into each ear and adjust them with her phone.

"I have plans with Tyler's family tonight," she says, once her aids are in. "He's picking me up at 5:30 for his dad's birthday dinner. We're doing build-your-own nachos and a game tournament. Their family goes crazy over games." She shoves the loose papers inside a notebook, then stands and moves toward her closet. "Can I get your opinion on an outfit really quick?"

"Sure." I pop up from the floor and hear a commotion going on in the dining room. Just as Gabby whirls to show me the cute blue fuzzy sweater and black denim combo on hangers, there's a knock on her door.

Again, her ceiling lights flash to indicate her brother's presence on the other side. There's a button August installed that I missed the first few times I was here.

"Hello?" he says through the door. "You ladies in there?"

I give Gabby a heads-up before I open the door a crack. My heart does a little hippity-hop maneuver at the sight of him in a quilted gray-and-black flannel that looks so cozy over his black undershirt. But more than that, he looks so . . . *happy.* Unusually so.

"I have a surprise out here for you both."

"For us both?"

He nods and stuffs his hands into his pockets. "Yes."

I widen my eyes, intrigued. "We were just finishing up a fashion consultation in here. Let me check where we are on that." I pull my head back into the room as Gabby slips out of her walk-in closet fully dressed in the outfit she showed me. She's let her hair down from her messy bun and is currently scrunching some kind of product in it with both hands. Oh, to have naturally curly hair. "August has a surprise for us out here."

Her eyebrows tick up as she gestures between us both. I laugh, given I'd done almost the exact same thing.

"That's what he says, yes."

"Hey." I pop my head back out the door to ask a question for his ears only, thinking, *Now or never.* "Do you think we can talk later on tonight?"

His face registers curiosity, but I don't miss the note of concern in his voice. "Everything good?"

I nod quickly and then wonder if that's actually true.

Gabby opens the door wider from behind me, and August's expression turns suspiciously delighted once again.

"You ready?" he asks. "It's in the dining room."

We follow him down the short hallway into the open living room and then turn left into a curtain of helium-filled balloons. There have to be a dozen or more of them tied together and floating at the end of their dining table—all brightly colored and many of them with the words *Congrats!* or *You're the Best!* printed on the latex. Gabby and I exchange confused glances, as I'm certain we're both thinking how today is not either of our birthdays. I know for a fact that Gabby doesn't turn seventeen until after the new year, in mid-February.

August beckons us around the mass of bobbing balloons to the broadside of the tables where there are two flat bakery boxes—each with one of our names scrawled across the lid in black Sharpie.

"Pizza cookies!" Gabby suddenly exclaims with a clap. "You went to Old Bay Bakery?!" She glances at me. "It's my favorite cookie shop ever!"

She reaches out to open her lid, but August stops her. "Sorry, sis. Sophie needs to open hers first. We are celebrating two special occasions tonight."

I'm staring between the two of them like I'm the party guest who wore the wrong costume to theme night.

"Go ahead." August's eyes gleam as he points to the box on the left. "Although, please don't judge me too harshly on the flavor choices. I didn't know your favorite, so I had to guess—and by guess, I mean I asked for a four-flavor combo."

I bite my bottom lip as I reach for the box and flip open the lid to reveal a giant combination cookie pizza with green and red piping in the center that reads *#Augie*.

I study the strange word and then slowly rotate to face him. "What does hashtag Augie mean?"

He laughs. "That was my question, too, when Chip first mentioned it at lunch today. Apparently, it's our *couple name*. Our audio performance of *Mistletoe Matrimony* has acquired somewhat of a large online fan base in the last couple of weeks."

Gabby steps between us, her phone already drawn like a loaded gun as she types in the strange hashtag. "Let's find it." And just like that, we do. I gasp as dozens and dozens of posts pull up on a single hashtag—the audio teaser being liked and shared tens of thousands of times. When Gabby taps on one popular post of her brother's face photoshopped under a branch of mistletoe with the words *All I Want For Christmas* underneath, I think I might actually hyperventilate. My laughs are more gasping inhales of air than anything else. As are Gabby's.

"Okay, okay. I think we all get the picture." He rolls his eyes and then turns to steady me between his strong hands. "The point is, we did it. We earned our bonuses and then some, and perhaps even better than that, Fog Harbor wants to negotiate more originals with us in the new year so hashtag Augie can grow in popularity."

"*Really*? Oh, August!" I throw my arms around his neck in an affectionate embrace, not caring that his baby sister is only a foot away. She seems just as thrilled for us as we are. "That's the absolute best news ever!"

"It's pretty darn close to it, but I think Gabby's cookie has ours beat," he whispers before he gently lets me go and then touches his sister's shoulder. "You're next."

Gabby sets her phone on the table face up, where my professional headshot is side-by-side with one of August in a wet suit next to a surfboard.

"What?" he all but shouts. "Where are they even finding these? That picture has to be at least five years old."

"Internet pics live forever," I tsk.

He shudders, and I stifle another laugh as Gabby leans down to open her lid.

Unlike mine, Gabby's cookie pizza appears to be a hundred percent one flavor—white chocolate chip macadamia. And also unlike mine, her white piped icing spells out a date: December 29th.

As soon as she looks to him for an explanation, a slow-searing dread begins to crawl up my spine.

He steps toward her. "I found a surgeon who can help you. She's already reviewed your scans and read all your medical reports, and . . ." He touches her shoulders and swallows the crack of emotion in his voice. "And she thinks she can repair the hearing in your left ear with a new procedure she's developed. You're scheduled for a consultation with her on December 29th at ten a.m. Her staff thinks they can get you in for surgery in February. Right before your birthday."

Gabby stays frozen, speechless, for some time, and I can't tell if it's because she's struggling to understand him or if—

"You've been talking to a surgeon about me?" Her question comes out flat and stilted, causing the dread in my core to enter my limbs.

"Yes," August confirms. "I found her a little over a year ago—Dr. Johnston—but I had to secure the funds before I scheduled anything. The surgery isn't covered by insurance yet."

Her eyes narrow, and she steps out of his hold, nearly falling as the backs of her knees bump against the bench seat under the table.

"Why not?" she asks. "Why isn't it covered?"

"Because it's . . ." August's pause makes me think he's considering his word choice carefully. "New."

Her breathing grows as rapid as her blinking. "Like an experiment?"

He says nothing to this, probably because there's no better terminology than the one she just used. And by the way her nostrils flare and her fingers ball into fists at her sides, it's the wrong one.

"*I am not broken.*" The fierceness of her voice causes me physical pain, and August flinches.

"I've never once said you were broken."

"But you think it all the time, don't you? You can't stand that I'm D-E-A-F." She fingerspells each letter in ASL, and my stomach rolls with nausea at the sight of her hurt. *Oh, August, this was not the way to do this.*

I place a hand on Gabby's upper back in hopes of de-escalating a conversation that, if left to its own devices, could spiral wildly out of control. Her heavy gaze meets mine and practically begs me to intervene on her behalf, to help her brother understand, but then her expression falls slack. "Did you know about this? Did you know what he was planning for me behind my back?"

Despite it being ages ago when August first mentioned another surgery as an option, I can't claim ignorance. Although, I so wish August would have discussed this with me before springing it on her. So much of my understanding of Gabby's situation, of her intimate thoughts and overall vision for her life, became clear when I listened to her voice memos. And I know beyond a shadow of a doubt that surgery is not what she wants.

"Did you?" she repeats a bit weaker now.

My chest squeezes at the note of betrayal in her tone. "I know your brother is hopeful that your hearing might be fully restored some day." Softly, I touch her cheek in hopes my words might reach her heart. "Because he loves you very much and wants the best for you."

Immediately, her eyes glaze with unshed tears, and when she speaks again, her voice is small. "I thought you understood me."

"I do, or at least, I think I do now," I fight to reassure her as I blink back tears of my own. I'd wrap my arms around her if it didn't mean compromising our communication. Instead, I make sure she can see me clearly when I say, "And if this is not what you want, then—"

"Of course it's what she wants," August cuts in, and both Gabby and I shift our attention to her big brother. "Doctor Johnston's success rate is nearly seventy percent. She thinks you have a promising case. We can discuss all your concerns with her at the consultation."

Gabby's laugh is dark and far from compliant. "My concerns?" She slashes her pointer finger through her hair above her left ear. "It's not *your* head she'll be experimenting on. I've already had brain surgery, remember? I'm not doing it again. I'm fine with the way I am, and so are the people who actually love and accept me!"

"And who's that?" he challenges coldly. "Tyler?"

"August," I warn, but he barrels full steam ahead.

"Tyler doesn't get a say in your future. You are still a minor under my care."

Despite her aids and her concentration, I can tell by the way she's angling her head she's struggling to keep up.

"Slow down," I hiss. "You're speaking too fast."

He repeats his statement, and I cringe when he doesn't take the opportunity to soften or revise a single word of it. I wish I could intercept them before they made impact.

Gabby's entire body goes rigid, her voice lethal. "Tyler would never ask me to change just so he could be more comfortable in my presence."

"That's not what's happening here, Gabby, and you know it. I'm offering you the chance to *hear* again—*forever*. Don't you think if Tyler was offered that same chance, he'd take it?"

303

"He *was* offered that chance!" she fires back. "His parents gave him the choice to get a cochlear implant when he was younger, and he didn't want one. If Mom and Dad were here, they would have given me the same choice. *They* listened to me, *they* asked me questions, *they* trusted me to know my own mind and heart. But how would you know any of that when you don't even let me talk to you about them!"

"That's not true," he says in a way that reveals just the opposite. "We talk about them plenty."

Gabby's openly crying as she pulls her phone from her pocket and begins furiously texting. I don't have to wonder who the recipient is.

"We talk about them plenty," August repeats in a far more frustrated tone, but her eyes are not on him, and whatever discussion is happening on her phone is of far more interest to her than what her brother is saying.

I gasp when August rips the phone out of her hand and watch in horror as he begins to skim through the text exchange between her and Tyler. Gabby tries to swipe it back from him, but August is too fast and too tall, and she has no chance.

"No way," he grounds out while reading the messages. "You are not going anywhere with him tonight."

"Wait a second, August," I cut in. I'm done pretending to be a neutral party when I grip his arm and force him to see me. "She already had plans to go to his house tonight for his dad's birthday dinner. It's why she's dressed up. Honestly, I think taking some space apart is a good idea for both of you tonight."

But August doesn't choose to hear me. Instead, he continues to glower at his sister. "Do you understand me? You are not to leave anywhere with him tonight. You're grounded. And this—" he tucks her phone in his back pocket—"is mine now."

"Oh, yeah?" She rips the aids out of her ears and tosses them on the chair. "Then you can take these, too."

Due to our proximity to the front door, I hear the hum of Tyler's engine as he rolls into the driveway. My eyes flick to the window for only a second, but it's enough for Gabby to realize that something has changed. In this case, her knight in shining armor has arrived.

She darts to the door and throws it open as August barks for her to come back, threatening her with heftier punishments if she so much as thinks of getting inside his car. But of course, Gabby hears none of these threats because her hearing aids are in the living room and the rumble of Tyler's engine drowns out whatever residual hearing she has left. She doesn't spare a backward glance in her brother's direction.

When August starts for the open door, I'm determined to block his path. The last thing he needs is a confrontation with Tyler. There is no scenario in any world where two heated men who love the same woman are going to see eye to eye.

I slam the door closed, lock it, and brace my body like a shield against the wooden frame.

"Open the door, Sophie."

"No. You need time to cool off before you talk to her again."

"What I *need*," he grinds out, "is to get my sister away from that punk." He tries to unlock the door around me, but I bat his hand away. He looks startled by the physical contact. *Good.*

"Listen to me, August. You are going to lose her if you go after her like this."

"Would you rather me call the police after they leave? Because that's well within my rights. He's about to take a minor in my care off my property."

I shake my head. "Do you even hear yourself right now? Look at me." I reach out and place my palm over his pounding heart. "Look at me, August. If you call the cops on her boyfriend, you might get her back physically, but you will lose her heart forever." My voice is strained but firm. "And we both know that's a much higher cost than you're willing to pay."

His chest rises and falls three times before I hear Tyler pull out of the driveway and down the street. I have every desire to sag against the door with relief, but then I take in August's stormy expression and know this night is far from over.

25

August

Out of the corner of my eye, I see the red flash of Tyler's brake lights at the four-way stop at the end of our street. It takes every ounce of self-control I possess not to bolt through Sophie's blockade and charge after him. Whatever this raging instinct is, it's all-consuming. Pulsing and physical. And it's pushed me too close to the edge.

I turn away from Sophie, needing movement. Needing space.

I rip open the sliding glass door at the far end of the dining room, hoping she won't follow me.

I cross over the dead grass looking for some wood to chop or perhaps a hole to dig with my bare hands, but the only thing close is the rotting, overgrown garden beds I'd planned to rebuild next spring. No time like the present.

I don't bother with gloves or even a hammer as I begin the dismantling process by kicking one board in the framed rectangle loose with my heel and then flattening it under my weight. I toss the weathered wood into the burn pile several yards from the greenhouse. By the fourth board, I'm huffing something fierce, and my heel is on fire.

Sophie moves into my periphery. Because of course she followed me. "If you would have discussed this possibility of surgery with her months ago, she would have told you she didn't want it." Each word Sophie speaks is evenly spaced and carefully devoid of emotion, but I'm an expert at plucking out even the smallest hint of judgment when it comes to my sister.

"She can't possibly know what she wants." I tear another board from a box with nails so rusted they break in half. "She's sixteen."

"So is your plan to strong-arm her into having brain surgery? Be reasonable, August."

I pause mid-kick to wipe my brow. "Oh? The same way I should *be reasonable* and allow her to date an eighteen-year-old who's likely filling her head with all sorts of nonsense right this second? I think it's fair to say you and I have two very different definitions of that word."

She crosses her arms over her chest, and I can't help but notice she didn't bother to grab a jacket on her way out. The thin thermal she's in might have long sleeves, but there's zero chance she's not freezing in this weather. "If you're insinuating I'm somehow to blame for encouraging her relationship with a guy who can understand her in a way neither one of us can, I don't buy it. You don't believe that any more than you believe Tyler's the enemy."

I jump to flatten another board under my weight, then bring my hands to my hips. "Gabby is my sister. I can handle her on my own."

"And was that back there—" she twists to point toward the dining room—"an example of you handling it? You cutting her off without listening to a thing she said? You confiscating her phone? You grounding her because she refuses to be a tally mark on some surgeon's chance at a medical breakthrough?" She marches toward me. "You told her what she was going to do without asking her a single question. And honestly, even if you had asked her, I doubt she would have felt safe enough to share her real feelings with you in that hostile environment."

I lift my gaze to her tense face. "And I suppose she's shared all those *real feelings* with you?"

Sophie hesitates a beat too long before she simply says, "Yes, she has."

This shouldn't rub me the wrong way—I have enough working brain cells to know that much—and yet the twisting sensation in my gut can't be ignored. Five months ago I was thrilled Gabby had a trusted female to confide in other than Aunt Judy and Tyler's mother. Back then, Sophie and I had felt like two players on the same team, a united front with the same goal: Gabby's best. But Gabby's best, as it turns out, is far more ambiguous than I realized before tonight.

I think about everything Gabby could have told Sophie in confidence—all the hours they've spent together carpooling from one place to another, taking ASL classes at the theater and attending church on Sunday mornings. Not to mention all the days Sophie has been here with me. With us.

Because in every way that matters, Sophie's become a part of us.

The revelation comes unbidden, and it's enough of a blow to my ego for me to launch the last plank of wood to the burn pile and shrug out of my flannel.

"Here," I say, extending it out to her. "Take this."

"I don't need your—"

"You're shivering." I don't lower my offering. "Please, just put it on." There are few things I can control at the moment, and regulating Sophie's body temperature so I can vent outside like an angry fool is one of them.

Our stare-down doesn't last long.

She takes the flannel.

I bend at the waist, hands on my knees as I catch my breath and fight to calm my racing thoughts when I hear her tug it on. "I know you're not the person I'm most angry at, Sophie—I'm sorry. I . . ." I make a study of my boots and release a frustrated growl that comes from somewhere deep. Somewhere dark. "I don't know how to fix this."

When she says nothing in reply, I lift my chin. And for the first time, the compassion I find in her gaze scares me.

"Maybe you need to ask yourself what you're really trying to fix, August."

"My sister's hearing," I retort immediately.

She wraps my shirt tighter around herself. "I think it's much more than that."

We're in a standoff again, only this time, I'm not sure which one of us will break first.

It's her.

"Are you going to burn that tonight?" She points to my pile of random, haggard wood. "It's supposed to rain most of next week, so tonight might be your only chance."

I drag my eyes from her to the garden shed, where I keep the lighter fluid. I march over to it, and within minutes, I've started a fire I hadn't planned on, tending to it with a long, skinny branch. Sophie made use of the time by carrying out two crusty garden stools from inside the greenhouse. The tops are hand-painted with mushrooms, caterpillars, and butterflies—my mother's handiwork from when I was still living under her roof. Seeing them out here is a painful reminder that she's no longer here and won't ever be again.

Sophie plants the chairs a safe distance away from the fire and gestures for me to join her.

She clasps her hands between her knees. "I've told you things about my brother and about my broken family dynamics that I've never shared with anyone," she starts as soon as I sit and poke the stick in the ground beside my stool. "I told you what happened to me at sixteen and about the realities of my life when I lived in New York. You know my failures as an actress and insecurities about returning to the stage and the fears I'm currently facing. And do you know how you've responded to me each and every time?"

I trace the angles of her face in the firelight and wait for her to answer her own question.

"With kindness and understanding."

I flick my eyes away from her as her cool hand closes around mine.

"Please give me a chance to show you the same. I hope you know you can trust me."

I want to tell her it's not as simple as she makes it sound. That some of these hurts are attached to strings with no ends. That if she tugs too hard on the wrong one, all of them, *all of me*, will unravel.

"I don't know what more you want me to say." It's an honest answer, even if it's not the one she's hoping for. "There are multiple reasons I think the surgery is the best thing for Gabby's future—"

"I don't want to talk about Gabby; I want to talk about *you*."

Her declaration stops me short, and I twist on my stool, catching her eyes in the glow of the fire. "Okay. What about?"

"Tell me the story of how your parents died."

The searing blade of a knife stabs me between the ribs. "You already know how they died."

"You've told me the facts, yes. The train accident in India. The phone call from your aunt. Gabby's hospital stays and diagnosis. An attorney informing you of your parents' wishes for Gabby's guardianship. The small inheritance they left to you both and your move back to Petaluma from LA." Her gaze is pointed as she presses her hand to her heart. "But none of those facts tell me anything about what happened in here—what's still happening *in here*. I'm your girlfriend, August. I want to know you. I *care* about you. I . . ." Her lips stop, but her silence speaks for her, and it's impossible not to feel every inch of the coward I've become. I drop my gaze to the patch of dry grass under my feet.

My head buzzes with the dissonance of conflicting thoughts. "*I want to know you*," she said. But what's lurking in my past is not a one-time confession. It's not something that was done to me, but rather something I did. Something I chose and continued choosing even after I knew the hurt my deception had caused. There's no light switch I can flip that will erase the years of heartache I caused my parents after I sold out my faith for a dream that never delivered. And there's no redemption plan that will bring my parents back after they died serving a God who hadn't bothered to answer their prayers.

"I don't see how dredging up the past will fix anything," I say, hoping the hitch in my voice is disguised by the crackling fire.

"It might not, but how can you heal if you're unwilling to face whatever it is you keep shoving down?"

"Not all fears are equal, Sophie." I can tell by her body language she doesn't miss the defensive edge in my tone. "I'd never force you to go down to hang out in the wine cellar or audition on a stage. Not even in the name of *healing*."

Sophie goes still beside me, and even when the fire pops and a board breaks, she remains tense. "I actually had an audition last week."

This stuns me. "What?"

"Technically, it was a callback. It wasn't on a stage, but it was in front of a casting director and his crew." I remain frozen as she twists her body toward me. Her knee bounces in time with my hammering pulse. "Dana sent in an initial audition video of me without my permission, and strangely enough, the director emailed to ask if I'd do a live audition over their online platform."

It's everything I can do to keep my voice level. "And you kept this from me because . . . ?"

"Because I didn't think anything would come from it. I wasn't even sure I'd be able to perform a full song, let alone that they'd have a lead role in mind for me. They've asked if I would fly down to LA for a final reading but—"

I stand and move toward the fire, gripping the poker stick so hard I'm sure it will snap. "Is that where the show is—LA?"

"No," she says softly. "It's a traveling production that requires a twelve-month contract."

Her words send a jolt of pain through me, and I wonder if she can see it on my face. "And you told them you'd go?"

"Of course I didn't." While firelight dances across her features, she stands and squares up to me. And without the slightest hint of reservation, she grips the poker stick, her closed fist brushing the top of mine. "I told them I needed time to talk to my boyfriend and figure a few things out before I gave them an answer. It's what

I wanted to talk to you about tonight before . . . well, before everything happened."

The reminder of the mess I created with my sister does little to steady my mind. But soon I'm studying the perfect swell of Sophie's lips, the thin line of her jaw, and the slight arch of her neck, and my desire for her flares brighter than the fire at my back.

I quickly tamp it down. "You want me to give you permission to go."

"No, August." She shakes her head and gives me a tentative smile. "I'm hoping you'll give me a reason to stay. I'm hoping you'll tell me you see a future for us. I'm hoping you feel the same for me as I feel for you." Her grip tightens on the branch as mine begins to yield. "Because I love you."

Her words are like oxygen to a dying soul, and it's simultaneously the best and worst thing to hear. Because I know what she can't possibly understand: that loving me is a mistake. Tonight should have clued her in on that, but Sophie is as resilient as she is forgiving. Which is ironically one of the qualities I love most about her.

For less than a second, I imagine what I'd do if I only had my own needs to consider. How I'd grip her waist and kiss her until she understood everything I felt without ever having to speak a single word of it. But I have more than my own needs to consider. That's what I understand about love now versus what I understood when I was only interested in chasing after my own selfish desires: I was hurting the very people who refused to give up even when I gave them zero reason to hope.

When I relinquish control of the poker, Sophie's beautiful bottom lip begins to tremble. It's the pain that crosses her features that spurs me to find a voice, even if it's not my own.

Because she deserves better from me. She's always deserved better.

"You asked me to be honest with you." I find her eyes and swallow the bitter taste on my tongue warning me not to do this. Warning me to lock these lying words up and to throw away the key before I ruin everything. "Are you sure that's what you want?"

Her nod is almost imperceptible, and I hate myself for the hurt I can already see blooming in her eyes.

"I told you in the very beginning that I'd never want to be the reason you missed out on an opportunity to use your talents."

"August, you can't be serious—"

"I think you should take the contract if it's offered to you."

For nearly a minute she studies me as if she doesn't know me at all, and maybe never did. "Is that all you have to say to me? That you hope I move away?"

No, I think. *That's not even close to all I have to say.*

But I know what will happen if she stays. I will disappoint her the same way I have disappointed everyone else in my life. And it will cost her something precious. Maybe not her life, maybe not her hearing, but perhaps the very thing that took my breath away the first time Sophie Wilder stepped into my life. Her light.

And that price tag is too much to bear.

"I think we both need to take some space and figure out what the future looks like . . . on our own."

After one last shattering look of disbelief, Sophie strips off my flannel, tosses it to the stool, and strides back toward my house. I nearly run after her then, but something in my subconscious holds me back. Because deep down I know that even if it kills me, letting Sophie go is the most loving thing I can do for her.

26

Sophie

I know it's none of my business, but . . . I can tell something's changed with you." Natalie eyes me as she hands me another scalding-hot wine glass from the industrial dishwasher in the staff kitchen. The clean-up portion of the first of many private December events hosted in our tasting room has given Natalie and I ample alone time tonight. The perfect breeding ground for a painful conversation I'd rather not rehash—though talking about the breakup with Natalie will be quite different than with Dana. For one, Natalie probably won't try to console me by suggesting my broken heart is likely a sign from the universe to go back into theater . . . even though I've told her more than once that I don't believe in "the universe."

"At first," Natalie continues hesitantly, "I wondered if it had something to do with the final quote Jasper gave you for the van rebuild. But you've been down for going on two weeks now."

Eleven days, I silently correct. I was rejected eleven days ago by the man I loved. By the man I *still* love.

"You don't owe me any kind of answer, I just—"

"August and I broke up." The phrase rubs me wrong. I had nothing to do with that breakup. It wasn't some mutual agreement or amicable arrangement. It was a hundred percent him, and I'd been a hundred percent blindsided. "No, actually," I correct myself as I set a dried glass into the storage container, "August broke up with me."

The death of a relationship has no body to bury or funeral to plan, but the absence of what could have been is a grief all its own.

"But why?" She crosses her arms. "And I'm not asking for whatever lame reason he gave first. That's never the real reason."

I straighten. Of all the questions Dana asked, this was not one of them. And yet, I know how to respond because it's been brewing inside me since that night.

"The real reason is . . ." A swell of emotion hits me dead-center in my chest, and I wait for the tears to pass before I speak. "I think he's afraid to let himself love me." I blink my blurring vision away. "I think he can't until he deals with stuff that happened long before I came into the picture."

Natalie exhales audibly. "I'm sorry, Sophie."

"Me too." I feel a tear slip down my cheek. I wipe it away.

"What does that mean for his sister? She's who you were learning ASL for, right? Have you seen her since?"

"Yes," I say, recalling how difficult that first meeting was for us both. We met at the theater under the pretense of rehearsing her monologue when in actuality we spent the majority of the night talking and trying not to cry. Eventually, we gave up the fight and gave in to the tears. "I've made a commitment to her. Regardless of where I end up, I know God put her in my life for a reason." I don't understand much at the moment, but I do know that. I love Gabby, and not only because she happens to be the little sister of my boyfriend—ex-boyfriend—but because she's an incredible human being who has blessed my life beyond what I deserve.

"Does that mean you're leaving California?"

"What?" I ask, veering into the present again.

"You said 'regardless of where you end up.'" There's a hint of something in Natalie's voice I can't decipher. "Do you have plans to leave?"

"Possibly," I say honestly. "I have an in-person audition in LA on December 11th with a reputable traveling theater company. If I land the part, I'll be relocating to company housing by New Year's and on the road by spring." I scheduled the flight for the morning after the winter showcase at Twilight Theater. It was the earliest I could leave without causing a disruption to the rehearsal schedule. The last thing I want to do is abandon Portia after all she entrusted to me. It was hard enough to tell her I might be leaving permanently depending on the outcome of my LA audition.

"But I thought you were *praying*," Natalie says, emphasizing the word, "about an opportunity at your friends' theater?"

Honestly, I forgot I shared that with her in the hot tub, but by the pointed look on Natalie's face, she hasn't. "I did pray about it." *A lot* is what I don't say. I journaled my prayers nearly every day, asking God to bless the Pimentels' vision for a deaf theater. Asking God to guide all their next steps. Asking God if He had a specific role in mind for me there. Thanking God for the provision He gave me in narration. Asking God to help me rebuild a life in California, full of thriving relationships, including the one that just disintegrated. "And I think God's answer is *no*."

Natalie doesn't say anything for several long minutes as we continue with our wash-dry-stack routine, and I wonder, not for the first time, what she's thinking about. I also wonder if she'd even be honest with me if I asked. While I haven't spotted that Clinton guy around the house again, it doesn't take a trained therapist to see Natalie is hiding a lot of secrets behind her flawless exterior.

"You can come to the winter showcase if you want; it's on December 10th. I can get you a ticket." I pause, hoping the discussion shifts away from my relationship woes. "There are some phenomenal acts, and Gabby is performing."

Natalie doesn't look up at me when she says, "I actually have plans that night with Jasper. A holiday art auction, for charity. But thank you for inviting me."

"Of course, I—"

"Natalie!" The sharp bark of my brother's voice turns both our heads toward the open doorway.

"I'm in here," she calls out, lifting one of our stacked boxes from the floor and shoving it on the counter in front of her. I can't help but notice how the exertion causes her to wince. Natalie is a runner— her build is lean and athletic. I've been hauling these storage boxes around for the better part of two days. They can't weigh more than twenty pounds apiece. So why—

Jasper fills the doorway. For a man who goes to great lengths to present a pristine appearance at all times, he is, at this moment, the antithesis of a public-facing business tycoon. His bloodshot eyes and unkempt hair are a precursor to his untucked, wrinkled dress shirt. I've worked hard to keep our paths from crossing over the last few weeks, but even still, I'm not sure I'd recognize my own brother if I ran into him on the street.

"I thought I told you to stay in the office today. You have paper-work that needs to be signed and overnighted," he says to his wife before his eyes shift to me and narrow.

"I know," Natalie starts, "but there was still too much clean-up work for Sophie to handle on her own after last night's event—"

"Your job is to assist *me*, not her." His forehead gleams with a fresh sheen of sweat, though this room is cool. "And I needed you up in the office hours ago."

My hackles rise at his degrading tone. I've never heard my brother speak to my sister-in-law like this before. But then again, I can count on one hand the number of times I've seen them interact openly since their wedding. If they're together, they're usually behind closed doors, unseen and unheard.

"We're almost done packing up the stemware—only a couple more boxes at most. I can come up after I take them down to the cellar and start a load of linens." She turns to me. "If you don't mind switching out the wash, I'll fold them after dinner."

"No, you won't," Jasper rebuffs. "You will let Sophie do her job, and you will do yours. Let's go." There's something inhumane about the way my brother is staring at Natalie. Like she's not a person, but an object. Like she's not his wife, but his servant.

It takes me a moment to place where I've seen this expression before, but then I recall my many years in New York food service, particularly the smug faces of men who chose to use their influence to degrade an underpaid server for a simple mistake. A wrong dish or drink refill—or heaven forbid, a smaller portion size than they deemed appropriate for the price—could set them off and result in the humiliation of a coworker.

I step up to Natalie's side. "She said she'll be up after she's finished."

His warning glare drags back to me. "This doesn't involve you."

It's a command, yet he has no authority over me.

"Actually, it does." I raise my arms and make a show of looking around. "According to the bylaws within our family trust, this entire property and the work it involves is as much mine as it is yours." I hope my expression looks as gritty as it feels. "You might be the operations manager and one of *three* trustees, but unless I commit a felony, forfeit my share, or am unanimously voted out, your authority over me is a moot point. And as a family member and cherished employee, the same rules and protections are true for your wife." I cross my arms over my chest. "I finally took your advice and brushed up on the business side of things around here. Made for some pretty boring bedtime reading this last week, but quite informative all the same."

But instead of the united front I'm anticipating from Natalie, there's terror in her eyes when her gaze cuts from me to Jasper. The silence that follows pricks my fear.

Natalie grips the storage box on the counter and moves toward the door with it in her hands. "How 'bout I run this next door to the cellar and then I'll be right up? You're right, honey, Sophie can manage the rest of this on her own without me."

The cords in my brother's neck constrict multiple times before he finally exhales. "Don't be long."

As soon as he exits the room, I start to speak again, but Natalie cuts me off with a single shake of her head. We wait until the last of his footsteps on the stairs fade and the door to his office slams closed.

Natalie starts for the outside door when I grab the storage container from her. "You're not taking this down there. I can see you're in pain."

"What? No." Her eyebrows scrunch in confusion as she keeps her voice low. "I know you haven't been down to the cellar since . . ."

"Maybe it's time I change that." It's a declaration, one I've been battling since August challenged me to face my own fears before asking him to face his. I set the box at my feet, take hold of my sister-in-law's shoulders, and speak with unrivaled fervor. "Natalie, listen to me, if you're in trouble I will help you—"

"It's not what you think," she whispers. "I promise, Sophie. I can handle myself." She throws a glance up the stairs. "Don't worry about the linens. I'll run a load of laundry after he falls asleep. It shouldn't be too much longer now. He never went to bed last night."

And then she twists out of my hold and scurries from the staff kitchen without a backward glance.

With Natalie upstairs with my brother, I take my time drying and boxing the last of the stemware alone. I listen carefully for any out-of-place creak or sharply spoken word. But there is nothing. After a while, my mind begins to play a riveting game of anxiety hopscotch, jumping over some squares while landing in the center of others. Each one marked with the name of someone I love.

Natalie.

Gabby.

August.

My prayers for each are simple, my words often fumbled and unsure, and yet I have faith enough to know they're heard.

By the time I load the second round of laundry into the washer and have the first folded and put away, I've convinced myself that my brother is too smart to do anything untoward to Natalie while I'm present on the property. At least, that's what I tell myself before I collect the storage boxes to carry across the path to the tasting room after dark.

When I enter the main dining area, I set the boxes on a table near the door and close myself in. It's far from the first time I've been alone in the tasting room since the attack, but somehow my body knows this time is different. There's a sticky anticipation building in my core, a tensing in my muscles, as if they've already begun to brace for an assault they've been overcompensating for since I was sixteen. I scan the familiar setting, not as it is now, but as it was back then, remembering the cloud of cheap cologne that hung in the air and the sound of clomping boots on the cellar stairs. And then the hushed duet of male voices—one more distinct than the other, hurling curses and insults at my unwelcome arrival.

I stop the memory there and grip the boxes like a shield at my chest. And then I cross to the far side of the room and stare down at the narrow staircase, proving to myself that there is no angry man about to assault me and no shards of glass beyond the door that once held me prisoner.

"I will not be afraid," I speak aloud, taking each step at my own pace and in my own time. When flashes of old memory threaten to steal my progress, I replace them with the here and now. My hip against the safety railing. The steps under my feet. The song I hum for comfort, the same one my grandmother sang with me as a child long before I had any real understanding of its meaning.

It takes me a full minute to build up the courage to pass the threshold into the cellar, and when I do, my lips begin to quiver. "I will not be afraid."

I think of Gabby's testimony, of the many times we've rehearsed her dramatic narrative in these last few weeks, and how the more I speak out this truth, the stronger my faith becomes.

On shaky legs, I move into the closet and set the boxes on the floor. I breathe through an overwhelming urge to bolt back up the steps and declare this a victory. But before I can, my mind turns to August once again, to whatever fear still holds him captive. To a prison so much worse than these four walls.

My pulse drums against my ribs as I take in my surroundings anew. Gone are the ominous shadows that scratched at the edges of my consciousness, replaced by the brightly lit display cases holding expensive wines framed by an art collection my brother has been curating since his promotion.

I will not be afraid.

Before I allow another negative memory to capture my thoughts, I part my lips and begin to sing. At first the verse is little more than a shaky rasp, but soon it becomes a prayer—*my prayer.*

> "Why should I feel discouraged,
> Why should the shadows come?
> Why should my heart be lonely,
> And long for heav'n and home?
>
> When Jesus is my portion,
> My constant Friend is he;
> His eye is on the sparrow,
> And I know he watches me;
> His eye is on the sparrow,
> And I know he watches me."

As my fear slowly ebbs, my voice builds and swells in full resonance. Not like an actress projecting a character on a stage, but like a woman who knows exactly who she is and why she sings. I also know I'm not alone. Not only in this moment, but on that dark night, too, and every night that came before and will come after.

> "I sing because I'm happy,
> I sing because I'm free;
> For his eye is on the sparrow,
> And I know he watches me."

The Voice We Find

With my eyes closed, I repeat the chorus once more as warmth blankets me from head to toe. And as the last line comes to an end, I remain still . . . until a quiet whimper alerts me to a presence not my own.

Natalie stands inside the doorway of the cellar, her arms wrapped around her middle protectively, as tears streak her cheeks.

"Natalie?" Alarmed, I move toward her.

But before I can say more, she pulls the heavy door closed behind her with a thud that echoes violently through the hollowed space, sealing us in.

"Do you really believe that?" Her accusation is a frantic sort of desperate, and it takes me a moment to grasp what's she asking. "Do you believe that God watches over us?"

"Yes," I say. "I do."

Her chin quivers as she fights to suppress her emotion. "I told you that I gave up on the idea of redemption for myself a long time ago." She wipes her face with the sleeve of her velour tracksuit. "But I want better for him."

At first, I'm certain she's speaking about my brother, her husband. But then she touches the small, rounding mound of her lower abdomen, and her tears fall in earnest.

"You're . . ." I lift shaky fingers to my lips.

"Pregnant." Her smile is the saddest kind of beautiful. "I'll be fifteen weeks tomorrow. It's a boy."

I hold my breath as several scenarios battle for territory in my mind. "Does—"

"Jasper know?" She gives a slow shake of her head. "No. You're the only person I've told."

Words fail me as I move to wrap her into the first hug I can recall us sharing. "I'll help you, Natalie. Whatever you need."

When she pulls back, her dark eyes fill with a resolve that seems to radiate inside my own chest. "I need you to pray for my baby."

And so I do.

27

August

I can count the number of words Gabby has spoken to me since our argument on one hand, not including the words she had Aunt Judy text me after packing her bags and leaving the house for several days. But even after she returned, she's only stayed long enough to sleep. So when I found the note Gabby scrawled on the theater ticket taped to my studio door this morning, her invitation caught me completely off guard.

August,
There's so much I need to say to you but don't know how. Will you please come tonight?

—Gabby

I hold the ticket in my hand now, backlit by the lights of the Twilight Theater, and note my aunt's Lexus in the parking lot. Her presence here tonight doesn't surprise me, and yet her unwavering support of Gabby exposes a raw nerve. Despite my role as my sister's legal guardian, it's our aunt she contacted after she accused me of not understanding her.

Of not *accepting* her.

The glint of my aunt's spotless sedan draws my attention once again. Perhaps I'd been wrong not to relinquish my legal rights to someone more capable.

Perhaps Gabby would have been better off if I'd stayed in LA.

Perhaps that's part of what Gabby wishes she could say to me but doesn't know how.

It's eight minutes until the show starts, but I find myself rooted at the stoop of the theater. My palms are sticky with sweat, as if I'm the one preparing to perform for an audience and not my sister and her friends. In truth, I don't know much about tonight's show other than what's printed on the ticket regarding the added accessibility for the deaf and hearing impaired. But I do know that Gabby started meeting with Sophie at the theater shortly after I blew everything up.

Sophie.

It's been twenty-two days since I've seen her, and exactly none of those days have felt any easier than the day I lied to her face and told her I didn't want her enough.

Even now, bile lurches up my esophagus at the memory.

For her sake, I hope to remain hidden within the crowd tonight. The last thing she needs is a reminder of the coward she dated.

I slip into the expansive lobby and into the auditorium with every intention to make a clean exit as soon as Gabby's act is finished. There are too many opportunities to risk hurting the people I care about most by staying any longer than necessary.

At five minutes to curtain, a high school–aged usher at the door hands me a program and offers to help me find the best seat available. I politely inform him that I'll be fine on my own. The place is packed—nearly every seat filled—but I'm hopeful to spy a spot near the back. I know Aunt Judy will be seated as close to the front as possible. I can't think of a single music recital of mine as a boy when she wasn't seated next to my parents in the front row, clapping for me with as much enthusiasm as if I'd just made the final touchdown in a championship game.

I locate an aisle seat in the second to last row. Head down, I do what I can to stay in the shadows, free from the gaze of the only blood relative I have in this auditorium. Once I've settled into my seat, I open my program in search of my sister's name and cast picture.

"Hey, I know you."

Dread prickles my spine. I haven't heard Bonnie Brewer's voice in months, not since that morning in church when she showered me with unsolicited advice. But I know it's her. She has the kind of distinct vocal quality a subconscious doesn't easily forget. And somehow, it's directed at me.

"Hello again." I rotate my neck just enough to give a diplomatic nod. "Ms. Brewer, isn't it?" Though I'm certain my face portrays I'm in no mood for small talk, she is not deterred.

"Just Bonnie is fine." She corrects me with a flick of her hand. "And you're a calendar month."

"Excuse me?"

She ticks at her fingers and mumbles, "Let's see, it's a weird one. Not October or March or . . ." She exclaims, "August! It's August, right?"

I blink. "Yes."

"I've been coming here for those ASL classes. Started a few months ago." She shrugs. "I like to challenge myself." Her fingers are hooked and arthritic, but even still, she finger spells her name—struggling on the N. "Turns out I'm not too old to learn new tricks after all."

"That's impressive," I say, before turning my attention back to my open program. I'm relieved when she does the same with her own. I slide my eyes down the show's lineup and then cringe. My sister's act is dead last. This is going to be a very long night.

"You know any of these youngsters performing?" Bonnie shakes her program like the youngsters she speaks of might fall out of the glossy pages onto her lap. It's an effort not to give in to my urge to lie so we can avoid finding a commonality of any kind.

"My sister," I admit after a moment's hesitation. There's no chance I'm going to tell her that I also know the woman whose headshot is on the second page. Sophie's photo and bio have her listed under the title of assistant director. A tiny, unexpected hope zips through my melancholy at the thought of her using her talent here, in this capacity. Of course, directing is not the same as acting. And I doubt the Pimentels are set up to offer her the kind of job security she desires, not with all the renovations they've done and still need to do.

Even still, I can't help the movie reel that plays in my mind at the hope of her choosing a life here. I see it so clearly: me, taking Sophie's face in my hands and begging her to forgive me, telling her how the idea of facing another hour, much less another week without her, makes me want to turn my skin inside out.

And yet I must face it. For her.

She deserves more than I can give her.

"Which one is she?" Bonnie asks, examining the cast's headshots and bios.

Before I can answer, Bonnie wagers a guess. She taps on a picture of a blond girl listed under the second act of the night. "Going off your looks, I'd guess this cutie with the dimples right here—Emily Adams. You two share a similar eye color."

I take the path of least resistance and point to a picture beside the eighth act of the night. "My sister is Gabby Tate." I watch Bonnie's eyebrows rise at the distinct lack of resemblance between me and my Colombian sister, and when she doesn't immediately comment on our differences, I wrongly assume this interaction has fulfilled the required small-talk quota for seatmates.

Bonnie continues to study Gabby's picture for longer than what feels comfortable. "I've seen her at the classes on Tuesday nights. Her smile is infectious." She presses two arthritic fingers to her chest. "It comes from her heart. My daughter had that same type of smile."

I note the past tense of her sentence and freeze.

"Cancer," she confirms softly. "A quick battle."

I shift my gaze to her profile. "I'm sorry."

"Me too," she amends. "Should have been me."

A feeling I know all too well.

As the theater lights dim and the curtain rises, Portia and her husband, Nick, take center stage. He signs a greeting to the audience in ASL first while Portia interprets. The two of them take turns welcoming us to the winter showcase, cracking multiple jokes to lighten the atmosphere and warm up the crowd. They teach the hearing-only crowd how to give applause in ASL—by raising both hands and shaking them in the direction of the stage. They then highlight the donation boxes in the lobby and the QR code on the back of the program allocated for their future efforts at commencing a deaf theater. A dream the two of them have shared since they married nearly twenty years ago. Despite the unsettled feeling in my gut since I walked in, their passion to create theater that can meld two worlds in a way I didn't even know existed draws me in.

By the time the couple exits stage left and a male narrator introduces the first act over the surround speakers, closed captioning of his words on the background screen, I've all but forgotten my resistance to being here. The lively song and dance number by two young people—one deaf and one hearing—invites audience participation as the two sign ASL to the lyrics in sync with each other. Bonnie leans forward in her seat, clutching at her program and squinting at the stage through her foggy glasses. I'm honestly not sure how she can see anything through those smeared lenses.

After the fourth act, Portia comes back on stage and announces a fifteen-minute intermission. I help Bonnie retrieve her walker. While I unfold it, I ask the young usher waiting nearby if there's a place Bonnie might satisfy her "hankering for a Snickers bar." She's only brought it up to me five times in so many minutes, so it's only fair I widen the circle of communication. Thankfully, the kid's brother is the one working the concessions table, and he offers to take her money and purchase her one while she makes use of the facilities closest to us. Not trusting myself to stay clear of the backstage area,

I remain exactly where I am, harboring a foolish hope that I might actually get out of here without running into Sophie.

Upon Bonnie's return, the same young usher approaches us again, carrying a king-sized candy bar in one hand and a tiny flashlight in the other. He leans toward me and speaks in a hushed tone. "Sir, I've just confirmed with our director that we have two open seats in the second row. Center stage." His smile makes no effort to hide his pride. "They're reserved for guests with your mother's specific accessibility needs."

"Oh, uh," I begin uncomfortably, "she's not my . . ."

"We'll take them," Bonnie exclaims loudly, clapping me on the back with a force that nearly knocks the wind out of me. "Don't leave your program behind, August. I don't like to share. Oh, and please grab my tissue pack from the armrest there. My nose tends to drip the later the night goes on."

And this is how I end up trailing after Bonnie as she navigates her walker down the center aisle of Twilight Theater at the speed of a tax audit. There's no chance we have not alerted every eye in the auditorium as our quest continues long after the theater lights flicker and signal the return of the show. As our eager usher shines his baby flashlight beam on the floor near Bonnie's feet, she sneaks her contraband Snickers bar from the basket of her walker and stuffs it into the pocket of her dress pants. She then has the audacity to tap a finger to her lips.

I'm still working on collapsing her walker for storage when the next act is announced on stage. I break into a sweat. When I finally take my seat beside Bonnie, the waving motion directly across the aisle from me catches in my periphery.

Even in this low lighting, Aunt Judy's smile is easy to discern. It costs me whatever pride I have left to wave back.

From these seats, everything appears larger than life. The faces and hands of the performers are sharper and more expressive, and I can't help but wonder how far along I'd be in my own ASL training if I hadn't chosen to pursue the path that made me a stranger in my own home.

Through the entire seventh act, my mind is everywhere but on the stage. I can't say if the act is a song or a drama or even a practiced comedy routine. But I do know that every minute that ticks by is another minute closer to whatever Gabby has planned for her performance.

As the applause hands come down and the clapping noise quiets, Portia and her husband introduce Gabby and ask her to please join them on the stage.

I sit up straighter. *This is different.*

My sister's posture is confident when she steps out from behind the curtain and waves at the audience. Both Portia and her husband take a step back, and I look to Bonnie as if she has an explanation. But she's too busy sneaking bites of her Snickers bar to weigh in.

"Hello," my sister says directly to the audience. "My name is Gabriella Tate, and I'm a cast member in tonight's showcase, as well as a student of the Pimentels." Gabby is speaking and signing at the same time, and I'm completely mesmerized by her poised stage presence. "Due to an accident I suffered two and a half years ago, I'm profoundly deaf. And in just a few minutes, I'm going to share a little bit of my story with you. But first I wanted to share a little about what Twilight Theater and the Pimentel family have meant to me."

She stops speaking for a moment and grins at Portia and Nick before resuming. "I'm still a student of ASL, but my growing vocabulary and immersive training is thanks to Portia and Nick, and their son, Tyler." She twists her head to the side of the stage and smiles. "This family has been so patient to teach me—along with many others in this room tonight—exactly why inclusivity matters to both the deaf and hearing communities and why we should hope for a brighter, more communicative tomorrow. Before you leave here tonight, I hope each of you will consider donating to this special theater and its special cause. Thank you for believing in their vision enough to become a bridge builder." Gabby bows slightly, and the packed auditorium erupts with applause when she encourages Portia and Nick to bow, as well. The couple hugs Gabby before they leave her alone on the stage. A spotlight illuminates her.

"For tonight's final act, I've asked a good friend of mine to be my voice in English so that I can focus on communicating this narrative in ASL without having to break up the natural flow to code-switch for interpretation, the way I'm doing now. We've rehearsed our respective scripts in each language. But though there will be two languages represented on this stage, there is only one story."

Pride swells in my chest, and I clap for her once again. It's then my sister catches my eye. Discreetly, she touches her chin with her fingertips and proceeds to thank me in ASL. I nod, hoping it somehow conveys that there's no place I would rather be than right here.

"Ladies and gentlemen," a male narrator says over the loudspeaker as the same words flash on the screen behind my sister. "Without further ado, the Twilight Theater proudly presents Gabby Tate and Sophie Wilder in an original dramatic narrative titled *The Rescue*."

Every cohesive brain cell in my head retreats to standby when Sophie's name is announced. And like the trained professional I know her to be, she all but floats across the stage—an actress who's performed in dozens of live productions in dozens of venues, who is actively standing up against the past I accused her of avoiding only three weeks ago.

My palms itch to applaud her. They itch to do a lot more than that.

The millisecond I detect a break in her focus, our gazes meld.

I love you. The words burst from the confines of my heart like an involuntary declaration, and I cannot take my eyes off her.

"That's your girl up there." Bonnie leans into me and points to Gabby.

No, I silently correct. *That's both of my girls up there.*

In a blink, the atmosphere in the theater changes. The lights are low when two separate spotlights capture them. Their heads are bowed as the large multimedia screen that stretches behind them brightens with a scenic picture of a country I've visited in a past life with my parents many years ago: Colombia.

The soft notes of a synth pad play a progression of four chords over a prerecorded track. D, A, G, B-minor.

When Gabby lifts her head and peers into the audience, she is not the sister I know today at sixteen. Her facial expression is young, and somehow it matches the movements of her hands, as well. And even before Sophie narrates word one, I know where she's starting: at the orphanage, on the day we came to take her home.

"You are so loved, Gabby girl. We are your family now—you don't need to be afraid." Sophie's narration is spoken in a reassuring tone meant to represent a man I wish I could beg forgiveness from.

Gabby moves the story along, skipping time like rocks in a lake. The screen pauses on a pool as Gabby acts out the day I taught her how to swim.

"Jump, Gabby, don't be afraid. I've got you!" Sophie's voice mimics my own this time as Gabby makes use of her entire body to show the scene vividly in ASL.

The words trigger my memories of her in real time, of teaching her to float on her back and then to doggy paddle from one end of the pool to another. It wasn't too long afterward that we took her to the beach for her first surf lesson.

Time fast-forwards again, the background switching to a garden where Gabby's spotlight dips to show her kneeling next to our imagined mother, who tries to calm her after a beetle startles her and crawls up her arm.

Sophie reaches down as if to pluck the invisible beetle off Gabby's shirt sleeve. She dangles it out to the audience, and a few young girls in the front squirm and shriek.

"Why would you fear this beetle when God made you so much stronger than him?" Sophie asks in a maternal voice that causes my throat to thicken. She cups the imaginary bug in her hands and sets it free in the garden bed next to Gabby.

The instant the two of them are back on their feet and the screen behind them morphs into a shot of rural India, I grip the armrests on either side of my chair.

"You okay, August?" Bonnie asks.

But I can't find the words to answer her, not as Gabby describes the details of a trip I declined. *Twice.* Once when my mother called to ask me to consider replacing their music pastor who dropped out last minute, and then again when my father called two days later. Our last phone call.

I'd just stepped out of a meeting with a killer music collaboration that had the potential to catapult all of Vanessa's weird morning meditations into reality when my dad called.

"You have a minute to talk, son?"

I didn't, but unlike my mom, my dad wasn't a big phone guy. When he called, it was usually as brief as it was important.

"Sure, everything good at home?" I speed-walked past the conference room and Vanessa's office toward the green room at the end of the hallway. I was famished. "You guys leave for India soon, right?" I slipped into our green room stockpiled with every kind of beverage and snack obsession known to mankind. Vanessa didn't believe in skimping on anything. She was a go-big or go-home type of woman—the very quality that reeled me in when she offered me a contract I couldn't refuse. That was the thing about Vanessa. She made it so you couldn't refuse her.

I could tell by the interference of the wind against my dad's phone speaker that he was somewhere outside. I checked the clock on the microwave to realize Dad was probably packing up for the day. "That's actually what I was hoping to talk to you about."

"India?" I beelined to the mini bags of trail mix. "Listen, I know Mom's bummed that I said no. But the studio is insane right now. Believe it or not, I just got out of a meeting with an artist whose last EP had a million streams in the first week. The first week! That kind of deal is—"

"Are you living with that woman?"

The bottom floor of my gut dropped to my feet. "What?"

"Your boss. Vanessa. Are you living with her?"

I dropped the bag of trail mix on the counter in front of me, watching as a green M&M plummeted to the tile below. All the lies I'd so carefully woven since I walked away from the band years before were now a tangled noose around my neck. "I still have my apartment." A technicality. At the moment it was more like a glorified storage unit. A place to collect my junk mail.

And my mom's monthly care packages from home.

"Your mother told me a little over a year ago that she knew you were hiding something from us. Said she felt something was off every time she prayed for you."

"What she feels is her hatred for LA," I countered bitterly.

"No," he growled. "If your mother hates anything, it's how quickly her only son turned from his faith to chase after all the shiny things of this world. You're squandering your God-given gifts."

"So now I'm the prodigal son?" I laughed darkly. "How many twenty-six-year-olds do you know who've made a half-mil in less than a year? How many do you know who drive a Porsche and work with some of the top talent in the music industry today? Vanessa has opened doors for me I never believed possible. She's the best thing that's ever happened to me."

"You're blind."

"No, I'm in love."

"Love doesn't hide!"

His sharply spoken words rattle through my bones. I could count on three fingers the number of times my father raised his voice at me. The first was when he was teaching me to drive, and I nearly rammed us into a concrete barrier. The second was when I rolled my eyes at my mother when she scolded me for leaving the trash out.

"You're settling for a counterfeit." My father's restraint was back, but I almost wished it wasn't because mine had just snapped.

"You don't know anything about her!"

"Then tell me, son. Tell me about her family, her friends, her past relationships, her future goals, her religious convictions."

He's asking questions, but something tells me he already knows the answers. Vanessa has no relationship with any of her family members, and the only friends she ever speaks about double as her employees. Vanessa doesn't have a religion, other than the mantras she speaks over herself after her morning meditation, but I suspect there's something else he wants me to confess. It's not enough for him to know I'm living with a woman I'm not married to. What he wants is for me to admit she's been married twice before and is hinting for me to pop the question before she turns thirty-eight.

"If it's her age you're getting at, I'm not concerned about being with an older woman."

"Then are you concerned about being with a woman who doesn't love the God you've claimed to serve? This isn't the life He desires for you."

I rammed a hand through my hair and squeezed my eyes closed as the guilt I worked so hard to suppress tugged at the edges of my mind.

"Come with us to India, son. It's not too late. We've been praying for God to do some big miracles on this trip—" His voice catches. "I love you, August. As soon as we're stateside again, I can fly back to LA with you. I can help you figure things out and—"

"I'm not going anywhere."

His silence was deafening.

"You can tell Mom to focus her prayers on someone who needs them."

"August . . ."

"Have a good time with God in India, Dad. If He still wants me, then He'll have to come and get me Himself."

When I blink out of the horrible memory, I'm not braced for the sight of a moving train or the screech of the tracks that follow, but as soon as the theater lights flicker a red warning, my pulse turns into a jackhammer.

The lights cut out.

For an eternity, there is no sound or movement at all, until a single blue spotlight illuminates my sister curled on the floor and an intense ringing sound fills the auditorium. She lifts her head and cups her hands to her ears, franticly looking around.

"Where am I?" Sophie voices what my sister's hands are asking in ASL from somewhere in the darkness. Her dialogue scrolls across the dark screen behind Gabby. "Why am I covered in mud? What's wrong with my ears? Where is the train? My parents?"

And then Gabby startles back, her eyes growing wide as the intense ringing in the auditorium drops away completely.

"Do not be afraid, Gabriella." The deep male voice is clear, resonant.

"How do you know my name? Your eyes—they're so blue, like my brother's. Where are you taking me?" The sleepy yawn in Sophie's acting voice is perfectly timed with Gabby's expression and signing in ASL. "My head hurts."

"I'm taking you to safety. Your brother will be with you soon."

"My brother? But where are my parents?"

"They are already home." The deep voice is reassuring. "Rest now and have faith, little one. There is nothing that can ever separate you from the love of God."

The theater lights turn off, and when they come up again, the screen shows a hospital bed.

Gabby's eyes are closed as Sophie narrates how the man found her in a muddy ravine, far down the hill from where the tracks washed out and the train car derailed. She explains how safe the man felt, how he spoke with gentle authority, and how his voice cut through the ringing in her ears. She explains how he carried her up the cliffside to the rescue team with ease and secured her transport on the next medical helicopter to a research hospital in Mumbai. Sophie recounts the details of Gabby's brain surgery and nerve damage and how none of the doctors could explain her survival, much less account for the story of the trained rescuer she insisted was real in a region with scarce medical supplies and resources.

Gabby opens her eyes on stage, and I read the ASL sign for the unique name Gabby gave me early on in her learning. It's a combination of surfer and brother. She looks right at me as Sophie speaks for her in English.

"My brother was waiting for me when I opened my eyes, just as my rescuer told me he would be. As soon as I was awake enough to speak, I told my brother everything I could remember about the American man with the shiny dark hair and ocean-blue eyes. But my brother had no idea who I was talking about."

Gabby shakes her head for the audience and holds up her hands to show her confusion.

The familiar conversation catapults me back into the memory of that moment.

I swallowed against the building sob in my throat as I sat at her bedside in an unfamiliar country. She'd been asleep on and off since I arrived three days ago, and now that she was finally stirring, I didn't know how I would bring myself to tell her. She was still too fragile, and the doctors here had cautioned me about the stress of too many emotions at once, especially considering the goal was to stabilize her enough for travel back to the States.

But how did I keep something like this from her? Our parents were dead.

"Is he here?" Gabby asked.

I shook my head, confused.

"My rescuer. Did he come back?"

I released an exhausted breath and shook my head. "Less is more," the doctors had told me. "Do everything you can to keep her from getting agitated." I supposed that meant keeping up this ruse about some mystery American with shiny black hair and crystal blue eyes who carried her from danger and secured help to get her on a helicopter.

She studied my face and tipped her head to the side. Could she read it in my eyes? Did she know what I was hiding?

"They're with Jesus, August," Gabby said without prompt. I was so shocked I barely reacted as she gripped my hand, despite the IV tapped into her vein. "The man told me." Her voice is raspy and holds an odd inflection. Perhaps her ears are still stuffed up; the surgeon warned that some of the side effects of her head trauma would last a few weeks. "I know we'll see them again," she encouraged as her tears fell. "That's our hope. The man said—"

"There was no man," I replied quietly, though I wanted to rage. This person she created was a figment of her imagination, something she dreamed during her concussion and drug-induced coma. The doctors assured me that there had to be a logical explanation for why she was found so late into the rescue mission and then provided exactly what she needed. I chose to believe them. I needed to believe them.

She tapped on my arm, her brow creased. "I can't hear you, August."

I met her gaze with a crushing weariness and shook my head in answer to her earlier question in order to keep the peace. Beyond that,

I didn't know what to do or how to help her. How could I when I didn't even know how to help myself?

Gabby wasn't deterred by my silence. "He told me you'd be here when I woke up."

I pressed my forehead to the mattress; my head throbbed. I'd barely slept since I got the call . . . was that four days ago? Five? I didn't know anymore. How would I take care of her, provide for her? How would I give her anything close to what Mom and Dad had given her? My tears pooled onto the white hospital sheet at her hip, and I felt the weight of her hand on my head.

She yawned. "He told me not to be afraid." She yawned again. "He said something else, too. A verse, maybe? Something familiar that Mom prays for you often."

Even in my sleep-deprived state, I knew I couldn't handle one more thing. So I shut it off. The train. The questions. The pain. The unknowns. The anger. All I knew for sure in that moment was that our parents were dead, and nothing about our lives would ever be the same.

Hot shame fills my core like acid as I realize just how right Gabby had been the night she accused me of never listening to her. I'd heard her, but I hadn't listened. Moreover, I hadn't believed her. Because believing her story would mean having to reconcile the worst part of mine.

Sophie's spotlight flicks off, and Gabby begins to speak into her wireless mic and sign for herself on stage.

"Our questions about the kind American man with the shiny black hair and ocean-blue eyes remain unanswered. There was no record of him on that train or with the medical personnel who assisted me and the other passengers involved in our tragedy. But I do have hope I will meet him again one day when I'm reunited with my parents." She takes a moment before slowly sweeping her gaze over the crowd. "I don't know why God allowed me to live when I should have died. And I don't know why He allowed me to hear the words of my anonymous rescuer when my hearing was lost during the accident. But I do know why He encouraged me to pray for the same miracle my parents died believing would come to pass."

I struggle to breathe as her gaze holds mine. The weight of my shame is nearly unbearable.

"Miracles come in many forms, and mine came in the form of a rescue I didn't deserve, and in a hope I never could have emulated before the accident. Hope covered me on the days I could hear with my ears, and it will cover me in the future when I can only hear with my heart." She places a hand to her chest. "The Scripture my rescuer partially quoted to me is from Romans, and I'd like to share it with you in closing." Gabby takes a deep breath and recites the verse from memory. "'And I am convinced that nothing can ever separate us from God's love. Neither death nor life, neither angels nor demons, neither our fears for today nor our worries about tomorrow—not even the powers of hell can separate us from God's love.'" She curtsies. "Thank you."

People jump to their feet, erupting in cheers and raised hands. But I am still frozen to my seat when Portia and Nick dismiss the audience to the lobby to meet the cast and enjoy refreshments.

"'Miracles come in many forms. . . .' What a treasure your sister is, August," Bonnie says as she steadies herself with a hand on my shoulder. "A beautiful reminder for a crotchety old soul like myself." She bends and stares me down. "You come find me at church on Sunday, you hear me? I'll be keeping an eye out."

I drag my gaze up to hers as she winks good-bye and exits the aisle at the same pace she came down it. My aunt approaches shortly after, touching my shoulder with the maternal compassion I've rejected out of my own self-loathing many times.

"Your parents loved you fiercely, August. They never stopped. I hope you can believe that." Tears clog my throat when she wraps her arms around my shoulders and plants a kiss on my head before continuing on to the lobby.

It's then I see Gabby make her way out from backstage. Her steps are tentative, but her eyes are searching.

Before I can process what I'm doing, I'm up from my seat and sprinting toward her, throwing my arms wide and wrapping her in an embrace so tight that it's not until I lower her to the ground that I realize how fiercely she was hugging me back.

I'm sorry, I say in ASL as soon as she's facing me. "I don't know how to sign everything else I need to say, but I promise you . . ." I choke up on the words. "I'm going to learn."

My sister's chin quivers. "I'm sorry, too, August." She looks behind her as cast members meander toward the lobby. "Will you wait for me to pack up my things? I'd like to go home."

"Of course." But of the dozens of half-processed thoughts circling in my brain, there is one that's complete. So before she turns for the stage, I say it. "I think it's time we open the box."

28

Sophie

Every endorphin I possess has been released sometime in the last hour, and it's all I can do to rein them back in and try to process even a single moment of it. There was no panic when I took that stage with Gabby tonight, no fear or worry or doubt. It was the same addicting thrill of theater I've always known. And yet . . . it was also something else entirely. Something I didn't even know existed before tonight.

And in the midst of it all, there was August.

It was impossible not to sense the cracking of his heart as he witnessed the miracle his sister portrayed on that stage. But it was equally impossible not to hope that this could be the beginning of something new for him and for the people he keeps in his orbit.

Emotion constricts my throat. I'm not one of those people anymore.

I'm the person he let go.

I'm the one he encouraged to board a plane in the wee hours of the morning tomorrow and try for a job that could keep us apart for more than a year.

It's that last thought that has me deciding to skip the meet-and-greet in the lobby and the possibility of a run-in with the man I can't seem to stop loving. Portia knows about my flight and the packing I have left to do. She also knows I've spent the last twenty minutes standing twenty feet from my ex-boyfriend while I fought to keep my composure during his sister's beautiful performance.

Portia will understand.

She's the one who loaned me Nick's spare pickup truck after I returned August's car to his driveway the day after we broke up.

I collect my bag from backstage and am out the back door in record time. My keys are in hand as I cross the parking lot when I hear the text tone coming from the zipped pocket in my purse. I hold my breath as I take my phone out, hoping in vain to see a name on my screen I haven't seen in over three weeks.

But it's not August. It's Natalie.

Natalie:

> I'm really sorry to bother you. I know you're at the theater, but something happened at the charity event. It's too much to text, but I'm at the police station. I'm okay and the baby is okay, but I could really use your support. Will you come?

Natalie:

> I have to turn my phone off for a while. But here's the address to the station. Tell the woman with the blue headscarf at the front desk that you're looking for me.

Only two steps from the driver's side door of Nick's old pickup, tiny ice crystals form in my abdomen as I read through her texts a second time and then check for a voicemail. Nothing.

What on earth happened at that charity event?

There's a slight shake to my hands as I unlock the doors and slip inside the truck cab. I tap the GPS link Natalie sent to the station, praying I have enough battery to make it all the way there before my phone dies. And then I pray that once I get there, I will be the support Natalie needs.

The only other time I've stepped foot inside a police station was to give a statement after the cellar attack when I was sixteen years old. But something tells me tonight will be different. Something tells me tonight will be worse.

Once I enter the front doors of the large brick building, I struggle to find a clear path through the chaos. The waiting area—if one can call it that—is oversaturated with people who clearly aren't here for the fun of it. The pungent aroma of unpleasant body odors causes my gag reflex to kick in as I search for a desk on the other side of a rowdy group of adolescent boys arguing over a stolen Xbox and gaming paraphernalia.

"Boys!" a woman barks from somewhere behind them. "Take a seat. I won't ask you again."

As soon as they shove to the side, I spot her.

The woman with the blue headscarf and no-nonsense expression.

I approach the desk, and she makes no effort to disguise her appraisal of me. I can only imagine how out of place my stage makeup must look under these fluorescent lights.

"May I help you?" Her voice sounds as craggy as I imagined it.

"Yes, hello. My sister-in-law asked me to meet her here. . . ." I look around the dirty room, making sure I haven't missed her by accident. "Somewhere. She told me to check in with you."

"Name?"

"My name is Sophie Wilder."

The woman arches an eyebrow. "I meant the name of your sister-in-law."

"Oh, right, of course." I lean onto the counter. "Sorry, this is only my second time in a police station, and things are quite different than I remember." At her beyond-bored expression, I swallow. "Her name is Natalie Wi—"

"Ms. Wilder." The voice at my back is brisk but holds an edge of familiarity.

Slowly, I rotate.

And my jaw falls slack.

It takes me a moment to place him in this new setting, seeing as he's no longer wearing a three-piece designer suit or asking me for a private tour of the wine cellar or chauffeuring my brother around in his brand-new Mercedes G-Wagon.

Or leaving my sister-in-law's house around midnight.

The Clinton Owens in front of me looks far too authoritative to discuss the finer points of a quality wine aerator.

"Clinton—?"

"I'm Agent Terrell." In a fluid movement, he extends his arm to indicate the hallway on the far left of the station. "I can take you to see Natalie now, if you'll please follow me."

A dozen questions ribbon through my brain at once. "Wait, you said agent . . . as in FBI?"

He confirms with a single bob of his head.

I can't quite catch my breath. "So then you don't work in stocks?"

"Afraid not, ma'am." I swear I spot a hint of a smile before he repeats himself. "Please, just follow me."

I clutch my purse to my abdomen and trail closely behind him.

"What is going on?" I ask in a hushed tone as I ignore the obnoxious catcalls coming from the waiting room we just crossed. "What happened tonight? Is Natalie hurt? Did my brother . . . ?" I don't finish as I picture the ultrasound image Natalie showed me last week. I wonder if Jasper found out. Even though she does her best to keep her baby bump covered, it's there. "Did he—" Stop. Don't go there.

When Agent Terrell answers exactly none of my questions, I get the distinct impression his silence is strategic. Okay, fine. I can play that game. For a time, at least.

The hallway he leads me down is narrow, with numbered doors on our left-hand side. As we pass door number six, it opens, and a woman in a navy blazer and slacks slips out. Only before she can close it behind her, I hear a voice that sends a shockwave down my spine.

"You're making a huge mistake, *Principessa*. This is *exactly* why a woman shouldn't be sent to do a man's job!"

I whip my head around just as the door latches closed, but the movement is disorienting enough to throw my entire equilibrium off balance. Or perhaps it's the voice that does that. I catch myself on the opposite wall, though it's not quite supportive enough to keep my knees from buckling under my weight.

"Miss? Miss, are you alright?" The woman rushes to my side as the tight-lipped Agent Terrell reverses direction to grip my opposite elbow and help me stand.

The woman with the slicked-back bun and blazer steps to my other side, shielding me from passersby.

"Are you hurt?" Agent Terrell asks.

I open my mouth, but when no sound comes out, I resort to pointing at the door across the hall.

The woman follows my finger, and then eyes the agent curiously. I don't miss the intrigue that flares in each of their gazes.

"W-w-who is that?" I ask. "The man inside that room?"

"Why?" Agent Terrell lowers his voice and speaks in a measured tone. "Do you know him?"

"No." I swallow, desperately trying to return the moisture to my mouth. "But I do know his voice." I'd bet the sizable balance of my family's trust on it. Italian accents aren't commonplace in our area, but it was the derogatory way he'd said the word *Principessa* that triggered my memory.

"Scream all you want down here, Principessa. Nobody will hear you."

I've replayed that statement a thousand times over the last decade. It was the same voice. The same man who was never convicted of locking me in a cellar for the thrill of a stolen vintage bottle of wine.

Despite the hard knock in my chest, I force out the rest. "Ten years ago, I was attacked in my family's place of business during a break-in. I was locked in a cellar for forty hours. The investigation was eventually dismissed, but I'm *positive* I remember that voice— *his* voice."

The woman tilts her head to the side appraisingly. "You're Sophie Wilder." There's something akin to awe in the way she says it, but I have absolutely no clue as to why. I'm certain I've never seen her before in my life. "I didn't recognize you through all that stage makeup."

"H-how do you know my name? Who are you?"

The inquisitive glance shared between these two professionals shifts into a nod of validation.

"I'll let Agent Terrell fill you in on the details, Sophie, but I think you just more than proved your worth in our investigation." She directs the gleam in her eye at me. "I'm Agent Trujillo, by the way."

A second FBI agent? There's a roadblock of information gathering too quickly for my mind to process, but a single word snags my attention: *investigation.*

Agent Terrell juts his chin toward the end of the hallway. "We'll be in nine if you need me."

"I'll check in when I'm finished in six," Agent Trujillo confirms.

The two agents offer each other cursory nods before I'm expected, once again, to trail after the first one with even fewer answers than I had before.

"What did she mean by 'proved my worth'?'" I'm officially done with the quiet game. "Can you please just tell me what is going on here?"

He stops in front of room nine. "Agent Trujillo believed you were a good egg from the start." He puts his hand on the doorknob. "That's a high compliment in our line of work."

"What line of work?" Frustration simmers low in my belly at his ambiguity. "You mean, back when you were pretending to be a pretentious stockbroker who propositioned me to join him for a night on his yacht?"

There isn't a shred of acknowledgment for my stellar memory recall or a hint of apology when he says, "I was building a case. Be grateful you were on the right side of it."

I'm about to comment when he swings open the door to reveal the back of Natalie's sparkly red ball gown. At the sight of her, adrenaline swamps my insides, and I forget all about the events in the hallway.

"Natalie." I plant myself in the hard plastic chair beside her and mentally prepare to see evidence of a physical altercation. But when she turns, there is no sign of dried blood. Just dried tears.

She rests a soft hand on the fabric covering her midsection. *The baby.* She offers me a tentative smile. "Thank you for coming. I know this couldn't be happening at a worse time for you." She flicks her gaze to the agent, who's just taken a seat across the narrow table from us.

It's then I scan the whitewashed walls and note the lack of furniture. *Is this an interrogation room?*

"What have you told her?" Natalie asks Agent Terrell.

"Not much. I figured you'd like to be a part of the discussion." His voice is notably softer when he speaks to her. "Although, she did hear Andre's voice in the hallway."

Andre.

Andre.

Andre.

Where had I heard that name before?

"Oh." My sister-in-law closes her eyes, exhales, and nods. "Okay."

"Natalie, please." A mix of desperation and fear churns in my gut. "Tell me what is going on here."

She takes a slow, measured breath. "Your brother was arrested tonight. For art fraud and embezzlement."

Of all the scenarios I'd imagined her telling me when I arrived, fraud of any kind hadn't even made it into my top one hundred guesses.

I sink back in my chair. Words have failed me many times in the last few weeks, but this time it's different. This time my speechlessness is because my brother is in jail and his wife appears as cool and collected as I've ever seen her.

Agent Terrell stakes his elbows on the tabletop and dips his chin. "We aren't at liberty to discuss certain details as the investigation is technically still open, but considering how pivotal Natalie's cooperation has been over the last three months, we decided to honor her request and loop you in as quickly as possible. She trusts you, and more importantly, so do I."

My jaw unhinges. "You trust me? How? You don't even know me."

"Actually," Natalie counters, "they know a lot more than you might think."

The only thing I can manage to move is my eyeballs, which are currently focused solely on Natalie.

"I know this must be a huge shock." She picks up my limp hand. "And I'm sorry I couldn't tell you sooner. I wanted to, but . . ." She shakes her head. "It would have put the investigation at risk."

Flustered, I make eye contact with the agent. "Can you please start from the beginning? When did all this begin?"

"Officially, seventeen months ago," Agent Terrell answers. "Unofficially, who knows. Your brother has been brokering questionable deals with a loyal partner he's known for some time—a friend he met in college with art connections both here and overseas. It started slow at first, with the two of them moving fraudulent pieces for a cut of the profits, but your brother—"

"Wants to be the one in control," I finish for him, only to realize there's another revelation that's risen to the surface. My eyes blink wide as I recall all the strange reactions the day after the storm last fall. "The van. Was that involved somehow?"

Agent Terrell nods. "Yes. Which is why we thought you might have been more involved than we originally thought. But like I said, we ruled you out after reviewing surveillance and conversing with you under false pretenses. It wasn't long after that the two men began curating their own orders and clientele and building a cover."

Lights are flickering on in my brain one by one. "The private art and wine events in the tasting room?"

"It was an almost perfect cover," Agent Terrell says before his gaze cuts to my sister-in-law. "With one minor flaw."

I twist in my seat, my knee bouncing of its own volition. "What?"

"Me," Natalie says. "And him." She pats the tiny baby bump hidden under the layers of her carefully selected gown.

"I don't understand. Why were you the flaw?"

"Who do you think Jasper put in charge of all the paperwork and the bills of sale at the end of those events?" Though the question is rhetorical, the answer is obvious: Natalie. "It was my signature on all those fraudulent documents. I had no idea that Jasper had acquired the art illegally, of course, but he was more than willing to pin me with the evidence that would have made me complicit to his crimes." Her eyes harden. "A favorite pastime of his."

"So after more than an entire year of stalemates in our investigation, we took a big but calculated risk," Agent Terrell continues.

"Agent Trujillo followed me into Target. It was the day after I took my third positive pregnancy test in early September," Natalie says. "And she watched me linger a bit too long in the baby department and buy the one and only baby item I have hidden away in my closet—a tiny lovey."

"A lovey?" I question.

"Like a miniature security blanket," Natalie clarifies. "Agent Trujillo met me at my car and asked me if I pictured raising my baby myself or letting the system raise him while I sat in jail."

I cover my gasp with my hand.

"Yeah." Natalie nods. "She gave me her card and told me to call when I was ready to discuss a few matters in a private location. But I handed it back and told her I could be ready right then. I didn't need an ultimatum to choose my baby." She lifts her head. "I followed her to a safe place, and there she told me of my husband's dealings, and in turn I gave her every passcode I knew to every account we shared, including my written permission for any and all law enforcement to access the security cameras around our property and on our vehicles. Once she knew she could trust me, she introduced me to Agent Terrell . . . or Clinton, as I'd known him up till then."

Shocked, I glance between them again. "You've been feeding him information since September?"

"Yes, which is partly how they knew about you." She gives me a meek shrug. "They also tapped the Escalades and the utility van."

I'm nodding, though my body doesn't quite feel attached to my head.

"I haven't known a life outside of Jasper's control since I was fifteen years old. He was my hero back then, a sanctuary outside my abusive home life. But then he became the abuser. Mentally, emotionally, and sometimes . . . physically." She swallows. "I've been a passive girlfriend and wife, but I refuse to be a passive mother."

I want to hate my brother for what he almost cost my sister-in-law and nephew, but instead of hate, I'm flooded with relief and love for the woman in front of me.

"I'm so proud of you, Natalie. You did the right thing."

"Your parents won't think so. They'll blame me for this."

I pull back. "My parents have refused to see the truth about their son for my entire life, but they can't deny these facts. This isn't about you—it's about him. He doesn't get to evade the consequences for his actions any longer."

Natalie's face crumples, and the atmosphere grows charged and uncomfortable once again. Agent Terrell must feel it, too, because he excuses himself a few seconds later. "I'll give you two ladies a moment."

As soon as he's gone, Natalie's voice begins to shake. "I've done a lot of things for Jasper I'm not proud of."

"Natalie, if anybody understands what it's like to live in his shadow, it's—"

"I lied to the cops about Jasper's whereabouts the night you were locked in that cellar. He needed an alibi, and I was too weak and brainwashed to stand up to him."

She must see from my expression that I'm struggling to make the connection. "What are you telling me, exactly?"

She blows out a weighty breath. "Your brother was a terrible student. He cheated his way through college, paying for essays and purchasing the answer sheets for every test and exam, all while continuing to party and mess around with girls behind my back. But then one day, he got caught. His business professor held him after class and told him he had less than twenty-four hours to tell your parents before the dean would expel him." She drops her eyes to her lap. "But instead, he concocted a plan with his new friend, Andre. Since the professor was a known wine connoisseur, Jasper offered him a deal: your dad's rarest wine for an A and a clean record.

The professor agreed, and your brother learned how to cheat the system on a whole new level." She takes my cold hands in hers. "It was Andre's voice you heard that night, and it was Jasper who left his only sister in that cellar without a second thought. But it was me who kept their secret for a decade and couldn't look you in the eye for almost as long." She studies our joined hands. "Out of all my sins, I know that one is the most undeserving of forgiveness. But I truly am so, so sorry."

I'm too numb to name the multiple emotions coursing through me at her confession or to feel the gravity of all my brother's grievances against me and my family, but I do know one thing: The same grace that set me free was given to Natalie, as well.

If this confession had come a year ago, or even six months ago, I can only imagine how I would have reacted. The resentment, the hurt, the bitterness, the re-victimization I would have clung to like a trophy of validation. None of those would move me any closer to a place of healing. And they certainly wouldn't do that for Natalie, either.

"I forgive you," I say quietly at first, and then again with deeper conviction. "I forgive you."

She covers her face with both hands, and for the first time since she told me of her husband's arrest, she falls apart.

I wrap her and her unborn child in my arms. "I told you I'd be here for you when you needed me. I meant it then, and I mean it now. You are not alone in this."

We stay this way for nearly a minute as the scratchy poof of Natalie's full skirt doubles as a protective shield against the world.

If only it could shield us against the familiar bellow we hear approaching, despite several authoritative protests for him to calm down.

We've just pulled apart when the door to our room bursts open and an angry pointer finger is jabbed at my sister-in-law.

"What did you do to my son?"

29

Sophie

Within a blink of my father's nasty accusation, Agent Terrell inserts himself into my father's personal space. Honestly, I'm beginning to like this guy more and more.

"As I warned you in the hall, Mr. Wilder, you can either behave in a reasonable and respective manner, or you can join your son in custody on a charge of disorderly conduct. I won't ask a third time. Are you clear on the expectations?"

By the way my father's wiry gray hair sticks up like the tail feathers on an unhinged rooster, I can tell he's in no mood to be trifled with. But Agent Terrell looks about as interested in my father's opinion as I am in making friends with the headscarf lady at the front desk.

"I'm clear," my father mutters.

"Good, then I'm going to suggest we relocate to a conference room better suited to fit the needs of your family. Please refrain from any conversation until I've secured us behind a closed door."

We all nod our agreement, even my sour-faced father.

Agent Terrell certainly knows how to command a room.

"Thank you, Agent Terrell." My mother steps out from around my father's back for the first time. "As you can imagine, Jasper's call to us came as quite a shock. We're just trying to get some answers on what exactly happened."

"I understand." He dips his chin, opens the door, and gives us a non-verbal cue to follow the leader. We walk single file to a room on the back side of the station. Upon entering, I note the fifty percent increase in furniture, including a long conference table with cushioned chairs and a slight upgrade to the dingy white walls.

These walls are painted the shade of a medical bandage.

Natalie takes a seat next to me and across from my parents. I don't miss the way she keeps her gaze low. I understand her trepidation; I've lived it. But whatever tensions I felt growing up in a home with Jasper as my older brother pale in comparison to what she must have dealt with as his wife. If I could go back in time, I would step in so much sooner. I would ask more questions. I would listen to her voice the way I wished someone would have listened to mine. But unlike me, Natalie didn't have an exit plan the minute she became a legal adult. She was sold a lie, and she's suffered because of it ever since.

"Mr. and Mrs. Wilder," Agent Terrell begins as he situates himself at the head of the table, a fact that must irk my father to no end. He hates losing control. "As I explained to you previously, your son was arrested on multiple charges—"

"I'd like to speak to my son," my dad grounds out in a somewhat restrained tone.

"I'm afraid that's not possible."

My father starts to stand. "Then who do I see about paying his bail and getting him out of this hellhole?"

"He's not here, Mr. Wilder. He's in federal custody. His bail won't be decided until after his arraignment, roughly forty-eight hours from now."

"Federal?" Mom gasps.

"Art fraud is a felony, Mother," I explain. "And like Agent Terrell said, fraud is not the only charge Jasper faces." Given that I was brought into a limited circle of trust due to Natalie's involvement in the investigation, I don't know what all I'm allowed to say. But repeating the agent's earlier statements in a way my mother might hear them seems harmless enough.

"But this has to be a mistake," my mother implores. "Jasper is a successful businessman and an esteemed leader in our industry. He and his wife have a beautiful marriage and a beautiful home." She turns her heartbroken gaze on Natalie. "They don't lack for anything. The family trust has always provided everything they could possibly need. Isn't that right, Natty? Tell him."

When my sister-in-law remains silent, Agent Terrell steps up in her defense once again. I wonder if this is the typical level of kindness he shows for an informant or if he's simply exceptional at his job. "With all due respect, ma'am, money is rarely the only motivating factor in crimes of this caliber."

"But then what could possibly be—"

"Say nothing more, Anita. I'm texting our lawyer," my father scolds, pulling out his phone and finger-pecking at the screen.

"He's guilty." Natalie's verdict reverberates inside the room. "Your son is guilty of every charge he's being held for tonight and many others he'll never be convicted of."

"You can't possibly mean that." My father lowers his phone and peers at his daughter-in-law as if she's lost all her senses. "How much did you have to drink at that party tonight?"

But just as I start to come to her defense, my mother asks, "What other crimes? What are you talking about, Natty?"

Natalie's eyes soften as her gaze lingers on my mother, and I can almost see the vulnerable teenager she was when she first came into our family's life as Jasper's girlfriend. She didn't grow up with a mother, and her connection to mine was as effortless as her connection to my brother. Her voice turns pleading. "I'm saying your son is not who you think he is, Anita. He's worked hard to convince you and everyone else that—"

"Stop this right now." My father slams a hand on the table. "Jasper has not been convicted of a thing yet, and we will not respond as if he has, Anita. Our job is to defend him, to protect him. *We are his parents.*"

"You are my parents, too." My declaration is raw but strong. "And yet I never once felt defended or protected by either one of you, not even when I was the victim of a crime that happened on *your* property."

"*Sophie.*" My mom's voice quavers as if she can't believe I would bring that up at a time like this. But denial can only last so long.

"This is not the same." My father shakes his head. "That investigation was dismissed on lack of evidence."

"Because you dismissed it. Because you refused to take the investigation to the next level and pay out of your own pocket. Because you told the detective I was nothing more than a dramatic attention-seeker who had likely staged the entire event." I watch as my father's lips pull tight. "I heard you. I heard you on the phone with him."

My mother covers her mouth. "Ronald?"

"That's . . . that's . . . there were other considerations. Factors outside of that phone call."

"You're right, there were." I stare into my father's eyes. "The first being that Jasper's word always took precedence over mine."

My father throws up his hands. "Do you really think this is the time to bring up every childhood woe?"

I eye Natalie, and she gives me a nod. It's all the permission I need to continue. "He lied to you about that night."

"What night?" my dad has the audacity to ask.

"The night he and his buddy broke into the tasting room, stole your prized wine, and locked your only daughter in a dark cellar for a day and a half. All so he could pay off his business professor at Stanford," I say.

"That's not true. He was with Natalie that weekend at a ski resort. The police verified their story."

"He wasn't with me. I covered for him," Natalie says with so much remorse my eyes sting. "I've been covering for him for a long time."

NICOLE DEESE

My dad shifts in his seat, and an uncomfortable silence fills the room. He glances down at his phone. "Our lawyer is on his way."

"That's it?" I insist. "That's all you have to say? Your son robbed you and deceived you and—"

"I won't believe that!" he fires off at Natalie and me. "I don't know why you two have decided to fabricate such a tale against him or why you've chosen to be disloyal to your family, but I won't stand for it. You hear me? *I won't stand for it.*" He bangs the table with a closed fist, sending Natalie's water bottle tumbling off the far edge.

"Careful, Mr. Wilder," Agent Terrell warns as he pushes back from the table to retrieve Natalie's water.

"This is why I left home at eighteen," I appeal to my mother. "This is why I forfeited the trust payout and the college plans and a future at the winery. This is why I chose to fly three thousand miles away from home. I have spoken the words of a hundred different characters on stage, but I've only recently found a voice of my own." My lips quiver as she locks eyes with me. "It's not too late for you to find yours."

My dad grips my mom's arm, but her eyes remain on me, unfocused and yet laser focused at the same time. "Anita, listen to me, honey. The two of us need to remain a united front when the lawyer gets here. We know our son—I've apprenticed him since he was thirteen. If he was capable of any of these things, I would know it. You would know, too. You're his mother." The wrinkle between my mother's eyebrows deepens. "He wouldn't throw away the life we built for him for a life of crime."

My mother is unresponsive to my father's impassioned words, and I wonder where her mind has taken her.

"My lawyer will demand to see proof of these allegations," my father directs at Agent Terrell, and I don't miss the desperate agitation in his voice. "I, for one, won't be leaving here until I see evidence of his crimes with my own eyes."

"Evidence?" Natalie asks in a tone that sends goose bumps down my arms. "Are you certain that's what you want, Mr. Wilder?"

"*Of course* that's what I want."

Agent Terrell shifts his attention to our side of the table and speaks Natalie's name with a softness that both intrigues and surprises me.

Yet, she is not deterred.

"Here's your evidence." She pushes away from the table and teeters slightly on her feet. Every muscle in my body tenses as she smooths the sparkly red tulle around her midsection to reveal the half-melon bump underneath. "This baby is not a product of two consenting, committed adults in a loving marriage. He was conceived out of coercion and manipulation—all orchestrated by the same man who refused to give up his one-night stands." There's venom in her voice when she speaks again. "So no, Anita, the family trust did not provide everything I needed. I needed help. I needed support. I needed someone to tell me I wasn't crazy and to stick around long enough to see the monster he really is behind closed doors." She turns to my father now. "He used me and tried to make me an accomplice in his art scheme, and if not for the help of Agent Terrell, I, too, would be in a holding cell tonight." She steels herself. "I will testify against your son in court, and I will pray for justice to be served. And if, after all of this, you still plan to defend him and throw your money at a lawyer who will partner with his deceptions, then please believe me when I say I will do everything in my power to keep my baby far away from his only set of grandparents."

Head held high, Natalie yanks open the door and exits the room. Agent Terrell follows soon after. But I hesitate, momentarily torn by the shame and devastation that hovers over this table like a storm cloud. My father's face falls slack and ashen while my mother weeps into her hands. But there is no muffling the sound of heartbreak.

For all the offenses committed against me in my youth, my earlier feelings of justification are sidestepped by empathy. I spent most of my childhood isolated in my pain, wishing I had someone to confide in, wishing my parents would see the truth. But perhaps the bigger truth is this: None of us have been spared from the tangled web of my brother's sins.

"I'm sorry," I say gently. "I'm sorry you're both suffering from the choices Jasper's made and the people he's hurt. And I'm sorry he's not the son you believed him to be." My mother's sobs rack her slender frame, and I want nothing more than to take away her pain. But instead, I pray that somehow God will use it. That He will bring purpose to this heartbreak in ways I cannot fathom. "This doesn't have to be the end of your story—or our family's story." I swallow the climbing tears in my throat. "And I sincerely hope it isn't."

When neither of them replies, I slowly push away from the table. "I'm taking Natalie home so she can rest."

And then I go in search of a woman who needs a family more now than ever before.

30

August

I'm standing outside Gabby's bedroom, waiting as she wipes the stage makeup from her face and transforms back into the girl I know best—the one who rarely remembers to wear her retainer without a reminder and prefers to stay in her pjs till noon. But when she opens the door wearing sleep pants with big strawberries printed all over them, I feel a physical ache in the center of my chest.

Sophie wore those pants the night she stayed over. She was up half the night eating chocolate and talking to me in those pants. She made me her famous scramble in those pants. And she'd finished narrating the last hours of *Mistletoe Matrimony* in those pants.

Gabby touches my arm, pulling me out of one memory and asking me to follow her into another. "You ready for this?"

The rush of nerves her question scatters throughout my body screams a resounding *no*, but I nod anyway. Because the persistent nudge I've felt since her performance overpowers this temporary discomfort. If Sophie could fight against her fear of the stage and

Gabby could fight against the ignorance of her brother . . . then isn't it time I fought against my fears, too?

Gabby stops at the end of the hall, and though I know she's entered this bedroom a hundred times before now, she steps aside for me to lead the way tonight. The doorknob is cold against my palm, and I feel every millimeter of its rotation.

We're a few steps inside when I realize I've been holding my breath. My first intake of air confirms every reason I've done my best to keep out of this space. I don't understand the chemistry behind a scent lingering for two and a half years, but it's here. The earthy aroma of two people who worked outdoors—Mom in the soil, Dad with fresh lumber.

As if it's the most comfortable place for her to be, Gabby climbs onto their king-size bed and wraps the worn quilt folded at the end of the footboard around her shoulders.

"I love this quilt. It still smells like Mom," she says, snuggling her face into the well-loved blanket. The colors and floral prints have faded with time, and there's a finger-length tear in one of the corners where a puff of cotton pokes out of the seam, but Gabby has never cared about the blemishes on this old blanket. She cares about what's been sewn into the layers: a blessing of unconditional love. The quilt is an heirloom that's been passed down from bride to bride in my father's family. From my grandmother to Aunt Judy and then to my mother on her wedding day to my father. My throat thickens as I imagine Gabby as the next recipient one day, as a bride. And then as I imagine my role in giving her away to a man I hope will possess the same depth of unconditional love we were shown in the example of our parents.

She looks up at me then, her expression soft and yielding. "Did you want me to get the box for you?" She slips off the bed and crosses to the closet, but I grip her elbow to stop her. When she grants me her full attention, I say the words that have taken me far too long to admit.

"I should have talked to you about the surgery. I should have asked you what you wanted . . . and what you didn't want. I'm sorry."

Her eyes shimmer. "I'm sorry, too. I know I shouldn't have run away to Aunt Judy's without talking to you first. I was angry—not only for the surgery stuff but also for what happened between you and Sophie."

Guilt charges through me like an electrical current, and I drop my hand. "What happened between Sophie and me is not your fault in any way."

"It felt like it was. Everything changed for the worse after that night."

I don't have to wonder which night she refers to. It's seared into my frontal lobe. "The blame lies solely on me, Gabs. No one else."

"But Sophie loves you, and I know you love her," she pleads. "There's still some time, you know? You can still fix this before—"

"No, Gabs. Stop." I shake my head. "I need you to let this go, okay? This is not your problem to solve. Promise me?"

"Fine," she huffs, "I promise, even though I think you made a big mistake."

"I've made a lot of big mistakes."

She gives me a resigned sigh. "Anyway . . . that's why I left without telling you and went to Aunt Judy's."

"I get it," I say. "Aunt Judy is a lot more nurturing than I am."

Gabby cocks her head to the side in a way that tells me she's missed a word or a meaning.

"Nurturing," I repeat as I attempt to finger spell the word in ASL. Halfway through, she swipes a hand through the air.

"Nurturing?" she clarifies.

I nod but her expression remains puzzled. "What are you not saying?"

Nothing like ripping the Band-Aid right off. I stuff my hands in my pockets and rock back on my heels. If she'd asked me a month ago, I'd have blown off such a question and told her everything was fine. But standing here now, in our parents' bedroom, I won't smudge the truth. And the truth is something I've never admitted to anyone.

"Sometimes I wonder if I made the wrong decision for you."

Gabby's eyes go wide. "About what?"

"After the attorney told me that Mom and Dad named me your legal guardian . . ." I release a hard breath. "Aunt Judy offered to take you."

Her eyebrows dip low. "You didn't want me?"

I'm quick to shake my head. "Of course I did, but I worried that I wouldn't be able to care for you the same way she could. She's motherly and kind, and I'm stubborn and shortsighted." I tug on her pigtail. "And she loves you."

"So do you." Gabby says this with enough conviction to pierce the gap between my ribs and stab straight into my heart. "You love me, too, August."

"I do." It takes a monumental effort to swallow. "I love you very much. But I want you to be able to make that choice for yourself now. You're mature enough to decide who you want to live with—"

"I choose you." Gabby throws her quilt-laden arms around me, and I hug her back, in the very space my mom once asked for my thoughts on being a summer host home for Gabby. But in my eighteen-year-old head, hosting her didn't make near the sense that adopting her did. The spunky little girl with the gap-toothed grin needed a family, and we had one to give her. Somehow even then I knew she was meant to be my sister, and I was meant to be her big brother.

I peek over her head, remembering how I sat at the foot of my parents' bed while my mom wrote her prayers for Gabby on pink three-by-five cards and stuffed them into the folds of her Bible, believing for the day they'd fly back and bring my sister home.

The recall of those days feels like someone else's life, from someone else's memory.

Little had I known then just how much our world would shift. I hold my sister a little tighter, thankful our mother's prayers were answered despite the unforeseen plot twists in her future. If nothing else, I could be grateful for that. And, of course, for whatever supernatural experience had kept my sister alive.

When we break apart, Gabby moves to the closet once again and lifts a box about the size of a shoebox from under our mother's gardening boots. I recognize it immediately; it had come without warning six months after our parents' death.

Gabby's recovery was finally on the upswing. Her recently fitted hearing aids were in, and she was watching a YouTube tutorial on ASL for beginners while Chip reclined on the sofa after dropping by with our favorite pizza cookies and suggesting some new action-adventure movie for after dinner. It was his every other Saturday afternoon routine, one I'd begun to look forward to at a time when there was little to feel that way about.

When the doorbell rang, I thought nothing of it. Aunt Judy's affinity for Amazon Prime equaled new girly knickknacks for Gabby every few days. There'd been stuffed animals and fancy nail polish kits and young adult book series and gobs and gobs of hair products. I expected to drop this shoebox-sized package at Gabby's feet like I had with all the others, but this one was addressed to me. So while Chip scrolled on his phone and Gabby practiced basic signs in ASL, I took the package to the kitchen table and used my pocket knife to cut through the thick tape.

The instant the first flap was free, blood rushed to my ears.

It was my parents' scent that hit me first—hard and fast like a punch to the jaw. I should have stopped there, should have closed it up then and waited for some inevitable day in the future when my self-loathing was high enough for such a punishment as this. But the card scrawled with my name was lying face up, and I couldn't leave the mystery untouched.

My fingers shook when I cracked the envelope open and pulled out a handwritten card by a pastor I'd never heard of—Pastor Bedi.

Dear August Tate,

   My church family has been praying for you and your sister in this difficult time of grief. We are saddened by the loss of your wonderful parents, but we rejoice in the truth of where they are today.

   Please forgive the delay in getting this package sent to you. Our mail service is unreliable, and we prefer to send our correspondence and care packages to the USA through our partner families and missionary friends. I pray this box finds you well and arrives without incident.

As you likely know, your parents, like many others who travel with our organization, signed a waiver to donate the majority of their packed personal belongings before the start of their trip. We are grateful to inform you that your parents' items (clothing, shoes, belts, toiletries, tools, books, suitcases) have recently been gifted to families in need. Hallelujah!

The contents we sent back are what we believe your parents would have taken home with them at the end of their visit. We hope they are a blessing to you and your sister, and a reminder of the faithful parents God gave you.

Blessings,
Pastor Bedi

I didn't know when Gabby joined me at the table, or what she said when she pulled the box toward her that day, but I do remember ripping it from her hands and stuffing the card back inside with a fury that scared us both. How dare this pastor reference a waiver and donate our parents' possessions without the permission of their children. They'd already donated their lives to his cause—was that not enough?

"Don't touch this," I scolded my sister.

"Why, what is it?" Gabby asked, scrutinizing my lips because once again she'd taken out her hearing aids.

"Where are your aids?" I tapped my ear, but she ignored me and swiped for the pastor's card. She got it on the first try and twisted away.

Chip's hand clapped me on the back before I could get it back. "Dude, what's up?"

"They donated their personal belongings is what's up," I growled as Gabby silently mouthed every word of the letter.

"Who did?" Chip asked.

"The church organization that killed my parents."

363

My friend's horrified expression at my bluntness was telling. "It was an accident that killed your parents, August. Not a church."

But I was in no mood to debate semantics. I knew exactly who and what had killed my parents. And regrettably, I knew the why, as well.

"This is all true." Gabby lowered the letter in her hands. "I donated my stuff, too. We all did. The people there have so many needs."

"And you don't?"

"Hey," Chip said quietly. "I think you should probably take a walk—"

"I don't need a walk. What I need is everybody to stop pretending that they chose this—that they willingly chose to become martyrs of the faith and leave their daughter as an orphan again. They never would have left Gabby behind."

If Gabby caught all that, she didn't react to it. Instead, she touched the box and looked up at me again. "You don't want to see what's in here?"

The lone tear that tracked her cheek was what cooled the fire in my lungs long enough for me to see this through her eyes. I didn't want to see the contents—because I couldn't. But I also couldn't deny Gabby what she needed.

Our grief was different. Hers wasn't stained by my shame.

I slid the box her way. "It's all yours."

She didn't move.

I took an unsteady breath and tried again as soon as her eyes found mine. "You can open it and keep whatever's inside, okay? It's fine."

She swiped a tear and nodded. But when she touched the box, it was to set the card inside and fold the two flaps into themselves. "I don't want to open it without you. I'll wait until you're ready."

I shook my head, trying to convince her otherwise. But even at fourteen years old, Gabby's faith was a hundred times what mine had ever been.

And two and a half years later, my opinion of her hasn't changed.

Gabby pushes the box toward me on our parents' rug, and my fingers twitch as I release the flaps. I lift the card out and set it aside. Strangely, the surge of anger I experienced the first time doesn't accompany it now.

Our parents' scent is faint but still there. I reach into the box. There are only a few items in total. Our father's slim-line New Testament he never traveled without, and the watch I bought him with my first big paycheck at the recording studio. It wasn't a high-end brand, but it caught my eye due to its claims of being "the timepiece for every tradesman." The ads had shown it being run over by a forklift, dropped from a high-rise, and even submerged in motor oil overnight. And still, it kept on ticking.

It's ticking even now.

"I remember when he opened that from you on video chat," Gabby says, sitting cross-legged on the floor. "I almost never saw him without it."

I touch the simple titanium frame around the analog clock face and examine all the nicks and dings on the band. He wasn't a smart-watch guy; he was too practical for the ever-changing technology. Something I'd ragged on him about for years.

I offer the watch to Gabby, but she shakes her head. "He'd want you to have it."

I push down my instinct to argue and slip the cool metal over my wrist, clasping the magnetic closure with ease.

"Go ahead." I gesture to the box, indicating it's her turn, even though there's only one more item to remove: our mother's thick, leather-bound Bible jam-packed with all sorts of bookmarks and sermon notes. Unlike our father's pocket-size New Testament, Mom could never be convinced to find a more suitable version for their travels. Gabby's lips tremble as she pulls it out and hugs it to her chest as if it were my mother herself.

The affectionate display clogs my airway for a moment, and I have to look away in order to regain my composure.

From my periphery, I see her open it on the floor. Gingerly, she flips through each marked section, until she stops.

"August. Look."

At the awe in her voice, I turn my head and peer down into the pages of my mother's worn Bible. Only it's not the Psalms I see, but a blue three-by-five card dated several months before the accident.

Father,

I thank you for my son and for how you're working in his heart even now. I believe you are trustworthy in all your promises and faithful in all you do. I believe your promises are for August and for his future. (Psalm 145:13)

Amen

Gabby flips to the next passage with a blue card, this one in the book of Luke.

Father,

I thank you for my son and for how you're working in his heart even now. I thank you that it's your kindness that leads us to repentance. I thank you that you've shown us how to run toward our son with open arms like the father in this parable, like you've always run toward us. (Luke 15:20–24)

Amen

My chest burns hot, not with the shame I usually feel, but with something much stronger. Even when I chose a life far from the one my mother had imagined for me, she didn't give up. She didn't let me go.

There are more than a dozen blue prayer cards tucked inside the folds of my mother's Bible, and with each one, the hard outer shell of my heart continues to crack. She prayed for me. As much for where I was in the moment as to where she hoped I'd be one day.

The last card we find is located in Romans. I pick it up, noting the familiar reference.

I read it out loud.

"'Father, I thank you for my son and for how you're working in his heart even now. I thank you that there is nothing that will ever separate August from your love. Neither death nor life, neither angels nor demons, neither our fears for today nor our worries about tomorrow. Thank you that your love for him is eternal. Romans 8:38. Amen.'"

"It's the same verse you read tonight," I say to Gabby. And it's the same verse her rescuer had spoken over her as he carried her to safety. But what's even more significant is the tiny date inked in the far right corner of the blue index card. The fault line that started at the base of my heart while Gabby performed on stage has now been cracked wide open. I can only stare in bewilderment as the card shakes in my outstretched hand.

"Look" is all I can manage.

I know the instant she sees it because her gasp sounds like the breath my lungs are still so desperate to take.

On the very day my mother met her Savior face to face, she prayed this benediction of love for me, her prodigal son.

My mother died believing that nothing could ever separate me from God's love, and yet I've spent more than two years living as if her death did just that. As if by refusing to accept my parents' invitation to go to India, I somehow disqualified myself from every other invitation offered to me by God. That the only way to lessen the pain was to try and fix all the brokenness around me without truly examining the point of my shame. Not because I didn't believe God could forgive me, but because I didn't believe I could ever forgive myself.

Much less love myself.

Or let anyone else try, for that matter.

As soon as Gabby rises from the carpet and excuses herself from the bedroom, I fall back against the bedpost, drop my head in my hands, and finally surrender the burdens God never asked me to carry.

When I come out of the bedroom, I find my sister reading our mom's Bible on the sofa. I can tell her eyes are glossy from tears, and I'm sure she can see the same in mine.

I sit on top of her feet, and she squirms and kicks the way she always does.

"Thank you for doing that with me," I say.

She smiles as if that's all I came out here to say, but it's not. Far from it. I jostle her leg until she's made eye contact with me again.

"What did you mean earlier when you said there was still some time to fix things with Sophie?"

Her eyes widen. "Because of her flight."

At my confusion, she says, "August, she leaves in the morning—for her audition in LA."

"*Tomorrow* morning?" I balk, and then promptly check the time on my dad's watch—*my* watch. It's just past ten.

Gabby shakes me. "Don't be stupid again, August. Don't think. Just go. Go now!"

And with those poetic words, I do just that.

In less than two minutes, I'm driving to Wilder Winery.

In the end, the choice will be Sophie's to make, but I at least need to be honest about the options she's choosing from.

By the time I arrive at the winery, the only lights around the property are security lights, which makes it feel like the set for a psychological thriller. That image provides little comfort as I cross the empty driveway and slip through the entrance gate.

I'm aware of every rustle of the wind and crunch underfoot as I tense in anticipation for someone to shout at me, but the property remains eerily quiet.

The mid-December chill is enough for me to zip my fleece to my chin.

The swoop in my chest drops even lower at the sight of Sophie's pool house. It's the kind of dark that says uninhabited, not asleep. If she has a flight in the morning, then where is she now? And what exactly is my plan if she is asleep? It's not like I had time to write her a song to serenade her with.

Regardless of the darkened windows, I approach the pool house, hoping I'm wrong. I knock several times before trying the doorknob. It's unlocked. I'm noticing a theme around here I don't much care for. Why are there security lights if we aren't locking doors?

I crack it open. "Sophie? Are you in here?"

A rustling sound greets my ears.

I push the door open wider. "Sophie?"

A furry black streak bolts over the top of my sneaker. *Dang it.* How did I forget about Phantom?

Of all the confessions I need to make to Sophie tonight, explaining how I lost her cat isn't one I'm counting on. Scanning the darkness with my phone light, I watch the shameless cat slide its hefty self through the—no surprise here—open pool gate. At least he's given me a way to contain him.

Careful not to spook the feline unnecessarily, I enter a backyard paradise suited for a celebrity mansion in the Hollywood Hills. The whole thing feels more like a status symbol than a refreshing escape. I know it well, seeing as Vanessa had a similar over-the-top setup at her place. Cascading waterfalls, cabanas, palm trees, a swim-up bar, and heated surround tile. I bend and touch the patterned tile under my feet to confirm.

At least it explains why Phantom is sprawled out on his belly without a care in the world.

"Hey, bud," I say, approaching the chaise he lies near with caution as he glares at me through his good eye. I raise my hands. "I'm just gonna take a seat right here. No tricks. That goes for you, too, okay?" I recline in the chaise as if I'm completely unbothered by the frosty air or the fact that I'm talking to a one-eyed cat.

I slip out my phone and tap out approximately ten messages I don't send before finally deciding on the one I do send.

> Hey, you were incredible tonight. I was hoping we could talk before you leave tomorrow. I'm actually here, at the winery. Chillin' with your cat, if you can believe that. If for some reason you've already left for LA, then I think Phantom's gonna be pretty disappointed you didn't take his favorite backpack along. But he certainly won't be the only one here who's disappointed.

I watch the screen for nearly five minutes, but the message stays on unread. So I do the next best thing and turn to Sophie's geriatric cat. "You know, I never much cared for the talking-animal movies as a kid, but I can definitely see how that particular brand of magic would come in handy right about now." Phantom looks at me with such indifference I try not to take it personally. "I bet you know a lot more than you let on around here."

I eye him curiously. "You don't happen to know where Sophie is, do you, bud?"

Phantom licks his paw.

"Blink twice if you think Sophie has already left for the airport."

But he doesn't blink at all. In fact, he glares at me for so long without blinking, I'm afraid he might be having some sort of old cat stroke.

He stands, stretches for an eternity, and then hops up into my lap. *Purring.*

I lift my hands like I'm in a hold-up situation. The only cat I've ever held prior to this one turned out to be a double agent for Satan, so this is all brand-new. He kneads my thighs like he's considering how much pressure it will take to put a claw through my femur before he finally plops down. *On my lap.*

"This is a little too personal for a second-chance meeting, chap. I mean, yes, we do love the same woman and all, but I do have boundaries."

The purring continues, and soon the outside air doesn't feel quite so cold. This chubby guy is a living heater. In what might be the most unnatural gesture of goodwill yet, I stroke a hand through the soft fur on his back. He seems to relax into me all the more. I imagine Sophie doing this very thing, and I do my best not to give in to the fear that I'm too late.

31

Sophie

I half expected Natalie to pass out as soon as she was buckled into the passenger seat. By the sounds of it, she hasn't had a full night's sleep since those two blue lines first appeared on her pregnancy test. And there's no wonder as to why. But instead, she has the alertness of a teenager at a sleepover after drinking one too many Red Bulls.

When Agent Terrell walked us out of the station, he promised he would keep us in the loop as the investigation progressed and encouraged us to call him if anything came up. He warned me privately to keep a close eye on Natalie in the coming weeks as the emotional fallout from these types of cases can hit hard, and he encouraged me to get her into counseling with a professional so she can find the healing she deserves.

I assured him I'd do everything in my power to help her walk this difficult road and thanked him for his concern and care.

By the time I navigate us through two different drive-throughs to appease Natalie's pregnancy cravings—chicken tacos with extra hot sauce and a vanilla soft serve ice cream cone—it's nearly midnight. Now, with cone in hand, she's finally trying to unwind by scrolling on her phone and watching funny reels. I'm glad that one of us still has some battery life left. My phone died hours ago.

She bolts straight upright. "What the—"

"What?" I squeal, fighting to stay in my own lane.

"There's a few notifications from the winery's security cameras." She's frantically tapping at her phone screen and zooming in on a grainy figure. "Someone's there, Sophie."

"Who?" My gut flips. "Is it one of the employees?" But even as I ask it, I have no clue why any of our employees would be on the property at this time of night on a Saturday. We're closed on Sundays.

"I don't know, I don't recognize him." She holds the screen up in the dark cab. "Do you?"

I slow the pickup truck as I spare a quick glance at her screen. My jaw slacks as soon as recognition sets in.

"What?" Natalie's voice has jumped several rungs on the panic ladder. "Do you know him? Maybe we should pull over so I can call Agent Terrell? He offered to provide us with a security detail if we—"

"It's August."

"August as in *your* August?"

"Yes," I confirm. *My August.* At least, that's what my heart still calls him.

She holds the phone closer to her face. "So why is he out there? And more importantly, why is he sleeping on a pool chaise with your cat?"

I twist my head and gawk at her. "He's doing *what*?"

"Hang on, let me rewind until . . . oh." She watches for several more seconds and then taps on the screen to pause it. "Looks like he had a chat with him first."

"I highly doubt that. August is not a cat fan."

"Hang on. Here." Natalie turns up the volume on her phone and soon, August's voice fills the cab.

"You know, I never much cared for the talking-animal movies as a kid, but I can definitely see how that particular brand of magic would come in handy right about now."

Natalie and I glance at each other and bust out laughing. This really is happening. August, the self-proclaimed cat nemesis, has been caught on video making small talk with Phantom. We eavesdrop on his one-way conversation the rest of the way home. Natalie oohs and ahhs when August asks Phantom if he thinks I've already left for the airport, and I can't help the fluttery, hopeful feeling that inflates my lungs.

Natalie beams at her phone screen as if she's watching a popular reality TV show, and I tuck this moment away for safekeeping. Natalie's last few years have been terrible, the last few weeks even more so, but tonight she's found a reason to smile again. And that feels like the beginning of something good.

"Looks like he dozed off out there," she says as I pull up to the house. "He's gonna freeze if you leave him out there too long."

"He'll be fine." I love the man, but at the moment, he has a lot of explaining to do before I run into his arms and forget all about what he said—and didn't say—the last night we spent together at the fire.

I unbuckle and come around to Natalie's door to help her out so she doesn't trip over all the excess fabric she's toting around in that dress. "Let's get you inside and up the stairs so I can help you out of this—"

"No." Her stare is resolved. "I'm not as fragile as I look, Sophie. I plan to take a hot bath and then fall asleep in a room I haven't slept in before." She gives me a quick hug. "Thank you for everything you did for me tonight. I'll never forget it."

I hold on to her arms as she starts to pull away. "I'm gonna stay in the main house with you. I'll take the couch downstairs, just in case you need something."

She opens her mouth as if to refute, then reconsiders. "I appreciate that." She plants one of her ruby red flats on the walkway to the main house before twisting back. "Feel free to bring Phantom inside with you. I'll see you in the morning."

I watch until she's through the door and has turned on the main light before I take a path I've walked a million times before—as a little girl who dreamed of acting on a big stage, as a teenager too afraid to use her voice in her own home, and now as an adult whose dreams and voice have changed in more ways than one.

I switch on the outside lights, located on the back side of the house. They illuminate August asleep on a lounge chair with my cat perched on his chest. Despite wanting to be near him more than I want anything else in the world, I cannot allow my emotions to take the driver's seat.

The dull patter of my shoes on tile is enough to perk Phantom's ears, but he doesn't move. His amber eye glows against the night sky, tracking me across the patterned tile as if to say, *I've found my new BFF.* Traitor.

There's a sliver of cushion next to August's right hip on the edge of the chaise, but I don't take it, even though I want to. Instead, I stand at the end of the narrow lounge chair by his feet and tap it with my boot. He doesn't budge. I tap it again. This time, Phantom looks at me like he's cussing me out. When I tap a third time, August jackknifes up, evicting my cat.

He blinks and blinks and blinks and then scrambles to his feet. "Sophie. You're home."

"Yes," I rasp, my throat tight at seeing him this close after so long of not seeing him at all. "And you're here."

A chill rips through the air, and August promptly unzips his fleece and drapes it over my shoulders around my back. I could suggest we go inside the giant, warm house across the path, but neither of us looks like comfort has been our top priority in the recent hours. Or perhaps the recent weeks. August is likely halfway frozen by now, and I'm halfway to brain fry after the night I've had.

And yet, my voice is still alive and well.

"You hurt me, August," I say.

He glances down at his feet and then finds my gaze again. "I know I did, and I . . . I'm trying really hard not to hate myself for that. For what I said to you that night, and especially for what I didn't say to you. I'm sorry. I've been a coward."

My heart beats double time at this. "I'd never want you to hate yourself."

The tiniest hint of a smile twists on his lips. "Does that mean it's not too late for me to give you a reason to stay?"

The tip of my nose begins to tingle with coming tears. "I suppose that depends on your reason."

He holds out his hand to me. "Will you sit with me a minute?"

And just that—just that small gesture alone—makes me light-headed with hope.

I give him my hand, and we find our seat on the chaise, our bodies angled to face each other. He keeps hold of my hand.

"I've lied to you by omission for months, thinking that if I held back what I really feel for you I would somehow protect you from the worst parts of me. But I'm learning that love doesn't work that way. I couldn't compartmentalize it like I could everything else. I couldn't compartmentalize *you*." He takes in a slow breath. "Somehow, you managed to shine a light on every dark place I've been too ashamed for you to see. And still . . ." He swallows hard. "You loved me anyway."

"*Love*," I correct softly as tears trail down my face. "What I feel for you is present tense."

He cups my cheek with his hand. "And what I feel for you is also present tense. So much so that if you hadn't come home tonight, I was planning to implement the buddy system and crash your audition tomorrow."

I crinkle my brow. "Who's your buddy?"

"Phantom."

I smile at this and lean into his touch all the more. "I'm not leaving, August."

"You're not?"

I shake my head. "I prayed that God would make it clear, and He did. Tonight. In more ways than one."

"Does it have something to do with the Twilight Theater?" he asks in a way that shows just how in-tune he is with the passion that makes my heart beat. So much has transpired over the last six months, and August has been there for all of it.

"That's one reason, yes, but also . . ." I exhale slowly, knowing this next statement will lead to a lengthy Pandora's box conversation. "I'm going to be an auntie soon, and I want to be here for him—for them both."

This, I can tell, was certainly not an announcement he was expecting. Which means he's about to be hit with a whole heap of surprises in just a matter of a minutes.

"Jasper's wife is pregnant?"

"Natalie, yes." I hesitate, trying to figure out how best to summarize the events of the last several hours. "I was at the police station with her just now and—"

"Wait—you were *where*?"

"Believe it or not, the location is the least weird part of this story." I take another deep breath while his eyes round. "Anyway, turns out my brother has been involved in a sophisticated art fraud crime ring. He was arrested tonight after the undercover FBI agent got the information he needed when Natalie—AKA their inside informant—blew the whistle on his operation during a charity event this evening." I breathe and start again. "Natalie called and asked me to come to the station after the show tonight, and while we were there my parents showed up."

At his bewildered expression I simply say, "Yeah, it's a lot. But I'm okay." I pause and consider this claim. "Well, I'm as okay as I can be with a brother who's been charged with multiple felonies, a pregnant sister-in-law in need of support, and two parents who are beyond devastated by my brother's deception."

His silence holds a thousand questions.

I stand and pull him up. "Do you mind if we continue this inside? I can make us something warm to drink and we can talk about . . . everything we've missed."

"Not everything I've missed involves talking." He pulls me into a hug so warm and protective I'm beginning to reconsider going indoors. "I'm so desperately in love with you, Sophie. And I promise to do my best to make up for all the times I didn't say it and should have." He looks down at me with so much longing my toes tingle. "I love you."

"And I love you."

He brushes his lips to the corner of my smile. "May I kiss you now?"

"You may indeed."

And he does so in a way that almost, *almost* makes up for the three weeks I spent hoping for a moment just like this.

Once we part, August laces his fingers through mine, and together we walk into the house I grew up in. While he fixes us warm drinks, I text Dana and tell her I won't be reading at the audition in LA tomorrow and promise to call her with an update as soon as I have a spare moment.

Nearly two hours later, I've filled August in on everything I know about the investigation and the recent revelations about what happened during the robbery when I was sixteen. In turn, August shares about the precious box in his parents' closet, his mother's prayer cards in her Bible, and his own moment of revelation that had me reaching for the tissue box more than once.

I'm still dabbing my eyes as he settles in beside me.

"I wish I could have met them—your parents," I say.

"They would have adored you." The muscles in his throat work double time when he speaks again. "No doubt about it."

August pulls me and the thin afghan I've been curled up with onto his lap. "I'd like to meet the rest of your family, too. Whenever you think the timing is right for that." I nod into his chest, certain I could sleep an entire night right here, just like this. I don't want August to leave yet.

"Okay, sweetheart." He sighs raggedly. "It's time for sleep."

"No," I protest weakly, trying and failing to cling to him. "I don't want you to go yet."

He chuckles and gently removes himself from my pathetic attempt to keep him close. "Where might I find a linen closet in this mansion?"

I yawn and curl up on the sofa. "Take a left out those double doors, and it's the second closet on the right."

He's back a moment later, and to my delight, he's carrying two blankets. He lays the first over me and then stretches out on the sofa parallel to mine and uses the second blanket for himself.

"You're not going home tonight?" My mind is fuzzy, but not fuzzy enough to forget Gabby. "What about your sister? Won't she be worried?"

"I texted her, she's fine." There's a smile in his voice. "Any other questions or thoughts that can't wait until morning?"

"I don't think so," I say through a yawn. "Good—"

"I have something," he cuts in.

I peek one eye open, though all I can see is the outline of his shadow. "What is it?"

"I love you."

"I love you, too."

I'm pretty sure I fell asleep with a smile on my face.

"Sophie? Sophie?" A hushed voice cuts through my subconscious.

I crack one eye open to find my mother's face looming over me. "Mom?"

She holds a finger to her lips and points at the couch opposite mine. She mouths the words, *Who is that?*

My blurry gaze lands on August and the chubby cat who has once again made a home on his chest. Not that I can blame him. "My boyfriend."

Her eyelashes flutter in response. "Oh. Oh my."

It takes a moment for me to process how weird this entire scenario is, but once the events of last night have a chance to surface in my brain, it seems less so. "Are you okay, Mom? What are you doing here so early?"

I struggle to sit up, and she lifts the blanket off me and then tucks it around my shoulders as if I'm six and not twenty-six. I look around and realize who I don't see. "Where's Dad?"

"He didn't come with me." Her answer has the punch of a double espresso to my system. "He's still . . . processing what happened. And I simply can't keep rehashing it." She pauses and looks at me. "I think I could use some caffeine. How about you?"

I nod and follow her into the kitchen. "Definitely."

It only takes me a second to realize I'm going to need to be the one to make the coffee. There might have been a day my mother knew where everything was in this kitchen, but that was long ago. Long before the events of last night rocked her entire world.

I touch her arm gently. "I'll get the coffee. Why don't you go take a seat."

"Thank you," she says.

As I pour the grounds into the coffeemaker, mom sits at the tattered round table tucked into the kitchen nook. It's surrounded on three sides with bay windows overlooking the smallest vineyard. That table is one of the only original items left in the winery from when Gigi built it. I've always been partial to it—scratch marks and all. A part of me is shocked my brother didn't get rid of it.

As if reading my mind, my mother addresses this very thing as she sits. "I told your brother he could get rid of anything in the estate but this. I have too many memories with my mother at this table to have it tossed due to aesthetic."

I want to tell her I'm surprised he agreed, as it seems out of character for him, but after so many heavy realities involving my brother, perhaps this table's presence can be a reminder of God's light in the darkness.

While the coffee brews, I study my mother's exhausted profile. She's wearing a sweatshirt and leggings with minimal makeup and hair that's been combed and clipped back. A far cry from how high society would know Anita Wilder.

"Did you sleep at all last night?" I ask.

"A power nap sometime around four. But it was fitful at best."

"I'm sorry." I set a full coffee mug down in front of her and take the chair beside her. "Do you want me to make you something to eat?"

She places a hand over mine. "I don't want you to make me anything. I just want to be near you." The instant she says it, her eyes puddle with tears. "I know there is nothing in the world that can make up for all the mistakes I made when you were still mine to raise . . . but I hope you'll let me try." Her voice trembles. "I have so many regrets, and if I could, I would go back and do so many things differently." She sniffs, then pulls a napkin from the crystal holder in the center of the table and balls it in her fist. "I thought a lot about what you said last night, how your brother's crimes don't have to be the end of our family's story. How we still have choices to make." She takes a slow sip of her coffee, then looks out at the vineyard. "My mother predicted this would happen."

"That what would happen?" Surely she hadn't predicted my brother's criminal activity; he was a pubescent teen when she passed.

"That your father's greed and lust for success would drive this place, as well as our family, into the ground." She continues to stare off into the distance. "That if we took God out of the equation, we'd lose more than we'd ever gain." She turns to me then. "Those were her parting words to your father and me the night before she passed. Little did we know then that she'd taken your dad's name off the trust and made the stipulations surrounding it nearly impossible for him to ever hold a place of ownership again."

"Is that why dad hated her so much?"

She lifts a shoulder. "They disagreed on many things—most of them having to do with me." She rubs her lips together before taking another half sip of coffee. "But his fate was sealed when he told her he would raise his family under the same atheistic mindset he'd been raised under." Her eyes cloud again, and she blots her cheeks as soon as the tears drop. "I should have pushed back years ago. I had known God as a child. My mother and my stepdad baptized me when I was a teenager during a church picnic. But when I met your father, I was so struck by his confidence and his no-nonsense approach to life and logic that it was difficult to keep my stance of faith. He thought it was nothing more than brainwashing and indoctrination. It's what started my rebellion. And my mother died praying I would turn back to the faith she had instilled in me as a girl. That was decades ago now."

Other than in the form of a curse, I've never once heard my mother reference God. So the fact that she was baptized as a teenager and then willingly chose to walk away is disorienting.

"You can come back, Mom," I say with a boldness not my own. "It doesn't matter how long it's been. My pastor says there's no expiration date when it comes to surrender. Or God's grace and forgiveness." I think of August then, of the years he spent too ashamed to be honest with himself, much less with God. And how all that shame and guilt and fear were broken the instant he surrendered.

She stretches out her hand to touch my cheek. "You've turned into such a beautiful woman, Sophie." She purses her lips and looks down into her coffee. "I've missed so much of your life."

I touch her arm. "Maybe we can start to get to know each other again."

She smiles and tips her head to the doorway. "We could start by you telling me a little about the man sleeping in the front parlor."

"His name is August Tate. He's been the producer on the narration projects I've been working on over the summer and I . . . I love him." Tears prick my eyes as this unfiltered truth pours out of me. "And I hope I'll get to spend the rest of my life loving him."

Mom makes a sound deep in her throat like a hiccup-sob. "Oh, Sophie." She blots her eyes with the napkin again. "And he's a good man?"

"He's a wonderful man," I confirm.

"Well, then." She sets her hand on the table. "I should probably go check on Natalie and freshen up before we meet this wonderful man at breakfast."

"Breakfast?" I ask.

"Yes," she says. "I thought we might have a bit of a family discussion."

Without Dad? is what I nearly voice, but seeing as absolutely nothing about the last sixteen hours has been normal, I simply nod and say, "I'll wake August so he can get going—"

"No," Mom says with a shake of her head. "He can stay."

"But—"

"If he's as important to you as you say he is, then I'd like you to invite him to join us. There's no use in trying to hide what will soon become national news." Mom's voice is stressed when she says this, but I'm surprised at the way she's still holding up her head. I'm even more surprised by how much taller she stands when she's not cowering under my father's big opinions.

When I finally wake August in the parlor, he's more than a little disoriented. But when I tell him he's invited to breakfast with my mother and sister-in-law, he's a step beyond mortified.

"What?" he croaks, scrubbing his face and getting to his feet. "You want me to meet your family *now*?"

I try not to laugh—really, I do. But something about a frazzled August on so little sleep is actually quite amusing.

"This is not funny."

"Okay." I press my lips together.

He looks himself over. "I have cat hair in places cat hair should never be."

"Phantom says he's very sorry."

August narrows his eyes at me. "So I'm supposed to shake your mother's hand and talk about my intentions toward her daughter when I haven't brushed my teeth since yesterday?"

"I probably wouldn't mention that part."

"Sophie." The exasperated way he says my name pushes me over the edge.

"Relax," I tease. "There's a guest bathroom on the far side of the staff kitchen, and you'll find oral care kits in the cabinet on the right."

His eyes flash with suspicion. "Why?"

"You'd be surprised how many people request them after wine tastings." I shrug and then make a shooing motion. "You better go. Breakfast will arrive any minute." And I also need some time to freshen up.

He nods and begins to exit the room when he stops and turns. "Sophie?"

"Yeah?"

"I love you."

Our breakfast is delivered from the bakery down the road just moments after August rounds the corner and introduces himself to my mom and sister-in-law. Not surprisingly, he's a hit with the Wilder women. Natalie taps my knee under the table after he pulls out her chair like a true gentleman.

Natalie's buttering her second croissant when Mom clears her throat. "I apologize, August, that your first impression of this family is happening during such distressing circumstances."

"No need to apologize, ma'am." August dips his head. "But if there's anything I can do to help, please don't hesitate to ask."

"I appreciate that," my mother says. "I will pass that on to Ronald, as well." My mother straightens. "Speaking of Ronald, we talked to Agent Trujillo after you girls left the station last night, which led to another lengthy discussion between the two of us on our way back to the condo."

I share a look of uncertainty with Natalie.

"Given the current state of things, not to mention our growing family"—her focus falls to Natalie's growing baby bump—"we've agreed it would be best to temporarily close the doors of the winery. I plan to call the family attorney later today and inform him of our decision once I find Jasper's bookkeeping records."

"*My* bookkeeping records," Natalie respectfully corrects. "Not Jasper's. I'm the one who's handled all the finances. I can show you anything you'd like to see, Anita."

"Thank you, Natty," Mom says, sounding a bit dumbstruck. "That would be helpful."

My mom isn't the only person at this table who didn't realize Natalie was so involved in the finances. I didn't have a clue.

"Thankfully," Natalie continues, "despite Jasper's terrible spending habits, the stocks Ron invested in years ago, plus the interest we've made on the assets owned by the winery itself, should be more than enough to float us long after we provide severance packages to the employees and pay off our current debts."

Mom's face reveals she's more than a little impressed with her daughter-in-law's insight. "That's . . . good. Yes."

"You likely didn't know I graduated top of my class," Natalie confirms before taking a sip of her water. "It wasn't something Jasper liked to mention, seeing as he barely passed economics." She shrugs. "Numbers are kind of my thing."

I beam at my sister-in-law. "I'm glad math is a skill for at least one of us at this table. It certainly isn't mine."

Natalie looks to me and seems to remember something. "As far as Sophie's trust payout is concerned, I'd like to propose she receive the full amount due to her next week as the van in question is now a key piece of evidence in a federal investigation. Maybe that's something you can bring up to the attorney?"

"Oh, well, yes. Certainly." My mom blinks. "But I think before I do that, I should bring up something else to him."

We all wait patiently for my mother to form her thoughts into words. "I'd like to propose we draft a revision to the board of trustees. We'll need a new quorum for future decision-making now that . . . now that things are different." She blinks away fresh tears. "Would you consider joining Sophie and me as trustee members, Natalie? We'll still have to vote, but I have no doubt our attorney will be in agreement." Her gaze falls on her mother's cross pendant around my neck. "I'd like for both you girls to have an active voice here. Gigi would want it that way."

Though it's impossible to wrap our minds around the future, Natalie thanks my mother in earnest, and I'm grateful when August takes my hand under the table and reminds me that he'll be with me through it all. Come what may.

Once breakfast is cleaned up, August asks me to walk him out to his car. I know he needs to get home to Gabby, but it's still difficult to see him go when I've only just gotten him back.

At his car, he presses my back against his door and leans in close. "What do you think about a date tomorrow morning?"

Elation sings through me until I remember what day it is. "Tomorrow is Sunday. I don't want to miss church." And I was hoping, given August's revelation last night, he wouldn't either.

"We won't. It will be a bit earlier than that."

I scrunch my eyebrows, and he kisses my nose. "How early?"

"I'll have to check the tide schedule and get back to you on that."

"A pre-church surfing date?" I throw my arms around his neck and then shiver involuntarily. "But won't the water be *so* cold this time of year?"

"Gabby won't care about the temperature. She's a freak when she's up on her board."

And just like that, the elation is back. "You're planning to invite Gabby to surf with us?"

"It's time." He nods in earnest. "I think it's probably time to say yes to a lot of things she's been asking to do. And before you say it"—he cocks an eyebrow and rolls his eyes good-naturedly—"Yes, I'm already planning to invite Tyler along, too."

I gasp and bite my bottom lip. "Are you trying to win the Best Brother of the Year Award?"

He cinches me closer. "I'd much rather win the Best Boyfriend of the Year Award. I hear the perks are much better. Although, I'm still waiting to collect on that VIP tour I was promised months ago."

"I think that can be arranged."

His wide grin spreads as he leans in just enough to whisper four words against my lips that I'm absolutely positive I'll never grow tired of hearing: "I love you, Sophie."

Voice Memo

Gabby

3 years, 3 weeks, 2 days after the accident

I'm absolutely exhausted after today's events, but I didn't want to forget any of the fun details, so I decided to make a memo. I haven't done one of these in a long time, but let's face it: I'm a better talker than I am a writer. So here we go.

Tonight I got to play my best role yet as the official proposal coordinator for Operation Engagement Day. (Yes, this is a self-appointed title.) The only title I have loved more is being Tyler Pimentel's girlfriend, which I hope will be updated to fiancée in just a couple of summers.

Anyway. . . . Today, July 10th, is the day when my brother finally made Sophie his fiancée!

The original plan started out simple enough. A quiet little surf date before sunset, followed by an on-bended-knee moment. Sure, it was a sweet idea, but I had a few suggestions to add. After probing my brother for some key facts he had to fish out of the depths of his memory bank, I helped him create a new plan. A better plan, in my humble opinion.

Don't worry, they still had their surf date, but when they came back to shore, there was little private about it. I mean, come on—Sophie is a thespian! She loves a big stage. So with the help of friends and family, we set up at least a dozen picnic blankets on the sand with to-go boxes filled with tacos, queso, salsa, and hot chips from her favorite Mexican restaurant in Bodega Bay. And of course Sophie's favorite salt-water taffy was also there.

Basically, we recreated their first date on a much larger scale, and it was fabulous.

My brother popped the question on bended knee in the surf while the golden sunset glowed behind them. Sophie screamed and jumped and cried and would have been swept right back out to sea if not for my brother picking her up and carrying her to the engagement party awaiting her. It was quite the sight, and I made sure Tyler got that shot—he's been taking a photography class at college, and his pics are amazing!

Anyway, Sophie was glad I'd thought all the details through, seeing as I knew she wouldn't want to attend such a special event in a sandy wet suit. I brought her a sundress, sandals, and her favorite pink headband and matching lip gloss to change into. She was stunning. No surprise there.

While the newly engaged couple mingled with guests and Tyler took their pictures alongside #Augie carefully written in the sand, I hopped from blanket to blanket visiting with some of our favorite people—like the world's sweetest baby boy, snuggled into the baby carrier strapped to Natalie's chest. Three-month-old baby Finn and his mama have had lots of help between Sophie and his doting grandma . . . as well as one very good-looking FBI guy Natalie insists is only a friend. Probably because her divorce isn't quite final yet, but I've seen the way he watches her when she's not looking. And I also saw the way he showed up to the winery with flowers and pregnancy snacks to "check in on her" more than a few times when I was there. Oh, I guess I should have mentioned Natalie hired me as her part-time personal assistant which also means I get to care for Finn when she's in meetings. That might be my favorite part of the job.

After all the media craziness died down about Sophie's brother's secret life of crime, the winery reopened in the spring for private events only. It's the perfect job for me, and I love it out there—especially now that I can drive myself in my dad's old Bronco. I'll never get over how my brother surprised me with that for my graduation gift in May. Best brother ever!

I see Sophie at the winery at least one day a week, but seeing as she and my brother just won a huge audiobook award for Allie Spencer's fantasy duology, they now have more requests for full-scale audio originals than they have time for. I love watching the two of them work together, and I love even more that my brother's been composing music again. And not only for his day job with Sophie, but also for the Twilight Theater. He's been consulting with Portia on ideas for our first all-access show with deaf and hearing cast members this coming winter! I absolutely cannot wait for that!

Okay, I got off track again. The engagement party. Right.

So Chip was also there, of course. He's not the biggest fan of the beach, but he's always a good sport. Although, I'm not gonna lie, when he told me about the booklovers cruise he got roped into going on next week . . . I couldn't help but laugh at the irony. At least he'll have some great stories to entertain us with during the wedding.

Which, of course, will be absolutely magnificent. In just a few months, August and Sophie will be married at the winery on a beautiful October day, and I absolutely could not be happier about it! I'm thrilled for my brother, but if I'm being completely honest, I am maybe the tiniest bit more thrilled for myself.

For Sophie's engagement gift, I gave her a name in ASL. It's a combination of several signs—sing, star, and my personal favorite, sister.

Discussion Questions

1. In the opening scene, August's encounter with the ocean mirrors his internal conflicts with grief, guilt, and shame. How does the ocean serve as a metaphor for his spiritual battle, and what can we learn about facing overwhelming circumstances?

2. How is the recurring theme of finding a voice reflected in August's, Gabby's, and Sophie's narratives?

3. Discuss the complications and conflicts between Gabby and August, and how their relationship changes and grows from beginning to end. Do you find their specific challenges to be realistic? Why or why not?

4. In what ways do Sophie's childhood trauma and fear affect her daily life at the start of the book? How does her new-found faith in God give her hope for healing? Do you have any personal experiences with overcoming difficult or traumatic events with Christ's help? Do you think healing from long-term wounds is possible?

5. Compare and contrast the different responses/reactions August and Sophie experienced during their first Seaside Fellowship service. Can you relate with one viewpoint more than another?

6. Gabby's resilience after her injury plays a significant role in August's life and his faith testimony. How did Gabby's audio journals impact the greater story and, eventually, help lead August to a place of full surrender?

7. Sophie's return to her family's winery brings her face-to-face with unresolved family tensions. How does her story explore the themes of forgiveness, reconciliation, and the search for belonging?

8. Sophie's artistic and creative passions are central to her character. How does her journey in rediscovering/redirecting her voice and her gifts reflect the spiritual call to use our God-given talents for a greater purpose?

9. How is the practice of biblical community demonstrated in *The Voice We Find*, and what is the impact on each of the characters and the community at large?

10. What valuable lessons can we find in Chip's friendship with August? Do you have a faithful friend like Chip in your life?

Acknowledgments

To my savior, Jesus Christ: Thank you for your faithful pursuit of my heart and for allowing me to partner with you in this beautiful ministry of story. To God be the glory.

To my husband, Tim: Can you even believe we've been married for twenty-one years? How did that happen? I know marriage to me is not always an easy gig, especially when I won't shut up about my fictional plot holes when you're trying to sleep . . . but I couldn't ask for a better encourager, supporter, lover, and friend. I'm so thankful you're mine for keeps.

To my writing sisters—Connilyn Cossette and Tammy Gray: Thank you for investing so much time and energy into every story I write and for your investment in me. I would never want to do any of this without you by my side. I love you both so incredibly much.

To my Coast to Coast Plotting Society—Christy Barritt, Connilyn Cossette, Tammy Gray, Amy Matayo: Ten years! We did it, girls! Our group has officially made it to a decade. I've said it before, and I'll say it again: Our plotting retreat is my favorite week of the whole year, and that has less to do with the awesome books we plot and everything to do with each of you. Thank you for being my people.

To my early readers/reviewers—Renee Deese, Hayley Elliot, Kacy Gourley, Rel Mollet, Joanie Schultz: Thank you for your insight and comments, and for supporting my efforts to bring this story to final publication. What an important treasure you are to this process!

To my publishing team at Bethany House Publishers and specifically to my editors—Jessica Sharpe and Sarah Long. Thank you for your expert feedback, brainstorming sessions, patience and flexibility with my schedule, as well as your sharp attention to detail. Thank you also for taking such good care of me as a writer as I work to balance my fiction life with my actual life.

To my church family at Real Life Ministries in Post Falls and specifically our small group: There is a reason I stress the value of community in every story I write . . . and all of you play a huge part in that.

And to you, my cherished readers: Thank you for taking a chance on my stories and for spending your precious time with these characters who have become like family to me. Your loyalty makes a huge difference in the life of an author, so thank you for continuing to keep my writing dreams alive. I love you all.

Special thanks to Dr. Nicole Rock for walking me through the details of August's medical emergency while simultaneously putting ice skates on your daughter in sub-freezing weather at the outdoor ice rink. You rock! (Pun definitely intended ☺))

Special thanks to Mike and Audra Trujillo for their expert guidance and advice on the fictional winery/estate scenario regarding Gigi's trust and payout plan. I referred to your bullet-point email multiple times. Love you both! (Also, any errors or oversights are mine to own. I do words, not numbers.)

Special thanks to Natalie Walters (award-winning romantic suspense author!) for responding to approximately one million panicked voice texts during each and every editing round of this story regarding all things crime, fraud, super bad dudes, and justice. You. Are. Awesome.

And a BIG special thanks to my friends—both in person and online—who have helped me understand a little more about the deaf and hard-of-hearing community at large and the needs within it. During the drafting and editing stages of this book, I tried my hardest to represent this community well, with grace, love, truth, openness, hope, and support. I apologize in advance for any error or misrepresentation found within this fictional storyline. Any mistakes are also mine to own.

If you enjoyed *The Voice We Find,*
keep reading for a sneak peek of

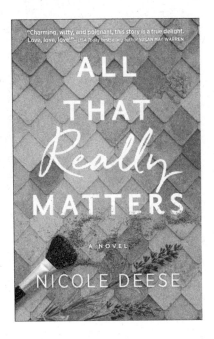

· 1 ·

Molly

I used to marvel at the way my Great Mimi's arthritic fingers would pinch her eyeliner pencil and trace a perfect stroke of midnight black along her upper lash line. The way her tired, nearly translucent skin would transform into a picture of regal elegance with only a few pats and swipes of color. For an eleven-year-old girl whose mother had never owned a single tube of mascara, it was a magical experience.

I'd watch my Mimi's routine with my elbows propped onto a gold-leaf vanity and eyebrows disappearing behind poorly cut bangs. My mouth would form an opera-worthy O as she became a living, breathing masterpiece, her best features showcased and enhanced, her flaws minimized and concealed.

And in those final few seconds before she closed her makeup drawer and blotted her ruby red lips, she'd hand me her blush brush and say with a wink, "Molly, when you feel good in your own skin, it's easy to help someone else feel good in theirs."

I'd tap the remaining rouge onto the apples of my pale cheeks and smile at the stringy-haired girl in the mirror, promising myself that one day I would do just that: I would help someone else feel the way my Mimi had always made me feel. And now, sixteen years and 606,000 Instagram followers later, I'd kept my promise to that often misunderstood little girl, one emboldened cat-eye and sheer lip tutorial at a time.

Beep! Beep! Beep!

I snapped the compact of my recently reviewed translucent face powder closed—four-out-of-five lip smacks, dinged for a shorter wear life than advertised—and primped my hair one last time in the mirror before following the sound of my oven's cry.

"See, Ethan? I told you I could finish getting ready before the oven preheated. That took what, five minutes? Hey, maybe that could be an idea for a future post series. 'How to Get Date-Ready in Five Minutes or Less.' Or wait—'How to Get Date-Ready in Five Minutes *and* Five Products or Less' is even better. Then I can feature that new Hollywood Nights collection that just came in. I'll have Val add it to the schedule." I rounded the corner into the kitchen, expecting to see my boyfriend on the recliner in my living room. Only he wasn't there.

"Ethan?" I slid the glass pan of chicken marsala into the oven and lifted the charcuterie board I'd spent nearly an hour preparing. There was something strangely satisfying about arranging cheeses, meats, nuts, figs, and olives.

"The chicken will take about forty minutes to bake, but our appetizers will go great with that wine you bought last month. I've been saving it." I wove around the island, gathering the glasses and balancing the cheese board on my palm like the trained waitress I was not. If my twin brother were here, this would be his cue to crack a joke about my propensity to drop plates of food, even though that had only happened *one time*. Granted, it had been on Thanksgiving Day, and granted, I had been carrying our twenty-five-pound stuffed turkey, but still, there should be a statute of limitations on bad family jokes.

I continued my balancing act into the living room. "I'm sure your appetite is still on East Coast time, but—" I stopped abruptly at the sight of my boyfriend stretched out on my sofa, eyes closed.

"Ethan?" I set both the appetizers and stemware on the coffee table and tiptoed over to him—quite a feat in four-inch cork-wedge heels. I approached him as if he were a wind-up toy ready to spring into action at any moment, which was perhaps the most fitting description of Ethan Carrington.

But there was no springing.

Apparently it didn't matter how much time a woman spent creating the perfect cat-eye if the man she wanted to impress was unconscious. I crouched low and waved a hand over his face before he released a snore that had me cupping a hand over my own mouth to stifle a laugh. This had to be the most anticlimactic start to a date ever.

I covered him with a vegan angora throw from a boutique in Canada I'd promoted last autumn, then decided to capitalize on the rare moment. After all, Ethan's favorite marketing motto was *Never miss an opportunity to relate to your audience.*

I whipped out my phone and proceeded to take a ten-second story, featuring my adorable sleeping boyfriend, a tray of untouched appetizers, and one pouty-lipped me. I captioned a post with *Jet lag is the thief of romance.*

Not even eight seconds later, my phone began to vibrate with notifications—likes, comments, emojis. An immediate endorphin boost. The temptation to scroll through them proved too much. After all, my manager-turned-boyfriend showed no signs of waking any time soon, and truth was, even if he had woken up, he'd tell me to reply to at least the first twenty or so commenters. Something to do with increased visibility and reach.

> You're so cute, Molly! And so is your boy toy! Hubba hubba . . .

> Ah, sorry girl! But at least that maxi dress is ADORBS on you! Link please???

Good hair days like that should never be wasted
tho. Wake him up already!

I liked a few dozen comments, replying in kind to their emoji strings and creative hashtags, then scrolled through the rest of my feed, hovering over the latest post by Felicity Fashion Fix, the snotty diva and ex-client of Ethan's who once stole an entire vlog series idea from me two days before mine went live. I breathed out my nose the way Val always encouraged me to and tried to let go of the negative static in my chest . . . but not before glancing at Felicity's latest follower count. 415,687. *What?* How on earth did she get such a big jump in followers so quickly? *What is she doing?* Besides stealing other people's ideas, of course.

When Ethan finally began to stir, it took a hefty force of will to silence my phone and shove it in the crack of the chair cushion. Yet I did it with a smile, because that was what committed couples did for each other. At least, that was what I'd read from a popular blogger I followed: *"Healthy couples ignore the pressures of social media to be socially present in their relationship."* I'd saved the pretty graphic to my photo reel just two days ago. Ethan and I didn't get much face-to-face time since he traveled for business roughly three weeks out of the month, but perhaps the strain of a long-distance relationship would dissipate if we practiced being more *socially present* with the time we did have together.

"Hey there, sleepyhead," I crooned from the recliner, where I'd kicked off my shoes and tucked my frozen feet under the skirt of my dress. Most days, springtime in northeast Washington was just a less snowy version of winter. "Welcome back."

He jolted at the sound of my voice and blinked. "Molly?"

"Happy date night."

Ethan rubbed at his eyes again. "What time is it?"

I glanced at the wall clock, surprised at how much time had passed while I'd been scrolling my feed. "A little after six."

He pushed himself up to a seated position. "You should have woken me. I don't even remember dozing off."

"No way, you looked way too peaceful to disturb." And it was nice to see him without a screen on his lap or in his hand. Ethan wasn't the greatest at leaving his work behind. Then again, neither was I. "Besides, you've been up since two in the morning Pacific time. Dozing off for a few minutes seems perfectly acceptable—even for someone as immune to naps as you are."

He ran a hand through his thick butterscotch-colored locks, and my breath actually hitched in my chest at the sight. In no way did he look like a man who'd spent his entire day traveling on an airplane. He smiled at me with those same midnight blue eyes that had won him many a client—myself included.

"Well, I hope you don't hold it against me, because I've been looking forward to tonight. To being with you." His expression cleared, then sharpened on my face. "There's actually something big we need to discuss. I wanted to tell you in person."

The professional tone made my palms grow damp. "Something to do with the agency?" There'd been a lot of changes happening within the Cobalt Group recently. Most had been great—bigger sponsors to partner with their contracted influencers, which, of course, meant bigger paychecks, bigger referrals, and a bigger bottom line. But nobody was immune to the volatile nature of our industry. There was always somebody waiting to rise to the top. Somebody willing to do more at whatever cost.

"Wait," I said, remembering the chicken. "Before you answer that, I need to check on our dinner first."

As if on cue, the oven timer buzzed as I scrambled to my feet to make for the kitchen. But Ethan's hand reached out for mine, and he tugged me toward him. He held out my arm to turn me this way and that. "You look really good, babe. That dress is on point. Did your fans choose it?"

"You'd know if you stopped by my pages more than every couple of weeks," I teased as I swiveled my hips to show the flare of the skirt as it swept over my bare toes. Once again, my online poll had proven itself accurate. This particular maxi dress had won over three other options categorized under "Best Home Date Dress" by nearly seven thousand votes.

I pecked his cheek and unhooked my hand from his. "I've got to get that chicken out or we'll be eating charcoal for dinner." I made my way from the sofa to the kitchen. "Oh, and don't think I forgot about your promise to take pictures for me while you were at Fashion Week."

He chuckled and slid out his phone from his back pocket. "I managed to take a few, but I doubt they'll meet your queenly standards. Not all of us can be top-trending influencers."

Ethan's hyperspeed mode usually left little time for snapping quality pictures of anything. Over the last nine months of our dating life, I'd received many a blurred selfie—Ethan in front of the Golden Gate Bridge for a triathlon, Ethan wearing his scuba gear on the coast of Fiji, Ethan jumping out of an airplane. There was never much context to his photos, other than his signature cheekbones and jewel-toned eyes, but even in the chaos of his shots, his zest for taking all that life could give him was palpable.

Ethan's all-gas-little-brake personality had found me at the perfect time.

After so many years of playing the role of outsider in a family who strived after intangible things, someone finally understood me—believed in me, even.

Allowing the pan of chicken to cool on top of the stove, I made him up a plate of smoked gouda and dry salami from the charcuterie board, arranging several crackers around the edges, and then poured him a glass of red wine. I placed both on the table and sat next to him. He didn't touch either offering.

Instead, he perched on the edge of my couch as if ready to sprint. "Babe, I had a meeting with Mr. Greggorio yesterday. About you."

About me? Mr. Greggorio was Ethan's partner at Cobalt, only he had about thirty years on Ethan in life and in running a successful marketing agency. His name always sparked a flurry of nerves. Maybe because Ethan had never once referred to him by a name other than Mr. Greggorio. Then again, perhaps wealthy, yacht-owning Italian men who agented all kinds of entertainment, talent, and business professionals didn't have first names? "But my numbers are on the rise. I just passed the six hundred thousand mark."

Ethan turned on the magnetism he was known for. "Oh, he knows. He's been keeping tabs on you himself. In fact, he's been doing a lot more than that."

I had no response for this. None. Mr. Greggorio didn't deal with influencer riffraff like me. He handled Cobalt's VIP clientele only—partnering with product lines associated with sponsors and companies that ranked in the top brands and corporations worldwide. I wasn't even certain he'd remembered me after our first meeting last year when I signed on as an influencer with them—a low-level one at that. My numbers had barely brushed the one hundred thousand mark, and my brand had been anything but focused. But Ethan had believed in my talent, in what I could do for the fashion and beauty industry as a whole, and he'd signed me on the spot.

We went on our first date just two months later. He'd flown me to dinner at the Space Needle—just under an hour flight from Spokane, Washington.

He stood now and paced my living room floor, his new flat-front chinos flexing with each step without a single wrinkle in sight—a fashion miracle considering his earlier state of hibernation. He stopped without warning and turned on the heel of his loafer. "He says you have the *It Factor*. The special quality that separates the fakes from the real thing." His grin revealed freshly whitened teeth. "Do you have any idea how many clients Mr. Greggorio has worked with in his lifetime?"

If I was stunned before, then I was practically catatonic now. I gave the tiniest shake of my head.

"Thousands." He laughed. "*Thousands*, Molly!" A wild spark ignited his gaze. "And I'm not the only one he told that to, either. He pitched you to the media moguls at Netflix. They're looking to recruit fresh talent for a new feel-good series slated for next year. And their response to him was, '*Molly McKenzie is already on our radar.*'"

"*What?*" I leapt off the sofa, unsure of what to do with my body other than gawk and flail my arms like a flightless bird. "No. No way. You're lying to me. This can't be real. Tell me you're lying." A scratchy, unrecognizable whisper escaped my throat. "Are you lying?"

He laughed. "Not even I could tell a lie that good."

I flung myself at him, and he caught my waist and spun me around. "Oh my goodness! I know you said it would happen someday, that you'd take my brand places I couldn't even begin to imagine, but I . . . I just can't believe it's actually happening!"

Ethan lowered me to the ground and cupped my face in his hands. "As long as you stay focused on the goals ahead, I will work to make your wildest dreams come true." He smiled as if to let his words soak in. "But before I can submit your official audition to the producers this summer, we need to eliminate every potential weak spot in your résumé to edge out your competitors."

"Sure, of course." Whatever cloud-like euphoria had inflated my entire being only moments ago had sprung a leak. Ethan reached for his briefcase, and just like that, Manager Ethan had shown Boyfriend Ethan to the door.

"I wrote some key targets down for you on my last flight. I know how much you like to visualize your goals."

"Right. Thanks." My gaze dropped to his briefcase as he popped open the lock. "Whatever I need to do, I'll do it."

A slight curve lifted the corner of Ethan's mouth. "That's exactly what I told Mr. Greggorio you'd say."

He scooted the appetizer board and wine glasses to a separate side table.

"So you're wanting to go over all this right now, then?" I asked, glancing back at our cooling dinner.

"Waiting time is wasted time." An Ethan quotable if ever there was one. Ethan was not someone who believed patience was a virtue.

"Right." I took the bullet point list from his hand, and my gaze immediately snagged on the first objective listed.

1 million subscribers

"A million subscribers? By the end of August?"

"Gaining the edge is never easy."

I raised my questioning gaze to his confident one. "But that's . . ." On principle, I didn't say the word *impossible*, but gosh, if there ever was a time for that word, it was right now. "That's almost four hundred thousand subscribers in just three months."

"Yes, it is. And I have a strategy for how to get us there."

"Does it include praying for a miracle?" My joke fell flat with a quick shake of Ethan's head.

"You know I don't believe in miracles. I believe in hard work, dedication, and plenty of grit. All things you have in spades. And all things that make us such great partners." He grabbed another document from his briefcase and laid it out flat. Pie graphs and algorithm reports I didn't have the first clue how to read stared back at me. "Between your campaign photo shoot next week with Hollywood Nights Cosmetics and the endorsement quotes Fashion Emporium is adding to their stores, I estimate your boost will be around twelve to thirteen percent." He traced a line with his finger, indicating the growth he'd already mapped out. "But that leaves a large gap to fill while I work on getting you some more widespread campaigns. We also need to find the right celebrity collaboration, someone who will take your hand and pull you up to their level—I have a few ideas already in the works. But there's something else as well." When he looked up at me, I got that strange woozy feeling I had whenever I glanced down in a glass elevator.

"What?"

"We need to show a different side of you to the public eye, work to expand the reach of the woman behind Makeup Matters with Molly. Which is why item two is so important."

I slid my focus down the page as his second point assaulted me in an entirely new way.

Partner with a human-interest cause

A burning sensation flared in my lower gut, a premonition I knew all too well. "What kind of human-interest cause?"

"It actually needs to be something quite specific." Ethan leaned in, as if the discovery he was about to share was too confidential for my living room. "After calling in a lot of favors and piecing together several off-the-record conversations, I was able to figure out the producer's hook for the show you'd be in the running to host." He held his breath for a full three seconds. "It's called *Project New You*, highlighting America's underprivileged youth. It will be a more holistic approach to the usual makeover show—not only focused on the physical side of things. The older teens who are featured will be chosen by a nomination system—teachers, mentors, foster parents, etc. The kind of show that leaves you reaching for a tissue and a tub of ice cream by the end of it."

The buoy keeping my hopes afloat sank inch by inch.

I opened my mouth to say something—anything—but then closed it tight again. So many thoughts spun inside my head at once, pinging against memories better left undisturbed. Though I "helped and supported" women on the other side of a digital screen several times a week via makeup tutorials and comparables and as-honest-as-I'm-allowed-to-be product reviews, helping people in the outside world was a different beast entirely. A much scarier, much more exposing beast. One I was quite familiar with, considering both my parents and my brother had given their souls to serve in full-time ministry.

Sometimes I wondered just how many prayer teams around the nation—perhaps the world, even—were committed to praying for the McKenzies' prodigal daughter, the girl who made a living profiting from one of the seven deadly sins: vanity.

Seeing as Ethan and I didn't share much about our pasts, he didn't take my silence for the fear that it was, the fear that stepping too close to the humanitarian line would only end in failure and disappointment for everybody involved. There was only one person in my life who would have believed otherwise, but Mimi had died nearly four years ago. Before I'd even hit five thousand subscribers on the channel she'd encouraged me to start. Had she known this day would come? Had she envisioned me hosting an on-demand show? I could almost feel her fingers rake through my hair as she said, "*Share your spark with the world, Molly. Stop trying to hide what God created to be seen.*" Was this the big break she'd been hoping I'd find?

"The producers are going to need to see more of your empathetic side. More heart. More compassion. More generosity and selflessness. They're impressed by your charm and wit, and no one would ever question your natural charisma on screen, but for this to move forward, we need to see the host of Makeup Matters with Molly get her hands a bit dirtier in the muck of real life. Because as it is right now, you're just a pretty face with an addictive personality."

The sting of his words throbbed in the back of my throat, and I swallowed against the ache. I'd never cried in front of Ethan, and I wasn't planning to start now. "I'm more than that."

He glanced up from the paperwork, brows crimped in confusion. "What?"

"I'm more than a pretty face."

"Oh, babe. I know that. Of course I know that." He touched my knee, squeezed, smiled. "But it's my job to assess how you might be perceived by the public eye, even though I know you have the potential to be so much more."

Only, his use of *potential* didn't quite pluck out the insult dart he'd thrown.

"You don't need to look so worried. I've got all this covered for you. It's not like I'm suggesting you go live in a homeless shelter for a month and serve rice and beans with the kitchen staff." He chuckled. "We'll find a good match for you somewhere. Something with older kids that you can pop in to see once a week. Hear some hard stories you can retell, take some heart-jerker pics, and then be done with it. Simple."

He paused, and I could almost feel the way he redirected the energy buzzing around us. "My assistant is already compiling a list of local charities and nonprofits for us to go through. The closest we can get to the premise of the show, the better. Plus, we'll need to steer clear from what other influencers in your space have going on right now. Felicity is—"

"Felicity?" Just the sound of her name made my hackles rise. "What does she have to do with this?"

"Have you seen her latest numbers?" he asked, as if I'd missed a presidential election.

"I may have glanced at them once or twice in the last few weeks."

"Well, since she added the no-kill shelters as a cause she supports, her numbers have skyrocketed. And it's no wonder why. People care *more* about successful people who pay it forward. Partnering with a cause will grow your influence, *and* it will give you a giant leg up in your audition submission."

I huffed a sigh. "I have a hard time believing that any self-respecting animal would choose to be in the same room as Felicity. She's basically the platinum blond version of Cruella de Vil."

"While that may be true," Ethan said, all managerial-like, "the numbers speak for themselves. She's grown nearly eighteen percent across all her platforms in the last four months."

"Eighteen percent?" I slumped back in my chair. "Wow."

"Yep. And," he said, tapping my knee, "I have no doubt you can do even better. You have more personality and charisma in your left earlobe than Felicity Fakes It."

"Felicity Fashion Fix," I corrected on a chuckle, my mood slowly on the rise again.

He curled a long piece of my hair around his finger and tugged gently. "I don't really care what her brand name is because she's not my client anymore, you are." He edged closer to me, taking my hands in his and rubbing his thumb over the inside of my wrists. "You've proven you know how to hook your viewers' loyalty, Molly. Now you need to hook them in the heart. If you can do that, then I can get you a makeover show in front of millions that will make everything you've done to build your brand to this point seem trivial in comparison."

I tried the phrase on for size—*hook them in the heart*—imagining how my twin brother would respond to such a statement.

"Oh!" I sat up straight and flattened my feet to the floor. "I've got it."

"What? A nonprofit we can contact?"

I shook my head. "Not exactly, but I do know the person who can lead me to one. Miles. My brother has a connection to every nonprofit organization within a hundred-mile radius of here." And beyond.

"Ah, yes. The preacher," Ethan said, finally reaching for his glass of wine and reclining back on the sofa. "Weren't the two of you supposed to do an interview together for your channels? I thought I suggested that a few months back—show your viewers the whole twin bonding thing you two have going. Did Val forget to put that on the schedule?"

I tried to ignore the raw way his tone rubbed against me whenever he spoke of my brother. Though he and Miles had only interacted twice, it was abundantly clear that neither of them was going to take up calling each other *bro* any time soon. Truth was, I often felt like a goalie between them, blocking any potential insult and negative jab.

I stood up, slipped between him and the chair, and made my way back to the kitchen. "He's not interested in doing an interview for Makeup Matters, and I'm totally okay with that. It's not his thing."

Ethan laughed. "Why not? Are preachers banned from social media? Is that one of the twelve commandments?"

"Ten."

"Ten what?"

"There are only ten commandments, not twelve."

He pulled out his phone and tapped on the screen, either not hearing me or not caring to respond. "You should really change his mind on that. It's a missed opportunity."

It probably was, and yet I knew my brother. The same way I knew my parents. Though at least Miles understood some of the benefits to social media and what my career as an influencer actually entailed. My parents, however, shared one flip phone between the two of them with no fancy apps or internet service—all in the name of frugality and stewardship.

As I pulled our plates down from the cupboard, I said nothing more on the topic of my family to Ethan. It was one of the clear boundary lines I'd drawn when we started dating. He hadn't known me as a child or as a lonely teenager searching for her place in a household she'd never quite measured up to. And I liked it that way. The two of us had come from two totally different lifestyles, two totally different histories, two totally different worlds, and perhaps that was what I enjoyed most about being with him. Our pasts didn't have to matter, because all we focused on was the future dreams we chased together. And in that aspect, we were very much the same. Ethan and I were a goal-making, goal-crushing machine. And signing on with his agency had been one of the best decisions I'd ever made.

He believed in me. And perhaps that was the only encouragement I needed to push toward my next goal.

"Hey." He came up behind me and put his hands on my shoulders while I reached for a spatula. "What do you think about skipping the chicken tonight and going out to eat instead? I'm craving that little Italian place downtown, the one with the breaded artichokes and fresh caprese salad." He brushed my hair off my back and planted a kiss to my neck. "We can continue this conversation over a nice plate of veal parmesan. And, bonus, there'll be no dishes needing to be washed."

I glanced down at the chicken I'd been marinating all day, based on a recipe I'd chosen a week ago when he told me he'd be flying into town tonight. "I do love that place, but I've been looking forward to trying this chicken out all week, and—"

He spun me around and touched my chin. "Babe, once this deal goes through, the only meals you'll ever want to try will be cooked by professional chefs. Come on, let me treat you tonight. I'm proud of you." He went to the door and shrugged on his jacket before removing my blush cardigan from the rustic wall hook and holding it open. "After all, it's not every day I get to celebrate the accomplishments of my best client, who also happens to be my beautiful girlfriend."